The Quiet Ones

Brad L Raby

The Quiet Ones

A Memory Series, Volume 1

Brad L Raby

Published by Orchard hill books., 2026.

Copyright

This is a work of fiction. Similarities to real people, places, or events are entirely coincidental.

THE QUIET ONES

First edition. March 21, 2026.

ISBN: 979-8995411512

Written by Brad L Raby.

Table of Contents

I keep friends whom are of an. opposite attitude and soul level from mine. I dedicate this to this friend for making me so angry, one day, i put this in writing on this novel, but gently.

The comfortable blindness was burning off. Not pleasantly — nothing about the process was pleasant — but burning off the way fog burns off a lake in the morning, leaving everything exposed and cold and more clearly itself than it was an hour ago.

Chapter One

THE QUIET ONES

Chapter One — Missy's Secret

I write fiction for a living which is a polite way of saying I lie professionally and sleep fine afterward. My desk faces the water because northern Michigan light in the morning does something to the brain that coffee only pretends to do. I have both going at seven a.m. — the light and the coffee — and for approximately forty minutes before the world remembers I exist, I am a man at peace with his particular corner of the universe.

I am seventy one years old. I have outlived two marriages, one engine fire at four thousand feet, a barn collapse, and whatever it was that lived in the dark at the edges of my childhood. I am not a large man. I am not a loud man. My daughter Nora says I have the social presence of good furniture — always there, comfortable, noticed only when absent.

I take this as a compliment. She does not entirely mean it as one.

The book I'm currently writing is about a man who discovers the universe is not indifferent to human suffering — it simply has a different timeline than we'd prefer. Chapter twelve was giving me trouble the way chapter twelves always give trouble, sitting on the page looking reasonable while secretly being wrong about everything. I was two sentences into fixing it when I felt her arrive.

I say felt because heard isn't accurate. Wren moves through a house the way smoke moves — present before you identify the source. She is six years old and has her mother's dark hair and eyes that have no business being in a six year old's face. Old eyes. Patient eyes. The kind that make strangers pause mid-sentence and forget what they were saying.

She appeared at my left elbow and leaned against the desk and watched me type with the focused attention she normally reserves for things most adults have stopped noticing.

I kept typing.

She kept watching.

This is our established language. It has no words in it.

Outside, a loon called once across the water and fell silent. The coffee had reached that temperature where it stops being excellent and begins its long sad decline toward acceptable. I saved the chapter document, which is what I do when chapter twelve is lying to me and I need a moment to let it think about what it's done.

Grandpa.

Mm.

She was quiet for a moment in the particular way she gets quiet when she's deciding whether to say the true thing or the easier thing. She always chooses the true thing. This is either her greatest gift or her most exhausting quality depending on the day and who's in the room.

Why does Missy say she loves going to see Marta.

I looked at my screen. *Does she.*

She says it every time. She says oh I just love visiting Marta, she uses that voice.

I knew the voice. Missy lived four houses down and had been performing cheerful contentment for the eleven years we'd been neighbors with the commitment of a woman who has confused the performance with the thing itself.

But, I said.

But I hear her say she hates going there. Not out loud. Just — I hear it.

I set my coffee down carefully on the coaster Nora bought me that says WORLD'S OKAYEST GRANDPA which I find both accurate and oddly comforting.

I turned and looked at my granddaughter.

She looked back at me with those eyes that had no business being in a six year old's face.

Here is what I did not say: *Wren, people often feel one thing and say another, it's called being polite, you'll understand when you're older.*

I did not say this because it would have been a lie and she would have heard it as one, and we had an unspoken agreement that I would not do that to her.

Here is what I did not say: *That's a very interesting observation sweetheart, would you like some breakfast.*

I did not say this because it was a deflection wearing a question's clothing and she would have heard that too.

What I said was: *What else do you hear.*

She considered this with the seriousness it deserved.

Lots of things. Cooper says he's fine about stuff when he's not. Mom says she's not worried when she is. Dad says he's not tired. She paused. *Dad is always tired.*

He works hard.

I know. I don't hear it mean. I just hear it true.

I hear it true.

Six years old.

I looked back at my screen where chapter twelve was still lying to me and felt something shift in my chest that wasn't quite grief and wasn't quite joy and wasn't quite fear. The closest word I have for it is recognition. The specific feeling of seeing your own face in a place you didn't expect to find it.

Does it bother you, I said. *Hearing it.*

She thought about this honestly the way she thinks about everything.

Sometimes. At school it's loud. Everyone saying things and meaning other things and I can't make it quiet. She looked at the water through the window. *Here it's quieter. You mostly say what you mean.*

Mostly.

You said mostly out loud, she observed.

I did.

Why mostly.

Because I'm not always brave enough for entirely.

She accepted this without judgment the way she accepts most things — completely, without the editorial commentary adults layer over every inconvenient truth. It is the quality I love most in her. It is the quality that keeps me awake some nights.

Mom says I shouldn't ask about it, she said.

I know.

She says it makes people uncomfortable.

It does.

Does it make you uncomfortable.

I looked at my granddaughter for a long moment. The dark eyes. The patience that belonged to someone much older. The complete absence of performance.

No, I said. *You don't make me uncomfortable.*

What I didn't say — what I wasn't ready to say on a Tuesday morning with coffee going cold and chapter twelve still lying on my screen — was that she made me remember. That standing next to her was like standing next to a version of myself so old I'd forgotten it existed. That somewhere in the particular frequency of her seeing I recognized the static of my own childhood like a radio station I'd spent fifty years trying to tune out.

What I didn't say was that I'd felt something three days ago standing in Gerald's empty house in the particular quality of air that remained after the ambulance left. Something I hadn't felt since I was nine years old walking corn rows in October with my hands bleeding from dry husks and the certainty — animal, wordless, correct — that something at the tree line was watching me that was not a deer.

I didn't say any of that.

Instead I closed my laptop on chapter twelve's lies and stood up from my desk with the careful architecture of a man whose knees have developed opinions.

Want to walk down to the water.

Her face did the thing it does — not quite a smile, something quieter and more complete than a smile. Agreement at a frequency below expression.

She took my hand.

We walked down to the water in the northern Michigan morning and the loon called again and I held my granddaughter's hand and thought about Gerald in his chair with his eyes open and the coffee still warm and the newspaper folded to the crossword he would never finish.

And I thought about a boy in a corn field who knew without knowing how he knew that something at the tree line had just turned its attention his direction.

And I thought about the notebook in the basement that I hadn't opened in fifty years until yesterday.

And I said nothing because the morning was beautiful and she was six and some doors once opened cannot be closed again and I wanted to give her one more ordinary morning before I opened this one.

The loon went quiet.

The water moved.

We stood at the edge of it together, an old man and a small girl, and I felt the last of the ordinary morning lift off the water like mist.

Behind us, four houses down, Missy was telling someone on her phone that she just loved visiting Marta.

Wren's hand tightened slightly in mine.

She heard it too.

Chapter 2

THE QUIET ONES

Chapter Two — What Gerald Left Behind

Gerald Hoffstead was the kind of neighbor civilization depends on and rarely acknowledges. He waved every morning from his porch with the reliability of a man who has decided that small gestures matter and stuck to that decision through eleven years of weather, politics, and the general deterioration of public courtesy that had settled over everything lately like a second winter that forgot to leave.

He drank his coffee black. He kept his gutters clean. He returned borrowed tools without being asked twice which puts him in a category occupied by fewer people than you'd think.

His wife Margaret had died four years ago and he had grieved her with the quiet dignity of a man who understood that love doesn't negotiate its exit and doesn't apologize for the mess it leaves. He kept her garden going. Not perfectly. But going. I respected that more than I ever told him.

We were not close friends. We were something more reliable than that. We were good neighbors, which is its own category of human relationship — present without demanding, concerned without intruding, the kind of connection that only reveals its value after it's gone.

I found him Tuesday morning.

His door was open two inches which was wrong. Gerald was a close-your-door man in the specific way that men of his generation are close-your-door men — not unfriendly, just private, a believer in the architecture of boundaries. In eleven years I had never seen his front door open at seven a.m.

I knocked anyway.

Then I pushed it open.

He was in his chair facing the east window the way he always sat in the morning, positioned to catch the first light off the water the way Margaret had taught him. The television was off. The newspaper was open in his lap to the crossword, three across filled in, four across blank, the pencil resting in the fold as if he'd set it down to think and simply forgotten to pick it up again.

His coffee cup was on the side table.

Still warm when I touched it.

His eyes were open.

He was looking at something just above the horizon that I could not see and that I understood with a certainty that arrived before thought, before reason, before the part of the brain that prefers comfortable explanations — he had not chosen to look at it.

I stood in the doorway for a long moment.

I am a man who has learned to be honest with himself about what he knows versus what he can prove. These are different countries with different languages and most people spend their lives pretending they share a border. I knew Gerald Hoffstead had not died of natural causes. I could not prove this. The warm coffee and the open newspaper and the peaceful expression and the complete absence of any sign of struggle would all testify against me.

I called 911 from his kitchen using his landline because my cell phone was on my desk next to my cold coffee and chapter twelve's lies and I wasn't going back for it yet. I told the dispatcher my neighbor appeared to have passed away in his chair. I answered her questions in the order she asked them. I was calm in the way people are calm when they are using calm as a tool rather than experiencing it as a condition.

Then I stood in Gerald's kitchen and waited for the ambulance and did what I do in moments that require it.

I got quiet.

Not the surface quiet of a man standing still in a dead man's kitchen. The other kind. The deep quiet I had learned in a childhood I rarely discuss and had spent five decades pretending was someone else's. The kind of quiet that has a frequency to it, a particular stillness that sits below thought and breath and the noise the body makes just by being alive.

I got quiet and I listened to the room.

What I felt was not grief, though grief was present. Not fear, though fear was present too, in the way fear is always present when you are standing in a place where something has recently happened that the visible world cannot fully account for.

What I felt was residue.

The closest analogy I have — and I am a man who makes his living from analogy so I have considered this carefully — is the feeling of a room after lightning has struck nearby. The air charged and altered. The smell of something that was one thing and became another. The sense that the atmosphere itself remembers what passed through it even after the event is over.

Something had been in this room.

Something that left the kind of trace that only certain instruments can measure and I happened to be one of them, a fact I had not advertised since approximately 1963 when I was nine years old and learned that advertising it was dangerous in ways I didn't yet have words for.

The residue had texture. Cold without temperature. Absence that pressed. The particular quality of a thing that has never been alive moving through a space where life used to be.

I knew this feeling.

I had not felt it in fifty years.

I had spent fifty years making sure I would not feel it again.

The ambulance arrived. The paramedics were kind and efficient and spoke to me in the careful voices people use with elderly neighbors who have found dead friends, which I found mildly insulting and also completely appropriate given what I must have looked like standing in Gerald's kitchen holding his landline phone like a man who had briefly forgotten what phones were for.

I answered their questions. I answered the police officer's questions. I watched them do what they do with the professional competence of people whose job requires them to see only what can be measured and recorded and I did not tell them what I had felt in the room because I am seventy one years old and have earned the right to choose my battles and this was not a battle I was going to win in Gerald Hoffstead's kitchen on a Tuesday morning.

The officer, a young man named Briggs with the careful eyes of someone smarter than his current assignment required, looked at me for a moment longer than the situation strictly demanded.

You doing okay sir.

Gerald was a good neighbor, I said. *Returned tools without being asked.*

Briggs wrote something in his notebook. I have no idea what.

Did he have any health problems you knew of.

He was seventy. Health problems come with the territory at seventy. I'm seventy one. I have opinions about my left knee that would fill a chapter.

Briggs almost smiled. Decided against it professionally. *We'll be in touch if we have more questions.*

I'll be four houses down, I said. *Facing the water.*

I walked home in the morning light that was no longer doing what northern Michigan morning light is supposed to do. I sat at my desk. I looked at the laptop without opening it. I drank cold coffee without tasting it.

Then I went to the basement.

I want to be precise about this because precision matters when you are describing something you have spent five decades not describing. I did not decide to go to the basement. The decision was made at a level below where decisions are usually made, in the same place that knew without knowing that Gerald had not chosen to leave, in the same place that recognized the residue in his living room before my conscious mind had finished forming the sentence *something is wrong here.*

The basement smelled of old wood and lake moisture and the specific dusty patience of stored things. Boxes from three moves ago. Nora's childhood books in a milk crate I kept meaning to ask her about. A box of tools I no longer had the projects for but couldn't bring myself to discard.

And one box in the far corner under the stairs that had survived six moves without my ever consciously choosing to keep it.

Brown cardboard. Water stained. Sealed with the kind of tape that yellows and loses faith in itself over decades. My handwriting on the side in the careful block letters of a child who had recently learned that neat handwriting was one of the few things that impressed adults regardless of what was written in it.

I looked at it for a while.

The residue from Gerald's house was still on me the way certain smells stay on clothing. Cold without temperature. Pressing absence.

I opened the box.

Inside, under a broken transistor radio and three arrowheads I'd found in a creek at age ten and a photograph of a dog I'd had briefly and lost and never replaced, was a notebook.

Black and white speckled cover. The kind that cost nineteen cents in 1962 and felt like serious equipment to a child who needed serious equipment.

I sat on the basement floor with my back against the wall the way I used to sit in corn fields when the rows were too long and the wind too cold and the day too much and I needed to make myself small enough that the world might forget to look for me.

I opened the notebook.

A child's handwriting. Careful. Deliberate. The handwriting of a boy who was putting something down because he needed it outside his head where he could look at it from a safe distance.

There is a thing, the first line said. *It does not have a inside.*

I read that line three times.

Then I read the next page.

Then I sat on the basement floor for a long time in the particular silence of a man who has just been handed proof that the thing he spent fifty years pretending wasn't real was real, has always been real, and has apparently been patient in a way that only things without a concept of time can afford to be patient.

On the fourth page, in the same careful block letters, a description.

An old man in a chair.

Facing a window.

Coffee on the table beside him.

Newspaper in his lap.

Eyes open.

Looking at something just above the horizon.

Written in 1963.

By a nine year old boy in northern Michigan who had never met Gerald Hoffstead and wouldn't for another sixty years.

I closed the notebook.

Held it in both hands the way you hold something fragile or something dangerous or something that is both simultaneously.

Upstairs, I heard Nora arrive, her key in the lock, her voice calling my name, the ordinary music of a daughter checking on her father after a neighbor has died, the beautiful unremarkable sound of a life that did not yet know what was in the basement.

I looked at the notebook in my hands.

I know, I said to no one.

Or possibly to the thing that had been in Gerald's house.

Or possibly to the boy who had written this fifty years ago and known, somehow, that the man he would become would need the warning.

I know.

I put the notebook under my arm and went upstairs to tell my daughter that Gerald was gone and accept her comfort with the gratitude it deserved and say nothing about the box under the stairs or the residue in the air or the nine year old boy who had apparently been trying to warn me across fifty years of careful forgetting.

Some doors once opened cannot be closed again.

I had opened this one now.

The question was what was going to come through it.

And whether I was going to be ready.

And whether ready was even a category that applied to what was coming.

Outside, four houses down, Margaret's garden was going to need tending now.

Nobody was going to do that.

I thought about that longer than made sense.

It was easier than thinking about the notebook.

Chapter 3

Chapter Three — What The Boy Knew

I have written fourteen novels..

I know how to pace a revelation. I know that information delivered too quickly is information wasted, that the reader needs time to lean into what they're about to learn the way you lean into a curve on a road you've never driven before — enough to feel the pull of it, not so much that you lose the wheel.

I know all of this professionally.

I read the rest of the notebook in one sitting on the basement floor and threw pacing out the window entirely because some things do not wait for craft.

Nora was upstairs making the kind of noise that means someone is cleaning a kitchen that doesn't need cleaning because they need something to do with their hands. The sound of cabinet doors and running water and the specific industry of a woman processing grief through domesticity. Margaret's garden. Gerald's crossword. Four across blank forever.

I sat on the basement floor and read what a nine year old boy had written in 1963 and tried to be a fair witness to my own history which is the hardest kind of witnessing there is.

The notebook had thirty one pages of content. Not thirty one consecutive pages — a child's notebook is not a disciplined document. There were gaps. Pages of nothing between pages of everything. Drawings that meant something to the boy and required translation from the man. Numbers that might have been dates or might have been something else entirely. The occasional unrelated entry about a dog or a creek or the particular quality of ice forming on the horse trough in November that only a boy with too much time alone and too little else to observe would bother recording.

But threaded through it, in the careful block letters of a child who needed his handwriting to be taken seriously, was something else.

Scenes.

Described with the flat precise specificity of someone reporting what they saw rather than imagining what might be. No drama. No embellishment. The way a good witness gives testimony — this is what was there, this is what happened, this is what I saw.

Gerald was the fourth page.

I turned to the fifth.

A woman with short gray hair sits in a classroom after the children leave. She has a garden at home she thinks about when the room gets hard. She is found the same way as the man in the chair. The police come again. They use the same words.

I sat with that for a while.

Vera Simmons had retired from thirty two years of teaching fourth grade at the elementary school three miles from where I was sitting. She had a garden that people drove past slowly in June just to look at. She was seventy three years old and sharp as a new pencil and had recently — publicly, at a town meeting I had not attended but heard about — said several true things that made several powerful people very uncomfortable.

She was alive as of this morning.

As of this morning I knew things about the next several weeks of Vera Simmons' life that I desperately did not want to know.

I turned to the sixth page.

The sixth page was a drawing.

I want to be careful here because careful is what the situation demands and because I am a writer and writers are supposed to find language for things and this is the one thing I have never found adequate language for in sixty two years of trying.

The drawing was in pencil. A child's hand — not artistically gifted, not trying to be, just trying to record. The figure in the drawing had edges that the pencil seemed to have trouble committing to, lines that started and stopped and started again as if the boy's hand kept losing confidence in the outline. Not because he couldn't draw. Because what he was drawing didn't hold still.

It had the shape of presence without the substance of it.

The outline of something that displaced no air.

Below the drawing, in the block letters:

It does not have a inside. I looked and looked. There is nothing in there. It is like a word that means nothing wearing the shape of a word that means something. It knows I can see it. It has started looking back.

I turned the page.

I am going to be very quiet now. I am going to be so quiet it cannot hear me. I am going to learn how to be part of the field. Rabbits do this. I watched a rabbit do this. The thing that was hunting it walked past three times and the rabbit was right there the whole time just being part of the field. I am going to be a rabbit. I am going to be so quiet I forget I can see it and maybe then it will forget it saw me seeing it.

I read that three times.

A nine year old boy in 1963 had independently arrived at the same defensive strategy that certain meditation traditions spend decades teaching. Not from wisdom. From necessity. From the particular intelligence of a child who has no adults available to solve his problems and therefore solves them himself with whatever is at hand.

Be the rabbit.

Be so still you become part of the field.

I had done this. I had done this so completely and for so long that I had forgotten I was doing it. Had forgotten there was something to hide from. Had built a life of deliberate ordinariness around a silence so practiced it became invisible even to me.

Fifty years of being the rabbit.

And now Gerald was in a chair with his eyes open and Vera Simmons was tending a garden she had left to tomorrow and something without an inside had left its cold residue in a dead man's living room four houses down.

The rabbit in the field.

And something walking past that had just remembered where it had last seen me.

I turned to the final pages of content. The last entries were different in character from the earlier ones — less precise, more fragmented, the handwriting of a boy who was in the process of doing what he had described. Becoming quiet. Letting the ability go still. Teaching himself to stop receiving what he did not ask to receive.

The last three pages were dated. November 1963. Three entries spread across two weeks.

November 4 — it has not looked this way in four days. The quiet is working. I do not look at it. I look at everything else.

November 9 — I think it has moved on. I am going to keep being quiet anyway. I am going to be quiet for a long time. Maybe forever. Some things are not worth seeing just because you can see them.

November 17 — I am not going to write in here anymore. I am going to put this somewhere and not look at it. Maybe someday when I am old and things make more sense I will read it and understand it better. Right now I am nine and I do not understand it and I want to go play.

I want to go play.

I sat on the basement floor and held the notebook and felt sixty two years collapse into the distance between those four words and this moment. The boy who wanted to go play. The man who had gone and played, had gone and built and flown and sailed and written and married and failed and gotten up and written some more and been, on balance, and against considerable odds, reasonably all right.

And had apparently left this waiting for himself.

This specific Wednesday morning.

This basement floor.

I heard Wren's voice upstairs. She had arrived while I was reading, had come in with Nora, was asking something about breakfast in the particular tone she uses when she is asking about breakfast and also about something else entirely.

I heard Nora answer.

I heard the gap between the answer and what the answer meant — I am fine, everything is fine, your grandfather is fine, this is a normal morning — and I heard it the way Wren hears everything and the way I had not let myself hear anything for fifty years.

Nora was afraid.

Not of what I was afraid of. She didn't know about that yet. She was afraid of the ordinary things — her father getting older, neighbors dying, the fragility of the life she had built on the assumption that the people she loved would remain in it.

Reasonable fears. The fears of a woman who sees clearly within the available light.

I thought about what it would cost her when I told her there was a different light available and what it illuminated was considerably more complicated than what she currently knew about.

I decided that conversation could wait until after breakfast.

I put the notebook inside my jacket, close to my body, the way you carry something you are not ready to put down but are not ready to display. Stood up from the basement floor with the architectural assistance of the wall and the careful negotiation with my knees that has become our morning ritual.

Climbed the stairs.

Emerged into the kitchen where Nora was making eggs with the focused competence of a woman who needs something to be under control and where Wren was sitting at the table with her dark eyes moving between her mother's face and the basement door I had just come through.

She looked at me.

I looked at her.

In her expression I saw the question she was not asking out loud in front of her mother — *what is down there, what did you find, what are you carrying inside your jacket that you weren't carrying before* — and I saw that she already knew the answer wasn't nothing.

I sat down at the table.

Smells good, I said to Nora.

Sit down and stop hovering, Nora said, which I was already doing, but this is the conversational music of daughters and fathers and I have learned to let it play.

Wren watched me across the table.

I poured coffee.

Outside the window, four houses down, Margaret's garden was going to need tending and nobody was going to do it and I was going to have to find a way to live with that alongside everything else I was going to have to find a way to live with.

Grandpa, Wren said quietly.

Mm.

She glanced at my jacket. Back at my face. The old eyes in the young face asking the question the young face was too careful to ask out loud.

Did you find something.

Nora turned from the stove. *Find something where.*

In the basement, I said. *An old notebook. From when I was young.*

What kind of notebook.

I looked at my granddaughter across the kitchen table in the northern Michigan morning with the water visible through the window and Gerald four houses down gone from the world and Vera Simmons tending a garden she had left to tomorrow and something without an inside moving through the ambient cruelty of the current age like weather finding the lowest ground.

The kind, I said, *where you write down things you're afraid you'll forget.*

Nora put eggs on plates.

Wren held my gaze for a moment longer.

Then she nodded, once, the small serious nod of someone who understands that some conversations happen at the table and some conversations happen later, in quieter rooms, between people who speak the same language.

She picked up her fork.

I picked up mine.

Outside, the loon called once across the water.

Neither of us looked up.

We already knew what it was saying.

Chapter 4

Chapter Four — The Distance Between Fine and Fine

Dinner at Nora and Dale's house happens at six thirty with the reliability of a well-maintained engine. This is Dale's doing. Dale Carver is a man who believes in the structural integrity of routine the way he believes in the structural integrity of everything else — you build it right, you maintain it honestly, it holds. He has applied this philosophy to his contracting business, his marriage, his friendships, and his dinner schedule with equal success and I respect him for it even when the six thirty rule catches me mid-sentence at my desk.

They live four minutes from my house which Nora arranged deliberately and has never admitted to deliberately arranging. I find this endearing. I find most things about my daughter endearing, including her conviction that subtlety is something she possesses.

I walked over at six twenty five with the notebook still inside my jacket and the specific expression I have worn at family dinners for fifty years — present, warm, mildly amused, giving nothing away. I have been told I have a good poker face. This is not a compliment I sought but it has served me adequately across seven decades of situations that required it.

Dale met me at the door with the handshake that has been our greeting for nineteen years. Solid. Brief. The handshake of a man who means it without making a production of it.

Harlan. He stepped back to let me in. *Heard about Gerald. Hell of a thing.*

Hell of a thing, I agreed.

Good neighbor.

The best kind.

We stood in the entryway for a moment in the comfortable silence of men who have run out of adequate words for loss and have mutually agreed not to fill the silence with inadequate ones. Then the kitchen produced a smell that required investigation and we investigated it.

Nora had made pot roast.

Pot roast means she is worried about something. Lasagna means she is angry about something. Roast chicken means everything is fine. In nineteen years of paying attention I have developed what I believe to be an accurate Nora Carver emotional weather system based entirely on protein and preparation method. I have never told her this. Some intelligence is worth protecting.

Cooper was at the table already, phone face down beside his plate in the performative compliance of an eleven year old who has been told twice to put it away and is demonstrating his virtue at maximum visible effort. He had his father's jaw and his mother's eyes and the particular energy of a boy who has recently grown two inches and hasn't finished being surprised by it.

Hey Grandpa. He said this to the table approximately.

Cooper. I said this to the top of his head approximately.

This is the full extent of our pre-dinner communication and we are both satisfied with it.

Wren was already in her chair with her hands folded on the table in the particular stillness she achieves that no other six year old I have encountered achieves. Most children at dinner tables vibrate at a frequency slightly above furniture. Wren sits with the settled patience of someone who has found her position and sees no reason to renegotiate it.

She watched me cross the kitchen and sit down.

I watched her watch me.

We did not say anything.

We did not need to.

Dale poured water. Nora brought the pot roast with the focused presentation of a woman who has made this particular dish as an act of emotional management and wants it acknowledged without wanting to explain why it needs acknowledging.

Smells incredible, I said.

It's just pot roast, she said, which means thank you.

We settled into the dinner the way this family settles into dinners — not loudly, not quietly, in the particular middle register of people who are comfortable enough with each other to leave spaces in the conversation without rushing to fill them.

Dale talked about a job in Elk Rapids. A foundation issue that the previous contractor had addressed with the specific combination of optimism and inadequate materials that Dale finds both professionally offensive and personally baffling. He has strong feelings about foundations. I find this appropriate in a man married to my daughter.

Nora talked about a situation at work involving a colleague she referred to only as *the one with the ceramic plant* in the tone that indicated the ceramic plant was the least of this person's offenses.

Cooper ate with the focused efficiency of a boy whose body is conducting a separate and urgent project that requires significant caloric input.

Wren ate small precise bites and watched everyone's faces with the dark patient eyes and said nothing, which is her default setting in group situations, the quiet that is not absence but its own form of presence — a tuning fork held still while everything around it vibrates.

Then Dale asked Cooper about his math test.

Cooper said he was fine.

He said it the way people say fine when they mean the other thing — with the slight upward inflection at the end that turns a statement into a question and a question into a small plea for no follow up. His eyes went briefly to his plate. His fork rearranged a piece of carrot with unnecessary attention.

I heard it.

Across the table, Wren heard it.

I did not look at her. I looked at my pot roast which was excellent and which Nora had made because Gerald was dead and the world felt unreliable and sometimes pot roast is the most honest response available.

Fine how, Dale said, because Dale is a man who checks foundations.

Just fine, Cooper said. *It wasn't that hard.*

The carrot received further attention.

Nora said *we can go over it after dinner if you want* in the careful voice of a mother who knows the answer is no and is making the offer anyway because the offer is the point.

Cooper said *I said I'm fine* with the specific emphasis of an eleven year old who has reached the limit of this particular topic.

Wren put down her fork.

You're not though, she said.

The table went briefly still in the way tables go still when a six year old states a true thing at the wrong moment.

Cooper looked at his sister with the expression brothers reserve for sisters who have just done the thing they always do at the worst possible time. *I am.*

You're not. No cruelty in it. No satisfaction. Just the flat precision of a fact being recorded. *You're worried about it. I can hear it.*

Wren, Nora said.

But he is.

That's enough.

Wren looked at her mother. Then at her plate. Then at her fork which she picked up and resumed using with the composure of someone who has said the true thing and accepted that the true thing is not always welcome and has made a separate peace with that fact.

Cooper stared at her for a moment with the complex expression of a brother who is simultaneously annoyed and unnerved and reluctantly aware that his sister is correct.

Dale looked at his pot roast.

Nora looked at me.

I looked at my pot roast.

The dinner resumed its forward motion the way dinners do when families have learned to navigate the particular geography of Wren's observations — not ignoring them exactly, not engaging them exactly, moving around them the way water moves around a stone, finding the path of least disruption.

I have watched this happen for six years. The small truths stated plainly. The room adjusting. Wren returning to her food without apparent distress, having said the thing she heard and accepted the family's need to unhear it.

What it costs her to do this I think about more than I let on.

After dinner Dale and Cooper retreated to the living room where a game of some kind was happening on the television with the volume at the level Dale pretends is reasonable and Nora pretends to accept. I helped Nora with the dishes because this is our time, the standing side by side at the sink time, the time when things get said that don't get said at tables.

Wren appeared in the kitchen doorway.

Can I show Grandpa the backyard, she said to Nora.

Nora looked at her daughter. Looked at me. The look of a woman who understands that something is happening between these two that she does not fully understand and has made a partial peace with not fully understanding because the alternative is a conversation she doesn't have the vocabulary for yet.

Don't stay out long, she said. *It's getting cold.*

The backyard in October in northern Michigan is a specific kind of beautiful that requires no editorial comment. The last of the color in the trees. The particular quality of the evening light off the water visible through the tree line. The smell of wood smoke from somewhere nearby and the cold coming in underneath it.

Wren walked to the middle of the yard and stopped.

I stopped beside her.

We stood in the cooling evening and she looked at the tree line with the focused attention she gives to things that deserve serious study and I stood beside her with the notebook against my ribs and Gerald four houses down gone from the world and waited for her to say what she had brought me outside to say.

It was on our street today, she said.

Everything in me went quiet.

Not the surface quiet. The other kind.

When, I said.

After school. Walking home. It was by the Millers' mailbox. She said this the way she says everything — flat, precise, no drama, just the fact of the thing. *It was looking at our houses.*

Did it see you.

I don't think so. I looked at the mailbox instead of at it. Like you said about the rabbit.

I had not yet told her about the rabbit.

I looked at her.

She looked at the tree line.

I haven't told you about the rabbit yet, I said carefully.

No, she agreed.

How do you know about the rabbit.

She was quiet for a moment in the way she gets quiet when she is deciding how to explain something that she experiences as obvious and understands is not obvious to everyone else.

I just knew, she said. *When I saw it I just knew not to look at it directly. It felt like the right thing. Like knowing not to touch a hot stove before anyone tells you.* She paused. *Is that the rabbit.*

That's the rabbit, I said.

She nodded. Filed it. Moved on with the efficiency of someone for whom confirmation of a thing they already know is useful but not surprising.

Grandpa.

Mm.

It's getting bigger isn't it. Not a question exactly. More like a hypothesis being tested. *Since Mr. Gerald. It's bigger than it was.*

I looked at the tree line. The last light going out of it. The cold coming in underneath the wood smoke and the dark following close behind.

Yes, I said. *I think it is.*

She stood beside me in the yard in the October evening and I felt her absorb this the way she absorbs all true things — completely, without flinching, with the particular courage of someone who has not yet learned that courage is supposed to be difficult.

Are we going to stop it, she said.

I looked down at my granddaughter. Six years old. Dark eyes reflecting the last of the evening light. Standing in a backyard in northern Michigan asking me the question I had been asking myself since I sat on a basement floor with a dead man's residue still on me and read what a nine year old boy had written about a thing that did not have an inside.

The honest answer was I don't know.

The true answer was we have to.

The answer I gave her was the one that sat at the intersection of both.

Yes, I said. *We are.*

She took my hand.

We stood in the yard until Nora called us in and the dark came all the way down and the wood smoke smell faded and the cold settled in with the permanence of a northern Michigan October cold that has made its decision and will not be argued with.

Inside, Cooper had apparently resolved his feelings about the math test because he was explaining to Dale at some length why his answer had technically been correct despite what the teacher's key suggested. Dale was listening with the expression of a man who is simultaneously proud of his son's conviction and aware that this particular conviction is going to require some careful management.

Nora handed me coffee.

I accepted it with the gratitude of a man who has been outside in October with the knowledge of what is moving through his granddaughter's street and needs something warm to hold.

Wren sat back down at the table with her hands folded and her dark eyes moving from face to face and her small mouth quiet.

Reading the room.

Reading all of us.

Knowing things she didn't say.

I watched her and thought about a nine year old boy in 1963 who had made the same calculation at a thousand dinner tables — what to say, what to keep, how to be present in the room without being fully visible in it.

The distance between fine and fine.

She caught me watching her.

Something passed between us that didn't have a name.

Outside, four houses down, the lights in Gerald's house were off for the first time in eleven years.

Chapter 5

THE QUIET ONES

Chapter Five — The Lowest Ground

I have lived long enough to watch the weather change.

Not the Michigan weather, which has its own opinions and expresses them without apology. The other weather. The kind that moves through communities the way rot moves through wood — invisible at first, detectable only by pressure, by the slight give where there used to be resistance, and then one day you put your hand on something that looked solid and it goes through.

I first noticed it two years ago. Maybe three. The specific timestamp is hard to fix because it didn't arrive as an event. It arrived as a accumulation. A town meeting that went ten degrees past disagreement into something that left a taste in the air. A neighbor who stopped waving not out of rudeness exactly but out of the particular exhaustion of a man who has decided that friendliness is a resource he can no longer afford to spend on people he isn't certain about anymore.

Certainty had become the currency. You had it or you didn't. And the people who dispensed it — loudly, confidently, with the specific righteousness of those who have found a way to make their fear look like conviction — had cornered the market.

I am a fiction writer. I notice things for a living. I noticed this.

I also noticed what it was doing to people.

Not the ones doing the dispensing. They were fine. Certainty is a remarkable analgesic — it numbs everything it touches, including the parts of the brain responsible for doubt and mercy and the productive discomfort of being wrong. The people doing the dispensing felt, I suspected, better than they had in years.

It was the others I watched.

The ones on the receiving end of it. The ones who had built their lives on the assumption that decency was a shared value and were discovering, incrementally and at some personal cost, that this assumption had been optimistic. The ones who said true things at town meetings and drove home afterward in a silence that was not peaceful. The ones who put signs in their windows and found the signs discussed in ways that made them feel like strangers in a place they had lived for thirty years.

Something was happening to some of those people.

Something I recognized.

The comfortable blindness was burning off. Not pleasantly — nothing about the process was pleasant — but burning off the way fog burns off a lake in the morning, leaving everything exposed and cold and more clearly itself than it was an hour ago.

They were starting to see.

Not what I see. Not the residue and the shade and the thing that moves through rooms without displacing air. Just — more. More than they'd seen before. The gap between what was said and what was meant. The performance beneath the conviction. The fear wearing the costume of certainty and hoping nobody looked too closely at the seams.

They were becoming visible.

And something had noticed.

The town meeting was on a Thursday.

I almost didn't go. Thursday evenings I write. Thursday evenings I have written for twenty three years with the reliability of a man who understands that the book does not care about your schedule but will accept the schedule if you offer it consistently enough. Chapter twelve was still lying to me but we had reached the stage of our negotiation where lying felt like progress.

Nora called at four thirty.

Are you going tonight.

I hadn't planned to.

Gerald would have gone.

This was not fair and she knew it was not fair and she said it anyway because daughters who love their fathers have a specific arsenal and they are not above using it.

I went.

The Antrim County community room smells of old coffee and the specific institutional optimism of a space that has hosted decades of meetings at which people came to be heard and left feeling otherwise. Folding chairs. Fluorescent lights with the patience of things that have outlived every argument held beneath them. A podium that has absorbed more certainty than any piece of furniture should reasonably be asked to absorb.

I arrived early enough to choose my seat with intention. Back row. Left side. Wall behind me. Sight lines to all three exits. This is not paranoia. This is fifty years of habit wearing the costume of preference.

The room filled.

I watched it fill the way I watch everything — with the particular attention of a man who has learned that the most important information is usually in the details people are not trying to present. The way someone sits. The distance they leave between themselves and their neighbor. The quality of the smiles, which smiles reached the eyes and which stopped at the mouth and why.

I saw people I knew. Rudy Marsh, who ran the hardware store on Bellaire's main street and had recently and publicly changed his mind about something he'd believed for years. He sat three rows ahead of me with his wife and the careful posture of a man who has learned that the room's temperature changes when he enters it. Agnes Pfeiffer, who taught piano to half the children in the county and had put a sign in her music studio window six months ago that had generated more discussion than she'd anticipated or wanted. She sat alone in the middle section with her hands folded and her chin at the angle of someone who has decided to stop apologizing for taking up space.

And others. The quiet ones — not quiet like Wren and me, quiet like people who have swallowed things they can no longer comfortably swallow and are sitting with the discomfort of that in a public room on a Thursday evening.

The meeting began.

I will not recount the specifics because the specifics are both particular to this place and this time and completely interchangeable with a hundred other places and a hundred other times. The content has become almost beside the point. What matters is the temperature. What matters is the way reasonable disagreement curdled somewhere in the second half hour into something that required a different word. What matters is the man three rows from the front whose voice climbed past conviction into the register where voices go when they have confused volume with truth. What matters is the woman beside him nodding with the specific rhythm of someone who has found in agreement a relief from the exhausting work of thinking.

What matters is what I felt.

Forty minutes into the meeting I felt it.

Cold without temperature. Pressing absence. The residue I had felt in Gerald's living room — not identical, not as concentrated, but related. The way a fire smells related to the smoke it produces. The source and its evidence occupying different spaces.

It was in the room.

I did not move. Did not look for it directly. Became very still on the frequency that stillness lives on and looked at the room through my peripheral attention the way you look at a faint star — directly at it and it disappears, shift your gaze slightly to the side and there it is.

There it was.

Not a figure. Not a shape a stranger would notice. A quality of the air in the back corner opposite me, near the emergency exit, that was wrong in the specific way a shadow is wrong when the light that should be casting it is absent. A concentration of the ambient wrongness that had been building in the room for forty minutes, drawn to it the way water is drawn to the lowest ground.

Finding the lowest ground.

That was what it did. That was how it moved. It did not create the cruelty. The cruelty was entirely human, entirely self-generated, requiring no supernatural assistance whatsoever — we are more than capable of that particular project without help. But it found the cruelty the way certain organisms find decay, the way certain weather finds certain valleys.

And it fed.

I watched it the way the rabbit watches the thing hunting it — without looking, without moving, with every available sense except the one the thing was monitoring.

It was larger than it had been in Gerald's house.

Not physically larger. Larger in the way a fire is larger when it finds more fuel. More present. More concentrated. The absence it carried with it deeper and colder and more itself than it had been four days ago.

Rudy Marsh said something three rows ahead of me. Something true and carefully worded and delivered with the restraint of a man who has learned to measure his words in this particular room. Something about the community he had lived in for forty years and what he believed it had been and what he was watching it become.

The man three rows from the front turned in his seat.

What followed was not an argument. An argument requires two people engaging with each other's meaning. This was one person using another person's words as raw material for a performance that had nothing to do with the words and everything to do with the audience.

Rudy sat with it. Absorbed it. Said nothing further.

In the back corner near the emergency exit the coldness deepened.

Agnes Pfeiffer looked at her folded hands.

I looked at the ceiling.

The meeting concluded thirty minutes later with the specific inconclusion of meetings that were never going to conclude in any way that satisfied anyone who came hoping for resolution. People filed out with the expressions they'd arrived with, slightly more compressed. The man three rows from the front shook hands with people near the exit. Rudy and his wife left quickly through the side door.

I sat in my folding chair until the room was mostly empty.

The corner near the emergency exit was empty too.

The residue remained, faint and cold, the way a smell remains after its source has left.

I sat with it for a moment.

I see you, I did not say out loud.

But I thought it.

And in the thinking of it felt, or imagined I felt — the distinction was becoming harder to maintain — the faintest response. Not acknowledgment exactly. More like the way a compass needle moves when you bring a magnet near it. An orientation. A registration.

It knew something in the room had noticed it.

It didn't know what.

Not yet.

I stood up from the folding chair with the assistance of my knees which had their usual opinions about folding chairs and cold rooms and men of my age who sit in them longer than necessary.

Drove home through the northern Michigan dark.

Went to my desk.

Did not open chapter twelve.

Opened the notebook instead.

Read the fourth page again.

A woman with short gray hair sits in a classroom after the children leave. She has a garden at home she thinks about when the room gets hard.

Called Nora.

I need you to do something for me.

Dad it's ten thirty.

I know. I need you to invite Vera Simmons to dinner.

Silence on the line. The silence of a daughter processing a request that doesn't make immediate sense and is deciding whether to ask why or trust the decades of her father not making requests without reason.

The retired teacher.

Yes.

Why.

Because she said a true thing at a town meeting and I'd like to know she's all right.

Another silence. Shorter.

I'll call her tomorrow.

Thank you.

Dad.

Mm.

Are you okay.

I looked at the notebook on my desk. At the cold feeling that had followed me home from the community room and was sitting in the corner of my study with the patience of something that does not experience time as a limited resource.

I'm working on it, I said.

I hung up.

Sat at my desk.

Outside the northern Michigan dark was complete and cold and indifferent in the way darkness is when it has been darkness for ten thousand years and has no particular feelings about one more night of it.

Inside, chapter twelve was still lying to me.

I closed the laptop.

Opened the notebook to the last page with writing on it.

Read the final line the boy had written one more time.

I am not going to write in here anymore. I am going to put this somewhere and not look at it. Maybe someday when I am old and things make more sense I will read it and understand it better. Right now I am nine and I do not understand it and I want to go play.

I want to go play.

I sat with that for a long time in the study with the cold in the corner and the dark outside and the notebook in my hands.

Then I picked up a pen.

Turned to the first blank page after the boy's last entry.

And for the first time in sixty two years, I wrote in it.

November, present day. I am seventy one. Things do not make more sense. But I understand it better. It is back. I think it has been back for a while and I was the last to know. There is a girl. Six years old. She sees it more clearly than I ever did. I don't know yet if that makes her safer or less safe. I am going to find out. I am going to write in here again because the boy was right to write things down. Some things need to be outside your head where you can look at them from a safe distance. This is one of those things.

It is larger than it was.

So am I.

I closed the notebook.

Put it in the desk drawer where I could reach it without getting up.

Made coffee.

Went to bed.

Lay in the northern Michigan dark and listened to the lake and thought about Rudy Marsh driving home in silence and Agnes Pfeiffer and her folded hands and Vera Simmons in a classroom thinking about her garden and Gerald in his chair with the crossword four across blank forever.

The ones who see clearly.

The ones it finds.

Thought about a six year old with dark eyes standing in a backyard saying *are we going to stop it* with the matter of fact certainty of someone who has already decided the answer and is simply waiting for the adult to catch up.

Yes, I had said.

We are.

I lay in the dark and hoped I had not lied to her.

The lake moved.

The dark held.

Somewhere out in it, patient as geology, something without an inside moved through the lowest ground and fed and grew and oriented itself toward the small warm lights of the people who were beginning to see.

I closed my eyes.

Got quiet on the frequency that quiet lives on.

Be the rabbit.

Be part of the field.

And tried to remember everything a nine year old boy had known before he decided not to know it anymore.

Chapter 6

THE QUIET ONES

Chapter Six — Sharp As A New Pencil

Vera Simmons arrived at Nora's door on a Friday evening with a bottle of wine she had clearly selected with intention and a potato salad she had clearly made from scratch and the specific energy of a woman who does not accept dinner invitations casually and wanted her hosts to know she understood the weight of the gesture.

She was seventy three. Short gray hair worn without apology. The posture of a woman who had spent thirty two years asking children to sit up straight and had absorbed the instruction herself so thoroughly it had become structural. Eyes that were brown and direct and missed approximately nothing and did not pretend otherwise.

I liked her immediately in the way you like people who have decided that pretending is a tax they are no longer willing to pay.

Nora took the wine and the potato salad with the warmth of a woman who had not known Vera Simmons well before this evening and was revising her estimate upward in real time. Dale shook her hand with the handshake he reserves for people he respects before he has been given specific reason to and I noted this and filed it.

Cooper said hey from the couch without looking up which Vera accepted with the equanimity of a woman who has spent three decades in rooms full of people who would rather be somewhere else.

Wren was at the kitchen table drawing.

She looked up when Vera entered.

Vera looked at Wren.

Something passed between them that I was probably the only other person in the room equipped to notice — a brief mutual recognition, the specific quality of two people who operate on a similar frequency encountering each other for the first time. Vera's eyes stayed on Wren a half second longer than the social situation required.

Then she looked at me.

You must be the father, she said.

Harlan, I said.

Vera. She shook my hand with a grip that meant it. *Nora says you write novels.*

I do.

I've read two of them.

I hope they held up.

The first one more than the second. She said this without cruelty, as simple assessment. *The second one you were being careful. I could feel you being careful. Writers shouldn't be careful.*

I looked at this woman for a moment.

No, I agreed. *They shouldn't.*

She nodded as if something had been confirmed and moved into the kitchen to help Nora with things that didn't need helping with, which is what guests do when they want to be useful and also want to see how a kitchen operates because kitchens tell you things about people that living rooms are too composed to reveal.

I sat down.

The notebook was in my jacket.

It had been in my jacket for four days. I was becoming accustomed to its weight the way you become accustomed to a stone in your shoe that you have decided for complicated reasons not to remove.

Dinner was roast chicken.

Everything fine then. Nora's weather system confirmed.

We settled around the table — Nora and Dale at their ends, Cooper beside his father with the resigned posture of a boy attending an adult dinner under the terms of a negotiated agreement, Wren beside me, Vera across from me with the bottle of wine open between us and her potato salad beside it looking exactly as good as something made from scratch by a woman who does things properly looks.

The conversation found its level the way good dinner conversation does — not immediately, not without the usual preliminary orbiting of safe subjects, but genuinely, by the salad course.

Dale talked about the Elk Rapids foundation job. Vera asked questions that revealed she understood load bearing walls better than most people who haven't built things and Dale's estimation of her climbed visibly.

Nora talked about the ceramic plant colleague. Vera listened with the focused patience of a woman who has heard thirty two years of staff room complaints and can identify the real problem beneath the stated one within two sentences. She identified it. Nora looked at her with the expression of someone who has just been understood more efficiently than expected.

Cooper ate.

Wren watched Vera.

Vera, I noticed, occasionally watched Wren back.

I watched all of it from the particular remove I have maintained at dinner tables since approximately 1963 and ate the roast chicken which was excellent and thought about the fourth page of the notebook and the woman with short gray hair who thinks about her garden when the room gets hard.

I heard you at the meeting Thursday, I said during a pause that presented itself between the chicken and whatever Nora had made for dessert.

Vera looked at me directly. *I didn't see you there.*

Back row. Left side.

Of course. Something in her expression acknowledged something without naming it. *Then you heard what came after.*

I did.

And.

And you said a true thing and the room made you pay for it.

She was quiet for a moment. Not the quiet of someone who has been hurt and is composing themselves. The quiet of someone taking an honest inventory.

It's become expensive, she said. *Saying true things. In ways I didn't anticipate when I was younger and less careful about the budget.*

Does it stop you.

No. Simply. No elaboration. *Does it stop you.*

I'm a fiction writer, I said. *I hide true things inside made up ones. It's less expensive and considerably more cowardly.*

She almost smiled. *At least you know which one it is.*

Dale was looking between us with the expression of a man following a conversation that is happening on two levels and tracking one of them. Nora was looking at me with the expression of a daughter who recognizes her father being more himself than he usually allows in company and is deciding how she feels about it.

Wren was looking at Vera with the dark patient eyes.

You think about your garden, Wren said.

The table went still.

Vera looked at Wren. Not startled. Something more considered than startled.

I do, she said carefully.

When things are hard. You think about it. Wren said this the way she says all true things — flat, kind, without performance. *I can hear it.*

Wren, Nora said.

It's all right, Vera said. She was still looking at Wren with the expression of a woman recalibrating. *She's right. I do.* To Wren: *How did you know that.*

Wren considered the question with the seriousness it deserved.

I hear what people mean, she said. *Not always the words. The underneath part.*

Vera looked at her for a long moment.

Then she looked at me.

I held her gaze and gave her what I could — which was not an explanation, not yet, but something. Acknowledgment. The specific look of one person telling another person across a dinner table that what they are experiencing is real and they are not alone in it and there is more to say but not here and not now.

She received it the way people receive things they have been waiting for without knowing they were waiting.

Your granddaughter, she said to me.

Yes.

She's something.

Yes, I said. *She is.*

Dessert arrived. The conversation found its way back to the surface and stayed there for the remainder of the evening — comfortable, warm, the pleasant specific conversation of people who have decided they like each other and are content to like each other on the surface for now with the understanding that there is more below it when the time comes.

Vera left at nine with the potato salad dish washed and returned and her coat buttoned against the October cold and a warmth in her expression that had not been there when she arrived.

At the door she shook my hand again.

Held it a half second longer than the leaving required.

You wanted to tell me something tonight, she said quietly. *And decided not to.*

I looked at this sharp pencil of a woman in my daughter's doorway.

Yes, I said.

Will you.

Yes. When I know how.

She nodded. Accepted this. Buttoned the top button of her coat.

I've been feeling something, she said. Very quietly. Not a question. Not quite a statement. The words of someone testing whether the ground will hold before committing their full weight to it. *For about two weeks. Since the meeting. Something I can't* — She stopped. *I was a science teacher before I was a fourth grade teacher. I have a particular relationship with things I can't explain.*

So do I, I said. *I was going to be a science teacher once.*

Something in her eyes.

And.

And I became something else instead, I said. *When I understood that some things don't wait for explanation before they require a response.*

She stood with that for a moment in the cold doorway.

Call me, she said.

I will, I said. *Soon.*

She walked to her car in the October dark. I watched her go with the notebook against my ribs and the cold thing that had followed me home from the community room still sitting in the corner of my study four minutes away and the fourth page of a child's notebook burning in my memory.

A woman with short gray hair. She has a garden at home she thinks about when the room gets hard.

I closed the door.

Stood in Nora's entryway.

Wren appeared beside me the way smoke appears.

She feels it too, Wren said.

Yes.

Is she safe.

I looked at my granddaughter in Nora's entryway with the October cold coming in under the door and the notebook in my jacket and the specific terrible arithmetic of a man who knows what is coming and has not yet found the mechanism to stop it.

I'm going to call her tomorrow, I said.

Wren looked at me with the eyes that were too old for her face.

She heard the gap between what I said and what I meant.

She always did.

She took my hand and we went back to the warmth of the kitchen where Dale was doing dishes and Nora was wrapping leftovers and Cooper was back on his phone with the focused relief of a boy released from adult obligations and everything was ordinary and warm and exactly as fragile as things are when something without an inside is growing in the lowest ground outside and has begun to notice the lights in the windows of the people who can see.

I held my granddaughter's hand.

And did not let go until it was time to walk home through the dark.

Chapter 7

THE QUIET ONES

Chapter Seven — The Frequency of Rabbits

The basement at two in the morning has a particular quality that no other room in the house achieves at any other hour. The world above it goes quiet enough that the basement becomes its own country — different air, different light, different relationship to time. I have always done my clearest thinking in basements. This probably says something about me that a qualified professional could articulate better than I can.

I sat on the floor with my back against the cold wall and the notebook in my lap and a flashlight beside me because the overhead bulb had burned out three weeks ago and I had not replaced it because replacing it required a trip to the hardware store and the hardware store required passing Gerald's house and I had been managing my route accordingly.

This is called avoidance. I am familiar with the concept. I have practiced it at a professional level for most of my adult life.

The flashlight made a circle of yellow light that held the notebook and my hands and not much else. Beyond the circle the basement was dark in the specific way basements are dark at two in the morning — completely, without apology, with the patience of a darkness that has been there longer than the house built over it.

I was not afraid of the dark.

I want to be precise about this because precision matters and because people who read about men sitting alone in dark basements at two in the morning tend to assume fear is the operating condition. It was not. I have been afraid in my life — genuinely, specifically, with cause — and I know what it feels like and this was not it.

What I felt sitting on the basement floor at two in the morning was the specific discomfort of a man attempting to remember something he taught himself to forget.

This is different from fear the way surgery is different from injury. Both involve pain. The origins and purposes are not the same.

I was nine years old the first time I understood that I was not like other people.

Not in the way children understand they are different — the wrong clothes, the wrong lunch, the wrong answer in class. That kind of different I understood earlier and managed accordingly, which is to say badly and with significant collateral damage. I mean different in the way that cannot be managed, cannot be concealed, cannot be reasoned with or reasoned away because it does not operate in the register where reason lives.

The farm in October.

I need you to understand the farm in October before I can tell you what happened on it.

Northern Michigan farms in October are not the farms of paintings or calendars or the selective memory of people who grew up on them and have had sufficient years to soften the edges. They are cold in the specific way that cold becomes personal — not the cold of a winter morning you walk through to get somewhere warm, but the cold of a place that has decided warmth is a temporary condition and October is when it gets honest about that.

The corn rows were long.

I know how that sounds. Corn rows are corn rows, they have a beginning and an end, a child can walk them. This is true. It is also true that when you are nine years old and small for your age and your hands are bleeding from the dry husks and the wind is coming across the field with nothing between it and you and the row ahead looks exactly like the row behind, the length of a corn row becomes something other than a measurement.

It becomes a condition.

My brother Chuck was two rows over. I could hear him but not see him, which was the geography of our childhood in general — close enough to know we were not entirely alone, far enough that close enough was its own particular loneliness.

I was thinking about nothing.

This is important.

I had learned early that thinking on the farm was a luxury the farm did not offer at market rate. Thinking required a portion of your attention that the farm had prior claim on. So I had developed, without naming it or understanding it as a skill, the ability to work from a place below thought. Hands doing what hands needed to do. Body moving through the row. Mind gone somewhere quieter and less present than the field.

It was in this state — hands bleeding, mind absent, body working the row in the October cold — that I first felt it.

Not heard. Not saw. Felt.

The way you feel a change in pressure before a storm arrives. The way the air becomes a different thing a moment before lightning finds the ground. Something in the field had changed and my body registered the change before my mind returned from wherever minds go when they leave the body to manage alone.

I stopped walking.

The corn moved around me in the wind.

Two rows over Chuck kept working, the sound of husks and the rhythmic thud of corn hitting the wagon, the ordinary music of the farm in October that I had heard so many times it had stopped being sound and become background.

I stood still in the row and looked at the tree line.

The tree line was forty yards away. Elm and oak and the first of the birch that would be bare by November, and behind them the deeper dark of older growth that the farm had never cleared because even farmers understand that some things should be left to themselves.

Something was at the tree line.

I cannot tell you what I saw because saw is not the right word and I refuse to use the wrong word for something I have spent sixty two years trying to find the right ones for. I can tell you what I perceived, which is a different country with a different language.

I perceived an absence.

Not the absence of something that had been there and left. The presence of an absence. The active, specific wrongness of a space that should contain what spaces contain — air, light, the ordinary physics of a field in October — and instead contained a deficit. A place where something was, defined entirely by what it was not.

It was at the tree line.

And it was looking at me.

I know how this sounds. I knew how it sounded at nine years old, which is why I never told anyone, which is why the notebook existed, which is why the notebook was in a box in a basement for sixty two years waiting for a morning when a neighbor died in his chair and the coffee was still warm.

I stood in the corn row.

The thing at the tree line — the absence, the deficit, the shape of nothing wearing the outline of something — oriented toward me with the specific quality of attention that has no human analogue because humans have insides and what I was perceiving did not and the attention of a thing without an inside is a different order of experience than anything with an inside can prepare you for.

I felt it notice me noticing it.

And then I did something that I did not decide to do, that arrived from below the level of decision, from the same place that had perceived the thing before my mind returned from its absence —

I got quiet.

Not surface quiet. Not the quiet of a boy standing still in a field. The other kind. The deep kind. The kind that has a frequency to it, a particular quality of stillness that exists below thought and breath and the noise the body makes simply by being alive.

I got quiet and I became part of the field.

Not metaphorically. I mean that something in me — the part that had been perceiving the thing at the tree line, the part that operated on whatever frequency that perception lived on — went still in a way that I can only describe as becoming unavailable. As if a light had been switched off in a room and the room had become indistinguishable from the dark around it.

I stood in the corn row and became part of the field.

And the thing at the tree line —

Stopped.

Not stopped moving. It had not been moving. Stopped attending. The orientation that had been directed at me shifted, imperceptibly at first and then completely, the way a compass needle shifts when the magnet is removed, swinging away from north and settling into the general indifference of a needle with nothing specific to point at.

It lost me.

I stood in the corn row for a long time after that. Long enough for Chuck to finish his row and start another. Long enough for the cold to work its way through my coat and find my bones and make its opinion known. Long enough for my hands to stop bleeding and start the specific aching that comes after bleeding stops.

Then I walked to the end of my row, threw the last of the corn into the wagon, and went in for supper.

I did not tell anyone.

I did not tell anyone because I was nine years old and had learned with considerable efficiency that the adults in my life had a limited appetite for things they could not see, and an even more limited patience for children who insisted on the reality of things they could not see, and that the intersection of these two limitations produced outcomes I preferred to avoid.

I told the notebook instead.

That night. In the cold bedroom with the wind finding every gap in the walls that gaps existed in and Chuck asleep in the other bed with the deep unconscious breathing of a boy who had not seen anything at the tree line and therefore had no obstacle between himself and sleep.

I wrote it down in the block letters.

There is a thing. It does not have a inside.

Sitting on the basement floor at two in the morning sixty two years later, I held the notebook and remembered the corn row and the October cold and the bleeding hands and the absence at the tree line with the clarity of a man who has spent five decades suppressing a memory and discovered that suppression is not the same as erasure.

The memory had been there the whole time.

Waiting with the patience of things that do not experience time as a limited resource.

I remembered the frequency.

This is what I had come to the basement to do. Not to read the notebook — I had read it. Not to sit in the dark — the dark was incidental. I had come to remember the frequency the way a musician comes to a quiet room to remember a piece of music they learned in childhood and have not played in fifty years. Knowing it is in there somewhere. Knowing the body remembers what the mind has filed away. Needing the quiet to hear it.

I closed my eyes.

Found the place below thought.

Below breath.

Below the ordinary noise of being alive in a body in a basement in northern Michigan at two in the morning.

Found the stillness.

And there it was.

Unchanged. Undiminished. Waiting with the patient availability of something that is not a skill exactly — skills can be lost, skills require maintenance — but a capacity. Something built into the original architecture and never removed, only unused. The way a door that has been painted shut is still a door.

I found the frequency.

Got quiet on it.

Became part of the field.

And sat in the basement in the dark feeling it the way you feel a familiar thing after a long absence — with the complicated emotion of recognition, which contains both the pleasure of finding and the grief of having lost in the first place.

The cold thing that had been in the corner of my study was not in the basement.

I noted its absence.

I noted that its absence felt different now that I was quiet on the frequency. More apparent. More specific. The way a smell is more apparent to someone paying attention than to someone who has been in the room long enough to stop noticing it.

I could feel where it wasn't.

Which meant with practice I might be able to feel where it was.

The rabbit does not only hide from the hunter.

The rabbit, if it is paying attention, knows where the hunter is.

I sat with this for a while in the dark.

Then I thought about Wren.

Six years old. Dark eyes. Hearing truth beneath words with the effortless precision of someone who has never learned to filter it out.

Standing in the backyard saying *are we going to stop it* with the matter of fact certainty of someone who has already decided.

She had found the frequency without being taught.

She had been born on it.

Which meant she had never learned to hide on it. Had never needed to. Had never had a morning in a corn row that taught her the specific terrible lesson that some things notice you noticing them.

She could see the thing clearly.

The thing did not yet know she could see it.

The gap between those two facts was the only weapon available to us and it would remain a weapon only as long as she learned to see without appearing to see. To look without looking. To be present on the frequency without being visible on it.

To be the rabbit.

I needed to teach her before it understood what she was.

I opened my eyes.

The basement dark held.

The flashlight circle held the notebook and my hands and the specific expression of a man who has just remembered something he needed and found it costs more than he anticipated and is going to pay anyway.

I stood up.

Knees.

Negotiations.

Conducted.

Climbed the stairs.

Made coffee at two thirty in the morning because sleep was a different country now and I had work to do before I could apply for a visa.

Sat at my desk.

Did not open chapter twelve.

Opened a new document.

And began to write down everything a nine year old boy in a corn field had known about the thing at the tree line. Everything the body remembered that the mind had filed away. Everything the frequency carried when you got quiet enough to hear it.

The notebook was the boy's record.

This was the man's.

Outside, the northern Michigan dark held its position with the confidence of a darkness that has been doing this since before there were windows to press against.

Somewhere in it, patient as geology, something without an inside moved through the lowest ground.

And for the first time in fifty years, something was moving in the other direction.

Toward it.

Quietly.

On a frequency it hadn't learned to listen for yet.

Chapter 8

THE QUIET ONES

Chapter Eight — Teaching The Rabbit

She appeared at the top of the basement stairs on a Saturday morning the way she always appeared — without announcement, without the preliminary noise that other humans generate simply by moving through space, as if the air made accommodations for her that it didn't bother making for anyone else.

I heard the door open.

Saw the small feet on the top step.

Grandpa.

Down here.

The feet descended. Carefully. One step at a time with the deliberate placement of a child who has been told about basements and stairs and the general wisdom of not rushing either. She reached the bottom and stood in the edge of the flashlight circle — I still hadn't replaced the bulb, the hardware store still required passing Gerald's house — and looked at me sitting on the floor with my back against the wall and my notebook and my coffee and the expression of a man who has been awake since two in the morning and has made a separate peace with that.

She sat down across from me.

Cross legged. Back straight. Hands in her lap.

Looking at me with the dark patient eyes.

We sat for a moment in the basement quiet.

You were down here a long time last night, she said.

You were asleep.

I woke up. No accusation in it. Simple fact. *I could feel you down here.*

I looked at my granddaughter across the flashlight circle.

What did it feel like, I said.

She thought about this with the seriousness she brings to questions that deserve it.

Like when someone is concentrating very hard on something in another room, she said. *You can't hear it but you can feel the shape of it.*

I nodded.

That's accurate, I said.

Were you practicing.

Yes.

The quiet thing.

Yes.

She looked at the notebook in my lap. At the coffee. At the general evidence of a man who had been on the basement floor in the dark for several hours working on something he considered important enough to lose sleep over.

Can I learn it today, she said.

Not can you teach me. Can I learn it. The distinction was hers, not mine, and I noted it the way I note all of Wren's distinctions — as information about the specific quality of her mind, which processes agency differently than most six year olds process agency, which is to say she understands that learning is something the learner does and teaching is something that merely assists.

I had been thinking about this moment since two in the morning.

I had been thinking about what it would cost her.

Here is what I had arrived at after four hours of basement floor consideration: the cost of teaching her was real and the cost of not teaching her was worse. This is the arithmetic of people who have no good options and are selecting the least bad one. I have made this calculation before. It does not get more comfortable with practice.

Yes, I said. *Today.*

She settled slightly. Not relaxing exactly — she was already still in a way most adults never achieve. Something more like a tree settling its roots before a wind it can feel coming.

First, I said, *I need to tell you something true.*

Okay.

What I'm going to teach you is real. Not a game. Not pretend. Real. I watched her face. *You know the difference.*

Yes.

And you know the thing on our street is real.

Yes.

So you understand that what I'm teaching you is for that. Not for fun. For that.

She looked at me steadily.

I know grandpa, she said, with the patient tone of someone who has been several steps ahead of this conversation since it started and is waiting with good manners for it to catch up.

I almost smiled.

Right, I said. *Of course you do.*

I set the notebook aside. Put the coffee down. Shifted to face her more directly, the cross legged configuration of a man whose knees had filed a formal objection that he had overruled on the grounds of necessity.

Do you know what a frequency is, I said.

She thought about it. *Like on the radio. Different stations.*

Exactly like that. Everything that exists operates on frequencies. The table. The wall. Us. All of it broadcasting on different channels simultaneously. Most people only receive a few of them. The ones they've been taught to receive. The ones that match the equipment they've been told they have.

She was watching me with the focused attention she gives to things that matter.

But some people, I said, *have equipment that wasn't on the standard list. They receive channels most people don't know exist. You're one of those people. You've always known this even if you didn't have words for it.*

The underneath part, she said. *What people mean.*

That's one channel yes. There are others. I paused. *The thing on our street broadcasts on one of those channels. Which is why you can perceive it when other people can't. Your equipment finds it.*

And it can find me.

Yes. Because you're broadcasting on the same range of frequencies. Two radios that can receive each other can also be received by each other. I watched her process this. *Do you follow.*

I'm a radio it can hear, she said.

Yes.

And I need to learn to turn down the volume.

I looked at my six year old granddaughter.

Not turn it down, I said. *Turn it off. Completely. So completely that it cannot distinguish you from the background. From the field.*

The rabbit, she said.

The rabbit.

She nodded. Filed it. Ready.

How, she said.

Here is what I told her.

I told her that the frequency she broadcasts on is connected to attention. That what the thing perceives is not her body or her physical presence but her awareness — the specific quality of consciousness that notices, that reaches out, that engages with what it perceives. That when she sees the thing she is also, in the act of seeing, sending a signal on the frequency that says *something here is aware of you.*

I told her the rabbit does not stop existing. The rabbit stops announcing its existence.

I told her the mechanism was stillness at a level below the physical. That it was not about not moving — you could stand perfectly still and still be broadcasting if your attention was active and reaching. The stillness required was the stillness of attention itself. The quieting of the reaching quality of consciousness. The difference between a searchlight and a pool of still water — both can show you what's there, but one announces itself and one does not.

I told her it was harder than it sounded and easier than she feared and that the difficulty was not in achieving it but in maintaining it while also continuing to function — to walk, to talk, to be apparently present in the ordinary world while being genuinely absent on the frequency.

She listened to all of this without interrupting.

When I finished she was quiet for a moment.

So I have to be in two places at once, she said.

Yes. Exactly yes.

Present here, she touched her own sternum, *and gone there.* She touched her temple.

Not gone, I said. *Still. The way water is still. Still water reflects everything. Still water announces nothing.*

She thought about this.

Can you show me, she said.

I'm going to try, I said. *Watch.*

I closed my eyes.

Found the place below thought.

Below breath.

Below the ordinary noise of being alive.

Found the frequency.

Got quiet on it.

I cannot describe what this looks like from the outside because I have only ever done it from the inside. I can tell you what Wren told me afterward, which was: *you didn't disappear but you got further away. Like when something moves to the back of a picture.*

I held it for thirty seconds.

Then I came back.

Opened my eyes.

Wren was looking at me with an expression I had not seen on her face before — not the patient assessment, not the quiet knowing. Something closer to recognition. The look of someone who has just seen something they have been trying to name for their entire life and have suddenly been handed the word for.

I felt that, she said.

What did it feel like.

Like you stepped back, she said. *But you didn't move.*

Yes.

I want to do that.

I know.

Show me how to start.

I looked at my granddaughter across the flashlight circle in the basement on a Saturday morning with the notebook beside me and the October light coming through the small window above the washing machine and the hardware store three minutes away that I still hadn't visited and Gerald four houses down still gone from the world.

I thought about a nine year old boy in a corn field learning this alone. With no one to show him. With nothing but necessity and a rabbit and the specific intelligence of a child who solves problems with whatever is at hand because the alternative is not solving them.

I thought about what it had cost that boy.

The hiding. The pretending. The long careful performance of ordinary that had lasted five decades. The life built on the foundation of a silence so complete it had swallowed not just the thing he was hiding from but parts of himself he hadn't intended to include in the burial.

I was about to teach my granddaughter to do this.

I was about to hand her the tool that had saved me and cost me simultaneously and tell her to use it and trust that her hands were steadier than mine had been.

Grandpa, she said.

Mm.

You look sad.

I looked at her.

I'm not sad, I said.

She heard the gap between what I said and what I meant.

She always did.

It's okay, she said, with the specific gentleness of a six year old who has decided to take care of someone older. *You can be sad and still teach me. I don't mind.*

I sat with that for a moment.

Then I said: *Close your eyes.*

She closed them.

Find where your thoughts are, I said. *Not what you're thinking. Where thinking happens. The place in you where attention lives.*

Silence.

Found it, she said.

Of course she had.

Now, I said, *imagine that place as a light. Bright. Reaching outward. The way a flashlight reaches.*

She nodded with her eyes closed.

Now, I said, *don't turn it off. Don't dim it. Just — stop it reaching. Pull it back inside itself. Let it be light that illuminates without projecting. The way a lamp lights a room without shining out the window.*

Silence.

Long silence.

I watched her face.

Watched the quality of her stillness change.

It is difficult to describe what I saw because what I saw was an absence of something rather than a presence, which is always harder to articulate. But I can tell you that the quality of her presence in the basement changed. That something in the frequency of the room shifted in a way I felt before I understood it. That the specific signature of her awareness — which I had been feeling since she came down the stairs, bright and clear and present the way her awareness always was, the way it had been since she was born and I had held her the first time and felt the specific frequency of her and recognized it — went quiet.

Not gone.

Still.

Still water.

Still water reflects everything.

Still water announces nothing.

I held my breath.

She held the stillness.

Ten seconds.

Twenty.

Thirty.

Then she opened her eyes.

Looked at me across the flashlight circle.

Like that, she said.

Not a question.

Like that, I said.

Something moved across her face. Not quite pride. Something quieter and more complicated than pride. The expression of someone who has just discovered a room in themselves they didn't know existed and is standing in the doorway looking at it.

It feels strange, she said.

Yes.

Like holding very still inside.

Yes.

But I can still see you. I can still see everything.

Yes. That's the point. You're not less aware. You're less visible to what's aware of you.

She thought about this.

Like a one way mirror, she said.

I looked at my granddaughter.

Exactly like a one way mirror, I said. *Yes.*

She nodded.

Looked at her hands in her lap.

Grandpa.

Mm.

When you learned this. Was someone teaching you.

I picked up my coffee. Cold now. Drank it anyway because some things you do for the ritual of them rather than the substance.

No, I said. *I learned it alone.*

How.

I watched a rabbit, I said. *In a field. Something was hunting it. The rabbit went still in a way that made it disappear without moving. I watched it and then I did what it did.*

She absorbed this.

That must have been scary, she said. *Learning alone.*

It was.

I'm not scared, she said. *Because you're here.*

I set the cold coffee down.

Looked at the flashlight circle and the notebook and the small window with the October light coming through it and my granddaughter sitting cross legged on the basement floor with her hands in her lap and her dark eyes and her six years of being exactly what she was without apology or concealment.

I thought about what was moving through the lowest ground outside.

I thought about Gerald and Vera and Rudy Marsh driving home in silence and Agnes Pfeiffer with her folded hands.

I thought about a boy in a corn field learning alone in the cold.

Practice it, I said. *Every day. Sitting here or anywhere. In and out of it. Find it and hold it and release it and find it again until it's as natural as breathing.*

How long did it take you.

Two weeks, I said. *To hold it reliably.*

I'll do it faster, she said.

Not boasting. Assessment.

She probably would.

One more thing, I said.

Okay.

When you practice — and when you use it out there — you are not hiding who you are. You are not making yourself smaller. You are not disappearing. I waited until her eyes were fully on mine. *You are choosing what you show and what you keep. That's not the same thing. Do you understand the difference.*

She looked at me for a long moment with the eyes that were too old for her face.

Yes, she said.

Say it back to me.

I'm not hiding, she said. *I'm choosing.*

Yes.

Like you, she said. *You chose for a long time.*

Yes.

But now you're choosing differently.

I looked at my granddaughter.

Outside the small window the October light moved across the basement floor between us like something trying to reach from one side to the other.

Yes, I said. *Now I'm choosing differently.*

She unfolded her legs. Stood up with the effortless architecture of someone whose knees have no opinions yet. Brushed off her pajama pants.

I'm going to practice upstairs, she said. *While I eat breakfast.*

Good.

Can I come back tomorrow.

The door's always open.

She went to the stairs. Put her hand on the rail. Paused.

Grandpa.

Mm.

The thing on our street.

Yes.

It was there again this morning. Before I came down here. She said this the way she said all true things — flat, kind, without drama. *By the Millers' mailbox again. But further up the yard than before.*

Everything in me went quiet on the frequency.

Did it see you.

No. I did the thing before I looked. A pause. *I wanted to see if it worked before lessons.*

I looked at my six year old granddaughter standing on the bottom step of my basement stairs in her pajamas in the October morning.

Did it work, I said.

Yes, she said. *It looked right at where I was standing and then looked away.*

She climbed the stairs with the careful one step at a time placement of a child who has been told about stairs.

The door at the top opened and closed.

I sat on the basement floor in the flashlight circle and held the notebook and listened to the small sounds of a six year old making breakfast in the kitchen above me and thought about what she had just told me.

It had looked right at her.

And looked away.

The rabbit had worked on the first try.

Which meant she was more capable than I had hoped.

Which meant we had less time than I had estimated.

Because the thing that had looked at her and looked away had been close enough to look.

And it was getting closer.

I picked up my pen.

Opened the notebook to the page where the man had begun writing after the boy stopped.

Added one line.

She is ready faster than I was. The thing is closer than I thought. These two facts are related and I have not yet determined if their relationship is fortunate or otherwise.

Closed the notebook.

Looked at the small window.

The October light had moved on.

The basement was its own country again.

I sat in it for a while longer.

Thinking about a one way mirror.

And what it meant that on one side of it stood a six year old girl in her pajamas who had just made herself invisible to something ancient and soulless on the first try.

And what it meant that the something ancient and soulless had been close enough to her front yard to look.

And what the boy in the corn field would have done with that information.

And what the man in the basement was going to do with it instead.

Chapter 9

THE QUIET ONES

Chapter Eight — Teaching The Rabbit

She appeared at the top of the basement stairs on a Saturday morning the way she always appeared — without announcement, without the preliminary noise that other humans generate simply by moving through space, as if the air made accommodations for her that it didn't bother making for anyone else.

I heard the door open.

Saw the small feet on the top step.

Grandpa.

Down here.

The feet descended. Carefully. One step at a time with the deliberate placement of a child who has been told about basements and stairs and the general wisdom of not rushing either. She reached the bottom and stood in the edge of the flashlight circle — I still hadn't replaced the bulb, the hardware store still required passing Gerald's house — and looked at me sitting on the floor with my back against the wall and my notebook and my coffee and the expression of a man who has been awake since two in the morning and has made a separate peace with that.

She sat down across from me.

Cross legged. Back straight. Hands in her lap.

Looking at me with the dark patient eyes.

We sat for a moment in the basement quiet.

You were down here a long time last night, she said.

You were asleep.

I woke up. No accusation in it. Simple fact. *I could feel you down here.*

I looked at my granddaughter across the flashlight circle.

What did it feel like, I said.

She thought about this with the seriousness she brings to questions that deserve it.

Like when someone is concentrating very hard on something in another room, she said. *You can't hear it but you can feel the shape of it.*

I nodded.

That's accurate, I said.

Were you practicing.

Yes.

The quiet thing.

Yes.

She looked at the notebook in my lap. At the coffee. At the general evidence of a man who had been on the basement floor in the dark for several hours working on something he considered important enough to lose sleep over.

Can I learn it today, she said.

Not can you teach me. Can I learn it. The distinction was hers, not mine, and I noted it the way I note all of Wren's distinctions — as information about the specific quality of her mind, which processes agency differently than most six year olds process agency, which is to say she understands that learning is something the learner does and teaching is something that merely assists.

I had been thinking about this moment since two in the morning.

I had been thinking about what it would cost her.

Here is what I had arrived at after four hours of basement floor consideration: the cost of teaching her was real and the cost of not teaching her was worse. This is the arithmetic of people who have no good options and are selecting the least bad one. I have made this calculation before. It does not get more comfortable with practice.

Yes, I said. *Today.*

She settled slightly. Not relaxing exactly — she was already still in a way most adults never achieve. Something more like a tree settling its roots before a wind it can feel coming.

First, I said, *I need to tell you something true.*

Okay.

What I'm going to teach you is real. Not a game. Not pretend. Real. I watched her face. *You know the difference.*

Yes.

And you know the thing on our street is real.

Yes.

So you understand that what I'm teaching you is for that. Not for fun. For that.

She looked at me steadily.

I know grandpa, she said, with the patient tone of someone who has been several steps ahead of this conversation since it started and is waiting with good manners for it to catch up.

I almost smiled.

Right, I said. *Of course you do.*

I set the notebook aside. Put the coffee down. Shifted to face her more directly, the cross legged configuration of a man whose knees had filed a formal objection that he had overruled on the grounds of necessity.

Do you know what a frequency is, I said.

She thought about it. *Like on the radio. Different stations.*

Exactly like that. Everything that exists operates on frequencies. The table. The wall. Us. All of it broadcasting on different channels simultaneously. Most people only receive a few of them. The ones they've been taught to receive. The ones that match the equipment they've been told they have.

She was watching me with the focused attention she gives to things that matter.

But some people, I said, *have equipment that wasn't on the standard list. They receive channels most people don't know exist. You're one of those people. You've always known this even if you didn't have words for it.*

The underneath part, she said. *What people mean.*

That's one channel yes. There are others. I paused. *The thing on our street broadcasts on one of those channels. Which is why you can perceive it when other people can't. Your equipment finds it.*

And it can find me.

Yes. Because you're broadcasting on the same range of frequencies. Two radios that can receive each other can also be received by each other. I watched her process this. *Do you follow.*

I'm a radio it can hear, she said.

Yes.

And I need to learn to turn down the volume.

I looked at my six year old granddaughter.

Not turn it down, I said. *Turn it off. Completely. So completely that it cannot distinguish you from the background. From the field.*

The rabbit, she said.

The rabbit.

She nodded. Filed it. Ready.

How, she said.

Here is what I told her.

I told her that the frequency she broadcasts on is connected to attention. That what the thing perceives is not her body or her physical presence but her awareness — the specific quality of consciousness that notices, that reaches out, that engages with what it perceives. That when she sees the thing she is also, in the act of seeing, sending a signal on the frequency that says *something here is aware of you.*

I told her the rabbit does not stop existing. The rabbit stops announcing its existence.

I told her the mechanism was stillness at a level below the physical. That it was not about not moving — you could stand perfectly still and still be broadcasting if your attention was active and reaching. The stillness required was the stillness of attention itself. The quieting of the reaching quality of consciousness. The difference between a searchlight and a pool of still water — both can show you what's there, but one announces itself and one does not.

I told her it was harder than it sounded and easier than she feared and that the difficulty was not in achieving it but in maintaining it while also continuing to function — to walk, to talk, to be apparently present in the ordinary world while being genuinely absent on the frequency.

She listened to all of this without interrupting.

When I finished she was quiet for a moment.

So I have to be in two places at once, she said.

Yes. Exactly yes.

Present here, she touched her own sternum, *and gone there.* She touched her temple.

Not gone, I said. *Still. The way water is still. Still water reflects everything. Still water announces nothing.*

She thought about this.

Can you show me, she said.

I'm going to try, I said. *Watch.*

I closed my eyes.

Found the place below thought.

Below breath.

Below the ordinary noise of being alive.

Found the frequency.

Got quiet on it.

I cannot describe what this looks like from the outside because I have only ever done it from the inside. I can tell you what Wren told me afterward, which was: *you didn't disappear but you got further away. Like when something moves to the back of a picture.*

I held it for thirty seconds.

Then I came back.

Opened my eyes.

Wren was looking at me with an expression I had not seen on her face before — not the patient assessment, not the quiet knowing. Something closer to recognition. The look of someone who has just seen something they have been trying to name for their entire life and have suddenly been handed the word for.

I felt that, she said.

What did it feel like.

Like you stepped back, she said. *But you didn't move.*

Yes.

I want to do that.

I know.

Show me how to start.

I looked at my granddaughter across the flashlight circle in the basement on a Saturday morning with the notebook beside me and the October light coming through the small window above the washing machine and the hardware store three minutes away that I still hadn't visited and Gerald four houses down still gone from the world.

I thought about a nine year old boy in a corn field learning this alone. With no one to show him. With nothing but necessity and a rabbit and the specific intelligence of a child who solves problems with whatever is at hand because the alternative is not solving them.

I thought about what it had cost that boy.

The hiding. The pretending. The long careful performance of ordinary that had lasted five decades. The life built on the foundation of a silence so complete it had swallowed not just the thing he was hiding from but parts of himself he hadn't intended to include in the burial.

I was about to teach my granddaughter to do this.

I was about to hand her the tool that had saved me and cost me simultaneously and tell her to use it and trust that her hands were steadier than mine had been.

Grandpa, she said.

Mm.

You look sad.

I looked at her.

I'm not sad, I said.

She heard the gap between what I said and what I meant.

She always did.

It's okay, she said, with the specific gentleness of a six year old who has decided to take care of someone older. *You can be sad and still teach me. I don't mind.*

I sat with that for a moment.

Then I said: *Close your eyes.*

She closed them.

Find where your thoughts are, I said. *Not what you're thinking. Where thinking happens. The place in you where attention lives.*

Silence.

Found it, she said.

Of course she had.

Now, I said, *imagine that place as a light. Bright. Reaching outward. The way a flashlight reaches.*

She nodded with her eyes closed.

Now, I said, *don't turn it off. Don't dim it. Just — stop it reaching. Pull it back inside itself. Let it be light that illuminates without projecting. The way a lamp lights a room without shining out the window.*

Silence.

Long silence.

I watched her face.

Watched the quality of her stillness change.

It is difficult to describe what I saw because what I saw was an absence of something rather than a presence, which is always harder to articulate. But I can tell you that the quality of her presence in the basement changed. That something in the frequency of the room shifted in a way I felt before I understood it. That the specific signature of her awareness — which I had been feeling since she came down the stairs, bright and clear and present the way her awareness always was, the way it had been since she was born and I had held her the first time and felt the specific frequency of her and recognized it — went quiet.

Not gone.

Still.

Still water.

Still water reflects everything.

Still water announces nothing.

I held my breath.

She held the stillness.

Ten seconds.

Twenty.

Thirty.

Then she opened her eyes.

Looked at me across the flashlight circle.

Like that, she said.

Not a question.

Like that, I said.

Something moved across her face. Not quite pride. Something quieter and more complicated than pride. The expression of someone who has just discovered a room in themselves they didn't know existed and is standing in the doorway looking at it.

It feels strange, she said.

Yes.

Like holding very still inside.

Yes.

But I can still see you. I can still see everything.

Yes. That's the point. You're not less aware. You're less visible to what's aware of you.

She thought about this.

Like a one way mirror, she said.

I looked at my granddaughter.

Exactly like a one way mirror, I said. *Yes.*

She nodded.

Looked at her hands in her lap.

Grandpa.

Mm.

When you learned this. Was someone teaching you.

I picked up my coffee. Cold now. Drank it anyway because some things you do for the ritual of them rather than the substance.

No, I said. *I learned it alone.*

How.

I watched a rabbit, I said. *In a field. Something was hunting it. The rabbit went still in a way that made it disappear without moving. I watched it and then I did what it did.*

She absorbed this.

That must have been scary, she said. *Learning alone.*

It was.

I'm not scared, she said. *Because you're here.*

I set the cold coffee down.

Looked at the flashlight circle and the notebook and the small window with the October light coming through it and my granddaughter sitting cross legged on the basement floor with her hands in her lap and her dark eyes and her six years of being exactly what she was without apology or concealment.

I thought about what was moving through the lowest ground outside.

I thought about Gerald and Vera and Rudy Marsh driving home in silence and Agnes Pfeiffer with her folded hands.

I thought about a boy in a corn field learning alone in the cold.

Practice it, I said. *Every day. Sitting here or anywhere. In and out of it. Find it and hold it and release it and find it again until it's as natural as breathing.*

How long did it take you.

Two weeks, I said. *To hold it reliably.*

I'll do it faster, she said.

Not boasting. Assessment.

She probably would.

One more thing, I said.

Okay.

When you practice — and when you use it out there — you are not hiding who you are. You are not making yourself smaller. You are not disappearing. I waited until her eyes were fully on mine. *You are choosing what you show and what you keep. That's not the same thing. Do you understand the difference.*

She looked at me for a long moment with the eyes that were too old for her face.

Yes, she said.

Say it back to me.

I'm not hiding, she said. *I'm choosing.*

Yes.

Like you, she said. *You chose for a long time.*

Yes.

But now you're choosing differently.

I looked at my granddaughter.

Outside the small window the October light moved across the basement floor between us like something trying to reach from one side to the other.

Yes, I said. *Now I'm choosing differently.*

She unfolded her legs. Stood up with the effortless architecture of someone whose knees have no opinions yet. Brushed off her pajama pants.

I'm going to practice upstairs, she said. *While I eat breakfast.*

Good.

Can I come back tomorrow.

The door's always open.

She went to the stairs. Put her hand on the rail. Paused.

Grandpa.

Mm.

The thing on our street.

Yes.

It was there again this morning. Before I came down here. She said this the way she said all true things — flat, kind, without drama. *By the Millers' mailbox again. But further up the yard than before.*

Everything in me went quiet on the frequency.

Did it see you.

No. I did the thing before I looked. A pause. *I wanted to see if it worked before lessons.*

I looked at my six year old granddaughter standing on the bottom step of my basement stairs in her pajamas in the October morning.

Did it work, I said.

Yes, she said. *It looked right at where I was standing and then looked away.*

She climbed the stairs with the careful one step at a time placement of a child who has been told about stairs.

The door at the top opened and closed.

I sat on the basement floor in the flashlight circle and held the notebook and listened to the small sounds of a six year old making breakfast in the kitchen above me and thought about what she had just told me.

It had looked right at her.

And looked away.

The rabbit had worked on the first try.

Which meant she was more capable than I had hoped.

Which meant we had less time than I had estimated.

Because the thing that had looked at her and looked away had been close enough to look.

And it was getting closer.

I picked up my pen.

Opened the notebook to the page where the man had begun writing after the boy stopped.

Added one line.

She is ready faster than I was. The thing is closer than I thought. These two facts are related and I have not yet determined if their relationship is fortunate or otherwise.

Closed the notebook.

Looked at the small window.

The October light had moved on.

The basement was its own country again.

I sat in it for a while longer.

Thinking about a one way mirror.

And what it meant that on one side of it stood a six year old girl in her pajamas who had just made herself invisible to something ancient and soulless on the first try.

And what it meant that the something ancient and soulless had been close enough to her front yard to look.

And what the boy in the corn field would have done with that information.

And what the man in the basement was going to do with it instead.

Chapter Nine when ready — Harlan goes to the police. Detective Briggs. The conversation that goes exactly as expected. The specific dark humor of a seventy one year old man sitting across a desk from a competent detective and trying to explain in the language of the visible world something that exists entirely outside it. And the moment Briggs, who is smarter than his assignment requires, says something that tells Harlan he is more rattled than he will officially admit.

10

1:39 PM

You skipped Chapter Nine — Harlan at the police station with Briggs. That chapter does important work — the dark humor of the impossible conversation, Briggs more rattled than he admits, and Harlan leaving alone with the confirmation that he has no institutional help available.

It also sets up everything that follows in Act Two.

Do you want Nine first to keep the sequence intact — or are you deliberately jumping to Ten for a reason?

Your call. I just don't want to lose Briggs. He earns his place later.

9

1:39 PM

THE QUIET ONES

Chapter Nine — The Limits of Visible Evidence

The Antrim County Sheriff's Department occupies a building in Bellaire that was designed by someone who believed that function and charm were mutually exclusive and chose function with the conviction of a man who has never been wrong about anything and doesn't intend to start. Concrete block. Institutional tan. Windows that admit light the way a bouncer admits people — grudgingly and only enough to maintain minimum standards.

I have driven past it for eleven years without going in.

I went in on a Monday morning at nine a.m. because nine a.m. on a Monday is when serious people conduct serious business and I wanted to be taken seriously for as long as the conversation would allow, which I estimated at approximately seven minutes.

The woman at the front desk had the specific energy of someone who has heard everything and filed it and is prepared to hear everything again without surprise or particular interest. I told her I wanted to speak with someone about the deaths of Gerald Hoffstead and Vera Simmons.

She looked at me.

I looked at her.

Vera Simmons isn't dead, she said.

No, I said. *Not yet.*

This bought me Detective Briggs in under four minutes which I considered a reasonable return on the investment.

Briggs had the careful eyes I remembered from Gerald's kitchen — the eyes of a man whose intelligence slightly exceeds his current context and who has made a working peace with that gap without entirely surrendering to it. Mid forties. The build of someone who was athletic in a previous decade and maintains enough of it to remember what it felt like. A desk with the specific organized chaos of someone who thinks in systems and is currently running more systems than the desk was designed to hold.

He looked at me when I sat down across from him.

I looked at him.

Mr. —

Harlan, I said. *Harlan Gage.*

Mr. Gage. He had a notepad. He wrote my name on it with the unhurried deliberateness of a man who uses the act of writing to buy himself thinking time. *You found Gerald Hoffstead.*

I did.

And you're here about his death and about Vera Simmons who is not dead.

Correct.

Why Vera Simmons.

Because I believe she's in danger.

He wrote something. I could not see what.

What kind of danger.

Here is the moment I had been preparing for since I decided to come. The moment where the language runs out. Where the available vocabulary of the visible world reaches its edge and everything beyond it requires either a leap of faith from the listener or a retreat to safer ground.

I have written fourteen novels. I understand the mechanics of how information lands. I understand that the same content delivered differently produces different receptions and that the difference between being heard and being dismissed often has less to do with the content than with the framing.

I had spent Sunday evening working on the framing.

Two people in this community have died in the past two weeks, I said. *Both found in their chairs. Both with the same presentation.*

Both individuals who had recently been publicly vocal about things that made certain people uncomfortable. I believe a third person who fits the same profile is at risk.

Briggs looked at me with the careful eyes.

You're describing Gerald Hoffstead and who else.

A man named Rudy Marsh. Hardware store on Main.

Rudy Marsh is alive.

Yes. I'm aware.

You said two people died.

Gerald Hoffstead and a woman named Vera Simmons.

Vera Simmons is alive. You said so yourself two minutes ago.

I looked at him.

He looked at me.

You're right, I said. *I misspoke. Gerald Hoffstead and one other person I'd prefer not to name until I have more information.*

Briggs wrote something. Put his pen down. Picked it up again. The behavior of a man whose instincts are pulling in a direction his training is not equipped to follow.

Mr. Gage, he said. *Gerald Hoffstead died of cardiac arrest. The medical examiner —*

I know what the medical examiner found.

Then you know there's no indication of —

I know what he found, I said again. *I'm not disputing what he found. I'm suggesting that what he found may not be the complete picture.*

Briggs sat back in his chair.

This is the posture of a man creating distance between himself and a conversation that is about to require it.

What do you think the complete picture is, he said.

And here is where fourteen novels and a lifetime of framing information for maximum reception ran directly into the wall that the wall was always going to be.

Because the complete picture was: there is something moving through your community that does not have an inside, that feeds on ambient cruelty and the clarity of people who have started seeing through the performance of certainty, that leaves a residue in the rooms where it has been that I can perceive on a frequency most people don't know exists, and that my six year old granddaughter can see more clearly than I can and has already been looked at directly by it twice from the end of her driveway.

I sat across from Detective Briggs in the institutional tan building on a Monday morning and considered my options.

Something is targeting people in this community who see clearly, I said. *Who say true things. Who have recently shed a comfortable blindness and become more themselves. I believe Gerald Hoffstead was one of those people. I believe others are at risk.*

Targeting how.

I don't know the mechanism in terms that would satisfy a medical examiner.

But you believe it's not natural causes.

I believe it's not natural causes.

Briggs looked at me for a long moment.

He had the expression of a man running two parallel processes — the official one, which had a protocol and a vocabulary and a filing system, and the other one, which was less organized and more honest and was currently generating results the official process had no folder for.

Mr. Gage, he said. *You're a novelist.*

I am.

Fiction.

Correct.

So you understand that what you're describing —

Sounds like fiction, I said. *Yes. I'm aware of how it sounds. I spent considerable time Sunday evening trying to find a way to make it sound like something else and was unsuccessful.*

He almost smiled.

Did not.

What would you like me to do with this information, he said.

I'd like you to keep Gerald's file open, I said. *And I'd like you to be aware of Vera Simmons and Rudy Marsh. Not surveillance. Just awareness. The kind that means if something happens you don't file it as coincidence.*

I can't open an investigation based on —

I'm not asking you to open an investigation, I said. *I'm asking you to keep a file open and pay attention. You're capable of both without institutional permission.*

He looked at me.

I looked at him.

The careful eyes doing their careful work.

How do you know Gerald's death wasn't natural causes, he said.

Not officially. Not for the notepad. The other process asking.

I considered my answer.

I was in the room after, I said. *Before the ambulance left. Something was wrong with the air in a way I can't quantify for you but couldn't misread.*

Wrong how.

Wrong the way a room is wrong after lightning has been in it, I said. *The air remembers.*

Briggs put his pen down.

Left it down.

Looked at his desk for a moment with the expression of a man who has been carrying something he hasn't told anyone and is deciding whether the person across from him is a safe place to put it.

The Simmons woman, he said. Quietly. Not for the notepad. *I drove past her house Friday evening.*

I waited.

The lights were all off, he said. *At six thirty. She's not the lights off at six thirty type.*

No, I said. *She's not.*

I slowed down. He said this the way people say things they're not sure they should be saying. *I don't know why I slowed down. I had no reason to slow down. I just* — He stopped.

The air, I said.

He looked at me.

Something felt wrong, he said. Very carefully. *From the street. With the lights off.*

Did you stop.

I knocked on the door. A pause. *She answered. She was fine. She'd fallen asleep on the couch.* Another pause. *She looked — tired. In a way that wasn't just tired.*

Yes, I said. *That's what it looks like.*

We sat with that for a moment.

The institutional tan walls held their position. The fluorescent light maintained its patient indifference. Outside someone was on a phone and a door opened and closed and the ordinary business of a Monday morning at the Antrim County Sheriff's Department continued without reference to what was happening at this particular desk.

I can't open an investigation, Briggs said again.

I know.

I have no evidence of anything actionable.

I know.

What you're describing isn't something I can —

I know, I said. *I'm not asking you to. I'm asking you to keep the file open and pay attention and call me if something happens that feels wrong from the street.*

He looked at me for a long moment.

Picked up his pen.

Wrote something on the notepad.

Tore the bottom strip off and slid it across the desk.

His cell number.

Not the official line.

The other one.

If something happens, he said. *That you think I should know about.*

I took the number.

Put it in my jacket pocket next to the notebook.

Thank you, I said.

I'm not doing anything, he said.

I know, I said. *Thank you anyway.*

I stood up.

My knees made their contribution to the proceedings.

Briggs watched me stand with the expression he'd arrived at somewhere in the middle of the conversation and hadn't left — not convinced, not dismissive, occupying the uncomfortable middle ground of a man whose official process and other process have reached a standoff and are waiting for more information before either one concedes.

Mr. Gage, he said as I turned to leave.

Harlan.

Harlan. He paused. *The other person. The one you didn't want to name.*

I turned back.

Yes.

They fit the same profile. Vocal. Clear-eyed. Recently more themselves than they used to be.

Yes.

Anyone I'd know.

I thought about Vera Simmons falling asleep on her couch with all the lights off at six thirty. About Rudy Marsh driving home in silence from the town meeting. About Agnes Pfeiffer with her folded hands.

Probably, I said. *This is a small county.*

Should I be worried about them.

You should be aware of them, I said. *There's a difference.*

What's the difference.

Worry, I said, *makes you slow. Awareness makes you ready.*

I left him with that and walked back through the institutional tan building and out into the October morning where the air was cold and clean and honest about what it was in the specific way October air in northern Michigan is always honest and I stood on the sidewalk for a moment and looked at the sky.

The sky looked back with the indifference of something that has been sky for longer than the current problem has existed and will continue being sky long after it resolves one way or another.

I found this comforting in the way that vast indifference is sometimes comforting.

Got in my car.

Drove home.

Past Gerald's house.

I looked at it as I passed.

The lights were off the way they were always off now. Margaret's garden going brown at the edges. The porch where he had waved every morning for eleven years empty in the particular way that specific absences are empty — not just without the thing but shaped by the thing that should be there.

I drove past.

Did not stop.

Went home.

Made coffee.

Sat at my desk.

Opened chapter twelve.

Read the first sentence.

Still lying.

Closed the laptop.

Took Briggs' number out of my pocket and looked at it.

Put it in the desk drawer next to the notebook.

Two things in the drawer now.

The boy's record and the detective's number.

The evidence of what I knew and the evidence of what the official world could offer.

I sat for a moment with the specific arithmetic of that.

Then I picked up my phone and called Vera Simmons.

She answered on the second ring with the voice of a woman who had been awake since before the call.

I was going to call you, she said.

I know, I said. *Tell me.*

And she did.

Chapter 10

THE QUIET ONES

Chapter Ten — What Vera Knew

There is a particular quality to the voice of someone who has been holding something alone for too long.

Not distress exactly. Not fear exactly. Something more precise than either — the specific compression of a person who has been carrying weight in a container not designed for weight and has reached the structural limit and is now, with great care and some relief, setting it down in front of someone they have decided can be trusted with it.

Vera Simmons had that voice on the phone.

I recognized it because I have had it myself. Because I know what it costs to carry something alone and what it feels like when the carrying becomes untenable and what the specific quality of relief is when you find the person you can hand it to.

I had found that person at nine years old and it had been a notebook.

Vera had found it now and it was a telephone and a novelist four minutes away who had looked at her across a dinner table and told her without words that what she was experiencing was real.

It started the night of the meeting, she said.

I had the notebook open on the desk. The man's section. I wrote the date and her name at the top of a fresh page and picked up my pen.

Tell me, I said.

I've been a science teacher, she said. *Fourth grade teacher. Thirty two years of asking children to observe carefully and report accurately and not confuse what they wish were true with what is actually there. I have a particular relationship with evidence. With the discipline of not seeing more than is present.*

I know, I said. *That's why I'm listening.*

A brief pause. The pause of someone deciding the ground will hold.

Walking to my car after the meeting, she said. *The parking lot behind the community room. You know it.*

Gravel lot. Two lights. One of them has been out for six months.

Yes. The dark side of the lot. She paused. *I had parked on the dark side because I arrived late and that was what was available. I was walking to my car and I — stopped.*

What stopped you.

I don't know, she said. *That's the honest answer. I don't know. Something changed in the air between one step and the next. A quality I don't have a word for. Not temperature. Not smell. Not sound. Something that registered on a sense I don't have an official name for and have spent my professional life being appropriately skeptical of.*

I wrote: *registered on unnamed sense. parking lot. dark side.*

What did you do, I said.

I stood still, she said. *Which was not a decision. My body stopped before my mind caught up. I stood still and looked at the dark part of the lot where the light was out and there was —* She stopped.

Take your time.

There was something there, she said. *In the dark. I want to be precise. I am going to be precise. There was something there that I perceived as present but that I could not see in any conventional sense. Not a figure. Not a shape. More like — the dark was doing something the dark wasn't supposed to be doing. Behaving differently than dark behaves.*

I wrote: *dark behaving differently than dark behaves.*

I underlined it.

What happened then, I said.

It — oriented, she said. *Toward me. That's the only word I have for it. It oriented the way something orients when it becomes aware of you. And I felt —* She paused. *I felt seen. In a way I did not want to be seen. In a way that felt like being looked at by something that has a very different idea of what looking is for than I do.*

I sat at my desk with the pen in my hand and the notebook open and the October light coming through the window and the cold certainty arriving in my chest the way cold certainty always arrives — quietly, completely, without asking permission.

How long did this last, I said.

Perhaps thirty seconds, she said. *Then I got into my car and locked the door which was a completely irrational response to something I cannot prove was there and which I did anyway without deliberation.*

Not irrational, I said. *Accurate.*

Silence on the line.

You know what it is, she said.

Not a question.

Yes.

Tell me.

I looked at the notebook. At the boy's section and the man's section and the careful block letters and the drawing with the edges that wouldn't hold still and the line that said *it does not have a inside.*

I'm going to tell you, I said. *But I want to ask you something first.*

All right.

Since that night. Two weeks. Has it happened again.

The pause before she answered was its own answer.

Yes, she said.

How many times.

Four, she said. *That I was certain of. Perhaps two more that I —* She stopped. *That I talked myself out of.*

Don't talk yourself out of them, I said. *Your first read is accurate. You've spent thirty two years training yourself to observe carefully. Trust the observation.*

Six times then, she said. With the precision of a woman recalibrating. *Six times in two weeks.*

I wrote it down.

Where.

The garden twice, she said. *Once at the grocery store. Once at the school — I still volunteer on Tuesdays. Once driving home from Agnes Pfeiffer's. Once —* She stopped.

Once, I said.

Once outside my bedroom window, she said. *At two in the morning. I was awake. I heard — not a sound. The absence of sound in a specific place. If that makes any sense.*

Complete sense, I said.

I turned the light on, she said. *It was gone. Or not gone. I don't know if gone is the right word for something I can't establish was there in any verifiable —*

Vera.

Yes.

Stop doing that.

A pause.

Doing what.

Qualifying every true thing with the framework you use to dismiss the things you can't verify, I said. *You're using your skepticism as a defense mechanism and it's slowing you down. The thing outside your bedroom window at two in the morning was there. You know it was there. The light didn't make it gone. It made it less convenient.*

Silence.

Long silence.

The kind that means something is being reconsidered at a fundamental level.

All right, she said finally. Quietly. The voice of a woman setting down a tool she has carried for thirty two years and finding her hands feel strange without it. *All right. It was there.*

Yes.

What is it.

I looked at the drawing in the notebook. The edges that the pencil had trouble committing to. The figure that had the shape of presence without the substance of it.

It's something that has never been alive, I said. *Not dead. Never alive. It exists in the way an absence exists — defined by what surrounds it rather than by what it is. It moves through the world on a frequency most people can't perceive. It's drawn to people who see clearly. Who say true things. Who have shed a comfortable blindness and become more themselves.*

Silence.

Why, she said.

Because being seen by someone who sees clearly is the one thing it can't tolerate, I said. *And the one thing it can't stop seeking. It has no soul. But it has something that functions like hunger. It needs to be near the ones who can almost see it. It needs the proximity.*

And the people it gets close to —

Die, I said. *Yes.*

The word sat on the line between us.

I did not soften it. Vera Simmons was not a woman who benefited from softened words and I had known this since she told me my second novel was careful.

Gerald, she said.

Yes.

The other one. The one you mentioned.

Yes.

Am I —

I don't know, I said. *I'm going to be honest with you because you've earned it. I don't know the timeline. I don't know the mechanism precisely. I know it's been close to you six times in two weeks and I know that Gerald died and I know that the notebook on my desk written by a nine year old boy in 1963 described Gerald's death before I was old enough to have met him.*

Silence.

A nine year old boy, she said.

Me, I said. *I was the boy.*

The silence that followed this was different from the previous silences. Fuller. The silence of a woman integrating multiple large things simultaneously with the focused efficiency of someone who has spent thirty two years teaching children that the universe is larger than the available textbooks and has always privately suspected this applied to herself as well.

You can perceive it, she said. *The way I can.*

Yes. Though differently. You perceive it the way a scientist perceives an anomaly — accurately, reluctantly, against your framework. I perceive it the way someone perceives weather. Directly. Without the intermediary of the framework.

Because you've always been able to.

Since I was nine years old in a corn field, yes.

And you've been hiding it.

For fifty years, yes.

Why.

Because the farm taught me that the things you can't explain are the things that get you hurt, I said. *And because hiding it worked and working things are hard to argue with.*

Until now.

Until Gerald, I said. *Until the notebook. Until —*

I stopped.

Until what, she said.

I looked at the window. At the October light. At the street beyond it where four houses down Gerald's porch was empty and Margaret's garden was going brown at the edges.

Until my granddaughter, I said. *She can see it more clearly than I can. She's six years old and she can see it completely and it doesn't know she can.*

That's — Vera stopped.

Yes, I said. *It is.*

Is she safe.

I'm working on that.

Harlan.

Yes.

What do I do, she said. *Specifically. Practically. I am a practical woman and I need practical instruction.*

I thought about the basement. The flashlight circle. The small feet on the stairs. The one way mirror.

I'm going to come and see you, I said. *Today if you're available. I'm going to bring the notebook and I'm going to show you something that a nine year old boy figured out in a corn field that I should have told someone about fifty years ago.*

What is it.

How to be invisible to something that's looking for you, I said. *Without moving. Without running. Without doing anything the world would notice.*

The rabbit, she said.

I stopped.

I'm sorry.

The rabbit, she said again. *That's what it feels like when I do it accidentally. When I go quiet in a particular way and it seems to — miss me. I've been doing it accidentally. I didn't know I was doing it until just now when you said that.*

I sat at my desk.

Held the phone.

Thought about a nine year old boy in a corn field watching a rabbit become part of the field and understanding without being told that this was the mechanism.

Thought about a retired schoolteacher in a dark parking lot going still in a particular way that she had been doing accidentally for two weeks without knowing she was doing it.

Thought about a six year old on the bottom step of my basement stairs saying *I wanted to see if it worked before lessons.*

Some people are born knowing.

Most of them spend their lives being told they don't.

Vera, I said.

Yes.

You've been doing it right, I said. *Trust what you've been doing. I'm going to come this afternoon and we're going to make it deliberate instead of accidental. That's all I'm going to do. Make the thing you already know into something you can use on purpose.*

A breath on the line.

The specific breath of a woman setting down something heavy.

Two o'clock, she said. *I'll make coffee.*

I'll bring the notebook.

Harlan.

Yes.

Gerald, she said. *Did he — was it fast. Did he —*

He was in his chair, I said. *Facing the window. The coffee was warm. The newspaper was open. He looked like a man who had set something down for a moment and forgotten to pick it up again.*

Silence.

That's not the worst way, she said quietly.

No, I said. *It isn't.*

But you're going to make sure it's not my way.

Yes, I said. *I am.*

Good, she said. *Two o'clock.*

She hung up.

I sat at the desk with the phone in my hand and the notebook open and the October light moving across the floor the way October light moves — with the specific unhurried quality of light that knows the days are getting shorter and has made its peace with that.

I wrote on the man's page of the notebook.

She's been doing it accidentally. The rabbit. Without knowing. The way I did at nine before I knew what I was doing. This means something. I don't know yet if it means she's safer or more at risk. I think it means she has been perceived as a possible threat and the thing has been circling her the way it circled me in 1963 before I learned to be still.

I think it has been deciding about her.

I think we are running out of the time in which it is still deciding.

I closed the notebook.

Looked at chapter twelve lying on my screen.

Thought about what Vera had said.

The second one you were being careful. I could feel you being careful. Writers shouldn't be careful.

I opened chapter twelve.

Read the first sentence.

Deleted it.

Wrote a new one that was not careful.

It was better.

Some things take the right person to see them clearly.

I saved the document.

Closed the laptop.

Got up from the desk.

Went to tell Wren I was going to see Vera at two o'clock and that she was coming with me because I was not leaving her alone in the house with the thing moving closer up the street and because Vera needed to meet her and because some things you don't explain you simply arrange and let the arrangement speak for itself.

She was at the kitchen table practicing.

Eyes closed. Hands in her lap. The stillness of still water.

I stood in the doorway and watched my granddaughter be invisible for a moment.

Then I said her name.

She opened her eyes.

Came back from wherever the still water goes when it is being still water.

Looked at me.

We're going to see Vera this afternoon, I said.

She nodded.

She can almost do the rabbit, Wren said.

Yes, I said. *How did you know.*

I could feel her trying, she said. *From here.*

I stood in the kitchen doorway.

Outside the October morning was doing what October mornings do in northern Michigan — being beautiful and cold and honest and completely indifferent to the specific concerns of the people living inside the houses it surrounded.

Get your coat, I said. *We'll go after lunch.*

She slid off the chair.

Went to get her coat.

I stood in the kitchen and thought about a nine year old boy who had known something and told nobody and a retired schoolteacher who had been doing the rabbit accidentally in dark parking lots and a six year old who could feel people trying from four minutes away.

And somewhere between the kitchen and the coat closet I understood something I had not understood before.

I was not the last of this.

I had never been the last of this.

There had always been others doing it alone in dark parking lots and corn fields and basements and bedrooms at two in the morning without knowing what they were doing or why or that there were others doing it too.

The ones who see clearly.

The ones it finds.

And the ones it hasn't found yet because they've been doing the rabbit accidentally and calling it something else and trusting it anyway because it works and working things are hard to argue with.

There were more of us than I knew.

I thought about what that meant.

I thought about what it meant that the thing had been growing.

I thought about what it meant that the growing and the waking were happening simultaneously.

Cause and effect running in both directions at once.

The sewage rising.

The ground getting higher.

I thought about all of this in the kitchen on a Monday morning in October in northern Michigan and then Wren came back with her coat and her dark eyes and her six years of seeing everything and I helped her with the zipper because she can do it herself but sometimes accepts help anyway and we went to make lunch.

Chapter 11

THE QUIET ONES

Chapter Eleven — Three Of A Kind

Vera Simmons lived on a street of modest houses that had been built in the fifties with the specific optimism of an era that believed in porches and believed in them structurally — wide enough to sit on, deep enough to be out of the rain, present enough to communicate that the people inside were available to the world in controlled doses.

Her porch had two chairs and a small table between them and a pot of late chrysanthemums that had no business still being alive in October and were alive anyway through what I can only assume was an act of mutual stubbornness between the flowers and the woman who tended them.

She was at the door before we reached the porch steps.

She looked at Wren.

Wren looked at her.

The specific mutual recognition I had seen at Nora's dinner table — the half second longer than social convention requires, the particular quality of two instruments recognizing they are tuned to the same register — happened again on Vera Simmons' porch steps on a Monday afternoon in October and I stood slightly behind it and watched it happen with the feeling of a man witnessing something he has been waiting for without knowing he was waiting.

You must be Wren, Vera said.

You have a nice garden, Wren said.

It's mostly done for the year.

The chrysanthemums aren't.

No, Vera said, looking at them. *They refuse to be.*

I like that, Wren said.

Vera looked at her for a moment with the brown direct eyes.

So do I, she said.

She stepped back and we went inside.

Vera's kitchen was the kitchen of a woman who uses it seriously. Not elaborately — seriously. The difference being that elaborate kitchens are designed to impress and serious kitchens are designed to work and the working ones always smell better. Hers smelled of coffee and the specific warm complexity of a house that has been lived in by one person who knows exactly how they like things and has arranged them accordingly over many years.

The coffee was already made.

There was a plate of something she had baked because she was the kind of woman who bakes when company is coming not as performance but as a practical expression of the belief that people think more clearly when they are not hungry.

I approved of this.

Wren approved of this more immediately and directly.

We sat at the kitchen table — Vera across from me, Wren beside me with the plate of baked things within reach which she navigated with the careful restraint of a child who has been told about taking too many and the complete inability to pretend she wasn't thinking about taking more.

I put the notebook on the table.

Vera looked at it.

That's it, she said.

That's it.

May I.

I slid it across.

She opened it with the careful hands of a woman who understands old things and what they cost to preserve. Read the first page. Read the second. Turned to the drawing and held it for a long time with the expression of someone looking at something they have seen before in a different form.

The edges, she said.

Yes.

That's exactly — She stopped. *That's exactly what it looks like. The edges that won't commit.*

Yes.

A nine year old drew this.

A nine year old who had been looking at it for two years by then, I said. *Familiarity improves the rendering.*

She turned to the page with the block letters. Read them slowly.

It does not have a inside, she read aloud. Quietly. The way you read something that lands in a place below language. *I looked and looked. There is nothing in there.*

She closed the notebook.

Pushed it back across to me.

Looked out the window at her garden for a moment.

I've been a science teacher, she said again. Not to me. To herself. The way people repeat the thing that defines them when the thing that defines them is being asked to expand.

Science teachers, I said, *are the best equipped people I know for this. You observe. You record. You follow the evidence without deciding in advance where it leads.*

Science teachers, she said, *are also trained to dismiss evidence that can't be replicated under controlled conditions.*

And yet, I said.

And yet, she agreed.

She looked at Wren.

Wren was on her second baked thing and looking out the window at the garden with the focused attention she gives to things that deserve serious study.

Your grandfather tells me you can see it, Vera said to her.

Yes, Wren said without looking away from the window.

Clearly.

Yes.

What does it look like.

Wren turned from the window. Considered the question with the seriousness it deserved.

Like a hole, she said. *But a hole that moves. Most holes stay where they are. This one moves around and looks at things.*

Vera sat with this.

That's more precise than anything I've managed, she said.

I've been looking at it longer, Wren said. *You look away. I don't.*

Why don't you look away.

Wren picked up her third baked thing and considered it.

Because if I look away it might do something, she said. *If I watch it it stays where it is. Like when Cooper does something he's not supposed to. If I watch him he stops.*

I looked at my granddaughter.

This was new information.

You've been watching it, I said carefully. *While you're doing the rabbit.*

Yes.

How long.

Since you taught me, she said. *Before I could only see it. Now I can see it and be still at the same time. Like you said. The one way mirror.*

Vera was looking at Wren with the expression of a woman recalibrating for the second time in twenty four hours. The expression of someone whose framework keeps being asked to expand and is expanding with the effortful grace of something built to last.

You can observe it, Vera said. *While it can't observe you.*

Yes, Wren said.

And when you observe it it stays still.

Mostly, Wren said. *Sometimes it moves anyway. But slower.*

Like a variable, Vera said quietly. More to herself than to us. *She's a variable it doesn't know it's accounting for.*

Yes, I said. *Exactly yes.*

Vera looked at me.

That's not nothing, she said.

No, I said. *It's not.*

We sat with that for a moment. The three of us in Vera's kitchen in the October afternoon with the coffee and the baked things and the notebook on the table and the garden going brown at the edges outside the window and something without an inside moving through the lowest ground of the community around us growing in the way things grow when the conditions are exactly right.

Three people who had been doing the same thing alone.

Finding out they hadn't been alone.

Now, Vera said. *The rabbit. Make it deliberate.*

Yes, I said. *That's why we're here.*

I looked at Wren.

Show her, I said.

Wren set down her baked thing. Folded her hands in her lap. Closed her eyes.

Found the stillness.

I watched Vera feel it happen — the slight change in the quality of the room, the frequency shifting, the specific signature of Wren's awareness going from projecting to reflecting. Vera's eyes widened fractionally in the way eyes widen when something registers on the unnamed sense that she had spent thirty two years being appropriately skeptical of.

I felt that, Vera said.

Now you, I said to Vera.

Vera looked at me.

Looked at Wren sitting in her stillness.

Closed her eyes.

She did not find it immediately.

This was expected. Vera had been doing it accidentally for two weeks — the body knowing the mechanism, the mind not yet having been formally introduced. Making it deliberate requires a conversation between the two that takes some negotiation.

I talked her through it the way I had talked Wren through it in the basement. The frequency. The reaching quality of attention. The lamp that lights the room without shining out the window.

She tried.

Found the edge of it.

Lost it.

Tried again.

You're thinking about finding it, Wren said quietly. Eyes still closed. Still in her own stillness. *Stop thinking about finding it. It's already there. You just have to stop announcing yourself.*

Vera opened her eyes and looked at Wren.

She's six, she said to me.

Yes, I said.

She just told me something that would take a meditation teacher forty minutes to explain.

She tends to do that.

Vera looked at her hands on the table.

Closed her eyes.

Stopped announcing herself.

And found it.

I felt it happen the way I had felt Wren find it in the basement — the quality of the room shifting, the frequency adjusting, the specific texture of a person's awareness going from searchlight to still water.

Not as deep as Wren's. Not yet. But there.

Real.

Deliberate.

Wren opened her eyes.

Looked at Vera.

Yes, she said. Simply. The way she confirms all true things.

Vera came back. Opened her eyes. Sat for a moment with the expression of someone who has just physically experienced something their framework has been arguing about for thirty two years and found the experience more convincing than the argument.

Well, she said.

Yes, I said.

That's — She stopped. Started again. *That's a room I didn't know I had.*

You've been in it accidentally for two weeks, I said. *Now you know where the door is.*

She nodded. Processing. Filing. The scientist adjusting the model to accommodate new data with the specific intellectual honesty of someone who believes that the model serves the evidence and not the other way around.

Practice, I said. *Every day. In and out. Find it and hold it and release it and find it again until* —

Until it's as natural as breathing, Wren said.

She was looking out the window again.

At the garden.

With the focused attention she gives to things that deserve serious study.

I looked at her.

Wren.

Mm.

What are you looking at.

A pause.

The specific pause of a child deciding whether the true thing is the right thing for this particular moment in this particular kitchen with these particular people.

She decided.

It was in the garden, she said. *This morning.*

The kitchen went very still.

Not the rabbit still. The other kind. The still of a room after something has been said that changes the temperature of everything in it.

This morning, Vera said. Very carefully.

Before we came, Wren said. *I felt it when we turned onto your street. I looked.* She paused. *It was by the chrysanthemums.*

Vera looked at her chrysanthemums through the window. The ones that refused to be done for the year through mutual stubbornness.

Was it still there, I said. *When we arrived.*

No, Wren said. *It left when we turned into the driveway. I think it felt grandpa.*

It knows me, I said. *From before.*

Yes, Wren said. *It remembers you.*

I sat at Vera Simmons' kitchen table in the October afternoon and thought about a thing without an inside that had been at the tree line in 1963 and had looked at a nine year old boy and been looked at back and had spent sixty two years being patient in the way only things without a concept of time can afford to be patient.

It remembered me.

Of course it did.

It had been waiting for me to stop being the rabbit and start being something else.

And now I had.

And now I had brought the something else directly to the house of the woman it had been circling for two weeks.

I picked up my coffee.

It had gone cold while we were doing the lesson.

I drank it anyway.

Vera, I said.

Yes.

I need to ask you something and I need you to answer it as a scientist not as a woman who is being polite.

All right.

Is there somewhere else you can stay. For a while. Someone you can be with so you're not here alone.

She looked at me with the brown direct eyes.

My sister, she said. *In Traverse City.*

Would she ask questions.

She would ask many questions, Vera said. *She is also a retired science teacher and we have been asking each other questions for seventy three years and showing no signs of stopping.*

Could you answer them.

I could answer some of them, she said. *The ones with available evidence.*

Go to your sister, I said. *For a week. Maybe two.*

And when I come back.

When you come back, I said, *I'll know more than I know now. And you'll have two weeks of deliberate practice and a sister who asks good questions.*

She considered this.

Looked at her garden.

At the chrysanthemums that refused to be done for the year.

I'll water them before I go, she said.

Water them twice, Wren said. *They'll be fine.*

Vera looked at my granddaughter.

The look of a woman who has spent thirty two years teaching children and can identify in approximately four seconds the ones who are going to be something the world wasn't fully prepared for.

You're something, she said to Wren. Not for the first time. As confirmation rather than discovery.

Grandpa says that too, Wren said. *I think it mostly means unusual.*

It means, Vera said, *that the world is going to have to adjust.*

It already is, Wren said. And looked back out at the chrysanthemums.

As if she could see something adjusting right now.

In the garden.

In the lowest ground.

In the cold October air that moved through the brown edges of things and found what was still alive and moved through that too.

I put my hand on the notebook.

Thought about the boy's last line.

Right now I am nine and I do not understand it and I want to go play.

Thought about what it had cost him not to.

Thought about what it was going to cost the man.

Thought about what it was going to cost the small girl beside him who was looking out a kitchen window in October with her dark eyes and her six years of seeing everything and had not once — not in the basement, not in the backyard, not here in this kitchen with the coffee and the baked things and the thing that had been by the chrysanthemums this morning — had not once asked to stop.

Ready, I said to no one in particular.

Yes, Wren said.

As if the question had been directed at her.

As if she had been ready since before the question existed.

Outside the October afternoon moved toward evening with the unhurried certainty of October afternoons that have somewhere to be and know exactly how long it takes to get there.

Inside, three people sat in a kitchen and drank cold coffee and practiced being invisible to something that was looking for them.

Getting better at it.

One afternoon at a time.

Chapter 12

THE QUIET ONES

Chapter Twelve — What Follows

The drive home from Vera's took eleven minutes.

I know this because I have driven every road in Antrim County enough times that the distances have become internal — not measured in miles or minutes consciously but felt, the way you feel the length of a familiar hallway in the dark. Eleven minutes from Vera's porch to my driveway on a normal evening in October with the early dark coming down and the headlights finding the road in the specific way headlights find northern Michigan roads — illuminating exactly enough and no more, the dark beyond the beam remaining entirely committed to being dark.

Wren was in the back seat.

She had been quiet since we left Vera's. Not her usual quiet — the settled, present quiet of a child who is comfortable with silence. This was a different quality. Concentrated. The quiet of someone paying attention to something outside the car.

I watched her in the rearview mirror.

She was looking out the side window.

Not at anything I could see. At something in the dark beyond the headlights that the headlights were not illuminating.

I drove.

She watched.

We passed the community room where the meeting had been. The gravel parking lot dark on the side where the light was still out. I did not look at the dark side of the lot. I looked at the road.

Grandpa.

Mm.

It's behind us.

I kept my hands on the wheel at the position my driver's education teacher had recommended in 1967 and which I have maintained through fifty four years of driving through the specific stubbornness of a man who was told to do something correctly and decided correctness was worth the effort.

How far, I said.

About a block, she said. *Maybe less.*

Is it moving.

Yes.

Toward us.

At the same speed we're driving, she said. *It's keeping the distance.*

I looked in the rearview mirror.

The road behind us was dark and empty and entirely ordinary looking in the specific way that things look entirely ordinary when you are not equipped to see what is actually there.

Are you doing the rabbit, I said.

Yes.

Hold it.

I am.

Don't look directly at it.

I'm not, she said. *I'm looking beside it. Like the stars.*

Like the stars. Shift your gaze slightly to the side and there it is. Six years old.

Good, I said. *Keep doing that.*

I turned left on Birch. Our street was two more turns. Eleven minutes total but we were at nine now, the last two minutes the ones between Birch and home that I had driven so many times the car could probably manage them without my specific input.

Is it still there, I said.

Yes.

Same distance.

Same distance.

I turned right on Maple.

Grandpa.

Yes.

It's not the same distance anymore.

I looked in the mirror.

Road dark. Empty. Ordinary.

Closer or further.

Closer, she said. *When you turned it got closer. Like it didn't expect the turn.*

How close.

She was quiet for a moment.

Half a block, she said.

I turned onto our street.

Pulled into the driveway with the specific efficiency of a man who has decided that the time between the car stopping and the front door closing should be as brief as physically achievable.

Still there, I said.

Yes, she said. *At the end of the driveway.*

I turned the engine off.

Looked at the end of the driveway in the rearview mirror.

Dark. Empty. Ordinary.

Wren, I said. *When I open your door I want you to walk directly to the front door. Don't look at the end of the driveway. Don't look toward it. Look at the front door.*

Okay.

Can you hold the rabbit while you walk.

Yes.

You're sure.

Grandpa, she said, with the patient tone of someone who has answered this question before and has decided to answer it again without visible irritation as a courtesy. *Yes.*

Right, I said. *Sorry.*

I got out.

Opened her door.

She slid out with the notebook I had handed her to carry — she had been holding it the entire drive without being asked, which I noted and filed — and walked to the front door with the unhurried deliberateness of a child who has been told not to run and understands that not running is the correct tactical decision even when every available instinct is suggesting otherwise.

I followed her.

Unlocked the door.

We went inside.

I locked it behind us.

Stood in the entryway for a moment.

Wren stood beside me.

Is it still at the end of the driveway, I said.

She was quiet for a moment. Eyes not closed — she had told me once that she didn't need to close her eyes to feel for it, that closing her eyes was a beginners technique she had moved past in the first week, which I had found simultaneously impressive and humbling given that I still occasionally closed mine.

Yes, she said. *It stopped at the end of the driveway.*

It didn't come up the drive.

No.

Why do you think that is.

She thought about it with the seriousness she brings to questions that deserve it.

Maybe it doesn't want to get too close yet, she said. *Like when you're fishing and you don't want to scare the fish before the hook is ready.*

I looked at my granddaughter in the entryway.

That's an unsettling analogy, I said.

Cooper taught me to fish, she said. *That's what he says about being patient.*

I'll have a word with Cooper about his fishing philosophy.

Grandpa.

Yes.

I don't think it knows I can see it, she said. *I think it thinks it's following you. It knows you from before and you stopped hiding and now it's* — She paused. Looking for the word. *Reacquainting.*

Reacquainting.

I stood in my entryway with my granddaughter and the notebook and the locked door and thought about a thing without an inside that had looked at a boy in a corn field in 1963 and spent sixty two years being patient in the way things without a concept of time can afford to be patient and had now, in the space of two weeks, moved from the distant circling of a thing deciding to the closer attendance of a thing that has decided.

It was following me.

It thought Wren was me.

No.

Worse than that.

It had followed me to Vera's house. Had been in Vera's garden this morning before we arrived. It was not just following me — it was learning my patterns. My people. The ones I went to. The ones I cared about.

The ones who could see.

It was mapping us.

Wren, I said.

Mm.

I need you to do something for me.

Okay.

I need you to tell me every time you feel it. Not just when it's close. When it's anywhere on the street. When it's at any of the houses. When it feels different than it felt the day before. I paused. *Can you do that.*

I've been doing that, she said.

I know. I'm asking you to tell me when you do. Every time. Even if it seems small.

She looked at me.

You're making a map, she said.

Yes.

Of where it goes.

Yes.

Because if you know where it goes you know what it's doing.

Yes.

And if you know what it's doing —

Then we're not reacting, I said. *We're anticipating.*

She nodded. Filed it. The small serious nod of someone who understands the difference between playing defense and playing offense and has been waiting for the conversation to arrive at that distinction.

It's gone now, she said. *From the driveway.*

Where.

I can't feel it anymore, she said. *It went quiet.*

It can do that.

Can we.

Yes, I said. *We've been practicing.*

So it's practicing too.

I looked at my granddaughter.

Outside the October dark had settled in completely with the permanence of northern Michigan October dark that has made its decision. The street was quiet. Gerald's house dark four houses down. Vera's chrysanthemums being watered twice for two weeks of absence.

Something without an inside practicing going quiet on a street in Bellaire Michigan.

Two people inside a house practicing the same thing.

Learning each other's mechanisms.

The question being which side learned faster.

Hungry, I said.

Yes, she said.

Soup.

Yes.

We went to the kitchen.

I made soup because soup is what you make when the world outside has gotten complicated and the world inside the pot is simple and governed entirely by heat and time and the reliable chemistry of things that become more themselves the longer they cook.

Wren sat at the counter and did her homework.

Ordinary. Warm. The specific ordinary warmth of a kitchen in October with soup on the stove and a child doing homework and the dark outside doing what dark does.

I stirred the soup.

Thought about the thing at the end of the driveway.

Thought about it learning my patterns.

Thought about Vera packing a bag for her sister's house in Traverse City.

Thought about Rudy Marsh and Agnes Pfeiffer going about their lives in the ordinary way of people who do not know they have become visible to something that feeds on visibility.

Thought about the notebook in my jacket.

Took it out.

Set it on the counter beside the stove.

Opened it to the man's section.

Wrote one line while the soup simmered.

It is no longer circling. It is following. There is a difference and the difference matters and I am going to spend tonight understanding exactly what it is.

Closed the notebook.

Stirred the soup.

Grandpa, Wren said from her homework.

Mm.

In my reading book today, she said. *There was a story about a boy who was afraid of the dark.*

What happened to him.

He turned on a light, she said. *And the dark went away.*

Did that satisfy you as a resolution.

She looked up from her homework.

No, she said. *The dark didn't go away. It just went somewhere the light wasn't.*

I looked at my granddaughter.

That's a better ending, I said.

I know, she said. *I don't know why they didn't use it.*

She went back to her homework.

I stirred the soup.

Outside the dark held its position with the confidence of a dark that knows exactly where the light isn't.

And somewhere in it, quieter now, practicing its own stillness, something without an inside waited with the patience of a thing that has already waited sixty two years and has made its peace with waiting a little longer.

Patient as geology.

Quiet as the space between heartbeats.

Learning.

Chapter 13

THE QUIET ONES

Chapter Thirteen — The Tree Line

I want to tell you about the farm.

Not the farm of memory softened by distance — I have no patience for that version and neither does the truth. The farm as it was. Cold and specific and unglamorous in the way that real work is unglamorous, which is to say completely, without apology, with the flat honesty of a thing that does not care how it looks because it has other concerns.

Northern Michigan farms in 1963 were not struggling toward something better. They were what they were with the settled permanence of things that have found their level and stopped moving. Ours sat on forty acres of field and tree line and the particular kind of silence that is not peaceful but empty — the silence of a place where the wind has more to say than the people and says it constantly and without invitation.

The house had four rooms and opinions about winter that it expressed through every gap in the walls simultaneously.

We were four people in it. My father, my mother, my brother Chuck, and me. Four people arranged in the specific geometry of a family that has stopped pretending to be something it isn't and hasn't yet figured out what it actually is. My father was a large man who became a different large man after the third drink and my mother was a woman who had learned to read the difference from a distance and position herself accordingly. Chuck had our father's jaw and our mother's eyes and the specific internal weather of a boy who remembers everything and forgives nothing. I had whatever was left which turned out to be enough but only barely and only in retrospect.

I was nine years old in October of 1963.

I am telling you this so you understand that what I am about to describe was not the perception of a child prone to imagination. I was not a child prone to imagination. Imagination requires a certain leisure and leisure was not a resource the farm offered at market rate. I was a child prone to observation, which is a different thing entirely — less creative, more accurate, and considerably more inconvenient when what you are observing does not fit the available explanations.

The corn rows that October ran north to south across the east field.

This matters because it meant the tree line was to my right as I worked — forty yards of open ground between the end of the rows and the beginning of the elms and oaks and the deeper dark of the older growth behind them. I had been looking at that tree line my entire life without seeing anything in it that required particular attention. Trees. The occasional deer. The light changing through the seasons in the specific ways that light changes through seasons when you have nothing else to watch.

That October it was different.

I noticed it first on a Tuesday.

Not an event. Not a sound or a movement or anything the eye could locate and report. A quality of the air between the corn rows and the tree line that was different from the air the day before in a way I could not name and could not dismiss. The way you notice a room has changed before you can identify what changed. The way you know someone has been in a space before you find the evidence.

Something at the tree line was paying attention.

I kept working.

This is what you do on a farm when something is wrong that you cannot fix — you keep working because the work does not pause for wrong things, has never paused, will not begin pausing on your account. You keep working and you pay attention in the sideways manner of someone who has learned that direct attention draws direct attention and that there are situations in which being noticed noticing is the worst available outcome.

I threw corn into the wagon.

The thing at the tree line paid attention.

Two rows over Chuck worked with the focused efficiency of a boy who had decided the farm was a problem to be solved rather than a life to be lived and was solving it with the grim thoroughness he brought to everything. He did not feel what I felt. I knew this without asking. Chuck felt everything that could be measured and nothing that couldn't and the thing at the tree line was entirely in the second category.

I was alone with it.

This was not a new condition. I had been alone with most of the important things in my life by that point. Aloneness was not something that happened to me. It was the weather I lived in. You do not complain about weather. You dress for it and keep moving.

I dressed for it.

Kept moving.

The second time was Thursday of the same week.

Same field. Same rows. Same tree line. The difference being that on Thursday I was ready for it — not in any strategic sense, not with any plan, but in the way you are ready for weather that came before and you know the feeling of now. I felt it before I consciously recognized I was feeling it. My body registered the change in the air and adjusted its posture before my mind had finished the sentence *it's there again.*

I kept throwing corn.

Breathed normally.

Did not look at the tree line directly.

Looked at it the way you look at something you are not supposed to be looking at — through the peripheral attention that sees without announcing itself, the sideways glance that registers without committing.

It was there.

Not in the trees. At the edge of them. In the specific place where the field ended and the shadow of the first elms began — the threshold, the border, the place that is neither open ground nor deep wood but both simultaneously.

It occupied that threshold the way thresholds get occupied by things that have not yet decided whether to advance or retreat.

I looked at it sideways.

It looked at me directly.

This is the part that is difficult to explain to someone who has not felt it. The quality of being looked at by something that does not have eyes in any conventional sense. Not the feeling of being watched — that is a human feeling, a social feeling, the awareness of another consciousness directed at yours. This was different. This was the feeling of being located. Of being found on a map. Of something that navigates by a method you don't have a word for fixing your coordinates in a system you didn't know you were part of.

It found me.

I felt it find me.

And I did something that I did not decide to do.

I threw another ear of corn into the wagon.

I breathed normally.

And somewhere below the level of decision, below thought, below the cold in my hands and the wind in my face and the smell of the dry field and the sound of Chuck two rows over — somewhere in the place that knows things before the rest of you catches up — I went quiet.

Not surface quiet.

The other kind.

I had never done this before. I did not know I could do it. I did not know it was a thing that could be done. I only knew that something in me understood the situation with a clarity that the rest of me had not yet achieved and responded to it with the only available tool which was a stillness so complete it changed the quality of my presence in the field.

The reaching quality of my attention — the part that had been noticing the thing at the tree line and being noticed back — pulled inward. Stopped projecting. Became something that received without broadcasting. Something that saw without announcing the seeing.

I became part of the field.

The thing at the tree line — and I watched it happen in my peripheral attention, sideways, without committing to the looking — shifted.

The orientation that had been fixed on me moved.

Not immediately. Not all at once. The way a compass needle moves when the magnet is slowly withdrawn — reluctantly, in increments, the needle swinging through the intermediate points before settling into the general indifference of a needle with nothing specific to point at.

It lost me.

I stood in the corn row and breathed and threw corn and was part of the field and watched the thing at the tree line from the sideways attention that sees without announcing itself and felt it lose me and felt something in my chest that was not triumph and not relief but the quiet specific satisfaction of a mechanism that has been tested and found to work.

A rabbit in the field.

I didn't know that yet. That came later, from an actual rabbit in an actual field on an afternoon when I needed to understand that what I had done had a name even if the name was borrowed from a smaller animal with less complicated problems.

That Thursday in October I only knew it worked.

I kept working until the row ended.

Went in for supper.

Did not tell anyone.

The third time was different.

Two weeks later. November now, the cold having made its decision and committed to it with the thoroughness of northern Michigan cold that has a job to do and intends to do it. The east field was done by then. My father had moved us to the woodlot, splitting and stacking for the winter with the specific urgency of people who understand that the wood you split in November is the warmth you have in February and that these two things are not metaphorically related.

I was carrying split wood to the stack.

Alone this time. Chuck had been sent to the barn for something. My father was at the far end of the woodlot where the older growth began, the sound of his axe a steady percussion that I tracked the way I tracked all sounds on the farm — as information about location, about mood, about the current temperature of the day's particular dangers.

The thing was not at the tree line.

It was closer.

This is what was different about the third time. The previous two times it had maintained the distance of the threshold — the edge of the field, the border of the open ground. It had been learning me from forty yards the way you learn something from a distance before you decide whether to approach.

It had decided.

It was in the woodlot.

Not near me. Thirty feet perhaps. Between two large oaks whose roots had been fighting for the same ground for a hundred years and had arrived at the specific compromise of trees that have decided to coexist rather than compete. Between those two oaks, in the shadow that their canopy made in the November afternoon, the thing was present in the way I had come to understand it was present — through the wrongness of the air, the pressure of the absence, the specific cold that was not the cold of November but the cold of a thing that has never been warm.

I kept carrying wood.

Breathed.

Found the stillness.

But it was harder this time.

Harder because it was closer and proximity has a quality that distance does not — it is louder, in a frequency that has nothing to do with sound, more insistent, more present in the way that a smell is more present when you are standing in the room with it rather than catching it through an open window.

I found the stillness.

Held it.

Kept carrying wood.

The thing between the oaks attended to the general woodlot without locating me specifically — I was there, my body was there, the physical fact of a nine year old boy carrying split wood was entirely visible, but the part of me it was looking for was quiet in a way the physical fact could not report.

It was learning this too. I felt it learning. The specific quality of frustrated attention that a thing has when the thing it is looking for is present but not findable — like a word on the tip of the tongue, like a name you know you know, like the specific maddening almost of something just beyond reach.

It attended to the woodlot.

I carried wood.

My father's axe kept its steady percussion at the far end.

Chuck came back from the barn with whatever he'd been sent for and said something to me about the stack being crooked and I said something back and the ordinary conversation of brothers doing farm work in November continued over the top of what was happening in the space between two oak trees thirty feet away and nobody in the world knew about it except me and the thing and the two oaks who had their own concerns.

Then it left.

Not gradually this time. Directly. The way you leave when you have made a decision. The presence of the absence simply ceased to press and the air between the oaks became ordinary November air again and the woodlot was just a woodlot and I was just a boy carrying split wood and the cold was just the cold.

Gone.

I stood with a piece of split maple in each hand and felt it go and felt the woodlot return to itself and breathed the ordinary November air and understood three things simultaneously with the clarity that sometimes arrives when the situation is simple enough that even a nine year old can read it without ambiguity.

One — it had been closer this time because it was testing the distance. Finding the limit of the approach before the thing it was looking for registered its presence and responded.

Two — it had not found me on the frequency because I had been still enough. But barely. The closeness had made the stillness harder and barely was a margin that would narrow if the distance continued to close.

Three — it was going to come back.

Not because I had done something to invite it. Not because of anything I was or wasn't. Simply because it had found a frequency it recognized and was interested in the way things without insides are interested in things — without curiosity, without malice, with the pure orientation of a compass needle toward the thing it is built to find.

It was going to come back.

And the next time the distance would be less.

I put the split maple on the stack.

Went back for more.

Did not tell anyone.

Wrote it in the notebook that night.

It came into the woodlot today. It was closer. The quiet worked but it was harder. It is going to come back. I think it comes back to everything it finds until it either gets what it wants or decides to stop. I do not know what it wants. I know I do not want to give it whatever that is.

I was nine years old.

I closed the notebook.

Looked at the ceiling of the cold bedroom with the wind finding the gaps and Chuck breathing in the other bed and my father's boots on the stairs and thought about the thing in the woodlot and the distance getting smaller and what a boy does when the distance gets smaller and the only tool he has is a stillness that worked barely.

What a boy does is practice.

What a boy does is get better at the barely until barely becomes enough and enough becomes reliable and reliable becomes the thing that saves him.

What a boy does is become the rabbit until the rabbit is not something he does but something he is.

I closed my eyes.

Practiced.

Sixty two years later in a house on a quiet street in Bellaire Michigan with soup on the stove and a small girl doing homework at the counter, the man who had been that boy sat with the notebook open on the counter and read what he had written and felt the specific complicated feeling of understanding something you experienced before you had the vocabulary for it.

The thing had come into the woodlot in November of 1963.

It had come onto our street in October of the present year.

The distance had been getting smaller for sixty two years.

What a man does is the same thing the boy did.

Practice.

Get better at the barely.

Make barely into enough.

Make enough into the thing that saves not just himself this time but the small girl beside him who is doing her homework with the focused efficiency of a six year old who has already decided that what is coming is coming and the only relevant question is whether you are ready.

Grandpa, Wren said.

Mm.

The soup.

I looked at the stove.

The soup was boiling.

I turned it down.

Stirred it.

Thank you, I said.

You were far away, she said.

1963, I said.

She nodded as if this was a perfectly reasonable place to have been.

Was it bad, she said.

The farm.

Yes.

I stirred the soup.

Thought about the corn rows and the cold and the bleeding hands and the thing at the tree line and the boy who had learned to be the rabbit because the rabbit was all he had.

Yes, I said. *It was bad.*

But you learned something there.

Yes, I said. *I learned something there.*

So it wasn't only bad, she said.

I looked at my granddaughter doing her homework at the counter in the warm kitchen in the October evening.

Thought about what the farm had cost.

Thought about what the farm had made.

Thought about the specific terrible arithmetic of experiences that break you into something stronger than you were before the breaking and whether the breaking is ever worth the strength and whether that question even has a clean answer.

No, I said. *Not only bad.*

She nodded.

Went back to her homework.

I stirred the soup.

Outside the October dark held its position.

Inside the kitchen was warm and the soup was almost ready and a nine year old boy in 1963 had learned something in a cold woodlot between two oak trees that a seventy one year old man was still using.

Still using.

Still enough.

For now

Chapter 14

THE QUIET ONES

Chapter Fourteen — Hardware

Rudy Marsh had owned the hardware store on Main Street in Bellaire for twenty three years.

I know this because he told me once while I was buying deck screws and he was the kind of man who tells you things like how long he has owned something not out of pride exactly but out of the specific satisfaction of a man who made a decision and stuck with it and finds the longevity itself to be the point. Twenty three years in the same building doing the same work with the same inventory and the same handwritten price tags on the bins of specialty screws that no big box store bothered to stock and that Rudy stocked because someone occasionally needed them and when they needed them they needed them specifically and he believed that was sufficient reason.

I liked him for the handwritten price tags.

I liked him for the specialty screws.

I liked him for the way he said twenty three years — not boasting, just noting. The way you note a thing that has lasted because lasting is its own achievement and deserves acknowledgment.

I went in on a Wednesday morning with no particular need for hardware.

The bell above the door announced me.

Rudy was behind the counter doing something with a parts catalog and a pencil and the focused attention of a man conducting an inventory of things that matter. He looked up when I came in.

Harlan.

Rudy.

This is the extent of our greeting. We are not men who elaborate on hellos. The hello is the information — I am here, I see you, we are both present in the same space and acknowledge it. Everything else is conversation and conversation comes after.

He went back to his catalog.

I went to the bin of deck screws I did not need and looked at them with the focused interest of a man who definitely needs deck screws and has come specifically for that purpose.

The store smelled the way hardware stores smell — metal and wood and oil and the specific dusty competence of a place that has been solving practical problems for twenty three years and has absorbed the solutions into its walls. I find hardware stores settling in the way I find certain other places settling — libraries, old barns, the particular kind of diner that has been making the same breakfast since before you were born. Places that know what they are.

I looked at Rudy from the deck screw bin.

He was thinner.

Not dramatically. Not the thinness of illness announced. The thinness of a man who has been not quite eating without noticing he has been not quite eating, the gradual subtraction that happens when something is drawing on your resources below the level of conscious awareness.

His color was wrong in a way I had seen before.

Gerald's color in the last weeks — I understood this now in retrospect — had been wrong in the same specific way. Not pale. Not ill looking in any conventional sense. More like the particular quality of a light that is burning from a diminishing source. Present. Functioning. But drawing down.

Rudy's light was drawing down.

I picked up a handful of deck screws I didn't need and went to the counter.

He looked up from the catalog.

How many do you need.

A pound, I said. *Three inch.*

He got the bag and the scale with the efficiency of a man who has done this ten thousand times and finds the repetition not deadening but reliable. The reliability of known things. The comfort of a motion so practiced it requires nothing from you but the motion.

Haven't seen you in a while, he said.

Been writing, I said. *Chapter twelve.*

Still.

Chapter twelves have opinions, I said. *They require negotiation.*

He almost smiled. The smile that almost happened was smaller than the smile I remembered from the town meeting, from the years of buying deck screws, from the specific warmth of a man who has decided that friendliness is worth the investment. Smaller and slower to arrive. As if it had to travel further than it used to.

How's business, I said.

Fine, he said.

There it was.

Fine with the specific inflation I had come to hear. Fine as a container into which a man puts everything that is not fine so he doesn't have to look at it directly. Fine as the sentence you say when the available sentences have been reduced to ones that don't require explanation.

Good, I said. *Glad to hear it.*

He weighed the screws. Wrote the price on a small bag in the handwritten way. Slid it across the counter.

I paid.

Did not leave.

Rudy looked at me.

Something else you need.

No, I said. *I wanted to ask you something.*

All right.

The meeting, I said. *Three weeks ago. What you said.*

Something moved across his face. Not quite pain. The expression of a man touching a bruise to check if it's still there and finding that it is.

What about it.

You said true things, I said. *And the room made you pay for it.*

That's the cost of true things lately, he said. *I knew the rate going in.*

Did you.

Harlan. He put the pencil down. Looked at me directly with the eyes of a man who has been not quite sleeping and has the specific clarity that not quite sleeping sometimes produces — stripped of the comfortable padding, seeing the edges of things with an accuracy that rest would soften. *What are you asking me.*

I looked at Rudy Marsh behind his counter in his hardware store of twenty three years with the handwritten price tags and the specialty screws and the scale and the parts catalog and thought about the fourth page of the notebook and the woman with short gray hair and the pattern that a nine year old boy had documented in 1963 without understanding what he was documenting.

The ones who see clearly.

The ones who say true things.

The ones it finds.

I'm asking how you're sleeping, I said.

He was quiet for a moment.

The specific quiet of a man deciding whether the question is safe to answer honestly.

Not great, he said.

Since when.

Since — He stopped. *Since the meeting, I suppose. Give or take.*

Dreams.

He looked at me.

How did you know about the dreams.

What kind, I said.

Another pause. Longer this time. The pause of a man standing at the edge of something he has been not looking at directly and being asked to look.

The kind where something is in the room, he said carefully. *That shouldn't be in the room. You know it's there before you see it. You look and there's nothing. But you know.*

Yes, I said.

You know that feeling.

I know that feeling.

It's just dreams, he said. But said it the way people say things they are attempting to convince themselves of, with the slightly elevated effort of someone pushing a door that is pushing back.

Rudy, I said.

Yes.

Has anything else been off. Not dreams. Waking. During the day.

He looked at his catalog.

At his pencil.

At the bin of specialty screws behind me that someone occasionally needed specifically.

There's a cold spot, he said. Very quietly. The voice of a man confessing something he has been refusing to confess to himself. *In the back of the store. Near the lumber. It started — I don't know. Ten days ago maybe. I thought it was the insulation. I checked the insulation. The insulation is fine.*

It's not the insulation, I said.

He looked at me.

What is it.

I looked at Rudy Marsh.

Thought about Gerald in his chair.

Thought about Vera going still in a dark parking lot accidentally.

Thought about the notebook and the pattern and the thing that had been at the tree line in 1963 and was on our street now and had been in this hardware store for ten days near the lumber with the cold that was not the cold of failed insulation.

Something found you, I said. *Because you see clearly. Because you said true things when the room wanted you to say comfortable ones. Because the kind of person who does that broadcasts on a frequency that something in this area has been following.*

He stared at me.

I waited.

This is the moment in these conversations where it goes one of two ways. The person finds the version of themselves that has always known there was more to the world than the available explanations and lets that version speak. Or they find the version that has spent a lifetime building the wall between the explicable and the rest and retreats behind it.

Rudy had been a hardware man for twenty three years.

Hardware men believe in what works.

The cold spot, he said slowly. *It moves.*

Yes, I said.

I thought I was imagining it.

You weren't.

What does it want.

To be near you, I said. *That's all it does at first. It finds the ones who see clearly and it gets near them and it — draws on them. The way a drain draws on water. You don't feel it happening. You just gradually have less.*

He was quiet.

I watched him process this with the methodical honesty of a man who has spent twenty three years solving practical problems and has just been handed one that requires a completely different set of tools.

Gerald, he said.

Yes.

He saw clearly, Rudy said. *Gerald saw everything clearly. He just never said much about it.*

No, I said. *He didn't.*

Is that why.

I think so.

Rudy put both hands flat on the counter. The gesture of a man steadying himself on a known surface while the ground rearranges itself beneath him.

What do I do, he said.

The same question Vera had asked.

The practical question. The hardware store question. What is the tool and how do I use it.

I thought about Vera in Traverse City with her sister who asks good questions.

Do you have somewhere you can go, I said. *For a week or two. Somewhere away from here.*

My son in Petoskey.

Go, I said.

I can't just close the store.

Rudy, I said. *You've lost eight pounds since the meeting. You're not sleeping. There is a cold spot near your lumber that moves. Close the store.*

He looked at me.

The careful eyes of a man who has always believed in showing up, in keeping the hours, in the specific reliability of a place that is open when it says it will be open because someone might need specialty screws and need them specifically.

A week, he said.

At least.

And when I come back.

When you come back I'll know more, I said. *And I'll tell you everything. Not the edited version. Everything.*

You know more than you're telling me now.

Yes.

Why.

Because there's a sequence to how much a person can absorb at one time, I said. *And I'm respecting the sequence.*

He almost smiled again. Closer this time to the full version.

You sound like a writer, he said.

Occupational hazard, I said.

He looked around his store.

The twenty three years of it. The handwritten price tags. The specialty screws. The scale. The parts catalog with his pencil resting in the fold like Gerald's crossword pencil resting in the fold and I pushed that thought down before it arrived fully because it was not a useful thought and I needed useful thoughts right now.

I'll call Danny tonight, he said. *My son.*

Good.

Harlan.

Yes.

The cold spot, he said. *Last night it was in the bedroom.*

Everything in me went quiet on the frequency.

Not the store cold spot.

The bedroom.

When did it move from the store, I said.

Two nights ago, he said. *I thought — I told myself it was the window. The bedroom window has a bad seal. I've been meaning to fix it.*

It's not the window.

No, he said. *I know it's not the window.*

Call Danny today, I said. *Not tonight. Today.*

He looked at me.

Read my face.

That bad, he said.

The sequence, I said carefully, *has accelerated.*

He nodded.

Picked up his phone from beside the catalog.

I took my bag of deck screws I didn't need.

Went to the door.

The bell announced my leaving.

Harlan, Rudy said.

I turned.

He was holding the phone. Looking at me across the twenty three years of his store with the expression of a man who has just been told something that rearranges the floor plan of his entire life and is choosing, with the specific pragmatic courage of a hardware man, to rearrange accordingly.

The specialty screws, he said. *The bins. Can you check them when I'm gone. Make sure nobody gets into them. People think because the store's closed —*

I'll check them, I said.

Every few days.

Every few days, I said. *I promise.*

He nodded.

Looked at his phone.

Dialed.

I went out into the October morning.

Stood on the sidewalk of Main Street in Bellaire with a bag of deck screws and the cold feeling in my chest that was not the cold of October and thought about Gerald and Vera and now Rudy and the pattern that kept completing itself in the same direction.

The bedroom.

When it reached the bedroom it was past the circling stage.

It had decided about Rudy the way it had decided about Gerald.

The difference being that Rudy was still alive and I was standing on his sidewalk and Gerald had not had anyone standing on his sidewalk who knew what the cold spot meant.

I walked to my car.

Sat in it.

Did not start it.

Took out the notebook.

Wrote quickly in the man's section with the specific urgency of someone recording information before the urgency of the moment erodes the precision of the details.

Rudy Marsh. Eight pounds. Cold spot moved to bedroom two nights ago. Gerald timeline from store to bedroom to chair was approximately ten days. Rudy is at eight days. I have sent him to Petoskey. If he goes today he has margin. If he waits he does not. The pattern is accelerating. Gerald first. Then the circling of Vera and Agnes and others. Now Rudy with the timeline compressed. It is getting more efficient. Things get more efficient with practice. This is not a comforting observation.

I closed the notebook.

Started the car.

Drove home past Gerald's house without looking at it.

Past the Millers' mailbox where the thing had stood watching.

Into my driveway.

Sat for a moment.

Thought about efficiency.

Thought about a thing that has been doing this for longer than I have been alive getting better at it.

Thought about what getting better at it meant for the ones it had not yet reached.

Thought about Agnes Pfeiffer.

Went inside.

Called Agnes Pfeiffer.

She answered on the first ring in the voice of a woman who had been waiting for someone to call without knowing who or why.

Agnes, I said. *It's Harlan Gage. I live on —*

I know who you are, she said. *I've been hoping someone would call.*

I sat down at my desk.

Tell me, I said.

And she did.

Chapter 15

THE QUIET ONES

Chapter Fifteen — The Space Between Notes

Agnes Pfeiffer had been teaching piano for forty one years.

Not as a fallback. Not as the thing she did while waiting for something else to happen. As a vocation in the original sense of the word — a calling, a life's work chosen with the specific clarity of a young woman who understood at nineteen that music was not what she did but what she was and had arranged everything else accordingly.

She taught in a studio attached to her house on Elm Street — a room she had built for the purpose with the careful investment of a woman who believes that the space where children learn something beautiful should itself be beautiful. Good light. A serious instrument. Bookshelves of music sorted by composer then period then difficulty with the quiet authority of a system that has been refined over four decades into something that works without effort.

On the wall beside the door, a small framed card in her own handwriting:

Listen to what is actually there.

Not what should be there. Not what you expect. What is actually there.

Forty one years of teaching children to hear the difference.

I've been hearing something for three weeks, she said on the phone. *In the studio. During lessons and after. I want to be precise about this because precision is the only tool I have for something I don't have a framework for.*

Be as precise as you like, I said. *I have time.*

It's in the rests, she said.

The rests.

In music a rest is not silence, she said, in the tone of someone who has explained this to children for forty one years and finds the explaining still worth doing. *A rest is held silence. Active silence. Silence that is part of the structure of the piece, that has weight and duration and meaning. It is not the absence of music. It is music expressed through absence.*

Yes, I said.

What I'm hearing is in the rests, she said. *Not during the playing. During the held silences. Something that occupies the rest the way — the way a wrong note occupies a chord. You feel it before you name it. The chord sounds almost right. Almost. And the almost is louder than anything else in the room.*

I had the notebook open.

I was writing.

Almost right, I wrote. *The rest occupied. Wrong note in the chord.*

How long has this been happening, I said.

Three weeks, she said. *Since the town meeting. I was there. I heard what was said to Rudy Marsh and I heard what it meant and I heard the difference and I said nothing because —* She stopped.

Because the room, I said.

Because the room, she agreed. *I drove home and sat at the piano and played for an hour because that's what I do when the room has been what it was and I need to remind myself what the world actually sounds like underneath the noise people make in it.*

And.

And it was there, she said. *In the first rest. I stopped playing and the held silence had something in it that held silence does not have. A quality. A presence. The almost of a wrong note that isn't quite a note at all.*

I thought about the residue in Gerald's living room. The cold without temperature. The pressing absence.

Agnes had felt the same thing.

Through the instrument she had spent forty one years learning to hear through.

Of course she had.

Agnes, I said. *Has it gotten closer since the first time.*

A pause.

Define closer, she said.

More present. More — concentrated. Does the almost get louder.

Yes, she said. *Each week. The first week it was only in the rests during lessons. The second week it was in the rests when I practiced alone. This week* — She stopped.

This week, I said.

This week it's there when I'm not playing, she said. *I sit in the studio in the evening and I can hear it in the ordinary silence of the room. Not a sound. The quality of the silence itself is wrong. The way a room sounds wrong after someone has been in it who shouldn't have been.*

Yes, I said. *That's exactly what it is.*

Silence on the line.

The specific silence of a woman who has spent forty one years listening to what is actually there receiving confirmation of something she had been hoping was her imagination.

It's real, she said.

Yes.

I'm not —

No, I said. *You're not.*

What is it.

I told her what I had told Vera. What I had told Rudy. The same information delivered to the same quality of person — someone who has spent a lifetime trusting careful perception over comfortable explanation and has arrived at a moment where that trust is being asked to extend further than the framework was designed to reach.

Agnes listened without interrupting.

When I finished she was quiet for a moment.

It's drawn to people who hear clearly, she said.

Yes.

The way I'm drawn to a student who actually listens, she said. *Rather than one who plays what they expect to hear.*

Yes, I said. *Exactly that.*

Except it doesn't want to teach them, she said.

No.

It wants to — what. Drain them.

It wants proximity to the ones who see and hear clearly, I said. *The proximity itself is the damage. You don't feel it happening. You just gradually have less. Like a battery that's always slightly cold and never quite charges to full.*

She was quiet.

I could hear her breathing. Even and measured. The breathing of a woman who practices stillness through music and has more resources for the current situation than she knows.

I've been tired, she said. *For three weeks. I thought it was the season. October always takes something from me.*

It's not the season.

No, she said. *I suppose not.*

Agnes, I said. *The card on your wall.*

A pause. *How do you know about the card.*

My granddaughter takes piano, I said. *She told me about it. Listen to what is actually there.*

Yes.

You've been doing that, I said. *For three weeks you've been hearing something in the rests that has no business being in the rests and you've been listening to it accurately and precisely and not talking yourself out of it.*

It didn't seem —

It seemed insane, I said. *I know. And you listened anyway because forty one years of listening to what is actually there rather than what should be there is not a habit you can switch off when the thing actually there is inconvenient.*

No, she said. Quietly. *It isn't.*

That discipline, I said, *is going to be useful.*

How.

I thought about Vera finding the rabbit accidentally in dark parking lots for two weeks. About Wren finding it on the first try in a basement. About Rudy who had been doing none of it and had a cold spot in his bedroom.

Can you come here, I said. *This afternoon if possible. There's something I need to show you. Something that involves a certain kind of stillness that you have been practicing for forty one years without knowing that's what it was.*

The rests, she said slowly.

I'm sorry.

The held silence, she said. *Active silence. Silence that is part of the structure. Not absence — presence expressed through absence.* A pause. *That's what you're talking about isn't it. That's the mechanism.*

I sat at my desk with the notebook open.

Thought about a nine year old boy in a corn field becoming part of the field.

Thought about Vera going still in a parking lot accidentally.

Thought about Wren describing it as holding very still inside.

Thought about Agnes Pfeiffer spending forty one years teaching children the difference between silence and held silence.

Active silence.

Presence expressed through absence.

Agnes, I said. *You've been teaching children the rabbit for forty one years.*

A long pause.

The rabbit, she said.

It's what my granddaughter calls it.

How old is your granddaughter.

Six.

She takes piano.

She does.

She's the one, Agnes said slowly. *Isn't she. The one you mentioned. Who sees it clearly.*

Yes.

She's been in my studio, Agnes said. *Every Tuesday for two years.* A pause that carried the weight of something being understood for the first time. *She sits very still during the rests.*

Yes, I said. *She would.*

I always thought she was just a serious child.

She is a serious child, I said. *She's also something else.*

She hears it too, Agnes said. *In the rests.*

She sees it, I said. *Completely. More clearly than either of us.*

The silence on the line was a held silence.

Active.

Present expressed through absence.

The silence of a woman integrating something enormous with the careful efficiency of someone who has spent a lifetime making room for what is actually there.

Three o'clock, she said. *I'll bring the card.*

You don't need the card, I said.

I know, she said. *But I've had it for forty one years and it seems relevant to bring it.*

I almost smiled.

Three o'clock, I said.

I hung up.

Sat at my desk.

Looked at the notebook.

Added one line to the man's section below the notes on Rudy.

Agnes Pfeiffer hears it in the rests. She has been teaching children the rabbit for forty one years and calling it held silence. She is the most prepared of any of them and doesn't know it yet. Three o'clock.

Closed the notebook.

Looked out the window at the October street.

Thought about what was gathering.

Not just the thing.

The other side of it.

Vera in Traverse City practicing every day. Rudy driving to Petoskey this afternoon if he had listened. Agnes coming at three with forty one years of active silence in her hands like a tool she had been sharpening without knowing what it was for.

And Wren.

Wren at the center of all of it with the dark eyes and the six years and the ability to see the thing completely while it thought she couldn't.

The one way mirror.

I had spent sixty two years thinking I was the last of this.

I was not the last of this.

I was perhaps the first to understand what this was.

There was a difference.

The difference felt important.

The difference felt like the beginning of something that the boy in the corn field had not had access to and the man at the desk was only now beginning to see the shape of.

Not one rabbit in a field.

A field full of rabbits who had found each other.

And something that had always hunted alone discovering that the field had changed.

Outside the October morning moved toward afternoon.

Inside chapter twelve sat on my screen still lying.

I opened it.

Read the first sentence.
For the first time in three weeks it didn't lie.
I started writing.

Chapter 16

THE QUIET ONES

Chapter Sixteen — One Note

I have an upright piano in the living room.

This requires explanation because I do not play piano and have never played piano and the piano arrived in my life the way certain things arrive — not chosen exactly, more accepted, the way you accept weather that has decided to happen in your vicinity regardless of your preferences on the matter.

My second wife played.

She played the way certain people do things — not for performance, not for accomplishment, but for the private conversation between herself and the instrument that she needed the way other people need sleep or food or the particular quality of morning light through a specific window. She played in the evenings after dinner and I would sit in the other room and listen without telling her I was listening because she played differently when she thought no one could hear and the difference was the best music I have ever been in the same house with.

She left. The piano stayed.

This is not a metaphor. She simply could not take it and I could not sell it and so it remained in the corner of the living room for eleven years, lid closed, occasionally dusted, present in the specific way that objects belonging to absent people are present — not haunting exactly, just occupying their space with the patient permanence of things that outlast the circumstances that brought them.

Wren had started lessons with Agnes two years ago.

She would practice on this piano.

She played differently than my second wife had played. Where my wife had played from feeling — fluid, searching, the music finding its shape in real time — Wren played with the focused precision of someone learning a language and taking the grammar seriously. Each note placed. Each rest held. The specific patience of a child who understands that the structure comes before the freedom and is willing to earn the freedom properly.

I had sat in the other room and listened to that too.

Agnes arrived at three o'clock exactly.

She was a small woman — smaller than I remembered from the town meeting, where she had occupied her folding chair with a presence that made the chair seem insufficient. In my doorway she was compact and precise with the posture of someone who has spent forty one years telling children to sit up straight and the gray hair of someone who stopped negotiating with gray hair at some point and found the not negotiating clarifying.

She carried a canvas bag and the card in a small frame and looked at me when I opened the door with the direct assessment of a woman who is updating her information about you in real time.

You look like someone who hasn't been sleeping, she said.

I've been sleeping, I said. *Selectively.*

That's what I said.

She came in.

Saw the piano immediately.

Went to it the way musicians go to instruments in rooms — not deliberately, more gravitationally, the specific pull of a thing that speaks your language in a room full of things that don't.

She touched the closed lid.

May I.

Please.

She opened it.

Looked at the keys with the expression of someone reading a face they haven't seen in a while — checking for changes, for wear, for the particular history that instruments accumulate from the hands that have played them.

It's been played recently, she said.

My granddaughter practices here.

I know her touch, Agnes said. *She's careful. More careful than most children. She treats the instrument like it has opinions.*

It might, I said.

Agnes looked at me.

You're serious.

I'm a writer, I said. *I assign consciousness to everything. Occupational habit.*

She almost smiled.

Wren appeared from the kitchen where she had been doing homework with the focused efficiency of a child who wants homework finished before interesting things happen.

She looked at Agnes.

Agnes looked at her.

The mutual recognition again — the half second longer, the particular frequency of two instruments tuning to the same note. But different from when Vera had looked at Wren, different from when I had looked at Wren the first time I understood what she was.

This recognition had a specific quality.

The quality of two people who have been in the same room with the same thing for two years and are only now being introduced to what they were both hearing.

Miss Agnes, Wren said.

Wren, Agnes said. *Your grandfather tells me you've been hearing things in the rests.*

Wren looked at me.

I looked at Wren.

He said it differently, she said to Agnes. *But yes.*

Sit down, Agnes said. *Both of you.*

We sat.

Agnes remained standing at the piano with the canvas bag over her shoulder and the card in its frame in her hand and the keys open in front of her and the specific authority of a woman in the room she has always been most herself in.

She put the card on top of the piano.

Listen to what is actually there, she read aloud. Not for us. For herself. The way you read a thing you have read ten thousand times because the reading is the reminder.

She set the canvas bag down.

Turned to face us.

I'm going to play one note, she said. *And I want you both to tell me what you hear in the rest that follows. Not what you expect to hear. Not silence. What is actually there.*

She turned back to the piano.

Found the note.

It was a middle C.

The most fundamental note. The center of the instrument. The note every beginner finds first because it is the beginning of everything and the point of return when you are lost.

She played it.

Clean. Full. The note filled the room the way a good note fills a room — completely, without apology, present in all the space available to it.

Then she lifted her finger.

The note ended.

The rest began.

Wren closed her eyes.

I got quiet on the frequency.

The rest held.

One second. Two. Three.

In the held silence — in the active silence, the presence expressed through absence — I felt it.

The cold without temperature.

The pressing absence.

The specific wrongness of a space that should contain what spaces contain and instead contained a deficit.

Not as strong as Gerald's living room. Not as concentrated as the parking lot or the woodlot in November 1963. But there. Present. Occupying the rest the way Agnes had described — the almost of a wrong note that isn't quite a note at all.

I looked at Wren.

Her eyes were still closed.

Her hand came up slowly.

She pointed.

At the corner of the living room to the left of the piano. The corner where the light didn't quite reach. The corner that had been slightly colder than the rest of the room for eleven days and that I had been navigating around the way you navigate around furniture in the dark — automatically, without looking directly at it, by the memory of where it is.

There, she said.

Agnes stood at the piano with her finger still on the key she had just released.

She did not look at the corner.

She closed her eyes.

And listened.

I watched her listen.

Watched the quality of her stillness change — not the stillness of a person being still but the stillness of a person who has spent forty one years practicing the held silence, the active silence, the presence expressed through absence, and is now applying that practice to something it was never designed for and discovering that it was designed for exactly this.

Her face changed.

Not dramatically. A musician's face changes when they hear something true — a small adjustment, a settling, the expression of someone whose instrument has just told them something and they are receiving it without intermediary.

She heard it.

I watched her hear it.

The almost of the wrong note that isn't quite a note at all.

She opened her eyes.

Looked at the corner Wren had pointed to.

The corner where the light didn't quite reach.

There, she said.

Not to us.

Confirming to herself.

The scientist and the artist arriving at the same coordinates by different instruments.

Wren opened her eyes.

Looked at Agnes.

You heard it, Wren said.

Yes, Agnes said. *In the rest after the note. Like a chord that's almost right.* She paused. *Almost right is the worst kind of wrong. In music and apparently in everything else.*

Can you hear it without the note, Wren said. *Just in the regular quiet.*

Agnes turned to face the room. Closed her eyes again. The held silence of a woman listening to what is actually there rather than what should be there.

Five seconds.

Ten.

Yes, she said. *Faintly. It's like — the room has a wrong note in it that nobody is playing.*

It's been there for eleven days, I said.

Agnes opened her eyes.

Looked at me.

In your living room.

Yes.

You've been living with it.

I've been watching it, I said. *Through Wren. She can see it. I can feel it. You can hear it. We all perceive the same thing through different instruments.*

Agnes stood at the piano and looked at the corner and then at Wren and then at me with the expression of a woman whose framework has just expanded for the third time in one conversation and is finding the expansion both uncomfortable and necessary in the way that all genuine learning is uncomfortable and necessary.

Show me, she said. *The rabbit.*

Wren, I said.

Wren turned to Agnes.

Close your eyes, she said.

Agnes closed them.

Find where the listening happens, Wren said. *Not what you're hearing. Where hearing lives.*

Agnes nodded.

Now, Wren said. *Make it a rest.*

Agnes was still.

I watched.

The held silence.

Active. Present. Structured.

Agnes Pfeiffer had been making rests for forty one years.

She found it in approximately eight seconds.

I felt the room shift. The frequency adjust. The specific texture of her awareness going from projecting to reflecting, from searchlight to still water, from the open listening of a woman who has spent her life receiving sound to the held silence of a woman who has just learned to receive without broadcasting.

Wren opened her eyes.

Looked at me across the room.

The look that needed no words.

Yes, I said.

Agnes came back.

Opened her eyes.

Stood at the piano in the afternoon light with the card that said *listen to what is actually there* beside her and the canvas bag at her feet and forty one years of held silence suddenly meaning something it hadn't meant this morning.

That's it, she said. *That's what I've been doing accidentally.*

Yes.

In the parking lot after meetings. When the room has been what it was and I need to remind myself what the world actually sounds like. She paused. *I go quiet in that specific way and it — stops pressing.*

Yes.

Because it loses me.

Yes.

She looked at the corner.

The corner where the light didn't quite reach.

It's in your living room, she said. *And you're going to let it stay there.*

For now, I said. *Yes.*

Why.

Because I need to understand its patterns, I said. *Where it goes. What it does. How it moves. And right now it thinks only I can sense it here.*

Agnes looked at Wren.

Wren looked at Agnes.

The two of them reached some understanding across the room that didn't require my participation.

It doesn't know about us, Agnes said.

No, I said. *It knows about me. It remembers me from a long time ago. It's been following me. But it doesn't know that Wren can see it clearly. And it doesn't know about you or Vera.*

We're variables it isn't accounting for, Agnes said.

Yes, I said. *Exactly yes.*

She turned back to the piano.

Played the middle C again.

Held the rest.

Listened to what was actually there.

Then she played it again. Different this time — not a single note but a chord. Three notes together. Full and resonant and present in the room with the authority of a thing that knows what it is.

The chord filled the living room.

I felt the thing in the corner shift.

Not retreat. Shift. The specific reorientation of something that has been attended to by a frequency it wasn't expecting.

The chord faded.

The rest held.

In the held silence the corner was different.

Quieter.

It moved, Wren said. *To the back of the corner.*

Yes, Agnes said. *I felt that.*

The sound bothers it, I said.

Not the sound, Agnes said. *The held silence after the sound. The rest.* She played the chord again. Let it fade. Held the rest with the full weight of forty one years of active silence behind it. *The rest is louder than the chord. To something that lives in the absence — a rest practiced by someone who knows how to hold it is the loudest thing in the room.*

She lifted her hands from the keys.

Turned to face us.

It can't hide in a rest I'm holding, she said. *Because I fill the rest completely. There's no room in it for a wrong note when the rest itself is right.*

I sat in my chair in my living room on a Wednesday afternoon in October in northern Michigan and looked at Agnes Pfeiffer standing at my dead wife's piano and thought about what she had just said.

It can't hide in a rest I'm holding.

Wren was looking at the corner.

It went further back, she said. *When you said that.*

It heard me, Agnes said.

It hears, I said. *I don't know how. It has no apparatus for it. But it perceives. Everything it needs to perceive.*

Then it knows I can affect it, Agnes said.

Yes.

Will that make it —

More cautious, I said. *For now. More interested later.*

How much later.

I don't know, I said. *Soon.*

Agnes looked at the card on top of the piano.

Listen to what is actually there.

She picked it up.

Looked at it for a moment.

Put it back down.

I've had that card for forty one years, she said. *I wrote it when I was thirty two and had my first studio and was trying to remember what I was teaching. I thought I was writing about music.*

You were, I said.

I was writing about this, she said. *Wasn't I.*

I looked at Agnes Pfeiffer in my living room.

Thought about the things that arrive before you know you need them. The notebook written in 1963. The piano that stayed when everything else left. The card on the wall of a music studio that a six year old girl read every Tuesday for two years while sitting very still in the rests.

Yes, I said. *I think you were.*

She nodded.

Filed it.

Sat down in the chair across from mine with the canvas bag in her lap and the October light coming through the window and the corner of the living room quieter than it had been in eleven days.

Tell me everything, she said. *From the beginning. Not the edited version.*

It's a long story, I said.

I have time, she said. *And apparently I've been preparing for it for forty one years.*

Wren came and sat on the floor between us.

Cross legged. Hands in her lap.

Facing the corner.

Watching.

So that Agnes and I could talk without watching.

So that we could tell the story without losing sight of the thing the story was about.

Six years old.

Already understanding the division of labor without being told.

I opened the notebook.

Started from the beginning.

The farm. The corn rows. The October cold. The tree line. The boy who became the rabbit because the rabbit was all he had.

Agnes listened to what was actually there.

The way she always had.

Outside the October afternoon moved toward evening with the unhurried certainty of October afternoons in northern Michigan that have somewhere to be and know the way.

Inside three people sat in a living room with a piano and a card and a notebook and the cold thing in the corner that had moved to the back of itself when the held silence got too loud.

Learning each other.

Preparing.

One afternoon at a time.

Chapter 17

THE QUIET ONES

Chapter Seventeen — What The Man Wrote

The house at eleven o'clock at night has a different character than the house at any other hour.

Not quieter exactly. The lake makes noise at night that it doesn't bother making during the day — a deeper conversation with the shore, lower frequency, the sound of water that has stopped performing and is just being water in the dark. The house settles around it. The refrigerator makes its periodic contribution. The old upright piano in the living room holds its silence with the specific weight of an instrument that has absorbed a day's worth of music and held silence and the presence of a thing in the corner that has moved to the back of itself and stayed there since Agnes left at six.

Wren was asleep.

She had fallen asleep at the kitchen table over her homework at eight thirty with the complete commitment of a child whose body has decided the day is over and is not accepting appeals. I had carried her to the couch with the careful architecture of a man whose back has opinions about carrying children and covered her with the blanket Nora kept folded on the armrest for exactly this category of evening.

She had not woken.

She was still there now. Small and certain under the blanket with her dark hair across the cushion and her hands folded under her cheek in the specific sleeping posture of a child who maintains her composure even unconscious.

I had checked the corner before I sat down.

Still there. Quieter. The quality of a thing that has retreated without leaving. Present at a lower frequency the way a fire is present as embers after the flame goes down — not gone, not harmless, waiting with the patience of something that understands that patience is its primary advantage.

I let it wait.

Sat at my desk.

Opened the notebook to the man's section.

Picked up my pen.

Wednesday. Late.

I am going to write down what I have because writing it down makes it real in the way that thoughts in the dark at eleven o'clock are not real — they are clouds, they are weather, they shift and reform and cannot be held. On paper they stay where you put them. On paper you can look at them from a safe distance and see if they are what you thought they were or something else.

What I have:

Vera Simmons in Traverse City. Two weeks of practice. A woman who found the rabbit accidentally in dark parking lots and is now making it deliberate with the methodical thoroughness of a retired science teacher who has decided that the evidence requires a response and is responding accordingly. She called this evening before dinner. She has been practicing four times a day. She said it feels more solid each time. Like a muscle. I told her that was exactly what it was. She said her sister has started doing it too without being taught. I asked what she meant. She said her sister watched her practice and went quiet in a similar way and when Vera asked about it her sister said she had been doing something like that since she was a child and had never told anyone. I wrote this down separately and underlined it. There are more of us than I knew. There have always been more.

Rudy Marsh in Petoskey. He called from his son's house. He sounded better. The specific better of a man who has removed himself from the proximity of something that was drawing on him and can feel the difference now that the drawing has stopped. He said he slept through the night for the first time in three weeks. He said he didn't realize how tired he had been until he wasn't. This is always how it works. You don't feel the weight until it's gone. He asked when he can come back. I told him not yet. He asked what I needed from him. I told him I would know when I knew. He accepted this with the equanimity of a hardware man who understands that some repairs require assessment before you can determine the correct tool.

Agnes Pfeiffer. She left at six with the canvas bag and the card and the specific expression of a woman who came to a conversation expecting to receive information and discovered she had been carrying half of it for forty one years without knowing what it was for. She is not going anywhere. I considered asking her to stay somewhere else temporarily the way I asked Vera and Rudy. I decided against it. Agnes is different from Vera and Rudy in one specific way — she can affect it. The held silence. The rest so completely filled there is no room for the wrong note. The thing in the corner moved when she played. Retreated when she held the rest with full intent. She is not just a person it finds. She is a person who changes the room it inhabits. That is a different category and I need to understand it before I ask her to leave.

Wren. Six years old. Asleep on the couch under Nora's blanket. She watched the corner from the floor between Agnes and me for three hours while we talked and did not once lose the stillness and did not once show fear and when Agnes played the chord and the thing retreated Wren described exactly how far and in what direction with the flat precision of a field observer reporting coordinates. She is the most capable of all of us and she is six years old and I keep writing that down because I keep needing to be reminded of it. Not because it diminishes what she is. Because it clarifies what I am responsible for.

What I do not have:

A mechanism. I understand what the thing is. I understand what it does. I understand that it finds the ones who see clearly and drains them and that it is growing more efficient and that the ambient cruelty of the current age is providing conditions in which it flourishes. I understand that it has been following me specifically since I stopped being the rabbit and started being something else. I understand that it does not know about Wren's ability and does not know about Agnes and does not know about the field of rabbits that is assembling itself in its hunting ground.

What I do not understand is how to end it.

Not drive it away. Not make it retreat to the back of the corner. End it.

The notebook has the boy's record and the man's record and neither of them contains an ending. The boy knew how to hide. The man knows how to hide and how to find others who can hide and how to understand the thing's patterns. Neither of them knows what happens when hiding is no longer sufficient and the distance closes to the point where the only available response is something other than stillness.

Wren said it cannot hide in a rest Agnes is holding.

Agnes said it can't because she fills the rest completely. No room for the wrong note when the rest itself is right.

I have been thinking about this since six o'clock.

A rest is held silence. Active silence. Presence expressed through absence. It is not the absence of music. It is music expressed through absence.

The thing is an absence. It exists as deficit. It is defined entirely by what it is not — the shape of nothing wearing the outline of something. It moves through the world by occupying the spaces between things. The threshold between field and tree line. The corner where the light doesn't reach. The rest after the note.

What happens when the rest is already fully occupied.

The wrong note has nowhere to be.

Not driven out. Not retreated. Nowhere.

I don't know if this is a mechanism or a metaphor and at eleven o'clock at night with Wren asleep on the couch I am not certain the distinction matters as much as it usually does.

What I know is that Agnes fills a rest completely and the thing moves away from it.

What I know is that Wren sees it completely and when she sees it it moves more slowly.

What I know is that I can feel where it is and track its patterns and understand its behavior in a way I couldn't at nine years old when the only thing I could do was hide.

What I do not know is whether these three things together constitute a mechanism or whether I am assembling comfort from available materials in the dark at eleven o'clock.

The boy in the corn field would have said they are the same thing.

Maybe the boy was right.

One more thing.

Nora called at nine. Checking in the way she checks in — warm, specific, the questions of a woman who wants to know her father is all right and has learned to ask sideways because asking directly produces answers calibrated for her comfort rather than her information. She asked how Wren was. I said fine. She asked what we had done today. I said Agnes Pfeiffer came by. She said oh that's nice, Wren loves her lessons. I said yes she does.

I did not tell her about the corner.

I did not tell her about the cold spot in Rudy's bedroom or Gerald's timeline or the pattern in the notebook or what Agnes heard in the rest after the middle C.

I am keeping the sequence.

The sequence being: understand it enough to explain it before you explain it. Nora is not Vera or Agnes. Nora is my daughter who has built a life on the assumption that the world operates within the boundaries of the visible and the explicable and who deserves to have that assumption challenged with care and evidence rather than panic and incomplete information.

But the sequence is getting shorter.

The distance is getting smaller.

And Nora's daughter is asleep on the couch having spent three hours watching a thing in a corner that Nora doesn't know exists and I am running out of timeline in which keeping the sequence is responsible rather than negligent.

Tomorrow.

I will tell Nora tomorrow.

Or the day after.

I will tell her soon.

I closed the notebook once before and put it in a box and left it for sixty two years.

I am not going to do that again.

I put the pen down.

Closed the notebook.

Sat at the desk for a moment in the eleven o'clock quiet of the house with the lake making its nighttime conversation with the shore and the refrigerator making its periodic contribution and the piano holding its silence and Wren breathing under the blanket on the couch.

Looked at the corner of the living room.

The thing was still there.

Quieter than it had been.

But there.

Patient as geology.

I looked at it for a long moment with the full attention of a man who has stopped pretending it isn't there and has not yet found what comes after the pretending stops.

I know you're there, I said.

Out loud.

For the first time.

Not to the notebook. Not in the privacy of my own frequency. Out loud in the eleven o'clock quiet of my house.

The corner did not respond.

The corner was not in the business of responding.

But something in the quality of the silence changed — fractionally, in the way that the silence in a room changes when someone in it has heard something they didn't expect to hear. A barely perceptible adjustment.

It had heard me.

I know what you are, I said. *I know what you want. I know what you've been doing and how long you've been doing it and why you came back.*

The corner.

The light that didn't quite reach.

The cold without temperature pressing in the specific way it pressed.

You're going to find, I said, *that the field has changed.*

I stood up.

Turned off the desk lamp.

Went to the couch.

Stood over my granddaughter for a moment in the dark.

She was deeply asleep with the complete commitment of a child whose body has decided and is not accepting appeals. Her face in the dark was the face of a six year old who had spent the day being something extraordinary and was now simply being six and asleep and small under a blanket.

I pulled the blanket up.

Went to my bedroom.

Lay in the dark.

Listened to the lake.

Thought about the field that had changed.

Vera practicing four times a day in Traverse City. Her sister doing it without being taught because there have always been more of us than any of us knew.

Rudy sleeping through the night for the first time in three weeks in his son's house in Petoskey.

Agnes at her piano in the studio on Elm Street, filling rests with forty one years of active silence, making rooms where the wrong note has nowhere to be.

And Wren.

Always Wren.

The one way mirror at the center of all of it.

I thought about what the boy in the corn field had known and what the man at the desk was beginning to understand and the distance between those two things which was the distance between hiding and something else that didn't have a name yet but was taking shape in the specific way that things take shape when you stop looking away from them.

I thought about the corner.

The field has changed.

I closed my eyes.

Found the frequency.

Got quiet on it.

Not hiding.

Something else.

Something that the boy hadn't had and the man was only now beginning to learn the name of.

Presence expressed through absence.

The rest held so completely there is no room for the wrong note.

I held it.

Held it.

The lake moved in the dark outside.

The house breathed around me.

In the living room the corner was what it was.

And I was what I was.

And for the first time in sixty two years those two facts occupied the same space without one of them retreating.

Sleep came eventually.

Slowly.

The way sleep comes to a man who has stopped running and is not yet sure what standing still in the open is going to cost him.

But it came.

Chapter 18

Chapter Eighteen — Four Minutes In The Dark

Nora was not a woman who acted on feelings she couldn't explain.

This is not a criticism. It is a description of someone who was built for the visible world and had built well within it — a good marriage, a good house, two children developing into people she was proud of in the specific complicated way parents are proud of children who are becoming themselves rather than becoming what the parents expected. She had built this life with the careful attention of someone who understands that good things require maintenance and had maintained accordingly.

She trusted what she could see.

She verified what she couldn't.

She did not drive four minutes in the dark at seven fifteen in the morning because a feeling told her to.

Except that she did.

I heard her car in the driveway before the knock. Recognized the specific sound of her engine — a sound so familiar it had graduated from information to background, the way certain sounds do when you have been hearing them long enough. I was at the kitchen counter with coffee and the notebook open to a blank page and the specific quality of early morning attention that comes after a night of not quite enough sleep and is sharper than it has any right to be.

Wren was at the table eating cereal with the focused efficiency of a child who has calculated the exact minimum time required for breakfast and is executing accordingly. Backpack by the door. Shoes on. The morning negotiation with the clock already resolved in the clock's favor.

She looked up when she heard the car.

Looked at me.

I looked at her.

Mom, she said.

Not a question. Information.

I closed the notebook.

The knock came before I reached the door. Three knocks with the specific rhythm of Nora's knock — not urgent, not casual, the knock of a woman who is maintaining composure as a matter of principle while everything behind the composure is doing something else entirely.

I opened the door.

She was in her coat. The coat she grabs from the hook by the door without thinking because it's the first coat her hand finds, which meant she had left in a hurry or in the dark or both. Her hair was the hair of someone who had done the minimum required and moved. Her face was the face I had been reading for forty three years — the face of my daughter, which I know the way you know certain landscapes, every feature mapped by time and attention, every expression catalogued by decades of paying the specific parental attention that doesn't stop when they grow up but changes frequency.

She looked tired.

She looked like a woman who had been awake since three in the morning.

She looked like a woman who had driven four minutes in the early dark because something told her to and was now standing in her father's doorway not entirely certain what she had come to say.

Nora, I said.

I know it's early, she said.

Come in.

She came in.

Saw Wren at the table.

Something in her face released — the specific release of a parent who has been carrying a fear they couldn't name and has just received the evidence that the thing they feared has not happened. Not relief exactly. The exhale before relief, the moment before the body believes what the eyes are showing it.

Hi Mom, Wren said. *I have seven minutes.*

I know, Nora said. *I'll drive you.*

She came into the kitchen. Accepted the coffee I poured without being asked because I have been pouring her coffee for thirty years and we are past the stage of asking. Sat at the table across from Wren with the coat still on and both hands around the mug and the expression of a woman who has arrived somewhere and is now figuring out why.

I sat down.

The three of us at the kitchen table in the early morning with the lake visible through the window and the October light doing what it does and the coffee and the cereal and the backpack by the door and Wren eating with the focused efficiency of a child who has six minutes now instead of seven.

Bad night, I said. Not a question.

Strange night, she said. *I kept waking up.* She looked at her coffee. *I had a feeling.*

What kind.

The kind I don't usually — She stopped. Started again with the precision of a woman choosing her words the way you choose tools — for fitness to purpose, not for comfort. *Something felt wrong. I couldn't locate it. I checked on Cooper. I checked on Dale. Everyone was fine. But the feeling didn't* — She paused. *It didn't go away when I found everyone fine. Which is not how feelings like that usually work.*

No, I said. *It isn't.*

So I drove over.

Yes.

Because she was here, Nora said. Looking at Wren. *I kept thinking about Wren being here and not at home and the feeling pointed here and I —* She stopped herself. The expression of a woman who has just heard herself say something that lives outside her usual vocabulary and is deciding whether to stand behind it.

You listened to it, I said.

I listened to it, she said. As if this were the unusual part. Which for Nora it was.

Wren finished her cereal.

Carried the bowl to the sink with the unhurried purposefulness of a child who has five minutes and has made her peace with five minutes.

I'm ready, she said to Nora.

One minute, Nora said.

Wren sat back down.

Looked at me.

The look that needed no words.

The look that said — *this is the moment, isn't it. The one you said was coming. The sequence ending on its own terms.*

I looked back at her.

Yes, I said. Not out loud. The frequency below words.

She nodded.

Picked up her backpack.

Mom, she said. *Can I tell you something.*

Nora looked at her daughter.

Of course.

Grandpa has been keeping a secret, Wren said. *Not a bad one. The kind you keep until the person is ready. I think you're ready.*

Nora looked at Wren.

Looked at me.

The expression of a mother who has just been told something by her six year old that requires her to update her understanding of what has been happening in this kitchen for the past several weeks.

Is that right, she said to me.

Yes, I said.

How long.

Three weeks, I said. *Give or take.*

She sat with that.

The specific sitting of a woman who is choosing not to be angry about the keeping because she can see on her father's face that the keeping was not carelessness and she has decided to hear the reason before she decides how she feels about it.

This is one of the things I have always respected most about my daughter.

She decides in the right order.

Wren, she said. *Go wait by the car.*

Okay, Wren said.

She stood up. Put on her backpack. Looked at me once more with the dark patient eyes.

Tell her about the corn field first, she said. *It helps to start there.*

Then she went out the door and I heard her feet on the porch steps and the specific sound of a six year old walking to a car in the morning with the unhurried certainty of someone who has done what she came to do and is at peace with the outcome.

Nora watched her go.

Turned to me.

She knows everything, Nora said.

Yes.

You told my six year old daughter before you told me.

She already knew, I said. *I didn't tell her. I confirmed what she had already perceived. There's a difference.*

Nora looked at her coffee.

At the window.

At the notebook on the counter that she had seen a hundred times in the past three weeks and had assumed was a writing journal and had not asked about because she respects my process the way children of writers learn to respect the process — as a weather system that operates independently and is best not interfered with.

The notebook, she said.

Yes.

It's not the new book.

No.

What is it.

I looked at my daughter in her coat with her hands around her coffee mug in the early morning kitchen with the lake behind her and forty three years of knowing her face and the specific expression on it now which was not fear and not anger but the expression of a woman standing at the edge of something and deciding whether to step forward or back.

I had seen that expression before.

In a corn field in October 1963.

In a mirror for fifty years after that.

In Gerald's doorway three weeks ago.

The edge of what you know looking out at what you don't.

Nora, I said. *Something has been happening in this neighborhood. Something I've been aware of since Gerald died. Something that Wren can perceive and that I can perceive and that I have been trying to understand well enough to explain before explaining it.*

Are you well, she said. First. Before anything else. The daughter asking before the skeptic.

Yes, I said. *I'm well.*

Is Wren safe.

I'm working to make certain of that, I said. *That's been my primary occupation for three weeks.*

She looked at me for a long moment.

Tell me, she said.

Not — *this sounds insane* or *Dad you're worrying me* or any of the available responses that would have been completely reasonable from a woman who trusts the visible world and has built well within it.

Just — *tell me.*

I picked up the notebook.

Thought about what Wren had said.

Start with the corn field, I said. *It helps to start there.*

And I did.

I told her about the farm. The corn rows. The October cold. The tree line. The boy who became the rabbit because the rabbit was all he had. I told her about the notebook and what it contained and what Gerald's living room had felt like after the ambulance left. I told her about Vera and Rudy and Agnes and the cold spot that moved and the rest that left no room for the wrong note.

I told her about Wren.

What Wren could see.

What Wren had been doing.

What I had been teaching her and why.

Nora listened.

She was still in the specific stillness of a person who is receiving something large and has made the decision to receive it completely before responding. Not agreeing. Not dismissing. Receiving. With the open careful attention of a woman who decides in the right order.

Outside Wren was waiting by the car.

Patient as the thing in the corner.

Patient as the October morning.

Patient as a six year old who has said what she came to say and is now simply waiting for the adults to catch up.

Nora looked at her coffee when I finished.

At the window.

At the notebook in my hands.

At me.

The feeling, she said finally. *At three in the morning. That pointed here.*

Yes.

That was real.

Yes.

It's been real before, she said quietly. *Other times. I always explained it.*

I know.

Cooper, she said. *When he was two. I woke up at two in the morning and went to his room and he had a fever of a hundred and four. I hadn't heard anything. I just —* She stopped. *I just knew.*

Yes.

I told myself it was maternal instinct, she said. *Biology. Something explainable.*

Maybe it is, I said. *Maybe the explainable and the other thing are the same thing and we've been treating them as separate because it was convenient.*

She sat with this.

The sitting of a woman whose framework is expanding with the effortful grace of something built to last.

The corner, she said. *In your living room.*

Yes.

It's there now.

Yes.

She stood up.

Walked to the doorway between the kitchen and the living room.

Stood there.

Looked at the corner where the light didn't quite reach.

I watched my daughter look at the corner.

She stood very still.

Not the rabbit. Not trained. Not deliberate.

Just still in the specific way that Nora is still when she is paying attention to something she has decided deserves her full attention.

She stood there for a long moment.

It's cold, she said. *That corner.*

Yes.

The rest of the room isn't.

No.

She turned back to me.

Her face had done something while she was looking at the corner. The specific thing faces do when the framework expands — a settling, a recalibration, the expression of someone who has just felt something with their own body that their mind had been considering abstractly and discovered that the body is a more convincing instrument than the mind in certain circumstances.

All right, she said.

Two words.

The two words of a woman who has decided.

All right, she said again. Quieter. To herself. The confirmation of a decision made.

She picked up her coffee.

Drank the last of it.

Put the mug in the sink.

I need to take Wren to school, she said.

Yes.

And then I'm coming back, she said. *And you're going to tell me what I can do. Not what to avoid. Not where to stay. What I can do.* She looked at me with the eyes that were her mother's and her own simultaneously. *I'm not Vera or Rudy. I'm not going to Traverse City. She's my daughter.*

I know, I said.

So tell me what I can do.

Come back at nine, I said. *I'll have coffee ready.*

She nodded.

Picked up her keys.

Went to the door.

Paused with her hand on the frame the way Wren pauses on stairs.

Dad.

Yes.

The corn field, she said. *Nine years old. Alone.*

Yes.

I'm sorry, she said. *That you were alone.*

I looked at my daughter in the doorway.

Forty three years of her face.

The daughter asking before the skeptic.

I'm not alone now, I said.

She held my gaze for a moment.

Then she went out to drive her daughter to school on an ordinary Thursday morning in October in northern Michigan and I stood in the kitchen and listened to the car back out of the driveway and heard Wren's voice saying something and Nora's voice answering and the specific sound of two people I love more than I have adequate language for driving away in the early morning.

I turned and looked at the corner.

The corner looked back in the way it always looked back.

The cold without temperature.

The pressing absence.

She's going to be a problem for you, I told it.

The corner did not respond.

It never did.

But something in the quality of the cold shifted fractionally the way it had shifted the night before when I spoke out loud.

It heard.

It always heard.

Good, I said.

I poured a second cup of coffee.

Opened the notebook.

Wrote one line.

Nora knows. She looked at the corner and felt the cold and said all right. She is her father's daughter and I should have told her sooner and I did not and I am telling her now and all right is exactly the right response.

All right.

The field keeps growing.

Closed the notebook.

Waited for nine o'clock.

Outside the October morning continued its business without reference to what was happening inside the house on the quiet street in Bellaire Michigan where a field was assembling itself around something that had always hunted alone.

Patient as geology.

Getting ready.

Chapter 19

Chapter Nineteen — What A Mother Knows

Nora came back at nine with a notebook of her own.

Not the speckled black and white kind. A practical spiral bound from the drawer in her kitchen where practical things live — the drawer with the batteries and the takeout menus and the good scissors that nobody is supposed to use for anything except what good scissors are for. She put it on the table beside my coffee and sat down and opened it to the first page and looked at me with the expression of a woman who has had forty five minutes to drive to school and back and has used every one of them.

I have questions, she said.

I expected you would.

Practical questions, she said. *Not philosophical ones. I've had forty five minutes with the philosophical ones and I've put them in a separate category for later. Right now I want the mechanics.*

This is Nora.

This has always been Nora.

When she was seven and her goldfish died she did not cry first. She asked first. What happened. Why. What could have been done differently. The crying came later, thorough and complete, after she had the information. She has always done things in the right order and the right order for Nora begins with understanding the situation accurately.

Ask, I said.

She looked at her notebook.

She had written questions on the drive. In her neat specific handwriting at red lights presumably, the handwriting of a woman who thinks in lists because lists are honest about what you know and what you don't and the space between them is where the work lives.

What does it do exactly, she said. *Not what it is. What it does. Specifically.*

It finds people who see clearly, I said. *Who perceive the gap between what is said and what is meant. Who say true things when the room wants comfortable ones. It gets close to them. The proximity draws on them the way a drain draws on water — slowly, without their awareness, until they have less than they started with. Energy. Clarity. The specific aliveness of a person who is fully themselves.*

How close.

It varies, I said. *It circles first. Learns the person. Then it gets closer. When it reaches the bedroom —*

That's when Gerald —

Yes.

She wrote something.

How long from circling to —

It depends on the person, I said. *And it's getting faster. Gerald was approximately three weeks from first contact to the chair. Rudy was compressing toward ten days when I sent him to Petoskey.*

Why faster.

Practice, I said. *And conditions. The ambient* — I paused. Chose the word. *The ambient cruelty in the community right now. It feeds on that the way a fire feeds on oxygen. More fuel, more efficient combustion.*

She wrote.

Can it be in multiple places at once.

I looked at her.

I don't know, I said. *I've been assuming it's singular. One thing. I don't have evidence either way.*

She wrote: *determine if singular or multiple.* Underlined it.

The handwriting of a woman making a list of things that need answering as distinct from things already answered. The specific intellectual honesty of someone who refuses to treat an assumption as a fact.

I felt something shift in my chest.

Not the cold thing.

Something warmer.

Cooper, she said.

He can't see it, I said. *He doesn't perceive it. As far as I can determine it has no interest in people it can't find on the frequency. Cooper is —*

Safe, she said.

For now, I said. *As long as he remains — himself. Ordinary. Not in the pejorative sense. In the sense of someone who hasn't yet developed the particular kind of clarity the thing is attracted to.*

He's eleven, she said.

Yes.

He's going to develop, she said. *Into a person who sees more clearly than he does now. All people do if they're paying attention.*

Yes, I said. *Which is why this needs to be resolved before that happens.*

She wrote something I couldn't see.

Dale, she said.

Dale is — I paused. Thought about Dale at the town meeting that I hadn't seen him at. Thought about Dale picking fights at the hardware store over nothing three weeks ago. *Dale is fine. He's been feeling the ambient pressure the way everyone has. But he doesn't operate on the frequency the thing is hunting. He's —*

Good, Nora said. *He's a good man.*

Yes.

He sees clearly in his way, she said. *He just sees things I don't see and I see things he doesn't. That's —* She almost smiled. *That's marriage.*

Yes, I said.

Me, she said.

The word sitting on the table between us with the weight of a question that has been waiting since she stood in the living room doorway and felt the cold corner.

You felt it this morning, I said. *In the corner.*

Yes.

That means you perceive it on some level, I said. *Not the way Wren perceives it. Not the way I perceive it. But the body registered it as real before the mind had a framework for it.*

The three in the morning feeling, she said.

Yes.

That's been happening my whole life, she said. *I've been explaining it my whole life.*

I know.

You knew.

I suspected, I said. *I didn't want to — complicate your framework before it was necessary.*

She looked at me.

The look of a daughter who understands what her father was protecting and has decided to accept the protection as the care it was rather than the withholding it could also be called.

Does that make me a target, she said.

It makes you someone who has been successfully not noticing for forty three years, I said. *Which means it hasn't found you on the frequency because you've been broadcasting on a very narrow band. The visible world, the practical world, the world of children and work and the good scissors in the drawer that nobody is supposed to use for anything else.*

That sounds like a limitation, she said.

I used to think so, I said.

She looked at me.

And now.

I picked up my coffee.

Thought about what I had been assembling since the night before. The thing I had written in the notebook at eleven o'clock and the thing Agnes had said about the rest and the thing Wren had said about the one way mirror and the thing Vera's sister had confirmed by doing it accidentally without being taught.

The thing lives in gaps, I said. *The space between what is said and what is meant. The space between what we value and how we treat each other. The space in a community where decency has been slowly replaced by performance. It finds these gaps and occupies them and grows in them.*

All right.

The people it hunts are the ones who see the gaps, I said. *Who name them. Who refuse to pretend they aren't there. Those people are dangerous to it in a way it can't ignore — which is why it targets them.*

Because they could fill the gaps.

Yes.

But, I said, *there is another kind of person who doesn't see the gaps because they don't leave them. Who is so completely present in the ordinary world — the visible, practical, real world of children and work and good scissors — that the gaps don't form around them in the first place.*

Nora looked at me.

You can't hunt a gap that doesn't exist, she said.

No, I said. *You can't.*

I'm not a gap, she said slowly. *I'm the opposite of a gap.*

Yes, I said. *Which is why it hasn't found you in forty three years. Not because you can't perceive it. Because you don't leave it the kind of space it needs to get close.*

She sat with this.

The sitting of a woman integrating something that reframes not just the current situation but forty three years of her own history. The three in the morning feelings she explained. The things she noticed and filed under maternal instinct and biology and coincidence. The gap she had always felt between her way of moving through the world and her father's way and her daughter's way — a gap she had sometimes felt as distance and sometimes felt as inadequacy and was now being told was neither.

Was armor.

Was its own kind of gift.

Wren got it from you, she said finally.

Wren got something from me, I said. *But she got something from you too. The groundedness. The way she comes back. She sees everything I see and she doesn't drift into it. She perceives the frequency and stays rooted in the ordinary world simultaneously.* I paused. *That's you. That's your gift in her.*

Nora looked at her notebook.

At the questions she had written on the drive.

She turned the page.

Started a new list.

What can I do, she said. *Specifically.*

You're already doing it, I said. *You've been doing it for six years without knowing that's what you were doing.*

Tell me anyway.

Stay close to Wren, I said. *Not helicopter close — Wren doesn't need that and you know it. The kind of close you already are. The presence that doesn't crowd but doesn't absent itself. She needs the ordinary world around her the way a diver needs the rope. You're the rope.*

She's been going pretty deep, Nora said.

Yes.

And you've been the rope.

I've been trying, I said. *But I'm not — I'm too close to the frequency she's operating on. I can hold the rope but I can also go under with her. You can't. The ordinary world is where you live. It doesn't pull you under.*

She wrote something.

What else.

Cooper, I said. *Keep his world ordinary. Don't tell him more than he needs. He saw something outside his window — he'll tell you when he's ready. When he does, listen without explaining it away. Don't confirm more than he brings. Let him lead.*

She nodded. Wrote.

Dale.

Tell him, I said. *Or don't. That's your decision. You know him better than I do. What I would say is that Dale is the kind of man who responds to a practical problem with practical response and this has become a practical problem.*

He'll want to fix it, she said.

Yes.

Is there something he can fix.

I thought about Dale and his foundations and his belief in structural integrity and the specific pragmatic courage of a man who responds to wrong things by correcting them.

There might be, I said. *I don't know yet what it looks like. But when I do I think Dale is the right person for that part of it.*

She wrote: *tell Dale when Harlan knows what Dale can fix.*

The handwriting of a woman who has taken the situation into her framework and is managing it with the same attention she manages everything — methodically, without drama, in the right order.

I looked at my daughter at my kitchen table with her practical notebook and her coat finally off and her coffee going cold the way coffee goes cold when you're thinking harder than you're drinking.

Thought about Gerald.

About Rudy.

About Vera and Agnes.

About the field assembling itself around something that had always hunted alone.

Thought about what the field had been missing.

Not more people who could see the thing.

Someone who could hold the ordinary world steady while the others did what they needed to do. Someone who could keep the ground solid under everyone's feet. Someone who understood that the visible world and the invisible one were not enemies — they were the warp and weft of the same cloth, and you needed both to weave anything that would hold.

The weaver.

Nora, I said.

Yes.

The feeling at three in the morning, I said. *That you've been explaining your whole life.*

Yes.

Stop explaining it, I said. *Just listen to it. You don't need to see what it's pointing at. You just need to go where it points.*

She looked at me.

Like this morning, she said.

Like this morning, I said.

She closed her notebook.

Put her pen down.

Picked up her cold coffee and drank it anyway because some things you do for the ritual of them rather than the substance.

All right, she said.

The same two words as this morning.

But different now.

This morning they were the words of a woman deciding whether to step forward or back from the edge of something.

These were the words of a woman who had stepped forward, found solid ground, and was ready to walk.

One more question, she said.

Yes.

Wren, she said. *In the end. Whatever the end looks like. Is she —* She stopped. *Is she going to have to be in the middle of it.*

I looked at my daughter.

Thought about the notebook. About what a nine year old boy had written about a drawing with edges that wouldn't hold still. About a six year old pointing at a corner saying *there* with the flat certainty of a field observer reporting coordinates.

Thought about what the child had written sixty two years ago.

It does not have a inside. I looked and looked.

Thought about Wren in the backyard.

Are we going to stop it.

Yes. We are.

Yes, I said to Nora. *She's going to be in the middle of it.*

The silence that followed was the silence of a mother receiving the thing she was most afraid of hearing and holding it with the specific courage of someone who knew it was coming and came anyway.

Is she ready, Nora said.

I thought about Wren on the first day in the basement.

Can I learn.

Yes. Today.

I thought about her on the stairs after.

I wanted to see if it worked before lessons.

I thought about her in the car.

It looked right at where I was standing and then looked away.

I thought about her on the floor between Agnes and me for three hours watching the corner so that Agnes and I could talk without watching.

Already understanding the division of labor without being told.

Yes, I said. *She's ready.*

Nora nodded.

Once.

The nod of a woman who has asked the question she needed to ask and received the answer she needed to receive and is now closing that particular file and opening the next one because there is work to do and she is a woman who does work.

Then let's get to it, she said.

Outside the October morning had fully arrived with the specific clarity of October mornings that have burned off the early mist and decided to be honest about what they are.

Inside a kitchen in Bellaire Michigan a field of people who saw clearly were having coffee and making lists and practicing held silences and sleeping in Petoskey and calling from Traverse City and teaching piano on Elm Street and doing homework at kitchen counters and waving from front porches and spinning wheels from miles away and sitting very still in the rests.

Getting ready.

One morning at a time.

The field had changed.

The ground was solid.

The weavers had found each other.

Chapter 20

THE QUIET ONES

Chapter Twenty — The Cost Of The Rabbit

The winter of 1963 into 1964 was the coldest winter I remember and I have lived through many Michigan winters so this is a statement made with the authority of someone who has a substantial sample size to compare against.

Not coldest in temperature necessarily though it was cold enough that the horse trough froze solid by November and stayed that way until March and the wind off the fields had the specific cutting quality of a wind that has been traveling a long distance over flat ground with nothing to slow it down and arrives at your face with the full energy of its entire journey intact.

Cold in the other sense.

The sense I had been practicing since October.

I want to tell you what happened to the boy that winter because I have not told anyone and because the chapter I am writing in my head about why I told Wren *you are not hiding you are choosing* does not make sense without it.

The rabbit had worked.

This was the problem.

The rabbit had worked so well and so completely that I kept doing it past the point where it was necessary and into the territory where it was something else. The way a medicine that helps in the correct dose begins to harm in the excess. The way a locked door that keeps the intruder out also keeps the occupant in.

The thing at the tree line had not come back after the woodlot in November.

I felt its absence the way you feel the absence of weather that has passed — the specific quality of air that is no longer doing what it was doing, the return of the ordinary atmosphere after something extraordinary has moved through it. By December I was reasonably certain it had moved on. Not gone — I was nine years old but I was not naive and I had learned enough about it by then to understand that gone was probably not a category it operated in. Moved on. Found other hunting ground. Decided the frequency it had been following had gone quiet enough to release.

I had gone quiet enough.

Too quiet.

Here is what I did not understand at nine years old that I understand now at seventy one with the clarity of a man looking back at a child with the specific heartbreak of someone who can see the mistake and cannot go back to correct it.

I understood the rabbit as a state to achieve.

I did not understand it as a tool to use and put down.

I kept being the rabbit through December.

Through January.

Into February.

Not because the thing was still there. It wasn't. Because the rabbit had become the default. Because the quiet on the frequency had become the quiet everywhere. Because a boy who had learned to make himself unfindable had found that unfindable was easier than the alternative which was being found — not by the thing, but by everything. By the farm and the cold and the screaming and the specific inventory of daily difficulties that a child in that house in that winter was subject to.

The rabbit kept you safe from all of it.

Not just the thing at the tree line.

Everything.

So I kept doing it.

And the boy who had been doing it started to become less.

Not all at once. Gradually. The way a photograph fades in a window — present every day, losing something every day, the change invisible in the moment and only apparent when you compare to what it was. I stopped arguing. Not because I had nothing to argue about — the farm provided abundant material. Because argument required a kind of presence that the rabbit didn't have. I stopped wanting things. Not because I had what I wanted but because wanting required broadcasting on a frequency the rabbit was not supposed to broadcast on. I stopped being visible even to Chuck who was two rows over and had always known where I was by the sound of me if not the sight.

Chuck noticed.

He was eleven that winter and had his steel trap mind and his perfect recall and the specific attentiveness of a boy who tracks everything because everything has proved to require tracking. He noticed that I had become quieter than the quiet he knew.

You're disappearing, he said one evening.

We were in the bedroom. I was on my cot looking at the ceiling. He was at the small table doing something with a piece of wire and the focused application of a boy who solves problems with his hands when his mind needs the rest.

I'm right here, I said.

That's not what I mean, he said. *You're here but you're not — you've been going away. For weeks. Since fall.*

I looked at the ceiling.

I'm fine, I said.

Chuck put down the wire.

Looked at me with the eyes that missed nothing and released nothing.

What happened in the east field, he said.

Nothing.

Something happened, he said. *You changed after that. I didn't say anything because you seemed — safer. Whatever you were doing seemed to make you safer. But now you're too far away and I don't* — He stopped. Chuck did not say things like I don't like it or I'm worried about you. He said them in the construction of his sentences — in what was left unsaid, in the specific pressure of the words around the gap. *Come back,* he said.

I looked at my brother.

Eleven years old.

Steel trap mind. Perfect recall. The boy who remembered everything and forgave nothing and had just told me in the only language available to him that he could see me fading and wanted me to stop.

I'm fine, I said again.

But I wasn't.

I was less than I had been in October.

Less than I had been before the east field.

The rabbit had saved me from the thing at the tree line and was quietly finishing what the thing had started — not by draining me from the outside the way the thing drained, but by teaching me to drain myself. To make myself small enough that nothing could find me. To exist at the minimum necessary volume.

Less is safe.

Less doesn't get found.

Less doesn't get the attention of things with edges that won't hold still.

Less also doesn't get to be a person.

I did not understand this at nine.

I understood it at seventeen when a teacher named Mrs. Beaumont — a woman with the specific directness of someone who has been watching children disappear into themselves for thirty years and has decided that watching without intervening is a choice she is not willing to make — kept me after class one afternoon in March.

You're going to tell me what's happening, she said.

Nothing's happening, I said.

You've been in my class for two years, she said. *In September you were here. In October you started going away. You're still going away and it's March and I want to know what happened in October.*

I looked at this woman.

Thought about the east field.

About the thing at the tree line.

About the rabbit.

About four years of being less as a strategy for survival.

I learned something, I said carefully. *To keep safe. And I didn't know how to stop doing it.*

She looked at me for a long moment.

What does it cost, she said. *This thing you learned.*

And I understood for the first time sitting in Mrs. Beaumont's classroom in March that the rabbit had a price that I had been paying without knowing I was paying it.

The cost was presence.

The cost was the full-volume aliveness of a person who is completely themselves.

The rabbit worked by reducing that. By turning down the broadcast. By making the self small enough and quiet enough that it couldn't be located.

It worked.

And it cost exactly what it saved.

You could not be the rabbit and be fully yourself simultaneously.

One or the other.

I didn't know how to put it down, I told Mrs. Beaumont.

She nodded.

Then let's figure that out, she said.

Sitting at my desk on a Thursday morning in October sixty years after Mrs. Beaumont kept me after class I thought about what I had told Wren in the basement.

You are not hiding. You are choosing.

I had said this because I knew what hiding cost.

I had paid it for four years before Mrs. Beaumont noticed and another decade after before I trusted the putting down enough to do it completely. I had paid it in ways I was still discovering — in the marriages that had suffered from a man who knew how to go quiet and sometimes went quiet when he should have been present. In the years of writing novels that the second wife said were careful and she was right because careful is what you write when you are still half-rabbit, still keeping some of yourself in reserve, still not entirely convinced that full presence is survivable.

I had paid it in ways I could not fully inventory even now.

And I had told Wren *you are not hiding, you are choosing* because the distinction was the difference between a tool and a trap.

A tool you pick up when you need it and put down when you don't.

A trap you step into once and spend years climbing out of.

The rabbit was a tool.

I had used it as a trap for forty years.

I was not going to let Wren do the same.

But here was the thing I had been turning over since the basement lesson. The thing I had not said to Wren because I didn't have the right words for it yet and I refuse to say important things in the wrong words.

Wren was not in danger of the trap.

Because Wren had never learned to be less.

She had come into the world at full volume — the dark eyes, the hearing of truth beneath words, the questions that made adults uncomfortable, the sitting very still in the rests at Agnes's piano. All of it present from the beginning. All of it unapologetic. All of it exactly what she was without reduction or concealment.

Nora had protected that without knowing that's what she was doing.

By being the ordinary world around her daughter. By saying *that's enough Wren* at dinner tables when the true things made people uncomfortable — not suppressing what Wren was, just teaching her the timing. When to say and when to wait. The difference between the full broadcast and the choosing.

Wren had never been the rabbit because she had never needed to be.

She had been something else all along.

Something the boy in the corn field had not had access to and was only now — at seventy one, in a kitchen in Bellaire Michigan with a notebook and cold coffee and a corner that was quieter than it used to be — beginning to understand.

Not the rabbit in the field.

The field itself.

So completely present. So entirely itself. That the thing moving through it could not find purchase.

Could not occupy a gap that wasn't there.

Could not plant its cold absence in ground that was fully occupied by what it was supposed to be.

I picked up the pen.

Wrote in the man's section.

The rabbit is a tool. I used it as a trap. I was less for forty years because less was safe and safe was all I understood how to want. Mrs. Beaumont saw me going away in March of 1964 and kept me after class and asked what it cost and I didn't have the answer then but I have it now.

It costs you.

The whole of you.

The rabbit works by making you smaller than the thing hunting you needs you to be. This works. And it is not the only way. There is another way that I did not know about until I had a granddaughter who never learned to be small.

She is not the rabbit.

She is the field.

The field does not hide. The field is simply so completely itself that there is no gap in it for the wrong thing to occupy.

I have been teaching her the rabbit because the rabbit is what I know.

I need to understand what she is so I can teach her that instead.

Or possibly so she can teach me.

I closed the notebook.

Sat at the desk.

Thought about a boy in a bedroom in February 1964 with Chuck watching him go away and not knowing how to come back.

Thought about Mrs. Beaumont in March.

Then let's figure that out.

Thought about Wren at the kitchen table this morning eating cereal with the focused efficiency of a child who has calculated the exact minimum time required and executing accordingly. Fully present. Fully herself. Not broadcasting at reduced volume. Broadcasting at exactly the right volume — which was all of it. Every frequency. The whole of what she was without apology or reduction.

Safe not because she was small.

Safe because she was complete.

I sat with the difference between those two things for a long time.

Outside the October morning was doing what October mornings do.

Inside the corner was quiet.

Not retreated.

Quiet.

The way a thing goes quiet when it is learning something new about the ground it has been hunting.

The ground had changed.

The rabbit had not changed it.

The field had.

And the field was sitting in a classroom four minutes away learning fractions with the dark patient eyes and the hands folded on the desk and the particular quality of presence that made teachers pause mid-sentence and forget what they were saying.

I should call Agnes, I thought.

I should tell her that the rest she holds completely is not a defensive technique.

It is the same thing as the field.

Presence so complete there is no room for the absence.

The wrong note has nowhere to be not because it was driven out but because the right notes are already there.

All of them.

Fully themselves.

I picked up the phone.

Called Agnes.

She answered on the second ring.

I've been thinking, I said.

So have I, she said. *About the rest. About what fills it.*

Yes.

It's not emptiness, she said. *A rest is not empty. A rest held properly is full. Full of all the music that came before it and all the music that comes after. It is the most concentrated point in the piece.*

Yes, I said.

So when I fill the rest, she said slowly, *I am not blocking it out. I am simply — being the music completely. In the silence.*

Yes, I said. *That's it exactly.*

And Wren, Agnes said.

Yes.

She's been doing that, Agnes said. *In lessons. For two years. She holds the rests differently than any child I've taught. Not empty. Full. I always thought she was just very serious about the structure.*

She is, I said. *She's also being the music completely. In the silence. She doesn't know that's what she's doing. She just does it because it's what she is.*

Agnes was quiet for a moment.

Harlan, she said.

Yes.

I don't think we're teaching her anything, she said. *I think she's been teaching us.*

I sat at my desk in the October morning with the notebook and the cold coffee and the corner that was quieter than it used to be.

Thought about a six year old in a basement saying *can I learn it today.*

Thought about her on the stairs after.

I wanted to see if it worked before lessons.

Thought about her pointing at the corner saying *there.*

Thought about her on the floor between Agnes and me watching so we didn't have to.

Thought about her in the car.

It looked right at where I was standing and then looked away.

Thought about her this morning.

Tell her about the corn field first. It helps to start there.

Yes, I said to Agnes.

Yes.

I think she has been.

Chapter 21

Chapter Twenty One — Thomas

I picked Wren up from school at three fifteen.

This is a recent arrangement. Three weeks recent. Before Gerald I had picked her up occasionally — the days Nora worked late, the days Dale had a job running long, the ordinary scheduling accommodations of a family that functions through coordination. Since Gerald I picked her up every day without being asked and without explaining why and Nora had looked at me once when the arrangement began and made the decision not to ask and I had looked back at her with the gratitude of a man whose daughter understands the difference between questions that need answering and questions that need waiting.

The school was a low brick building on Maple that had been a low brick building on Maple since 1958 and had the specific settled confidence of an institution that has been doing what it does long enough to stop worrying about whether it's doing it right. Good trees out front. A playground in back that smelled of wood chips and the specific outdoor cold of Michigan October that children generate immunity to and adults merely endure.

I parked on the street.

Waited.

The doors opened at three fifteen and the children came out in the specific way children come out of schools — not the orderly exit of the institution's imagination but the actual exit of forty separate urgent agendas finding the door simultaneously. A controlled detonation. Teachers at the edges like people who have accepted that their job for the next four minutes is containment rather than direction.

I watched for Wren.

She came out in the middle of the flow but not of it — present in the stream of children without being carried by it, moving at her own pace with the settled purposefulness of someone who knows where she is going and sees no reason to hurry or to dawdle. Backpack on both shoulders. Coat zipped. The dark eyes scanning the street with the specific efficiency of a child who locates what she's looking for without appearing to search.

She found me.

Walked to the car.

Got in.

Hi, she said.

Hi, I said.

This is our greeting when I pick her up. Two letters. All the information necessary. We are both here, we are both fine, we can walk to the water now or get in the car and drive home and either way the day is over and the next part has begun.

I pulled out.

How was it, I said.

Fine, she said.

I heard the gap between what she said and what she meant the way I always heard it — not dramatically, just present, the slight inflation of fine that means something specific happened and is being carried.

Fine how, I said.

She looked out the window at the October street.

There's a boy, she said.

I drove.

Thomas, she said. *He sits in the back. He doesn't talk much. The other kids have started — not being mean exactly. Just not including him. They don't know why. I don't think they know they're doing it.*

But you know why, I said.

He feels wrong to them, she said. *Not bad wrong. The wrong of something that doesn't fit. He's too quiet. He sits too still. He looks at things too long.* She paused. *He reminds me of me.*

I kept driving.

Kept my hands on the wheel at the position my driver's education teacher had recommended.

What do you hear in him, I said. Carefully.

She was quiet for a moment.

The specific quiet of a child searching for accurate language for something she perceives more clearly than she can describe.

He's very far away, she said. *Even when he's right there. Like he's in the room but most of him is somewhere else. Somewhere quieter. He only comes all the way forward when he thinks nobody is watching.*

I stopped at the light on Main.

Looked at the light.

Is he doing the rabbit, I said.

Wren turned from the window.

Looked at me.

I didn't think of it that way, she said. *But —* She stopped. *Yes. He's doing the rabbit. All the time. Even when there's nothing to hide from.*

The light changed.

I drove.

How old is Thomas, I said.

Seven, she said. *He got held back.*

Where does he sit at lunch.

Alone, she said. *At the end of the table by the window. I've been sitting with him.*

Does he talk to you.

Not much, she said. *But he doesn't go as far away when I'm there. I can feel him coming a little more forward.* She paused. *I don't think anyone has sat with him in a long time.*

I turned onto our street.

Drove past Gerald's house.

Past the Millers' mailbox.

Into the driveway.

Turned the engine off.

Sat.

Wren sat.

The October afternoon held itself around the car with the specific quality of October afternoons that have gone past their best warmth and are heading toward the cold that comes later but haven't arrived there yet. The in-between time. Still enough light to see clearly. Enough cold to know the dark is coming.

Grandpa, Wren said.

Yes.

Is Thomas like us.

I looked at my granddaughter in the passenger seat with her backpack on her lap and her dark eyes and her six years of seeing everything.

Thought about a boy in a bedroom in February 1964 with Chuck telling him *you're disappearing* and not knowing how to come back.

Thought about Mrs. Beaumont in March.

Thought about forty years of being less as a strategy for survival.

Thought about what it had cost.

I think, I said carefully, *that Thomas might have learned something that was necessary once. And is still doing it past the point of necessity. The way you keep taking medicine after the fever breaks because stopping feels dangerous.*

He's hiding from something that isn't there anymore, she said.

Maybe, I said. *Or maybe it was never the thing we hide from. Maybe it was something else. Something closer to home.*

She sat with this.

The sitting of a six year old who understands more than the words and is being patient with the words catching up.

Can we help him, she said.

I looked at the house.

At the front door.

At the ordinary October street where something without an inside had been moving and growing and where a field of people who saw clearly were assembling themselves around it.

Thought about what Agnes had said on the phone.

I don't think we're teaching her anything. I think she's been teaching us.

Thought about what I had written in the notebook.

She is not the rabbit. She is the field.

Thought about a seven year old boy in the back of a classroom going further away every day while the other children felt the wrongness of it without being able to name it and responded the way children respond to things they can't name — with the unconscious cruelty of avoidance.

The same avoidance the world had practiced on me.

On Wren before she learned to be the field.

On every person who had ever been too much of what they were for the room they were in.

Yes, I said. *I think we can.*

How.

The same way you've been doing it, I said. *By sitting with him. By not going away just because he has. By being so completely present that going away stops being the only available option.*

I've been doing that, she said.

I know.

Is that — She paused. *Is that what you needed. When you were Thomas.*

I looked at my granddaughter.

Thought about Chuck saying *come back* in the February bedroom.

About Mrs. Beaumont keeping me after class.

About the long cold winter of 1963 into 1964 and the boy who had learned to be less and didn't know how to stop.

Yes, I said. *That's exactly what I needed.*

Did you get it.

Eventually, I said. *Later than I should have. From people who noticed and stayed anyway.*

She nodded.

Filed it.

The small serious nod of someone adding information to a picture that is becoming clearer.

Grandpa.

Mm.

Thomas isn't the only one, she said. *There are others. In my class and the other classes. I can hear them going away. It's* — She searched for the word. *It's very common.*

I sat in the car in the October afternoon and thought about what she had just said.

Not one Thomas.

Many.

Children learning to be less. Learning the rabbit before they had words for it or reasons for it that made sense. Learning it from homes where the cost of visibility was too high and the safety of smallness was the only available math.

Going away.

Every day.

A little further.

Yes, I said. *It's very common.*

Why doesn't anyone do anything, she said.

Because most people can't hear them going, I said. *They see the quiet. They don't hear the frequency underneath it.*

We can, she said.

Yes.

So we should, she said.

Not a question.

Not a proposal.

The flat matter of fact certainty of a six year old who has identified a true thing and sees no reason to treat the acting on it as optional.

I looked at my granddaughter.

Thought about what was assembling itself around the thing in the corner.

Thought about what it had started as — a man and a small girl and a notebook and a cold spot in a dead man's living room.

Thought about what it was becoming.

Vera practicing four times a day in Traverse City.

Rudy sleeping through the night in Petoskey.

Agnes filling rests on Elm Street.

Nora with her practical notebook and her three in the morning feelings and her two words — *all right* — that meant everything.

And now Thomas.

Seven years old.

In the back of a classroom.

Going further away every day.

While a six year old with dark eyes sat with him at the end of the table by the window and stayed present and didn't go away just because he had.

Being the field.

Quietly.

Without being asked.

Yes, I said. *We should.*

She opened the car door.

Got out.

Walked to the front door with the backpack and the October light on her dark hair and the unhurried purposefulness of someone who has decided something and is getting on with it.

I sat in the car for a moment longer.

Thought about the thing in the corner.

About the pattern in the notebook.

About the mechanism I still didn't fully understand.

And then I thought about something else.

Something I had been assembling without knowing I was assembling it.

The thing fed on the gap between what people were and what the world allowed them to be. On the accumulated residue of visibility punished and presence reduced and true things swallowed and children learning to go further away every day in classrooms all over Antrim County and everywhere else.

It grew as the gaps grew.

As the going away accumulated.

As the rabbits multiplied.

But the field diminished it.

Presence so complete there was no gap to occupy.

The right notes already there.

No room for the wrong one.

And if the field could be taught — if a six year old could sit with a seven year old at the end of a table by a window and stay present and not go away — then the field could grow.

Not just around the corner in my living room.

Everywhere the gaps were.

Which was — as Wren had just observed with the flat certainty of someone stating the obvious —

Very common.

I got out of the car.

Went inside.

Found Wren at the kitchen table with her homework and a glass of milk and the focused efficiency of a child who wants homework finished before interesting things happen.

Grandpa, she said without looking up.

Yes.

There's something else about Thomas.

I put my jacket on the hook.

Turned around.

What.

She looked up from her homework.

The dark eyes.

The patience that belonged to someone much older.

He sees things, she said. *At the tree line behind the school. He told me today. He said he's been seeing something there for two weeks and he doesn't know what it is and he hasn't told anyone because —*

Because no one would believe him, I said.

Yes, she said.

I stood in the kitchen doorway.

The October afternoon doing what it did outside the window.

The corner of the living room quiet in the way it had been quiet since Agnes.

Wren, I said.

Yes.

Tomorrow at lunch, I said. *Tell Thomas your grandfather would like to meet him.*

She looked at me for a moment.

Then she went back to her homework.

I already told him today, she said. *He said okay.*

I looked at my granddaughter.

Of course she had.

Good, I said.

He's scared, she said. *But he's been doing the rabbit for two years already and he's only seven so he's actually pretty good at it.*

Yes, I said. *He would be.*

I went to put the kettle on.

Thought about a boy in an east field in October 1963.

Thought about a boy behind a school in October of the present year.

Two different boys.

Two different tree lines.

The same thing at the edge of both.

And in between them sixty two years of a man who had learned the rabbit alone and paid the cost alone and was only now — standing in a kitchen in Bellaire Michigan with the kettle filling and his granddaughter doing homework and Thomas coming to lunch tomorrow — understanding that alone was the variable that needed changing.

Not the rabbit.

Not the frequency.

Not the seeing.

The alone.

The field is not one rabbit.

The field is all of them.

Finding each other.

Chapter 22

THE QUIET ONES

Chapter Twenty Two — The Boy On The Porch

Thomas arrived at nine o'clock on a Saturday morning with his mother's permission and his own terror and a jacket that was slightly too large for him in the specific way that certain children wear clothes — not from poverty necessarily but from the particular economy of a household that buys ahead of the growth rather than for the size that currently exists.

He was small.

Not small the way Wren is small — Wren's smallness has the quality of something concentrated, dense, present in a volume that belies the container. Thomas's smallness was the other kind. The smallness of a child who has been making himself smaller than he is for long enough that the body has begun to cooperate with the project.

He stood on my porch with his hands in the pockets of the too-large jacket and looked at the door with the expression of a boy who has decided to do something and is now standing at the threshold of doing it and finding the threshold considerably more substantial than it appeared from the decision end.

I had watched him come up the walk from the window.

Watched him stop at the bottom of the porch steps.

Stand there for a moment.

Have the conversation with himself that children have at the bottoms of porch steps when they are about to do something that requires more of them than they currently have available.

Then climb the steps anyway.

Knock.

Three knocks with the specific rhythm of a child who has been taught to knock properly and is executing the instruction with more precision than the situation strictly required because precision is what you do when everything else feels uncertain.

I opened the door.

He looked up at me.

I looked down at him.

Seven years old.

Brown hair that needed cutting in the way boys' hair needs cutting when there is no one paying attention to it. Eyes that were — I noted this and filed it carefully — not the dark patient eyes of Wren but a lighter brown, almost amber, and in them the specific quality I had been told to expect but still felt in my chest like a hand pressing when I saw it.

The rabbit.

Present in his eyes the way it had been present in mine for forty years.

The distance. The removal. The part of himself he was keeping in a safer location than the front porch of a stranger's house on a Saturday morning in October.

Most of him was somewhere else.

A small brave fraction of him had knocked.

Thomas, I said.

Yes sir, he said.

The yes sir of a child who has learned that formality is a kind of armor and wears it accordingly.

I'm Harlan, I said. *Wren's grandfather.*

I know, he said. *She talks about you.*

Good things I hope.

She says you understand things, he said. *That other people don't.*

I looked at this seven year old boy on my porch in his too-large jacket.

Come in, I said. *I have hot chocolate.*

Something moved in his face.

Not quite relief.

The fraction of him that had knocked becoming slightly larger.

He came in.

Wren was at the kitchen table.

She looked up when Thomas came in and did the thing she does — the assessment that isn't unfriendly but is completely honest, the inventory of a person taken without pretense or social lubrication. She looked at Thomas the way she looked at the corner. Directly. Completely.

Thomas looked at Wren.

Something passed between them that I was probably the only other person in the room equipped to understand — the specific recognition of two instruments on the same frequency encountering each other in a context where that frequency is not supposed to exist. Not the warm recognition of Vera and Agnes. Something more tentative. The recognition of two children who have both been the strange one in the room for their entire lives and are not yet certain that finding another strange one is safe rather than simply a different configuration of the same danger.

Hi, Wren said.

Hi, Thomas said.

This was apparently sufficient.

He sat down at the table across from her with the careful placement of a child who chooses his position in rooms with more attention than most adults bring to the exercise.

Back to the wall.

Sight lines to the door.

I noted this without showing that I noted it.

Made the hot chocolate with the focused attention of a man who understands that hot chocolate on a Saturday morning is not a beverage it is a communication — *you are welcome here, this is a place where things are warm, you can come a little further forward* — and brought it to the table with the seriousness the communication deserved.

Thomas wrapped both hands around the mug.

The hands of a child who is cold in a way that has nothing to do with October.

Wren says you've been seeing something, I said. *At the tree line behind the school.*

He looked at his hot chocolate.

The specific looking-at-the-mug of a child deciding whether the ground will hold.

Yes, he said. Very quietly.

Tell me, I said.

He looked up.

The amber eyes with the rabbit in them.

You won't think I'm making it up, he said. Not a question. Checking.

No, I said. *I won't.*

My mom thinks I have an overactive imagination, he said. *She says it in a nice way. But she thinks that.*

Mothers often do, I said. *It's not their fault. They can only work with the information they have.*

He considered this.

Found it acceptable.

It's at the tree line, he said. *Behind the school. Near the big oak on the left side. I first saw it — felt it — about two weeks ago. During recess. I was* — He stopped.

You were being quiet, I said.

He looked at me.

Yes, he said. *I do that sometimes. Go to the edge of the playground where it's quieter and just — be quiet for a while.*

I know, I said.

The other kids think it's weird.

The other kids, I said, *are not wrong that it's unusual. They are wrong that unusual is the same as bad.*

He sat with this.

The sitting of a child receiving a reframe he has been needing for two years and is not yet certain he can trust.

I was being quiet, he said. *At the edge of the playground. And I felt something change. In the air. Behind the fence. At the tree line.* He paused. *It felt like being looked at. But not by a person.*

No, I said. *Not by a person.*

What is it, he said.

I looked at this seven year old boy at my kitchen table with his too-large jacket and his cold hands around the mug and the rabbit in his amber eyes.

Thought about what I had told Vera.

About the sequence. The right amount at the right time.

Thought about what I had told Nora.

Thought about what Wren had told me without being asked on the day I told her we were going to stop it.

Yes. We are.

Thought about Thomas on the porch steps having the conversation with himself.

Then climbing anyway.

He had already done the hardest part before he knocked.

He deserved the full answer.

It's something that has no inside, I said. *It moves through the world looking for people who see clearly. People who hear the difference between what is said and what is meant. People who go to the edge of the playground when they need to be quiet because quiet is where they think most clearly. It finds those people and gets close to them.*

Why.

Because being near someone who sees clearly is the only thing it has, I said. *It has nothing else. No warmth. No thought. No feeling. It is the shape of an absence. And it is drawn to presence the way cold is drawn to warmth.*

He looked at his hot chocolate.

Is it dangerous, he said.

It can be, I said. *To people who don't know it's there. Who don't know what the cold feeling means. Who don't know how to* — I paused. *How to be still in a particular way that makes them hard to find.*

He looked up.

The amber eyes.

Something in them shifting.

I do that, he said quietly. *I don't know what it is but I do something — when I feel it at the tree line I go very still and it stops — finding me. Like I step back behind something that isn't there.*

Yes, I said. *I know.*

How do you know.

Because I learned to do the same thing, I said. *When I was nine years old. In a field not very different from the one behind your school.*

He stared at me.

You've seen it, he said.

I've felt it, I said. *For sixty two years.*

The fraction of him that had knocked became more than half.

Something in his face — in the careful composed face of a seven year old who has been maintaining composure as a survival strategy for two years — shifted in the specific way that things shift when the weight you have been carrying alone is acknowledged by someone who knows the exact shape of it.

Not relief.

Something before relief.

The moment before the exhale.

The moment when you realize the carrying is about to be shared.

I thought I was crazy, he said.

I know, I said.

My mom —

I know, I said. *You're not.*

Wren said — He looked at Wren across the table. *She said you understand things. She said you would know what it was.*

Yes, I said.

She said — He stopped.

What did she say, I said.

He looked at his mug.

She said I wasn't alone, he said. Very quietly. The voice of a child saying a thing he has needed to say for a long time and is only now finding the container large enough to hold it.

I looked at Wren.

Wren was looking at Thomas with the dark patient eyes.

Not the assessment. Something warmer than the assessment. The specific expression of a child who has identified something that needs sitting with and is sitting with it.

She had told him he wasn't alone before she knew if that was true.

Because she had decided it was going to be true.

And had brought him here to make it so.

Six years old.

You're not alone, I said to Thomas.

He looked up.

There are others, I said. *People who feel what you feel and see what you see and have learned to be still in the particular way you've taught yourself to be still. More than you know. More than any of us knew until recently.*

Kids, he said.

Some, I said. *And adults who were once kids like you and learned what you're learning and kept going.*

Did they — He stopped. Started again. *Was it always* — He couldn't find the end of the sentence.

I understood what he was asking.

Was it always this. The alone. The too-quiet. The going away. The rabbit practiced past the point of necessity until it became the default and the default became the shape of a life.

No, I said. *It got better. Not all at once. Not without cost. But better.*

He sat with this.

The sitting of a seven year old boy who has been carrying something alone for two years and has just been told that the carrying has an end and is deciding whether to believe it.

Deciding.

Can you teach me, he said. *To do it properly. What Wren does. She told me a little but* —

Yes, I said. *I can teach you.*

The rabbit, he said.

I looked at him.

She told you about the rabbit.

On Tuesday, he said. *At lunch. She said her grandfather taught her and she could teach me the beginning but I should come here for the rest.*

I looked at Wren.

She was eating a piece of toast with the focused efficiency of a child who has arranged the morning exactly as intended and sees no reason to draw attention to the arranging.

Wren, I said.

Mm, she said.

You've been busy.

Thomas needed help, she said. *You knew things that would help. It seemed efficient.*

The specific tone of a six year old who has decided that modesty about effective action is a luxury the situation doesn't offer.

I almost smiled.

Looked at Thomas.

He was watching Wren with the expression of a boy who has found something he didn't know he was looking for and is in the early stage of understanding what he found.

Not the rabbit.

Not the frequency.

Something simpler and more fundamental than either.

Someone who sat with him at the end of the table by the window.

Someone who stayed present and didn't go away just because he had.

Someone who heard him going and came anyway.

Finish your hot chocolate, I said to Thomas. *Then we'll go to the basement.*

Why the basement, he said.

Better acoustics, I said.

He considered this.

For what.

For quiet, I said. *The right kind.*

He looked at Wren.

She nodded.

He drank his hot chocolate.

I watched him drink it and thought about a nine year old boy in a cold bedroom with Chuck watching him disappear and nobody knowing how to stop it.

Thought about Mrs. Beaumont in March.

Thought about what it would have meant — what it would have changed, what it would have cost less of — if someone had sat across a kitchen table from that boy on a Saturday morning and said *you are not crazy, I know what you feel, you are not alone, there are others, it gets better, I can teach you.*

Thought about what it meant that a six year old girl had identified the need and filled it before I knew there was a need to fill.

Thomas finished his hot chocolate.

Put the mug down with both hands.

Looked at me.

The fraction of him that had knocked was most of him now.

Still the rabbit in the amber eyes.

But less of it.

The very beginning of less of it.

Which was all that was needed to start.

Ready, he said.

Yes, I said.

We went to the basement.

The three of us.

An old man and two children descending the stairs into the specific quiet of a basement on a Saturday morning in October where the only light came through the small window above the washing machine and the flashlight on the shelf that I still hadn't replaced with a working overhead bulb.

Thomas looked at the basement.

At the flashlight circle on the floor.

At the wall where I sat.

At the window with the October light.

Sit down, I said. *Back against the wall. Both of you.*

They sat.

Cross legged. Side by side. Backs against the wall.

Wren with her hands in her lap and her stillness that was the field.

Thomas with his hands in his lap and his stillness that was the rabbit.

Both kinds of quiet in the same basement.

The difference between them visible to me in a way I didn't yet have complete language for but was beginning to understand was the most important thing I had learned in sixty two years of carrying a notebook and a frequency and the specific loneliness of a person who sees something nobody else can see.

Thomas, I said.

Yes.

What you've been doing, I said. *The going still. The stepping back behind something that isn't there. That's real. It works. It's been keeping you safe.*

Yes, he said.

It's also been costing you, I said. *You know that.*

He looked at his hands.

Yes, he said. Very quietly.

I know because it cost me, I said. *For a long time. More than it needed to.*

Can you — He stopped.

Can I what.

Can you teach me to do it without — He searched for the word. *Without paying so much.*

I looked at this seven year old boy.

Thought about what Agnes had said.

I don't think we're teaching her anything. I think she's been teaching us.

Thought about what Wren was.

Not the rabbit.

The field.

Yes, I said. *That's exactly what I'm going to teach you.*

I looked at Wren.

She looked at me.

The look that needed no words.

Actually, I said. *I'm going to teach you the beginning. And then Wren is going to show you the rest. Because she knows something about it that I'm still learning.*

Thomas looked at Wren.

Wren looked at Thomas.

Okay, he said.

Close your eyes, I said.

He closed them.

Wren closed hers.

The basement held its quiet.

The October light came through the small window and made its circle on the floor between us.

And I began.

The same words I had said in this basement to Wren six weeks ago.

Find where your thoughts are. Not what you're thinking. Where thinking happens. The place in you where attention lives.

Thomas was quiet.

Found it, he said.

Faster than I had.

Faster than Vera.

Almost as fast as Wren.

Of course.

He had been living in that place for two years.

He knew exactly where it was.

He just hadn't known what to do with it once he got there.

Now, I said. *I'm going to tell you two things. The first thing is what I learned when I was nine. The second thing is what she learned when she was six. They are both true. They are both useful. But only one of them is the whole answer.*

I paused.

The first thing, I said, *is how to be the rabbit.*

Thomas nodded with his eyes closed.

The second thing, I said, *is how to be the field.*

He was quiet for a moment.

What's the difference, he said.

I looked at Wren sitting beside him with her eyes closed and her hands in her lap and her six years of being exactly what she was without reduction or concealment.

Completely present.

Completely herself.

Not broadcasting at reduced volume.

Broadcasting at exactly the right volume which was all of it.

The rabbit, I said, *makes itself smaller than what's hunting it.*

The field, I said, *is so completely itself that there's no room for the hunt.*

Silence.

The basement held it.

Thomas sat with both eyes closed and both hands in his lap and the too-large jacket and the amber eyes behind their lids and sixty two years of a man watching a boy who was himself at nine and feeling something in his chest that was not grief and not joy but the specific complicated emotion of a door being opened that should have been opened a long time ago and is being opened now and now is what is available and now is enough.

Start with the rabbit, I said. *Because it's what you already know. And then —*

I looked at Wren.

Then she'll show you the rest.

Wren opened her eyes.

Looked at Thomas.

It's like the difference, she said quietly, *between hiding from the rain and being the ground the rain falls on.*

Thomas opened his eyes.

Looked at her.

The ground doesn't hide, he said.

No, she said. *The rain just becomes part of it.*

He sat with this.

A seven year old boy sitting with a metaphor that a six year old had produced without apparent effort and that I was still working on understanding completely.

Okay, he said.

He closed his eyes again.

I watched two children in a basement learn something that a man had spent sixty two years learning alone.

In forty minutes.

On a Saturday morning.

With hot chocolate still warm upstairs.

The field was growing.

One child at a time.

In the only direction that mattered.

From the inside out.

Chapter 23

THE QUIET ONES

Chapter Twenty Three — Briggs Calls

Thomas walked down the street at ten forty five with his too-large jacket and his hands in his pockets and something different in the way he moved.

Not transformed. I want to be honest about that. Two hours in a basement does not undo two years of the rabbit practiced past necessity. The coat was still too large. The hands were still in the pockets. The distance was still in the amber eyes when he had said goodbye at the door with the careful formality of a child who has been taught to say thank you and means it more than the words can carry.

But.

He walked down the street at ten forty five with his spine slightly more vertical than it had been at nine o'clock on the porch steps.

A fraction.

The fraction of a boy who has been told he is not crazy, not alone, not wrong about what he perceives. Who has been given the name for what he does and shown that the name belongs to a thing that can be used rather than merely endured. Who has sat in a basement with two people on the same frequency and felt the specific relief of instruments in tune.

A fraction.

Which was everything.

I stood at the window and watched him go until he turned the corner onto Maple and the too-large jacket disappeared from view and the street resumed its ordinary Saturday morning character — a dog on a leash, a car backing out of a driveway, two houses down a man raking leaves with the resigned thoroughness of someone who understands that October in northern Michigan is a raking proposition that does not resolve until November and possibly not then.

Ordinary.

Specific.

Real.

The visible world going about its business with the indifference of a world that does not know about basements and notebooks and children learning to be the field on Saturday mornings.

He'll be okay, Wren said.

She was at the table with her homework again. The perpetual homework. The homework that appeared to regenerate overnight like certain organisms that cannot be fully eradicated only managed.

Yes, I said. *I think he will.*

His mother should know, she said.

Yes.

Will you talk to her.

When I know how, I said. *The sequence.*

The sequence is getting shorter, she said.

I looked at my granddaughter.

Yes, I said. *It is.*

I went to the kitchen.

Made coffee.

Stood at the counter with the notebook open to a blank page and the pen in my hand and the specific quality of a Saturday morning that has already contained more than most full days and is apparently not finished.

Wrote:

Thomas. Seven years old. Two years of the rabbit already. Faster than I was — found the frequency in forty minutes. Wren showed him the field. He understood it better than I did when she explained it. The ground doesn't hide. The rain becomes part of it. I've been teaching the rabbit because it's what I know. She's been teaching the field because it's what she is. Between the two of them in that basement this morning I understood something I have been circling for three weeks without landing on.

The rabbit is defense.

The field is something else.

Not offense exactly. Completion. Wholeness so thorough that the absence has nothing to work with. No gap. No reduced frequency. No space between what you are and what the world has pressured you to perform.

The thing feeds on the gap.

Thomas has been living in the gap for two years.

An hour with Wren and the gap got smaller.

This is the mechanism.

Not confronting the thing directly. Not driving it away. Filling the space it occupies with what should have been there all along.

Gerald couldn't do this because nobody showed him.

Vera is learning.

Agnes has been doing it in music for forty one years.

Rudy will learn when he comes back.

Thomas is learning.

There are others.

There are always others.

The field grows as the gaps close.

The thing diminishes as the field grows.

This is how it ends.

Not with confrontation.

With completion.

I put the pen down.

Stood at the counter.

Felt something settle in my chest that had been unsettled since Gerald's living room three weeks ago.

Not resolution.

The shape of resolution.

The moment before you can see the end when you can see the direction and the direction is clear and the work between here and there is substantial but the work is possible.

The kettle was boiling.

I poured the coffee.

My phone rang.

The other line.

Briggs.

I looked at it for a moment.

Answered.

Briggs.

Harlan. His voice had the specific quality I had learned to read in our two conversations — the official process and the other process running simultaneously, the careful management of a man keeping both systems operational while they pull in opposite directions. This morning the other process was louder. *Are you home.*

Yes.

I need to tell you something, he said. *Not officially.*

All right.

There was a death last night, he said. *On Birch Street. Woman named Carol Demming. Fifty four years old. Found by her husband this morning.*

I set the coffee down.

In a chair, I said.

Silence on the line.

How did you —

Facing a window, I said. *Eyes open. Something nearby that should have been warm was still warm.*

Her coffee, he said. Very quietly. *On the table beside her.*

I stood at the kitchen counter.

Thought about the notebook.

About Gerald's timeline.

About Rudy at eight days.

About what I had written three weeks ago.

The pattern is accelerating.

Carol Demming, I said. *Tell me about her.*

Schoolteacher, he said. *Retired two years ago. Volunteered at the library. Ran a book club.* A pause. *She was at the town meeting three weeks ago. I didn't notice her there until I pulled the sign-in sheet this morning.*

Did she say anything at the meeting.

Not from the floor, he said. *But her neighbor says she talked about it afterward. Loudly. At the neighbor's kitchen table. Said some things about what she'd witnessed that* — He paused. *The neighbor said she'd never heard Carol talk that way. Said it was like something had opened up in her.*

Yes, I said. *That's what happens.*

The opening up.

Yes.

That's when it finds them, he said. Not a question. The other process making a statement it had been building toward for three weeks.

Yes, I said. *That's when.*

Silence.

The specific silence of a detective sitting with a conclusion his official process cannot file and his other process cannot dismiss.

How many is that, he said.

That I know of, I said. *Three.*

Gerald. The other one you wouldn't name.

A man named Roy Higgins, I said. *Seventy years old. Lived on Spruce. Died eleven days ago. I didn't tell you because I wasn't certain of the connection and I didn't want to* —

You didn't want to tell me something you couldn't prove, he said.

Yes.

And now.

Now there are three, I said. *And the timeline between them is compressing. Gerald to Roy was eleven days. Roy to Carol was nine.*

It's accelerating, he said.

Yes.

Why.

I thought about what I had written in the notebook.

About the ambient cruelty finding its level. About the sewage rising. About the conditions becoming more favorable.

The environment, I said. *The conditions in the community right now. The — anger. The contempt. The gaps between what people say and what they mean getting wider. It feeds on those gaps the way* — I paused. *The way a fire feeds on oxygen. More fuel. More efficient.*

So it's getting stronger, he said.

And faster, I said. *Yes.*

Briggs was quiet for a moment.

I heard him breathing on the other end of the line. The steady breathing of a man who is maintaining composure as a professional requirement while everything behind the composure is doing something that composure was not designed to manage.

Harlan, he said.

Yes.

I have three deaths I cannot explain to the medical examiner's satisfaction, he said. *I have a pattern I cannot put in a report. I have* — He stopped. *I drove past Vera Simmons' house this morning and the lights were on which means she came back from wherever she went and I felt — I needed to check.*

She's not back, I said. *She's still in Traverse City.*

Then someone is in her house, he said.

Everything in me went quiet on the frequency.

Are you certain.

I saw movement, he said. *Through the front window. A shadow. I almost stopped. Then I told myself it was the light changing and kept driving because it was six thirty in the morning and I had a death scene to get to.*

Go back, I said.

Harlan —

Briggs, I said. *Go back to Vera's house. Now. And call me when you're outside.*

What am I looking for.

You're not looking for anything, I said. *You're going to stand on the sidewalk and tell me what the air feels like.*

Silence.

The air, he said.

Yes.

You want me to —

Trust the thing you've been dismissing for three weeks, I said. *The other process. The one that made you slow down in front of her house two weeks ago and knock on the door. The one that made you keep Gerald's file open. The one that called me this morning from the other line instead of the official one.*

Silence.

Longer this time.

All right, he said.

Call me when you're there.

Five minutes, he said.

He hung up.

I stood at the kitchen counter with the coffee going cold and the notebook open and the pen beside it and the specific quality of a Saturday morning that had started with Thomas on the porch steps and had arrived somewhere considerably further than I had calculated when I woke up.

Grandpa, Wren said from the table.

Yes.

Something happened.

Yes.

Bad.

Yes.

She was quiet for a moment.

Is Vera okay.

I looked at my granddaughter.

I don't know yet, I said. *I'm going to find out.*

She nodded.

Went back to her homework.

The specific composure of a six year old who has decided that homework is what you do while the adults handle the part that requires adults and you stay ready for the part that requires you.

I picked up the coffee.

Drank it cold.

Waited for Briggs to call.

Thought about Carol Demming in her chair with her coffee still warm.

Thought about the timeline compressing.

Nine days between Roy and Carol.

Which meant the next one was not three weeks away.

The next one was close.

And the field was not yet ready.

Not complete enough.

Not full enough.

The gaps still there.

The thing still finding its level in them.

I looked at the corner of the living room.

Quieter than it had been.

But there.

Patient.

Learning.

I know, I said to it.

The corner said nothing.

It never did.

My phone rang.

Briggs.

Outside his voice when he spoke had the specific quality of a man standing on a sidewalk in October at ten fifty on a Saturday morning feeling something in the air that his official process has no folder for and his other process has been trying to file for three weeks.

Harlan, he said.

Yes.

The air, he said.

Yes.

It's wrong, he said. *In front of her house. The air is wrong in the specific way you described in Gerald's living room.*

Yes.

It was here, he said. *Last night or this morning.*

Yes.

She's not home, he said. *You said she's not home.*

She's in Traverse City, I said. *She's safe.*

Then why was it at her house.

I stood at the kitchen counter.

Thought about the thing learning my patterns.

Learning my people.

Mapping us.

Thought about what I had told the corner three nights ago.

The field has changed.

Thought about what the thing had been doing since then.

Learning the field.

Finding its edges.

Probing for the gaps.

It's mapping us, I said. *It knows about Vera. It went to her house to find her and she wasn't there.*

Is that good, he said.

It means she's safe, I said. *It also means it's looking.*

For her.

For all of them, I said. *It's learning who is connected to me. Who is in the field.*

The field, Briggs said. As if testing the word.

The people who see clearly, I said. *Who I've been — gathering. Around this.*

How many.

Enough to matter, I said. *Not enough yet.*

What do you need.

I looked at the corner.

Thought about Thomas walking down the street with his spine slightly more vertical.

Thought about Wren at the table doing homework while the adults handled the adult part.

Thought about the mechanism I had written in the notebook twenty minutes ago.

Not confrontation, I said. *Completion.*

I don't know what that means, Briggs said.

I'm still working it out, I said. *But I think I know the shape of it.*

Tell me when you know the whole thing, he said.

Yes.

Harlan.

Yes.

Carol Demming, he said. *She had a daughter. Thirty years old. Lives in Elk Rapids. I called her this morning.*

Yes.

She said her mother had been — different. For the past three weeks. Since the town meeting. She said her mother had started saying things. True things. Things she'd been keeping quiet for years. She said it was like something had opened up.

Yes, I said. *That's what happens.*

She also said, Briggs said quietly, *that she'd been feeling it herself. Since she came to see her mother two weeks ago. A coldness. A wrong quality in certain rooms. She said she thought she was picking it up from her mother's anxiety.*

She wasn't, I said.

No, he said. *I didn't think so.*

What's her name, I said.

Ellen, he said. *Ellen Demming.*

Can you give me her number.

A pause.

Officially I shouldn't, he said.

Briggs.

I'll text it to you, he said. *From the other line.*

Thank you.

Harlan, he said. *The timeline.*

Yes.

Nine days, he said. *Between the last two.*

Yes.

Who's next, he said.

I stood at the kitchen counter in the October morning with the notebook open and the pen beside it and the cold coffee and Wren doing homework at the table and the corner of the living room quiet in the way that things go quiet when they are learning something new.

Thought about Vera in Traverse City.

Rudy in Petoskey.

Agnes on Elm Street.

Nora four minutes away.

Thomas walking home with his spine slightly more vertical.

Ellen Demming in Elk Rapids who had been feeling it for two weeks and thought she was picking up her mother's anxiety.

The field not yet complete.

The gaps still there.

The timeline compressing.

I don't know, I said.

Which was true.

But I'm going to find out, I said.

Which was also true.

And considerably more importan

Chapter 24

THE QUIET ONES

Chapter Twenty Four — Ellen

I called Ellen Demming at eleven thirty.

I want to be honest about the timing because the honesty matters. Eleven thirty on a Saturday morning is four and a half hours after her husband found her mother in a chair facing a window with coffee still warm on the table beside her. Four and a half hours is not long enough for grief to settle into its permanent configuration. It is still in its first form — the sharp disorienting form, the form that makes the world look like a photograph of itself rather than the thing itself, the form where the walls between what we know and what we allow ourselves to know develop the specific permeability of freshly cracked plaster.

I called anyway.

Because the timeline was nine days and compressing.

Because the thing had been at Vera's house this morning.

Because Ellen Demming had been feeling it for two weeks and didn't know what it was and not knowing was the most dangerous condition available.

She answered on the third ring.

Her voice had the quality I expected — the careful composure of a person who has been making phone calls all morning and has developed a version of themselves for phone calls that sits slightly above the actual grief the way a thin layer of ice sits above cold water. Present. Functional. One careful step from breaking through.

Ellen Demming, she said.

My name is Harlan Gage, I said. *I live in Bellaire. I knew your mother.*

A pause.

Detective Briggs gave you my number, she said.

Yes.

He said you might call, she said. *He said* — She stopped. *He said you understood some things about what's been happening that he doesn't have a framework for and that I might.*

I'm sorry about your mother, I said. *Before anything else. She was a woman who said true things when the room wanted comfortable ones and that's a rare quality and the world is smaller without it.*

Silence on the line.

The silence of a woman receiving something she needed to receive that she hadn't known she needed.

Thank you, she said. Very quietly. *Most people have been saying she was at peace. That she looked peaceful. That it was a good way to go.*

Was that useful, I said.

No, she said.

No, I agreed. *I wouldn't think so.*

Detective Briggs said you lost a neighbor, she said. *The same way.*

Gerald Hoffstead, I said. *Three weeks ago. Good man. Returned borrowed tools without being asked.*

She almost made a sound that in different circumstances would have been a laugh.

My mother used to say that was the truest test of a person, she said. *Whether they returned things.*

Gerald passed, I said.

Mom would have liked him.

Yes, I said. *I think she would.*

We sat for a moment in the specific quiet of two people who have established enough human ground between them to now walk across it toward the harder thing.

Ellen, I said. *Briggs told me you've been feeling something. For two weeks. Since you visited your mother.*

The careful composure thinned.

Not breaking. Thinning. The ice over the cold water becoming more translucent.

Yes, she said.

Tell me.

I thought — She stopped. Started again with the precision of a woman who has been telling herself a story about what she's been feeling and is now, in the specific raw state of this particular morning, too tired to maintain the story. *I thought I was picking up her anxiety. She'd been different since the meeting. More — open. More herself in a way that was wonderful and also frightening because she was saying things she'd kept quiet for thirty years and I kept thinking something is going to happen, some cost is coming, and I thought the feeling was that.*

But, I said.

But it was there when she wasn't in the room, she said. *I'd be in her kitchen making tea and she'd be in the garden and I'd feel it. The cold. The — pressure. Like something was in the room that shouldn't be.*

Yes, I said.

And when I drove home, she said. *It followed me. That's* — She paused. *That sounds insane.*

It doesn't, I said.

It was in my apartment for three days, she said. *Then it faded. I thought I'd imagined the whole thing. Then last week it came back. Faint. Like something circling.*

I stood at the kitchen counter.

Thought about the timeline.

About the thing mapping the field.

Learning who was connected.

Following the connections.

Ellen, I said. *How old are you.*

Thirty, she said. *Why.*

Your mother, I said. *The way she changed after the meeting. More open. More herself. More willing to say true things.*

Yes.

Did that ever describe you, I said. *At any point. Before or after the meeting.*

Silence.

Longer than the previous silences.

The specific silence of a woman standing at the edge of something and feeling the pull of it.

My whole life, she said. Quietly. *It describes my whole life. I've been — I've always been too much. Too aware of the gap between what people say and what they mean. Too likely to name things that rooms want left unnamed. I learned to manage it. To be — careful. To choose when.*

Yes, I said.

Mom was the same, she said. *She managed it for thirty years. Then the meeting happened and she stopped managing and I watched her and I thought — she looks the way I feel on the inside. She looks like what I would be if I stopped being careful.*

What happened to her when she stopped being careful, I said.

She was — Ellen stopped. *She was more alive than I'd seen her in years. She was fully herself. She was —* The composure thinned to almost nothing. *She was my mother the way I remembered her when I was small. Before she learned to be less.*

The words landed in the kitchen like something dropped from a height.

Before she learned to be less.

I stood at the counter.

The notebook open.

The pen in my hand.

Ellen, I said. *I need to tell you some things. They are going to sound — extraordinary. I need you to receive them the way a person receives things on a morning like this one, when the walls are down and the truth has more room than usual.*

All right, she said.

And I told her.

Not the edited version.

Not the sequence I had been keeping.

Everything.

The corn field. The notebook. Gerald. The frequency. The rabbit. The field. Vera and Rudy and Agnes. Thomas in the basement this morning. The thing mapping us. The timeline compressing.

Carol Demming who had stopped being less and become fully herself and been found in a chair with her coffee still warm.

Ellen listened the way her mother had listened at the town meeting — fully, without interrupting, with the specific open quality of a woman who has spent her life hearing the gap between what is said and what is meant and has decided that this particular speaker means what he says.

When I finished she was quiet for a long moment.

It killed her, she said. *Because she stopped being less.*

Yes, I said.

Because she became visible.

Yes.

It kills the ones who see clearly, she said. *The ones who become fully themselves.*

Yes.

And you're — She paused. *You're building something that makes that safe. Being fully yourself. Being visible.*

I'm trying, I said.

The field, she said.

Yes.

And I — She stopped.

You've been feeling it for two weeks, I said. *Which means it has already found you on the frequency. Which means you are already in this whether you choose to be or not. The choice available to you is whether you understand what you're in.*

You're not trying to frighten me, she said.

No, I said. *I'm trying to give you the information your mother didn't have.*

Silence.

She didn't know, Ellen said. *She had no idea what was happening.*

No.

She just — opened up. Became herself. And it found her.

Yes.

If she had known —

Yes, I said. *If she had known.*

The silence that followed was the most painful silence of the conversation. The silence of a daughter sitting with the specific grief of a preventable thing — not preventable in the sense that her mother could have been saved by being less, by going back to managing, by swallowing the true things again. Preventable in the sense that knowledge changes the equation. That the field changes the equation.

That Carol Demming might have been alive this morning if someone had sat across a table from her three weeks ago and said *what is opening in you is real and it has a cost and here is how to be fully yourself and be safe simultaneously.*

I'm going to help you, I said. *If you'll let me.*

Yes, she said. Without hesitation. The word of a woman who has just lost her mother to something she now understands and has made the decision that understanding produces in people who are built the way Ellen Demming was built.

Not retreat.

Forward.

Can you come to Bellaire, I said. *Today if possible. I know it's —*

I'll come this afternoon, she said. *I need to —* She paused. *I need to make some calls first. There are arrangements.*

Of course.

Harlan, she said.

Yes.

My mother, she said. *In the end. The last three weeks. Was she —* She stopped. *Was she right to open up. Even knowing the cost. Was it worth it. Being fully herself.*

I stood at the kitchen counter in the October morning and thought about Carol Demming saying true things at her neighbor's kitchen table. Talking the way she hadn't talked in thirty years. Being the mother her daughter remembered from when she was small.

Thought about what it costs to be less.

Paid across decades.

In the currency of the self.

Thought about what it costs to stop.

Yes, I said. *She was right to open up. The cost was the thing's. Not hers. She didn't do anything wrong. She did everything right. She became fully herself and it found her and that is the thing's crime not hers.*

She was happy, Ellen said quietly. *The last three weeks. Genuinely happy. I hadn't seen her that way in —*

I know, I said.

She was right, Ellen said. *Even knowing.*

Yes, I said. *She was.*

Another silence.

Softer than the others.

Three o'clock, Ellen said. *I'll be there at three.*

I'll have coffee, I said.

She always said — Ellen stopped. Started again. *She always said coffee was the most honest beverage. Because it doesn't pretend to be anything other than what it is.*

Your mother, I said, *was a woman worth knowing.*

Yes, Ellen said. *She was.*

She hung up.

I stood at the counter.

Put the phone down.

Picked up the pen.

Wrote in the notebook.

Ellen Demming. Thirty years old. Carol's daughter. Has been feeling it for two weeks. Came to it through her mother. She is built the same way — hears the gap, sees clearly, has been managing it carefully for thirty years. She is already in the field whether she chose it or not. She is coming at three.

Carol Demming spent thirty years being less. Then stopped. Then was fully herself for three weeks. Then died in a chair facing a window.

This is the thing's method. Wait for the opening. Move in during the opening. The moment of becoming more yourself is the moment of maximum visibility.

Which means the most dangerous time is the best time.

The opening.

The becoming.

The moment you stop being less and start being the field.

That is when it strikes.

Which means the field needs to be established before the opening. The protection needs to be in place before the visibility increases. You cannot open up and then learn the rabbit. You have to know the field before you let yourself be seen.

Carol didn't know.

Ellen will.

The others will.

This is what I've been missing.

The sequence isn't — tell people what's happening and then teach them the rabbit.

The sequence is — teach them the field first. Make the ground complete before the opening. So when they become fully themselves the wholeness is already there and the thing has nothing to work with.

The gap never forms.

The rain just becomes part of the ground.

I put the pen down.

Looked at the notebook.

At what I had just written.

Thought about Thomas walking down the street with his spine more vertical.

Two hours in a basement.

The gap already smaller.

Not because we had taught him to hide better.

Because we had started teaching him to be more completely himself.

Thought about Vera practicing four times a day.

Not just the rabbit.

The field.

Both things simultaneously.

Thought about Agnes filling the rests.

Not blocking the wrong note out.

Being the music so completely there was no room for it.

Thought about what would have happened if someone had found Carol Demming three weeks ago.

Before the opening.

Before the visibility increased.

Before the thing moved from circling to deciding.

I thought about this for a long time.

Then I called Vera.

She answered on the second ring.

Harlan.

Are you practicing, I said.

Four times today already, she said. *My sister has started. Her neighbor came over this morning and watched and went quiet in a similar way and —*

Vera, I said. *I need to change the instruction.*

All right.

It's not just the rabbit, I said. *The rabbit is one part. There's another part that's more important. I've been teaching the defensive thing and not the* — I paused. *Not the thing that makes the defense unnecessary.*

The field, she said.

Yes.

I've been doing both, she said. *I didn't realize I was doing both until now but — yes. The rabbit is one thing. But there's another thing I've been practicing that feels less like hiding and more like — being very completely here.*

Yes, I said. *That's the one.*

They work together, she said.

Yes, I said. *The rabbit for the moments when you need to be unfindable. The field for everything else. The field is the condition. The rabbit is the tool. I had them backwards.*

Harlan, she said.

Yes.

A woman died, she said. It wasn't a question.

Yes, I said.

Someone like us.

Yes.

Her daughter is coming this afternoon.

Yes.

How many of us are there now, she said.

I looked at the notebook.

At the list that had been growing since Gerald's living room three weeks ago.

Vera. Rudy. Agnes. Nora. Thomas. Ellen.

Briggs who ran two processes simultaneously and called from the other line.

Vera's sister. The sister's neighbor.

The field was growing.

Enough, I said. *Not yet enough. But enough to see the shape of enough.*

What does enough look like, she said.

I thought about what I had written.

About the gap never forming.

About the rain becoming part of the ground.

About Carol Demming's thirty years of being less and three weeks of being fully herself and the specific terrible arithmetic of that.

Enough, I said, *looks like nobody having to choose between being fully themselves and being safe.*

Silence on the line.

The specific silence of a retired science teacher in Traverse City receiving a statement and running it through the framework she has spent a lifetime building and finding that the framework, expanded as it has been in the past three weeks, accommodates it completely.

That's not a small thing, she said.

No, I said. *It isn't.*

It's rather the whole thing.

Yes, I said. *I think it is.*

Outside the October afternoon was making its way toward three o'clock with the unhurried certainty of time that has somewhere to be and knows the way.

Inside the corner of the living room was quiet.

The field was growing.

The gap was closing.
One person at a time.
In the only direction that mattered.
From the inside out.

Chapter 25

10:03 AM

THE QUIET ONES

Chapter Twenty Five — What Wren Said

Ellen Demming arrived at three o'clock exactly.

I had expected someone who looked like grief. Grief has a recognizable presentation — the careful composure, the slight hollowness around the eyes, the specific way the body carries itself when it is managing something heavy and has decided that managing it visibly is not an option available to a person who has phone calls to make and arrangements to coordinate and a mother to bury.

Ellen had all of that.

She also had something else.

She was tall. Her mother's posture — I knew this without having known Carol Demming well, knew it the way you know family resemblances when they arrive in a doorway unexpected. The same quality of presence that Briggs had described as a woman who said true things at a neighbor's kitchen table. Present in the daughter as potential — the thing that Carol Demming had spent thirty years managing and three weeks releasing, present in Ellen as something carefully contained, a fire banked low but not out.

She had driven from Elk Rapids with the specific focus of a woman who has decided that forward is the only available direction and is executing accordingly.

I opened the door.

She looked at me.

The direct assessment of a woman who hears the gap between what people present and what they are and is taking my measure before deciding how much of herself to bring into the room.

She found whatever she was looking for.

Came in.

I took her coat.

She stood in the entryway and looked at the living room with the careful attention of someone who has been told what is in the corner and is now experiencing the information physically rather than intellectually.

There, she said. Quietly. Pointing.

Yes, I said.

It's smaller than I expected.

It varies, I said. *It's been quieter since* — I paused. *Since we've been doing what we've been doing.*

The field.

Yes.

She stood for a moment longer.

Not afraid.

Something more precise than afraid.

The expression of a woman confronting the thing that killed her mother this morning and finding it smaller than her grief and larger than her anger and exactly as real as she had known it was for two weeks while telling herself she was picking up anxiety.

All right, she said.

The same two words as Nora.

The same decision inside them.

I brought her to the kitchen.

Coffee on the table. The notebook. The afternoon light doing what October afternoon light does in northern Michigan — golden, specific, the light that knows it's temporary and is not apologizing for it.

Wren was at the table.

She had been there since two thirty, doing homework with the focused efficiency of a child who wanted homework finished before interesting things happened and had correctly calculated that three o'clock was when interesting things would happen.

She looked up when Ellen came in.

Ellen looked at Wren.

I watched it happen.

Not the mutual recognition of Vera or Agnes. Not the tentative frequency-matching of Thomas. Something different. Something I had not seen before in any of the meetings that had happened in my kitchen over the past three weeks.

Ellen looked at Wren and her face did something that faces do when they see something they have been trying to remember for a long time and have suddenly been shown.

Not recognition of another person.

Recognition of a lost version of themselves.

She stood in my kitchen doorway looking at my six year old granddaughter and I watched thirty years of careful management become briefly transparent and behind it — behind the managing, behind the being less, behind the thirty years of choosing when and measuring the room and swallowing the true things when the cost was too high — behind all of it was a six year old girl with dark eyes who heard truth beneath words and asked questions that made adults uncomfortable and had not yet learned that the world had a limited appetite for what she was.

Ellen had been that girl.

Had learned what the world's appetite was.

Had adjusted accordingly.

Had been adjusting for thirty years.

And here was the girl she had been, sitting at a kitchen table doing homework, unadjusted, complete, fully herself at six in the way that Ellen had stopped being fully herself at approximately six, and the meeting of those two things in my kitchen doorway on a Saturday afternoon produced something in Ellen Demming's face that I did not have adequate language for and did not try to name.

Wren looked at Ellen.

The dark patient eyes.

The assessment.

Then something shifted in Wren's expression. The assessment becoming something warmer. The specific warmth of a child who has identified something that needs sitting with and has decided to sit with it.

Hi, Wren said.

Hi, Ellen said. Her voice slightly different than it had been in the entryway. Something in it opened a fraction.

I'm Wren.

I know, Ellen said. *Your grandfather told me about you.*

He tells everyone about me, Wren said. *I don't mind.*

Ellen almost smiled.

Came to the table.

Sat down.

I poured coffee.

Sat across from her.

We talked for forty minutes about the practical things first because Ellen needed the practical things first — the same way Nora had needed the mechanics before the metaphysics, the same way Vera had needed the framework before the feeling. The what and the how and the what do I do now.

I told her about the field. About the rabbit. About the distinction between the two and why the distinction mattered and why her mother's death was not the consequence of becoming more herself but of becoming more herself without the field already in place.

She listened with the focused attention of a woman who processes information the way her mother had processed it — completely, without the defensive filtering of someone who needs the information to fit a predetermined shape.

She asked good questions.

Precise ones.

The questions of a woman who has been hearing the gap between what is said and what is meant for thirty years and applies the same precision to her own understanding.

Wren did homework.

Or appeared to do homework.

I noticed that she had been on the same page for forty minutes.

She was listening.

Not intrusively. The quiet listening of a child who understands that some conversations need witness more than participation.

At the end of the forty minutes Ellen sat back in her chair with both hands around her coffee mug and the specific expression of a woman who has received a large thing and is now sitting with the weight of it redistributed.

My mother, she said. *In the last three weeks. She kept saying — she kept telling me she felt like herself for the first time in years. I kept being happy for her and frightened for her simultaneously and I couldn't explain the frightened part. I thought it was just —* She stopped.

You felt the thing, I said. *You felt it getting closer. You didn't have the name for it but the body knew.*

Yes, she said. *And I kept thinking if I could just get her to be a little more careful. A little less —*

Less, I said.

She looked at me.

I was going to say less visible, she said. *But that's the same thing isn't it.*

Yes.

I was going to ask my mother to be less, she said. *To protect her.*

Yes.

And being less was what had been hurting her for thirty years.

Yes.

She sat with this.

The sitting of a woman who has just understood something that reframes not just her mother's death but her mother's life and her own life and the thirty years of careful management and what it had cost both of them.

She was right to stop, Ellen said.

Yes, I said. *She was.*

And if the field had been in place —

Yes, I said.

She could have been fully herself and been safe.

Yes.

Both.

Yes, I said. *Both. Simultaneously. That's the whole point of the field. You don't have to choose.*

Ellen looked at her coffee.

At the window.

At the October light.

At Wren.

Wren looked up from the page she had been on for forty minutes.

They looked at each other.

And then Wren said the thing.

I want to be careful about how I record this because careful is what it deserves and because I have been a writer for forty years and I know the difference between a thing that is said and a thing that arrives and this arrived.

Wren put her pencil down.

Looked at Ellen Demming with the dark patient eyes.

And said:

You've been being less for a long time.

Not a question.

Not an accusation.

The flat precise kindness of a true thing stated by someone who hears truth beneath words and has decided that this particular truth is one Ellen needs to hear out loud.

Ellen looked at Wren.

The ice over the cold water.

Thinning.

Yes, she said. Very quietly.

Your mom stopped, Wren said.

Yes.

And it found her, Wren said. *Because the field wasn't there yet.*

Yes.

But she was happy, Wren said. *Those three weeks. You said she was happy.*

Yes, Ellen said. The composure thin as paper now. *She was.*

She was herself, Wren said. *The whole of herself. For three weeks.* She paused. *That's not nothing.*

No, Ellen said. Her voice very careful. The voice of a woman holding something that is very close to breaking and has decided to hold it a moment longer. *It's not nothing.*

It's everything, Wren said. *Three weeks of everything is more than thirty years of less.*

The kitchen was very quiet.

The October light moved across the table between them.

Ellen Demming looked at my six year old granddaughter and the ice went through and the grief came and she did not apologize for it and Wren did not look away from it and I sat across the table and held the space the way you hold space when something necessary is happening that requires witness more than intervention.

Wren reached across the table.

Put her small hand on Ellen's hand.

Did not say anything else.

Did not need to.

The field is not only stillness.

The field is also this.

A six year old girl who has never learned to be less sitting with a thirty year old woman who has been less for thirty years and lost her mother to the cost of finally stopping.

Not fixing.

Not explaining.

Just present.

Fully.

The whole of herself.

No gap between what she was and what she offered.

The rain becoming part of the ground.

I watched my granddaughter hold Ellen Demming's hand across my kitchen table on a Saturday afternoon in October and thought about the thing in the corner.

About the gaps it fed on.

About the accumulated residue of people being less than they were.

About what fills the gaps.

Not argument.

Not confrontation.

Not the rabbit.

This.

Presence so complete that there is no room for the absence.

The right notes already there.

A six year old girl who learned to be the field before she learned to be afraid.

Showing a thirty year old woman what her mother had found for three weeks.

What was possible.

What had always been possible.

What the field protected.

Not the hiding.

The whole of yourself.

Ellen cried for a while.

Not the managed grief of the phone calls and the arrangements and the careful composure of a woman who has been keeping it together since six thirty this morning when her husband called.

The other kind.

The real kind.

The kind that knows what it has lost and does not pretend otherwise and does not apologize for the knowing.

Wren held her hand.

I drank cold coffee.

The October light moved.

The corner was quiet.

When Ellen was done she sat for a moment with the specific quality of a person who has put something down that they have been carrying since morning and is feeling the specific lightness and ache of hands that have been holding something heavy and have finally let go.

She looked at Wren.

How old are you, she said.

Six, Wren said.

You're something, Ellen said.

People say that, Wren said. *I think it mostly means unusual.*

It means, Ellen said, *that you never learned what most of us learned.*

What did you learn, Wren said.

Ellen looked at her.

Thought about it with the honesty of a woman who has just cried in a stranger's kitchen and has passed through the point where anything less than honesty is worth the effort.

That being fully yourself is dangerous, she said. *That the world has a limited appetite for it. That being less is safer.*

Is it, Wren said.

No, Ellen said. *It turns out it isn't.*

No, Wren agreed. *It just feels like it is.*

Ellen looked at this six year old girl.

How do you know that, she said. *At six.*

Wren considered the question with the seriousness it deserved.

Grandpa told me, she said. *Not in words. He just — showed me what being less costs. By being less for a long time and then stopping. I could feel the difference.*

Ellen looked at me.

I looked at my coffee.

He stopped being less, Ellen said.

When Gerald died, Wren said. *Something opened in him. Like your mom. Except he knew about the field so it was —* She paused. *Different.*

He was safe, Ellen said.

He knew the field first, Wren said. *Then he opened.*

Ellen looked at me.

That's the sequence, she said.

Yes, I said.

Field first, she said. *Then open.*

Yes.

My mother had it backwards.

Yes, I said. *Most people do. Because nobody tells them. Because most people don't know the field exists.*

You're going to tell them, Ellen said.

Not a question.

The statement of a woman who has been listening carefully for forty minutes and has understood not just the what and the how but the why and the toward what.

Yes, I said.

How many, she said.

As many as possible, I said. *Before the timeline closes.*

She nodded.

Put both hands flat on the table.

The gesture I had seen in Rudy's hardware store.

A person steadying themselves on a known surface while the ground rearranges.

Teach me, she said. *Today. Right now. The field first.*

Yes, I said.

And then I'm going to help you, she said. *Tell me what you need.*

I looked at Ellen Demming across my kitchen table.

Thirty years old.

Thirty years of being less.

Her mother's posture.

Her mother's directness.

Her mother's specific quality of presence that the thing had found and fed on and that was present in the daughter as potential — as the fire banked low but not out — and was about to become something else.

Something the thing had not calculated.

Carol Demming's daughter.

Fully herself.

Field in place.

The gap that had cost her mother everything closing before it could cost Ellen anything.

I need someone, I said, *who can talk to people. Who can find the ones who are opening up. Who are becoming more themselves. Who are visible on the frequency before they know the field exists. I need someone who can find them before the thing does.*

And tell them, she said.

And teach them, I said. *The field first. Then open.*

She looked at me.

How do I find them.

The same way you've always found them, I said. *You hear the gap. You've been hearing it your whole life. The gap between what people say and what they mean. Start listening for the gap closing. People becoming more themselves. More honest. More present. The opening.*

That's when they're visible.

Yes.

And I find them before it does.

Yes.

How much time do I have, she said.

Between when someone opens and when it finds them, I said. *Days. Sometimes less. It's getting faster.*

She nodded.

No drama.

No hesitation.

The nod of a woman who has understood the assignment and has decided that the assignment is worth doing and is already thinking about how to do it.

My mother's book club, she said. *Twelve women. They've all been — changing. Since the meeting. I've been watching it happen and not knowing what I was watching.*

Yes, I said.

They're opening, she said.

Yes.

Some of them may already —

Yes, I said. *Call them today.*

She pulled out her phone.

Looked at me.

After you teach me, she said. *Field first.*

Field first, I said.

Wren had already put her homework away.

Was sitting with her hands in her lap.

Waiting.

Knowing.

The division of labor understood without being assigned.

Wren, I said.

I'll start, she said.

She looked at Ellen.

Close your eyes, she said.

Ellen closed them.

And Wren began.

Not with the words I had used in the basement with Thomas.

Not with the words I had used with Vera or Agnes.

Different words.

Her own words.

The words of a child who has never been less showing a woman who has been less for thirty years how to come all the way forward.

How to be the ground the rain falls on.

How to be so completely herself that there is no gap for the wrong thing to occupy.

How to be the field.

I sat at my kitchen table in the October afternoon and listened to my granddaughter teach and thought about Carol Demming.

Three weeks of everything.

More than thirty years of less.

That's not nothing, Wren had said.

It's everything.

Outside the October afternoon was moving toward evening with the unhurried certainty of October afternoons that have somewhere to be.

Inside the field was growing.

One person at a time.

In the only direction that mattered.

From the inside out.
The gap closing.
The ground becoming whole.
The rain becoming part of it.
The weavers finding each other.
One Saturday afternoon at a time

Chapter 26

THE QUIET ONES

Chapter Twenty Six — Still Standing

The house at nine o'clock on a Saturday night.

Ellen had left at six with the specific purposefulness of a woman who has received something and knows immediately what to do with it. She had stood at the door with her coat on and her phone in her hand and the list of her mother's book club members already open on the screen and looked at me with the expression of a person who has been handed a task that is also a grief and has decided that the task is how she will carry the grief.

I'll call you tomorrow, she said.

Call me tonight if you need to, I said.

I won't need to, she said. Not arrogance. Assessment. The specific confidence of a woman who has just spent three hours learning something and knows the difference between what she knows and what she doesn't and has correctly identified which category this falls into.

She looked at Wren.

Wren looked at her.

The look between them had changed since three o'clock. Something had passed between them in the kitchen that afternoon that had reconfigured the distance. Not friendship exactly — the age gap was too large and the circumstances too specific for friendship in the ordinary sense. Something more particular. The specific bond of two people who have sat together in the same true thing and come out the other side changed in the same direction.

Thank you, Ellen said to Wren.

Your mom was right to stop, Wren said. *I want you to know I think that.*

Ellen stood at the door for a moment.

I know, she said. *Thank you for saying it out loud.*

She left.

I watched her car until the tail lights turned onto Maple.

Then I made dinner.

Soup again because soup is what October requires and October had been requiring a great deal of it lately and I had no complaints about that. Wren ate with the focused efficiency of a child whose body has conducted a substantial day and is presenting the invoice. She fell asleep on the couch at eight fifteen with the complete commitment of the truly spent — not the gradual negotiation of a child being put to bed but the sudden departure of a child whose body has simply closed the door without asking permission.

I covered her with the blanket.

Stood over her for a moment.

The dark hair across the cushion. The hands folded under her cheek. The specific stillness of a child who is the field even in sleep — completely herself, completely present, no gap between what she was and what she rested as.

I thought about what she had done today.

Thomas in the basement this morning. The ground doesn't hide. The rain becomes part of it. Forty minutes to teach a seven year old boy what I had spent sixty two years learning imperfectly.

Ellen in the kitchen this afternoon. Three weeks of everything is more than thirty years of less. Her hand across the table. The field held so completely that Ellen's grief had somewhere to land that wasn't the cold floor of her own managed composure.

Six years old.

I turned off the kitchen light.

Went to my desk.

Sat down.

Looked at the laptop.

Thought about chapter twelve.

Opened it.

Read the first sentence.

It was not lying.

For the first time in three weeks chapter twelve was not lying to me. It was sitting on the screen with the specific quality of a thing that has been wrong and has corrected itself in the night the way certain problems correct themselves when you stop looking directly at them and let the peripheral attention work.

I read the whole chapter.

It was almost right.

Almost was fixable.

I started writing.

I want to tell you about almost right.

In forty years of writing novels I have learned that almost right is not the enemy of right. Almost right is the map to right. The almost tells you exactly what direction to go — not toward it, not away from it, but through it. The almost is the door.

Chapter twelve had been almost right for three weeks because I had been being careful with it. Vera had told me that in my living room on the first evening — *the second one you were being careful. Writers shouldn't be careful* — and she had been right and I had not understood what she meant until I sat down at nine o'clock on a Saturday night with Wren asleep on the couch and Ellen driving back to Elk Rapids and Thomas somewhere with a slightly more vertical spine and the field growing in ways I was only beginning to understand and wrote three pages without stopping.

Not careful.

Present.

The full broadcast.

All of it.

The chapter was about a man who discovers that the universe is not indifferent to human suffering — it simply has a different timeline than we'd prefer. I had been writing this carefully. With the managed distance of a man who understands the idea intellectually and is rendering it faithfully without being inside it.

Tonight I was inside it.

Tonight I knew what it felt like to be the man in the chapter.

Because I was the man in the chapter.

I had been the man in the chapter for sixty two years and had been writing around it rather than through it and tonight I wrote through it and the chapter stopped lying and became what it had been trying to be the whole time.

Three pages.

Without stopping.

The specific forward movement of writing that is happening at the right frequency — not constructed, not managed, not careful. Arriving.

I saved it.

Closed the laptop.

Sat for a moment with the specific feeling of a chapter that has finally told the truth.

Then I opened the notebook.

Saturday. Late.

I am going to write down what happened today because today was the kind of day that requires the outside of the head rather than the inside.

Thomas came this morning. Seven years old. Too-large jacket. Amber eyes with the rabbit in them. Left with his spine slightly more vertical and the beginning of understanding that the rabbit is a tool not a condition. Wren taught him the field in the basement in the specific language of a six year old who has never been less — the ground doesn't hide, the rain becomes part of it. He understood it faster than I did because he has not yet accumulated the decades of the rabbit as default.

The rabbit is still new enough in him that it has not yet become the shape of a life. We caught him early.

That matters.

Catching them early matters.

Ellen came at three. Carol Demming's daughter. Thirty years old. Thirty years of careful management. Her mother's posture and her mother's directness and her mother's specific quality of presence that the thing had found and fed on — present in Ellen as potential, as the fire banked low but not out.

She cried in my kitchen.

Wren held her hand.

I am going to write that again because it deserves to be written twice.

Wren held her hand.

Six years old. The field held so completely that Ellen's grief had somewhere to land. No gap between what Wren was and what she offered. The whole of herself extended across a kitchen table to a woman she had met forty minutes earlier who needed exactly that and nothing else.

I have been thinking about what Wren said.

Three weeks of everything is more than thirty years of less.

I have been thinking about whether that is true.

I have been thinking about my own thirty years of less. The farm. The rabbit practiced past necessity. The marriages that suffered from a man who knew how to go quiet and sometimes went quiet when presence was what was needed. The careful novels. The long careful life of a man who learned at nine that less was safe and spent five decades unlearning it at the pace of someone who is not entirely convinced the lesson is wrong.

Three weeks of everything.

I did not have three weeks before Gerald.

I had been opening gradually, slowly, the way old wood opens in a fire — reluctantly, with a great deal of smoke before the flame. The writing. The moving to this house. The granddaughter who arrived and sat beside me and asked questions I had been not asking myself for fifty years. The slow return of the frequency I had buried.

I had been opening for years without knowing I was opening.

And then Gerald.

And then the notebook.

And then the corner.

And then the field.

Am I the man in chapter twelve, I wrote. *The man who discovers that the universe is not indifferent to human suffering but simply has a different timeline than we'd prefer.*

Yes, I wrote. *I think I am.*

The timeline of my life looks like damage from the inside. The farm. The rabbit. The cost of less paid across decades. The marriages. The careful novels. The long careful performance of a man who was always slightly less than he was.

From the outside — from the distance of a man sitting at a desk on a Saturday night with his granddaughter asleep on the couch and the field growing around him and chapter twelve finally telling the truth — it looks different.

The farm taught me the frequency.

The rabbit taught me the stillness.

The cost of less taught me what the field protects.

The marriages taught me that presence is not optional.

The careful novels taught me what careful costs.

The granddaughter taught me the field.

The corner taught me that the field was always the point.

Everything I was taught wrong I needed to have taught wrong in order to understand the right thing when it arrived.

I do not know if this is consolation or truth.

I think it might be both.

I think the man in chapter twelve would say it is both.

What I know for certain is this.

The thing in the corner has been hunting me since I was nine years old in a corn field.

It found me at the tree line in October 1963.

It waited while I was the rabbit.

It came back when I stopped.

And here I am.

Seventy one years old.

Still standing.

Not despite the farm. Not despite the rabbit. Not despite the thirty years of less and the cost of it and the long careful life of a man who learned too early that visibility was dangerous.

Because of all of it.

Every bit of it.

The steel is tempered by the fire it has passed through.

You don't get the strength without the fire.

You don't get the field without the rabbit.

You don't get the knowing without the cost.

Carol Demming had three weeks of everything.

I have had seventy one years of the fire and I am still standing at the desk and the chapter is finally telling the truth and my granddaughter is asleep on the couch and the field is growing and the thing in the corner is quieter than it has ever been.

Three weeks of everything.

I have had seventy one years.

And I am still standing.

That is not nothing.

That is everything.

I put the pen down.

Sat at the desk.

Looked at the notebook.

At the boy's section and the man's section and the sixty two years between them.

At the drawing with the edges that wouldn't hold still.

At the block letters.

It does not have a inside.

At what the man had added above it three weeks ago.

I know you're there.

At what I had written tonight.

Still standing.

I closed the notebook.

Sat for a moment in the specific quiet of a house at nine o'clock on a Saturday in October with the lake making its nighttime conversation with the shore and the refrigerator making its contribution and the piano holding its silence and Wren breathing under the blanket.

Thought about what I felt.

Tried to name it accurately the way you try to name things when you are a writer and naming things is the work and accuracy is the only standard that matters.

Not safety.

Not victory.

Not relief.

Something quieter and more fundamental than any of those.

Something that did not have a common name because it was not a common condition.

The specific feeling of a man who has been less for a long time and has stopped being less and is still standing.

Not triumphant.

Not healed.

Not arrived.

Still standing.

Still here.

Fully himself.

The whole of it.

The farm and the rabbit and the cost and the marriages and the careful novels and the granddaughter and the corner and the field and the notebook and Gerald and Vera and Rudy and Agnes and Nora and Thomas and Ellen and Carol Demming's three weeks of everything.

All of it.

Present.

Broadcasting at exactly the right volume.

Which was all of it.

Every frequency.

The whole of what I was without reduction or concealment.

Still standing.

I looked at the corner of the living room.

The corner was quiet.

Quieter than it had been since Gerald.

Not gone.

But quiet in the specific way of a thing that is learning something new about the ground it has been hunting.

The ground had changed.

The field was real.

The gaps were closing.

One person at a time.

From the inside out.

I looked at the corner for a long moment.

Then I said something I had not said since I was nine years old in a corn field in October when I first understood that the going quiet on the frequency was not the end of the story but the beginning of it.

I said it out loud.

In the nine o'clock quiet of the house.

To the corner.

To the thing that had no inside.

To the sixty two years between the corn field and this desk.

To myself.

I'm still here, I said.

The corner was quiet.

The lake moved in the dark outside.

Wren breathed under the blanket.

The piano held its silence.

Chapter twelve had finally told the truth.

And a man who had been less for a long time was sitting at his desk at nine o'clock on a Saturday night in October in northern Michigan and was not less anymore and was still standing and knew the difference between those two things and knew what the difference had cost and knew that the cost was exactly and precisely what it needed to have been.

Not less.

The whole of it.

Still here.

Still standing.

The field.

Chapter 27

THE QUIET ONES

Chapter Twenty Seven — Going To Them

Sunday morning arrived the way the best Sunday mornings arrive in northern Michigan — without announcement, without urgency, with the specific quality of light that comes off the lake in October when the mist is still on the water and the sun is finding it and the world looks briefly like something that has just been made and hasn't yet had time to develop opinions about itself.

I was at the window at six thirty with coffee.

The street was empty in the Sunday morning way — not the empty of absence but the empty of rest, the specific pause of a street that is occupied by people who are still in bed and will emerge later with the particular unhurried quality of people who have given themselves permission to be unhurried for one morning of the week.

Gerald's house dark.

The Millers' mailbox.

The ordinary geography of a life.

I had slept better than I had any right to.

Not the sleep of a man without concerns — I had concerns, specific and pressing and growing more specific and pressing by the day. The sleep of a man who has put his concerns in the right order and knows what he is doing when he wakes up. There is a specific quality to that sleep. It is not peaceful exactly. It is purposeful. The sleep of a body that is being used correctly and is restoring itself accordingly.

I sat at the window with the notebook open on my knee.

Did not write.

Just looked at the street and the lake beyond the houses and the October light doing what it did and thought about what was coming.

Not with dread.

I want to be precise about this.

For three weeks I had been thinking about what was coming with the specific quality of a man who is reacting — to the thing, to the pattern, to the compressing timeline, to the corner and the notebook and Gerald's cold living room. Responding to what arrived rather than moving toward what needed to happen.

This morning was different.

This morning I was thinking about what was coming with the specific quality of a man who has decided.

There is a difference between those two modes of thought the way there is a difference between a man standing in a current and a man swimming in one. Both are in the water. One is being moved. One is moving.

I had been in the current for three weeks.

This morning I was swimming.

Ellen called at eight.

I had been expecting it.

Not because I doubted her — I did not doubt her, had not doubted her since she arrived at three o'clock yesterday with her mother's posture and her thirty years of careful management and her decision made before she knocked — but because some people when they leave with purpose call early the next morning and Ellen Demming was that kind of person.

I talked to eleven of the twelve, she said. *Last night. Until midnight.*

And.

Three of them are already feeling it, she said. *The cold. The pressure. The wrong quality in certain rooms. One of them — Margaret, she's sixty eight, retired nurse — has been feeling it for ten days. She said she thought she was getting sick. She said the feeling has a texture like —* Ellen paused. *Like being slowly drained. That was her word. Drained.*

Ten days, I said.

Yes.

Gerald's timeline from first contact to the chair was approximately three weeks, I said. *But it's been compressing. Rudy was at eight days when I sent him to Petoskey. Carol —*

Don't, Ellen said. Quietly. Not sharply. The quiet of a woman who knows the sentence and has decided that she does not need to hear it completed this morning.

Yes, I said.

Margaret needs to know today, Ellen said.

Yes.

The other two are at earlier stages. A week or less. But they're opening — becoming more themselves — and the visibility is increasing.

Yes.

There are four more in the club who aren't feeling anything yet but have been changing since the meeting. More present. More honest. More —

Visible, I said.

Yes.

They will start feeling it, I said. *When the opening reaches a certain point.*

How long.

Days, I said. *Maybe less for some.*

Ellen was quiet for a moment.

The specific quiet of a woman doing arithmetic she does not enjoy but will not avoid.

Twelve women, she said. *My mother's book club. Twelve women who have been changing since the meeting. At various stages of opening. At various stages of visibility.*

Yes.

And the field needs to reach all of them, she said. *Before it does.*

Yes.

How, she said.

I looked at the street.

At the ordinary Sunday morning emptiness of it.

At Gerald's dark house.

At the Millers' mailbox.

Thought about what I had been doing for three weeks.

Waiting for people to come to me.

Vera had come because Nora had called her.

Rudy had come because I had walked into his hardware store.

Agnes had come because I had called her.

Thomas had come because Wren had sat with him at the end of the table by the window and not gone away.

Ellen had come because Briggs had called her and told her I might.

All of them — every person in the field — had come to me or been brought to me by someone else.

The field had been growing by arrival.

People finding their way to the basement and the kitchen table and the notebook and the flashlight circle.

One at a time.

At the pace of coincidence and connection and the specific accidents of a small county in northern Michigan where people know each other and word travels slow but far.

Margaret the retired nurse had been feeling it for ten days.

The timeline was compressing.

There was not time for arrival.

I'm coming to them, I said.

Silence on the line.

You're —

I'm going to stop waiting for people to find me, I said. *The field doesn't grow by staying still. It grows by spreading. And I have been sitting at this desk for three weeks reacting to what arrives when what I should have been doing is going to what needs me.*

Harlan, Ellen said.

Yes.

You're seventy one years old, she said. *And you've been —*

Less, I said. *For a long time. Yes.* I paused. *I'm not less anymore.*

Silence.

No, she said. *You're not.*

I need Margaret's address, I said. *And the other two. And the four who are opening.*

All seven, she said.

All seven, I said. *Today if possible.*

I'll come with you, she said.

Ellen —

She was my mother's book club, she said. *I know all of them. They trusted my mother. They'll trust me.* A pause. *And I need to do something with today that isn't arrangements.*

I understood this.

Yes, I said. *Come at nine.*

I'll be there at nine, she said.

She hung up.

I sat at the window for a moment longer.

Watched the October light move across the water.

Thought about the thing in the corner.

About Carol Demming in her chair.

About the timeline compressing.

About twelve women in a book club who had been opening up since the town meeting and were becoming more themselves in the specific way that increased visibility and only some of them knew what that meant and none of them had the field yet.

I thought about the boy in the corn field.

Who had learned the rabbit alone.

Who had written in the notebook alone.

Who had carried it alone for sixty two years.

I thought about what alone had cost.

I thought about what the field meant.

Not one rabbit.

Not one person in a basement with a flashlight.

All of them.

Finding each other.

The ground becoming whole.

One conversation at a time.

I finished my coffee.

Went to wake Wren.

She was already awake.

This did not surprise me.

She was sitting cross legged on the couch with the blanket around her shoulders and her hands in her lap and the dark patient eyes looking at the corner of the living room with the focused attention of a field observer who has been at her post since before I came to wake her.

It was active last night, she said without looking away from the corner. *After you went to bed. It moved around the room for a while.*

Did it find you.

No, she said. *I held the field.* She paused. *It seemed frustrated.*

Things without insides, I said, *do not get frustrated.*

This one does something that works like frustrated, she said. *It moves differently when it can't find what it's looking for. Faster. Less — deliberate.*

I sat down beside her.

Looked at the corner.

Quiet now in the Sunday morning light.

The specific quiet of a thing that has been active in the night and is resting in the day which was a new behavior and I noted it and filed it.

It's learning our schedule, I said.

Yes, Wren said. *It moved around the room for two hours. Then it went still. I think it went outside.*

You think.

I couldn't feel it in the house anymore, she said. *But I could feel it on the street. Faint. Like it was —* She paused. *Like it was making a map.*

Yes, I said. *That's what it's doing.*

Of all of us.

Yes.

Which means it knows about Ellen now, she said.

Probably, I said. *Yes.*

And Thomas.

Yes.

It's learning the field, she said. *The way we're learning it.*

I sat with this on the couch beside my granddaughter in the Sunday morning light with the blanket and the corner and the lake visible through the window.

Thought about two things learning each other simultaneously.

The field growing.

The thing mapping the field as it grew.

A race between completion and being found.

Then we need to move faster than it maps, I said.

Yes, she said. *That's what I was thinking.*

I'm going to go to people today, I said. *Instead of waiting for them to come. Ellen is coming at nine and we're going to visit seven women from her mother's book club.*

I'm coming, Wren said.

Nora —

Mom already knows, Wren said. *I called her at six thirty.*

I looked at my granddaughter.

You called your mother at six thirty on a Sunday morning.

She was already awake, Wren said. *She had the feeling again. She said she's been awake since five.* She paused. *She's coming too.*

I sat on the couch.

Thought about Nora.

Four minutes away.

Awake since five with the feeling that points rather than explains.

She's driving, Wren said. *She said you shouldn't drive when you're thinking this hard because you go through stop signs.*

This was accurate.

I had gone through two stop signs in the past three weeks.

Fair point, I said.

Also Dale is coming, she said.

Dale.

Mom told him last night, she said. *Everything. She said she decided the sequence was over.* Wren paused. *He didn't say much. He went to the basement and looked at the corner for a while and came back up and said what do you need me to do.*

Of course he did.

A man who believes in the structural integrity of things.

Who checks foundations.

Who fixes what is wrong without requiring the wrong thing to fit his previous understanding of what wrong things look like.

What did Nora tell him he could do, I said.

Drive, Wren said. *And hold the ordinary world steady while the rest of us do what the rest of us do.*

I looked at my granddaughter.

She said that.

Yes.

Those exact words.

Yes.

I sat with that for a moment.

Nora.

Who had driven four minutes in the dark at seven fifteen on a Thursday morning because something told her to.

Who had stood in the living room doorway and felt the cold corner and said *all right.*

Who had come back at nine with a practical notebook and practical questions and two words that meant everything.

Who had told her husband everything in the right order — the sequence over, the time for it past — and received in return a man who went to the basement and looked at the corner and came back up and asked what do you need me to do.

She's something, I said.

Yes, Wren said. *People say that about her too.*

What do you think it means when they say it about her.

Wren considered this with the seriousness she brings to questions that deserve it.

It means, she said, *that she never learned to be less either. She just learned to be a different kind of more. The ordinary kind. The kind that holds things together while other people do the unusual things.*

I looked at my granddaughter.

That's exactly right, I said.

I know, she said. *She taught me.*

We sat on the couch together in the Sunday morning light with the blanket and the corner and the lake and the October light doing what it did.

Wren leaned against my arm.

I let her.

The field between us.

No gap.

The whole of both of us.

Present.

Grandpa, she said.

Mm.

Today is going to be a lot of people.

Yes.

Some of them are going to be scared.

Yes.

Some of them are going to think we're —

Insane, I said. *Yes. Some will.*

What do we do with those ones.

I thought about this.

Thought about Mrs. Beaumont in March of 1964.

What you already know how to do, I said. *We sit with them. We stay present. We don't go away just because they have. Eventually the truth doesn't need defending. It just needs someone willing to stay in the room with it long enough for the other person to catch up.*

She nodded.

Filed it.

And the ones who are really scared, she said. *The Margaret ones. The ones who have been feeling it for ten days and don't know what it is.*

Those, I said, *are the ones we go to first.*

She nodded again.

Unfolded herself from the couch.

Stood up.

Held out her hand.

I took it.

We stood in the living room on a Sunday morning in October with the field between us and the corner quiet and the lake doing what it did and seven women in a book club who needed to know what was happening before the thing got there first.

Ready, she said.

Yes, I said.

We went to make breakfast.

Nora arrived at eight forty five.

Dale was driving.

He pulled into the driveway with the specific careful placement of a man who parks with the same attention he gives to foundations — deliberately, correctly, in the right position the first time. Got out. Came to the door with the expression of a man who has received extraordinary information and has decided that extraordinary information requires ordinary response because the ordinary response is what holds everything else up.

He shook my hand.

Harlan, he said.

Dale, I said.

Nora told me, he said.

Yes.

The corner, he said.

Yes.

He looked past me at the living room.

At the corner where the light didn't quite reach.

He looked at it for a long moment with the eyes of a man assessing a foundation.

It's real, he said. Not a question. The statement of a man whose body has just confirmed what his wife's words described.

Yes, I said.

All right, he said.

The same two words.

Third time I had heard them in this house in three weeks.

The Carver family and their two words that meant everything.

Nora came in behind him.

Looked at me.

The look of a daughter checking on her father before the day begins.

You slept, she said.

Yes.

Chapter twelve, she said. *Did you —*

Three pages, I said. *Without stopping.*

She nodded. Something in her face that was not quite a smile but was related to one.

Good, she said.

Wren appeared from the kitchen with toast and the expression of a child who has organized the morning and is ready for it to begin.

Ellen arrived at nine exactly.

Stood in the doorway.

Looked at the assembled group — me, Nora, Dale, Wren — with the expression of a woman who came expecting a man and a child and has found something larger.

Oh, she said.

The field, Wren said. *It keeps growing.*

Ellen looked at Wren.

Something moved across her face.

Yes, she said. *It does.*

She came in.

I introduced everyone with the efficiency of a man who has limited time and seven addresses and a compressing timeline and the specific morning clarity of someone who has slept purposefully and woken with direction.

Dale shook Ellen's hand.

I'm sorry about your mother, he said.

Thank you, she said. *She was* — She stopped. Started again. *She was the most fully herself she had ever been in her last three weeks. That matters.*

Yes, Dale said. *It does.*

He said it with the simple directness of a man who means things and says them and does not require more words than the meaning needs.

Ellen looked at him for a moment.

You're the ordinary world, she said.

Dale looked at her.

Nora says that's what I do, he said. *Hold it steady.*

It's the most important thing, Ellen said. *My mother didn't have that. She opened up alone. Nobody holding the ordinary world steady around her while she became more herself.*

Dale was quiet for a moment.

The quiet of a man receiving information about his purpose and finding it fits.

Then let's go, he said.

We went.

Dale driving.

Nora in the front with the addresses and the practical notebook and the three in the morning feeling that points rather than explains.

Me in the back with the notebook and Wren beside me and Ellen on the other side of Wren with her phone and her mother's book club contacts and the specific purposefulness of a woman who has decided that today is how she carries the grief.

Seven addresses.

Margaret first.

The retired nurse who had been feeling it for ten days and thought she was getting sick.

Dale pulled onto Birch Street.

The street where Carol Demming had died last night in a chair facing a window with her coffee still warm.

He did not point this out.

He drove past it with the careful attention of a man who holds the ordinary world steady by continuing to drive on ordinary streets and not making them into something else.

I looked at the house as we passed.

The lights on now.

Someone inside making the morning.

I thought about Carol Demming.

Three weeks of everything.

More than thirty years of less.

That's not nothing.

That's everything.

I looked at the street ahead.

At the October morning.

At the town of Bellaire waking up around us in the specific Sunday morning way of small northern Michigan towns — unhurried, specific, the quiet industry of people who live in a place they have chosen and are at ease in the choosing.

The town I had lived in for eleven years.

The town that had three dead people in it who had died in chairs facing windows with their coffee still warm.

The town where something without an inside had been moving through the lowest ground and feeding on the gaps and growing more efficient.

The town where a field of people who saw clearly were assembling themselves around the thing that had been hunting alone.

How far, Dale said.

Three blocks, Ellen said. *Left on Elm.*

Got it.

We turned onto Elm.

Past Agnes Pfeiffer's music studio where the light was on and I could almost hear through the walls the held silence of a woman who fills rests so completely there is no room for the wrong note.

Past the elementary school where Thomas had stood at the edge of the playground going quiet and feeling something at the tree line that nobody else could name.

Two more blocks.

A white house with a porch and a garden that had been put to bed for winter with the thorough attention of someone who tends things properly and believes in doing it right.

A light in the kitchen window.

A woman visible through the glass.

Moving.

Present.

Alive.

For now.

There, Ellen said.

Dale pulled over.

Turned off the engine.

We sat for a moment in the car on Elm Street on a Sunday morning in October.

Six people.

The field.

Going to the ones who needed it before the thing got there first.

Wren looked at the house.

At the woman visible through the kitchen window.

She's scared, Wren said. *But she's strong.*

Yes, I said.

Like Thomas, she said.

Yes.

She'll be okay, Wren said. *Once she knows.*

Yes, I said. *She will.*

I opened the car door.

Got out into the October morning.

The specific cold of it.

The specific light.

The specific smell of a northern Michigan Sunday in October that is both ending and beginning simultaneously the way October always is — the last of one thing, the first of another, the particular moment of the year when you can feel the turn happening and choose whether to face the cold or turn your back to it.

I faced it.

We walked up the path to Margaret's door.

Six people.

The field.

Going to the ones who needed it.

The ground becoming whole.

One Sunday morning at a time.

One door at a time.

One person at a time.

The weavers finding each other.

The gaps closing.

The rain becoming part of the ground.

I knocked.

Chapter 28

THE QUIET ONES

Chapter Twenty Eight — Always There

Margaret Ellison opened the door in the specific way that people open doors when they have been expecting someone but not this many someones — a half second of recalibration, the social arithmetic of a woman who had prepared herself for one conversation and was now facing six people on her porch on a Sunday morning and was deciding in real time whether to revise her preparation or simply proceed.

She revised.

In approximately two seconds.

The specific efficiency of a woman who has spent thirty years as a nurse and has therefore been recalibrating in real time for most of her professional life.

Ellen, she said. *And —*

Friends, Ellen said. *Good ones. Can we come in.*

Margaret looked at the six of us.

Her eyes moved across us with the practiced assessment of someone who has been reading people's conditions for thirty years — not their social presentation, their actual condition. The thing beneath the thing. The vital signs of the self rather than the body.

She looked at Wren last.

Held on Wren a half second longer than the others.

Something moved across her face.

Yes, she said. *Come in.*

Margaret's kitchen was the kitchen of a woman who had fed people for a long time and had opinions about how it should be done. Large table. Eight chairs. The specific worn quality of furniture that has been used seriously and maintained honestly. A window over the sink that looked onto the garden she had put to bed for winter. Coffee already made in the specific quantity of someone who had expected company even if not this much of it.

She poured without asking.

This is the highest form of hospitality — the assumption that you are welcome before you have proven it.

We sat.

The specific arrangement of six people at a table built for eight — Harlan, Ellen, Nora, Dale, Wren, and Margaret herself, with two empty chairs that did not feel empty so much as reserved for something not yet arrived.

Margaret sat across from me.

Looked at me directly with the eyes of a woman who has been afraid for ten days and has decided that fear is not going to prevent her from looking at the thing she is afraid of.

You know what it is, she said.

Yes, I said.

Ellen said you would. She wrapped both hands around her mug. The hands of someone who has spent decades using them with precision and purpose — strong, steady, slightly rough at the knuckles in the way that hands get rough when they have been washed many times because washing your hands is what you do when other people's lives depend on your cleanliness. *Tell me.*

I told her.

Not the full version — not the corn field and the sixty two years, not yet, there would be time for that and this was not the morning for the whole history. The operational version. What it is. What it does. Why it found her. What the field is and how it works and why knowing changes the equation.

She listened with the focused attention of a woman who receives information the way good nurses receive information — completely, without the defensive filtering of someone who needs it to confirm what they already think. She asked three questions. Precise ones. The questions of a person who has identified the three things she doesn't understand and is addressing them in order of importance.

When I finished she sat for a moment.

Ten days, she said.

Yes.

I've been feeling it for ten days and I thought I was getting sick, she said. *I took my blood pressure every morning. Normal. I took my temperature. Normal. I checked my iron because I had a patient once with severe anemia who described a similar — draining sensation.* She paused. *Everything normal. I couldn't explain it.*

No, I said.

It's not something medicine finds, she said.

No.

Because it's not medicine's territory, she said.

No.

She looked at her coffee.

At the window.

At the garden put to bed for winter.

I knew it wasn't physical, she said. *I knew that by the third day. The feeling has a quality that physical things don't have. Physical illness has — a relationship with the body. A conversation. This was more like —* She stopped.

Something bypassing the body entirely, I said.

Yes, she said. *Going straight to the source.*

Yes.

I've felt something like it before, she said. *In thirty years of nursing. Twice. Patients who were — I don't have the clinical language for it. Patients who were dying not from their illness but from something else. Something that had been drawing on them long before the illness arrived. The illness was almost incidental. Something had already been taking from them for a long time.*

I looked at Margaret Ellison across her kitchen table.

Tell me about those patients, I said.

She looked at me.

The specific look of a woman who has been carrying something professionally for thirty years and is deciding whether the person across the table is a safe place to put it.

The first one was a man, she said. *Sixty years old. Admitted for pneumonia. Should have recovered easily — healthy otherwise, good vitals, responded well to treatment. But he got worse. Not the pneumonia. Something else. He described it as a coldness. A pressure. He said something was in his room at night.* She paused. *I believed him. I didn't tell anyone I believed him because I was a junior nurse and believing patients who said something was in their room at night was not a career-advancing position.*

What happened to him, I said.

He died, she said. *The pneumonia was gone. His labs were fine. He died anyway.* She looked at her hands. *I filed it under unexplained. It stayed there.*

The second, I said.

A woman, she said. *Seventy two. Different hospital. Different decade. Similar presentation. The draining. The coldness. The thing in the room she couldn't see but couldn't stop feeling.* She paused. *I was a senior nurse by then. I had the standing to ask different questions. I asked her who in her life made her feel that way — that specific draining quality, that coldness.*

What did she say, I said.

She described her husband, Margaret said quietly. *Forty years of marriage to a man who had — nothing inside. Her words. She said it took her forty years to understand that the coldness wasn't her. That the drain wasn't her fault. That she had been giving everything she had to fill a space that could not be filled because there was nothing there to receive it.* She stopped. *She died three days later. Her husband sat in the chair beside her bed the entire time and I watched him and I understood something I have never been able to put in a report.*

The kitchen was very quiet.

Wren was looking at Margaret with the dark patient eyes.

Not the assessment.

Something deeper than the assessment.

The recognition of a woman who has been carrying two deaths for thirty years in a folder marked unexplained and has just been handed the explanation.

He was like it, Wren said. Quietly.

Margaret looked at Wren.

Yes, she said. *That's exactly what he was like.*

Not the same, Wren said. *But related. People can become like it. When they give up enough of their inside. When they stop being themselves for long enough.* She paused. *The thing outside is what happens when it goes all the way.*

The kitchen held the silence of a room in which something true has just been said that everyone in it has been circling without landing on.

I looked at my granddaughter.

Thought about what she had just said.

People can become like it.

The thing outside is what happens when it goes all the way.

I had been thinking about the thing as separate. As other. As something that arrived from outside and fed on the gaps.

Wren was saying something different.

Wren was saying the thing was not separate from the human cruelty that fed it.

It was the destination of the human cruelty.

What contempt becomes when it goes all the way.

What the contraction of a soul produces when the contraction is complete.

Not a separate entity that feeds on the gaps.

The gap itself.

Made autonomous.

Made mobile.

The absence of inside given the shape of presence and sent out into the world to find what it had lost and could never recover because you cannot recover what you chose to give away.

I sat at Margaret's kitchen table on a Sunday morning in October and felt something shift in my understanding of what we were dealing with the way tectonic plates shift — slowly, completely, with the specific inevitability of a thing that has been building toward this moment for longer than the moment knows.

Margaret, I said.

Yes.

In thirty years of nursing, I said. *The patients you described. The unexplained ones. Were there others.*

She looked at me.

Yes, she said.

How many.

She was quiet for a moment.

More than I reported, she said. *Less than I felt.* She paused. *I learned to recognize it. The quality of the drain. The specific coldness that wasn't physical. The patients who were dying from something that didn't show up on labs or imaging.* She paused again. *I learned to recognize the ones who had been living beside something like that man. The ones who had been giving themselves to something that could not receive. Who had been less for so long that the less had become a condition rather than a choice.*

And, I said.

And I learned, she said slowly, *to do something. I didn't know what I was doing. I didn't have the name for it. I would sit beside them and just — be very present. Completely myself. Completely there. And something would shift in the room. The quality of the air would change. The patient would breathe differently.* She looked at her hands. *I thought I was just being a good nurse. Being present with a dying patient. Standard practice.*

She looked up.

It wasn't standard practice, she said. *Was it.*

No, I said. *It wasn't.*

I was doing the field, she said.

Yes.

Without knowing.

Yes.

For thirty years.

Yes.

She sat with this.

The sitting of a woman integrating something that reframes not just the current situation but thirty years of professional practice and the two deaths she had carried in the unexplained folder and the specific quality of presence she had brought to every patient in every room for three decades without knowing it had a name.

It's always been there, she said.

Quietly.

Not to me specifically.

To the room.

To the thirty years.

To the unexplained folder.

The field, she said. *It's always been there. People doing it without knowing. Nurses and teachers and —* She stopped. *The ones who stay present with the frightened ones. Who don't go away. Who fill the room so completely that there's no room for the wrong thing.* She looked at me. *They've always been there.*

Yes, I said.

We've always been there.

Yes.

We just didn't know we were the same thing, she said.

I looked at Margaret Ellison across her kitchen table.

Thought about Vera doing the rabbit accidentally in dark parking lots.

Agnes filling rests with forty one years of active silence.

Thomas at the edge of a playground going still because still was what he knew.

Ellen managing her clarity carefully for thirty years.

Nora with her three in the morning feelings that pointed rather than explained.

Dale holding the ordinary world steady.

Wren being the field since before she could name it.

And now Margaret.

Thirty years of doing it in hospital rooms beside dying patients without knowing it had a name.

Yes, I said. *You've always been there. All of you. Doing it alone. Without the name. Without each other.*

And now, she said.

And now you have each other, I said.

Margaret looked around the table.

At Ellen who had lost her mother to the thing last night and was here this morning because forward was the only direction available.

At Nora who had driven four minutes in the dark because something told her to.

At Dale who had gone to the basement and looked at the corner and asked what do you need.

At Wren who had been the field since before she could speak.

At me.

Seventy one years old.

The notebook in my jacket.

The corn field and the rabbit and the cost of less and sixty two years of carrying it alone.

Not alone anymore.

The field, Margaret said. *We've been building it our whole lives without knowing.*

Yes, I said.

It's not something new, she said. *It's something remembered.*

I looked at this woman.

Thought about what she had just said.

Not something new.

Something remembered.

The field had always been there.

In every person who stayed present when leaving would have been easier. Who sat at the end of the table with the one sitting alone. Who filled the room beside a dying patient and changed the quality of the air. Who held a rest so completely there was no room for the wrong note. Who went quiet in dark parking lots and felt the thing move past without finding them. Who drove four minutes in the dark because something pointed.

The field had always been there.

We had been building it our whole lives.

Without knowing.

Without each other.

Until now.

Teach me, Margaret said. *Properly. What I've been doing accidentally for thirty years — teach me to do it on purpose.*

Yes, I said.

I looked at Wren.

Wren was already looking at Margaret.

The dark patient eyes.

The field present in them like still water.

Close your eyes, Wren said.

Margaret closed them.

The Sunday morning kitchen held its quiet.

The October light came through the window over the sink and moved across the table between them.

And Wren began.

The same words she had used with Thomas.

Her own words.

The words of a child who had never been less showing a woman who had been doing the field in hospital rooms for thirty years how to do it on purpose.

How to make the accidental deliberate.

How to make the unconscious known.

How to be not just what you have always been but what you have always been with full awareness of what that is and what it does and why it matters.

I sat at the table and watched and thought about Margaret's word.

Remembered.

Not built.

Remembered.

The field had always been there.

We were not creating something new.

We were finding each other.

Naming what we had always been.

Coming together around what we had always known and always done and always paid the cost of alone.

The weavers.

Not building the cloth.

Finding the other threads.

Discovering that the cloth had been there all along.

Waiting for them to find each other.

To weave together.

To become what they had always separately been.

The field.

After Margaret, the second address.

A woman named Ruth who had been opening up since the meeting and was six days into feeling the cold and was convinced she had developed a late-onset anxiety disorder and had already called her doctor.

We knocked on Ruth's door at ten forty five.

She opened it.

Looked at the six of us.

Looked at Wren.

Something in her face.

I've been expecting someone, she said. *I didn't know who.*

That's how it works, Wren said. *You feel it before you know what it is.*

Ruth looked at this six year old child on her porch.

Yes, she said. *That's exactly how it works.*

She stepped back.

We went in.

The third address.

A woman named Patricia. Sixty five. Retired librarian. Four days into feeling it. Had rearranged her living room furniture twice trying to fix the cold spot she couldn't locate.

She had moved every piece of furniture except the chair in the corner.

She looked at the chair when we came in.

It's not the furniture, she said.

No, I said.

I knew that, she said. *I moved the furniture anyway because I needed to do something.*

Yes, Dale said from the doorway. *That's exactly the right instinct.*

Patricia looked at Dale.

You're the ordinary one, she said.

Yes, he said.

I'm glad you came, she said. *I've been needing someone ordinary.*

I know, he said. *That's why I'm here.*

The fourth.

The fifth.

The sixth.

The seventh.

Seven kitchens on a Sunday morning in October in Bellaire Michigan.

Seven women who had been opening up since the town meeting.

Who had been becoming more themselves.

Who had been feeling the thing without knowing what it was.

Who had been doing the field accidentally, imperfectly, in the specific ways that their lives had taught them to do it — in hospital rooms and libraries and music studios and garden beds and book club discussions and thirty years of quiet reliable presence in a small northern Michigan town.

Who had been doing it alone.

Without the name.

Without each other.

Not anymore.

By two o'clock we were back in Dale's car.

Seven kitchens.

Seven women who knew.

Seven women who were practicing on purpose what they had been doing accidentally their entire lives.

Seven more threads in the cloth.

Dale drove.

Nora in the front with her practical notebook.

Ellen in the back with her phone already open texting the remaining five members of the book club because the sequence was over and the timeline was compressing and forward was the only direction available.

Wren beside me.

Leaning against my arm.

Eyes closed.

Not asleep.

Doing the field.

Monitoring the street.

Watching for the thing that had been mapping us last night.

I looked out the window at Bellaire going by in the Sunday afternoon light.

The ordinary town.

The ordinary Sunday.

The ordinary geography of a place where people knew each other and word traveled slow but far.

A place where something without an inside had been moving through the lowest ground.

A place where a field had always existed without knowing it was a field.

Until now.

Grandpa, Wren said without opening her eyes.

Yes.

Margaret was right, she said. *It's always been there.*

Yes, I said.

We just needed to find each other.

Yes.

We're finding each other.

Yes.

She leaned a little more against my arm.

The field between us.

No gap.

The whole of both of us.

Present.

Outside the October afternoon was doing what October afternoons do.

Inside the car the field was present in six people who had spent a Sunday morning knocking on doors and sitting in kitchens and saying *close your eyes* and *this is what you've always been* and *you've been doing it your whole life you just didn't know it had a name.*

Seven kitchens.

Seven threads.

The cloth growing.

The gaps closing.

The ground becoming whole.

Dale, I said.

Yes.

There's a book club meeting on Thursday, I said. *The remaining five members. Ellen is arranging it.*

Where, he said.

My house, I said.

I'll be there, he said.

No hesitation.

No question.

The response of a man who holds the ordinary world steady by showing up where showing up is needed.

Thank you, I said.

Harlan, he said.

Yes.

The corner, he said. *In your living room.*

Yes.

It's going to end, he said. *Isn't it.*

I looked at the back of Dale Carver's head.

The man who checks foundations.

Who fixes wrong things without requiring them to fit his previous understanding of what wrong things look like.

Who went to a basement and looked at a corner and asked what do you need.

Who drove six people to seven kitchens on a Sunday morning without asking for explanation.

Who held the ordinary world steady while the rest of us did what we needed to do.

Yes, I said. *It's going to end.*

Good, he said.

He drove.

The October afternoon went past the windows.

The field rode home in a station wagon on a Sunday in Bellaire Michigan.

Growing.

Remembering itself.

Finding its threads.

Becoming the cloth it had always been.

Chapter 29

THE QUIET ONES

Chapter Twenty Nine — Tuesday

Thomas didn't come to school on Tuesday.

Wren told me at three fifteen when I picked her up. Not dramatically. The flat precise delivery she uses for all true things. She got in the car and put her backpack on her lap and said:

Thomas wasn't there today.

I pulled away from the curb.

Did he call in sick, I said.

Mrs. Aldrich said he was absent, Wren said. *She used the voice she uses when she doesn't know why.*

I drove two blocks.

Stopped at the light on Main.

Is he okay, I said.

Wren was quiet.

The specific quiet of a child checking something on the frequency the way you check a signal on a radio — turning the dial carefully, listening for the station beneath the static.

He's scared, she said. *I can feel it from here.*

How scared.

Very, she said. *The kind of scared that makes you go further away instead of less far.*

The rabbit pulled tight.

The light changed.

I did not go through the intersection.

Grandpa, Nora said from behind me in a car that wasn't there.

I heard it anyway.

Address, I said to Wren. *Do you know where he lives.*

Birch Street, she said. *The blue house with the broken gutter on the left side.*

How do you know that.

I walked home with him last week, she said. *To make sure he got there.*

I looked at my granddaughter.

She looked at the windshield.

You didn't tell me, I said.

You had a lot going on, she said.

I turned left instead of right.

Toward Birch Street.

Toward the blue house with the broken gutter.

Toward the street where Carol Demming had died in a chair facing a window four days ago.

The house was quiet in the way that houses are quiet when something is wrong inside them. Not the quiet of rest. The quiet of held breath. The specific quality of a building that is managing something it doesn't have the vocabulary for.

I parked.

Looked at the house.

He's inside, Wren said. *Upstairs. He went as far back as he could.*

Is it in there, I said.

She was quiet for a moment.

It was, she said. *Last night. I think it came back this morning.* She paused. *That's why he didn't go to school. He was afraid to leave his room.*

I thought about Thomas on my porch steps three days ago.

The too-large jacket.

The careful knock.

The amber eyes with the rabbit in them.

The fraction of him that had knocked becoming most of him by the time he left.

The spine slightly more vertical.

Two hours in a basement.

Not enough.

Two hours in a basement was the beginning of the field not the field itself and the thing had known that and had come for him before the field could take hold.

Of course it had.

It had been mapping us.

It knew about Thomas.

It knew he was the newest and the youngest and the least established and the most vulnerable.

It had gone for the weakest point in the field the way cold goes for the gap in the insulation.

The broken gutter.

I got out of the car.

Stay here, I said to Wren.

No, she said.

I looked at her.

He needs to see me, she said. *Not just you. He trusts you. He trusts me more.*

She was right.

She was six years old and she was right and I was going to have to get comfortable with that faster than I had been getting comfortable with it.

Stay beside me, I said.

Always, she said.

We walked up the path.

I knocked.

Thomas's mother was a woman named Diane who opened the door with the expression of someone who has been inside with a frightened child since yesterday morning and has been cycling between worried and frustrated and back to worried and has arrived at a state that is simply exhausted and is trying not to show it.

She looked at me.

At Wren.

You're the grandfather, she said. *Thomas told me about you.*

Yes, I said. *I'm sorry to come without calling. I heard Thomas wasn't at school today and I wanted to check on him.*

She looked at me for a moment.

The look of a mother deciding whether the man on her porch is a help or a complication.

He won't come out of his room, she said. *Since yesterday morning. He says there's something in the house. I've checked every room. There's nothing.* She paused. *He's been like this before. When he was five. We saw someone. It got better. Then it stopped.* She paused again. *I thought it had stopped.*

It did stop, I said. *For a while.*

She looked at me.

You know what it is, she said.

Yes, I said.

The same words as Margaret.

The same quality in them.

The relief of a woman who has been alone with something inexplicable and has just been told it has a name.

Come in, she said.

The cold spot was in the hallway.

Not the corner this time.

The hallway between the kitchen and the stairs.

The threshold.

The place between spaces.

It occupied it the way it always occupied thresholds — with the specific quality of an absence that has found a border and is using it. Neither here nor there. Both simultaneously. The precise location that is hardest to defend because it belongs to neither room.

Wren felt it the moment we came through the front door.

I watched her feel it.

The slight adjustment in her posture. The field going from ambient to deliberate. The still water becoming intentional rather than natural.

She looked at the hallway.

Did not look at it directly.

The sideways attention.

It's smaller than yours, she said quietly. *The corner one is bigger.*

Because it's been at mine longer, I said.

It's been here long enough, she said.

I looked at Diane.

How long has Thomas been feeling it, I said.

He said two weeks, she said. *But I think longer. He started —* She stopped. Started again with the honesty of a mother who has decided that honesty is what the situation requires even when honesty is uncomfortable. *He started going further away about a month ago. I thought it was school. I thought it was the other kids not including him. I thought —*

You thought the right things, I said. *The school, the other kids — those were real. They were also —*

Cover, Wren said.

Diane looked at Wren.

Yes, I said. *The other things were real. They just weren't the whole story.*

What is the whole story, Diane said.

Can I talk to Thomas first, I said. *And then I'll tell you everything. I promise everything. But he needs to know we're here before he can come forward enough to hear it.*

She looked at me.

At Wren.

At the hallway.

At the cold spot she couldn't see and had been unable to find with her eyes and had therefore been telling herself wasn't there.

He's in his room, she said. *Top of the stairs. Left.*

I knocked on Thomas's door.

Wren stood beside me.

Silence.

Thomas, I said. *It's Harlan. And Wren.*

Silence.

Then the specific sound of a child moving. The creak of a bed. Feet on the floor. The particular careful footsteps of a boy moving toward a door he is not certain he should open.

The door opened three inches.

One amber eye.

Looking at Wren first.

Then me.

The door opened wider.

Thomas stood in the doorway in his pajamas — it was three thirty in the afternoon — with the too-large jacket pulled over them because he had not taken the jacket off apparently since Sunday and his hair in the condition of hair that has not been attended to because attending to it would require the kind of presence that had not been available and his face with the specific drawn quality of a child who has not slept properly and has been as far back as he could go for thirty six hours.

He looked at Wren.

You came, he said.

Yes, she said. *Of course.*

It was here last night, he said. *In my room. Not just the hallway. In my room.*

I know, she said. *I felt it from school.*

Why didn't it — He stopped.

Because you did the rabbit, she said. *It didn't find you.*

I did the rabbit all night, he said. *I didn't sleep.*

I know, she said. *You can sleep now. We're here.*

Something in his face.

The fraction of him that had knocked on my porch door three days ago.

Present again.

A little larger than before.

Because she was there.

Come downstairs, I said. *Your mother needs to hear some things. And then we're going to work on something that will mean you don't have to do the rabbit all night anymore.*

The field, he said.

Yes.

I've been trying, he said. *Since Sunday. But it keeps* — He paused. *I keep losing it when I'm scared.*

Yes, I said. *That's normal. The field takes practice under pressure. The rabbit is easier under pressure because fear makes you want to be small. The field requires something different.*

What, he said.

I looked at this seven year old boy in his pajamas and his too-large jacket in the doorway of his bedroom on a Tuesday afternoon.

Thought about what the field required.

Not smallness.

The opposite.

Full presence.

The whole of yourself.

Courage, I said. *Not the loud kind. The quiet kind. The kind that says I am completely here even though I am frightened.*

He looked at me.

I don't know if I have that, he said.

You knocked on my door on Saturday, I said. *Alone. Frightened. Not knowing what you'd find.*

He was quiet.

That was courage, I said. *The quiet kind.*

He stood in the doorway.

Processing.

The amber eyes with the rabbit in them.

And something else.

Something that had been there on Saturday too but was clearer now.

The specific quality of a child who has been less for a long time and is beginning — slowly, at great cost, against the considerable resistance of two years of practiced smallness — to remember what more feels like.

Okay, he said.

He came out of his room.

Put his hand in Wren's.

We went downstairs.

Diane sat at her kitchen table and listened the way Diane listened — with the focused attention of a mother who has been frightened for her child for longer than she has admitted and is now being given the explanation she has needed and is receiving it with the specific gratitude of someone who has been told they are not imagining things.

Thomas sat beside her.

Still in the pajamas and the jacket.

Wren on his other side.

Her hand still in his.

I told Diane what I had told the others.

She asked two questions.

Both about Thomas.

Nothing about herself.

The questions of a mother.

When I finished she looked at her son.

Why didn't you tell me, she said.

Because you would have taken me to someone, he said. *And they would have said I was imagining it. And then I would have had to pretend I believed them.*

Diane looked at her son.

The specific look of a mother understanding something about her child that she had missed and deciding not to spend time in the guilt of the missing but instead in the action that the understanding makes possible.

I believe you, she said.

Thomas looked at his mother.

You do.

Yes, she said. *I should have sooner. I'm sorry.*

He looked at her for a moment.

Then he leaned against her.

Just that.

The specific small surrender of a child who has been very far away for a very long time and has just been given permission to come back.

Diane put her arm around him.

Looked at me over his head.

What do I do, she said.

The same thing you're doing right now, I said. *Stay close. Stay present. Don't go away just because he has. And* — I paused. *Come to my house Thursday evening. There are people you need to meet.*

The field, she said. She had been listening carefully.

Yes.

Thomas too, she said.

Thomas too, I said.

Wren looked at Thomas against his mother's side.

Thomas, she said.

He looked up.

The field is easier when you're not alone, she said. *That's why it came for you first. Because you were the newest and the most alone in it.* She paused. *You're not alone anymore.*

He looked at her.

The amber eyes.

The rabbit still there.

But beside the rabbit now — present, small, new, like the first green thing after a long winter — something else.

The beginning of the field.

Not the practiced field of Agnes.

Not the thirty year field of Margaret.

Not even the deliberate field Vera had been building for two weeks.

Just the beginning of it.

The fraction that had knocked on my door on Saturday.

The fraction that had come downstairs in pajamas and a too-large jacket.

The fraction that had put his hand in Wren's and come down anyway.

I know, he said.

Outside on Birch Street the October afternoon was doing what it did.

Inside the cold spot in the hallway was still there.

But the kitchen was warm.

And a boy in pajamas was leaning against his mother.

And a six year old girl with dark eyes had her hand in his.

And the field was present in the room in the specific way that the field is present when people who have been alone find each other and stay.

I looked at the hallway.

At the cold spot.

At the thing that had come for the weakest point in the field.

It had found Thomas alone and frightened and had spent thirty six hours pressing closer.

It had not found what it was looking for.

Because Thomas had done the rabbit all night.

Because Wren had felt it from school.

Because I had turned left instead of right.

Because the field had moved faster than the mapping.

This time.

Harlan, Wren said.

Yes.

She was looking at the hallway.

At the cold spot.

At the thing.

It knows we're here, she said.

Yes, I said.

It's angry, she said.

Things without insides, I said, *do not get angry.*

This one, she said, *does something that works like angry.*

She had said this before.

About frustrated.

Now angry.

The thing was developing responses it hadn't had three weeks ago.

Or had always had them and we were only now getting close enough to feel them.

I wasn't certain which.

Both possibilities were concerning.

Let's go, I said.

We said goodbye to Diane.

To Thomas who stood in the doorway of the kitchen in his pajamas and his too-large jacket and watched us leave with the amber eyes and the beginning of the field and the specific expression of a child who has been found and is not certain yet that being found is permanent but is choosing to believe it might be.

Thursday, Wren said to him from the door.

Thursday, he said.

We went out into the October afternoon.

The cold spot in the hallway watched us go.

Or did what watching is when you have no eyes.

We walked to the car.

I opened Wren's door.

She got in.

I got in.

Started the engine.

Drove two houses down Birch Street past the house where Carol Demming had died in a chair four days ago.

Past the ordinary house.

The ordinary street.

The ordinary Tuesday afternoon.

Grandpa, Wren said.

Yes.

It's following us again.

I looked in the rearview mirror.

The street behind us.

Empty.

Ordinary.

Yes, I said.

It's closer than before, she said.

Yes, I said.

It's not mapping anymore, she said.

I drove.

Kept my hands at the position my driver's education teacher had recommended.

What is it doing, I said.

Wren was quiet for a moment.

The specific quiet of a child reading something on the frequency that she is translating into available language.

Deciding, she said.

I drove.

The October afternoon went past the windows.

Deciding what, I said.

She looked at me.

The dark eyes.

The field in them.

Clear and still and complete.

Which one of us to go for first, she said.

I kept driving.

Kept my hands exactly where they were supposed to be.

All right, I said.

All right, she said.

Neither of us said anything else.

The car moved through the October afternoon toward home.

Behind us, on Birch Street, on the ordinary Tuesday, something without an inside made its decision.

Chapter 30

THE QUIET ONES

Chapter Thirty — Wednesday

I called Vera first.

This is not a hierarchy. It is the order in which the calls needed to happen — Vera who had been practicing longest and had her sister and the sister's neighbor and was in Traverse City and needed the most lead time to get back.

She answered on the first ring.

I know, she said. *I felt something shift this afternoon.*

Yes, I said.

It's decided.

Yes.

When.

Tomorrow night, I said. *I'm moving the meeting to Wednesday. Tomorrow. Can you be here.*

I'm already packing, she said.

I called Agnes.

She answered from the studio. I could hear the piano in the background — not playing, the specific silence of an instrument recently played, the resonance still in the air.

I heard it in the rests today, she said before I could speak. *Different than before. More — directed.*

Yes, I said. *Tomorrow night. My house.*

What time.

Seven.

I'll bring the card, she said.

Agnes —

I know I don't need it, she said. *I'm bringing it anyway.*

I called Rudy.

He answered on the second ring with the voice of a man who has been sleeping well in Petoskey and eating his son's cooking and has the specific restored quality of someone who has been removed from proximity to the thing long enough for the drain to reverse.

I'm coming back, I said. *Tomorrow. Can you be there by seven.*

I've been ready to come back for four days, he said. *Danny keeps feeding me casserole. There are only so many casseroles a man can eat before he needs to go home.*

Rudy.

Yes.

It's moved past the mapping stage.

Silence.

The silence of a hardware man receiving information about a structural problem and calculating the implications.

How bad, he said.

Bad enough that I need everyone in one room tomorrow night.

I'll leave at noon, he said. *I'll be there by three. I can help set up.*

There's nothing to set up, I said. *Just chairs.*

Harlan, he said.

Yes.

In the store, he said. *Before you sent me away. The cold spot near the lumber.* He paused. *I've been thinking about it. About what it felt like before I understood what it was.*

Yes.

It felt like being watched by something that didn't want anything from me, he said. *Not threatening exactly. Just — attending. The way you attend to something you're considering.*

Yes, I said. *That's right.*

But when it moved to the bedroom, he said. *It felt different. Not attending anymore.*

What did it feel like, I said.

He was quiet for a moment.

It felt like being selected, he said.

I stood at my desk with the phone in my hand.

Yes, I said. *That's exactly what it is.*

So tomorrow night, he said. *We need to make sure it selects wrong.*

Yes.

How, he said.

I'm still working that out, I said.

Work faster, he said. Not unkindly. The directness of a hardware man who understands that some problems have a closing time after which the solution is no longer available.

Yes, I said.

Harlan.

Yes.

The selection, he said. *It selected Gerald. It selected Carol Demming. It selected Vera and me before we knew to move.* He paused. *What made it select them over others.*

They were the most visible, I said. *The most open. The most fully themselves.*

So the most complete ones, he said.

Yes.

The ones with the least gap, he said.

Yes.

Which means, he said slowly, *the one it selects next is the most complete person in the field.*

I stood at my desk.

Thought about this.

Thought about what Rudy had just said with the specific clarity of a hardware man who looks at a structure and identifies immediately where the load is greatest.

The most complete person in the field.

The one with the least gap.

The one who is most fully herself.

Who has never been less.

Who is the field in its purest form.

Rudy, I said.

Yes.

I need to write something down, I said. *I'll call you back.*

I put the phone down.

Opened the notebook.

Wrote what Rudy had said.

The selection goes to the most complete. The least gap. The most fully themselves.

Underlined it.

Which means.

Underlined that.

Wren.

Underlined it three times.

Sat at the desk.

The October night outside.

The lake.

The specific quiet of a house where a six year old was asleep on the couch under the blanket.

I sat with what I had written for a long time.

I called Ellen.

She was already organizing. Had spent the afternoon calling the remaining book club members and had reached four of them and was working on the fifth.

Tomorrow night, I said. *Seven o'clock. My house. Everyone.*

How many is everyone, she said.

I counted.

Vera. Rudy. Agnes. Nora. Dale. Ellen. Margaret. Ruth. Patricia. The other four book club members. Thomas and Diane. Vera's sister if she could make the drive. The sister's neighbor.

Possibly twenty, I said.

Your living room holds twenty, she said. Not a question. She had been in my living room.

With chairs from the kitchen and the basement, I said. *Yes.*

I'll bring food, she said.

Ellen —

People think better when they're not hungry, she said. *My mother's book club ran on food. It's non-negotiable.*

I thought about Carol Demming.

Who had said coffee was the most honest beverage because it didn't pretend to be anything other than what it was.

All right, I said. *Thank you.*

Harlan, she said.

Yes.

What are we doing tomorrow night, she said. *Specifically. What does it look like.*

I looked at the notebook.

At what I had written.

At the three underlines.

I'm still working that out, I said.

Work faster, she said.

The same words as Rudy.

The same directness.

The hardware man and the daughter both arriving at the same instruction from different directions.

Yes, I said.

I hung up.

Called Nora.

I know, she said. *Dale already told me. We'll be there at six to help set up.*

There's nothing —

Chairs from the basement, she said. *And someone needs to make sure the corner is — managed before people arrive. So it doesn't frighten anyone before they understand what they're looking at.*

I had not thought about this.

The corner.

Twenty people in my living room.

Some of them new to the field.

Some of them still finding the frequency.

All of them in the same room with the thing that had been in my living room for three weeks and had moved past mapping to deciding.

Nora, I said.

Yes.

That's a good point.

I know, she said. *Six o'clock.*

She hung up.

I sat at the desk.

Opened the notebook.

Started writing.

Not the record.

The plan.

Tuesday night. Late.

What I know:

The thing has moved from mapping to selecting. Rudy identified the logic correctly — it selects the most complete. The least gap. The most fully themselves. Gerald. Carol. Both of them in the full opening of becoming who they were. Both of them without the field in place before the opening.

The field changes the equation. Vera and Rudy and Agnes and the others — they are opening AND have the field. The field does not make them invisible. It makes the opening survivable. The gap never forms because the ground is complete before the rain falls.

But.

Rudy's logic runs to its conclusion.

The most complete person in the field is the one who has never been less.

Who has no gap to form.

Who is the field in its purest form.

Wren.

The thing knows this. It has been in this house. It has been on our street. It has felt the field in twenty forms now — Vera, Agnes, Margaret, Thomas, all of them — and it has felt what Wren is in the middle of all of them.

It is going to come for her.

Not because she is the weakest.

Because she is the strongest.

This is the reversal I did not see coming and should have.

The thing does not only hunt the ones who are opening.

It hunts the ones who are most complete because those are the ones whose loss would damage the field most severely.

Gerald was complete. Carol was complete. Both died not because they were opening but because they were fully themselves.

Wren is the most fully herself of anyone in the field.

She is six years old.

And the thing has decided.

What I do not know is when.

What I do not know is how to protect her without making her less.

Because making her less is what the thing wants.

If she contracts — if she learns to be less to avoid being selected — she becomes a gap.

And the thing moves into gaps.

There is no version of this where making Wren smaller keeps her safe.

There is only the version where she is completely herself and the field around her is complete enough that the selection cannot land.

Which means tomorrow night is not a meeting.

Tomorrow night is the field becoming what it needs to be.

Complete enough.

Whole enough.

Every thread woven tight enough that the thing that comes for the most complete person in it finds not a target but a ground so thoroughly itself that there is no purchase.

The rain becomes part of the ground.

All of it.

Every drop.

Every person in that room.

Completely themselves.

Simultaneously.

For the first time.

Together.

That is what tomorrow night needs to be.

Not a lesson.

Not a meeting.

The field becoming the field.

Complete.

For Wren.

I put the pen down.

Sat at the desk.

The October night outside.

The lake.

The corner of the living room quiet in the Tuesday night quiet.

I looked at it.

I know what you're doing, I said.

The corner.

The cold without temperature.

The pressing absence.

She is not Gerald, I said. *She is not Carol. She is not alone and she is not without the field and tomorrow night the field is going to be complete around her and you are going to find that there is nowhere to land.*

The corner said nothing.

It never did.

But the cold shifted fractionally.

The specific fractional shift I had learned to read over three weeks of living with it.

Acknowledgment.

It heard.

It always heard.

Good, I said.

I closed the notebook.

Went to check on Wren.

She was asleep on the couch.

The dark hair.

The folded hands.

The field present in her even in sleep.

Complete.

Whole.

The most fully herself of anyone I had ever known.

Six years old.

I stood over her for a moment.

Thought about a nine year old boy in a corn field learning the rabbit alone because there was no one to show him anything else.

Thought about what it would have meant if someone had been there.

Not to protect him from the field.

To be the field with him.

I am here.

We are here.

You are not alone.

The ground is complete.

There is nowhere for the wrong thing to land.

I've got you, I said.

Quietly.

Not waking her.

To the field around her.

To the twenty people who would be in my living room tomorrow night.

To the thing in the corner that had decided.

We've got her.

I went to bed.

Did not sleep immediately.

Lay in the dark and thought about tomorrow night.

About twenty people in a living room.

About the field becoming complete.

About what complete looked like and felt like and did when the thing came for the most whole person in it.

About a six year old girl who had never learned to be less.

Who was the ground the rain fell on.

Who was so completely herself that there was no gap for the wrong thing to occupy.

Who was going to stand in the middle of a room full of people who had found each other and be exactly what she was.

The field.

In its purest form.

Without reduction.

Without concealment.

The whole of herself.

Offered without reduction to the thing that had been hunting the whole of her.

Not as bait.

As answer.

The thing had been hunting completeness its entire existence because completeness was the one thing it had never had and could never have and could not stop seeking.

Not to destroy it.

To be near it.

To occupy the space beside it.

To fill itself with borrowed wholeness because it had no wholeness of its own.

The gap made autonomous.

Seeking the ground.

And tomorrow night the ground was going to be complete enough that seeking was all it would ever be.

The seeking without the finding.

The almost without the right note ever arriving.

Because the field would be whole.

Every thread.

Every person.

Completely themselves.

Simultaneously.

Together.

For the first time.

I lay in the dark and held this.

The shape of it.

The specific shape of what tomorrow needed to be.

Not a battle.

Not a driving out.

A completion.

The field becoming what it had always been trying to become.

What it had been in pieces across thirty years of hospital rooms and music studios and hardware stores and corn fields and dark parking lots and book clubs and kitchen tables.

Always there.

Never whole.

Until tomorrow.

I closed my eyes.

Found the frequency.

Got quiet on it.

Not the rabbit.

The field.

The whole of myself.

Present.

Broadcast at exactly the right volume.

Which was all of it.

And slept.

Chapter 31

Chapter Thirty One — The Chapter He Finished

I woke at five.

Not from a dream. Not from the corner or the frequency or the specific anxiety of a man with a compressing timeline and an evening that needed to be everything it needed to be.

From the specific clarity that sometimes arrives before dawn when the mind has been working through the night on something the conscious self was not aware of and presents its findings in the grey light before the lake has started its morning conversation with the shore.

The chapter was done.

Not done the way chapter twelve had been almost done for three weeks — almost right, almost honest, almost through the door instead of around it. Done the way things are done when the person writing them has finally stopped being careful and written the true thing without the managed distance of a man who understands the idea intellectually and is rendering it faithfully without being inside it.

I knew this before I sat down.

The way you know sometimes before you check.

I made coffee.

Carried it to the desk.

Opened the laptop.

Read the chapter from the beginning.

It was done.

Three weeks of chapter twelve lying to me and one night of sleeping with the shape of tomorrow in my chest and it was done.

Not because I had solved a craft problem.

Because I had stopped protecting myself from the material.

The chapter was about a man who discovers that the universe is not indifferent to human suffering — it simply has a different timeline than we'd prefer. I had been writing this carefully. With the specific distance of a man who had spent sixty two years being less and had not yet fully trusted that the page could hold the full weight of what he knew.

Last night I had trusted it.

And the chapter had told the truth.

I read it twice.

It held.

I saved it.

Closed the laptop.

Sat with the coffee and the grey morning light and the specific feeling of a thing finished that has been trying to finish for a long time.

Not triumph.

Something quieter.

The specific satisfaction of a lock that has finally found its key.

Wren woke at seven.

She appeared in the kitchen doorway with the blanket around her shoulders and the dark hair and the hands not yet folded, still in the loose morning configuration of a child who has not yet assembled herself for the day.

She looked at me.

You finished it, she said.

Yes.

Chapter twelve.

Yes.

I could feel it from the couch, she said. *Something went quiet in the house around three in the morning. I thought it was the corner but it wasn't. It was you.*

Yes, I said. *It was me.*

She came to the kitchen.

Accepted the toast I made without being asked because some things you do from pattern and some things you do from love and the best ones are both simultaneously.

She ate.

I drank coffee.

The morning assembled itself around us in the specific way that Wednesday mornings assemble in northern Michigan in October — without ceremony, with the solid specific quality of a day that knows what it is and intends to be it without apology.

Wren, I said.

Mm.

I want to read you something.

She looked up from her toast.

The dark patient eyes.

The assessment.

Then the other thing. The warmth beneath the assessment.

Okay, she said.

Come to the study.

She carried her toast.

We went to the study.

She sat in the chair across from my desk — the chair where Vera had sat, where Agnes had sat, where Ellen had sat, where all of them had sat across the weeks while I told them what I knew and they told me what they knew and the field assembled itself one conversation at a time.

I opened the laptop.

Found the chapter.

Read it to her.

I want to tell you what the chapter said.

Not all of it. A chapter is a chapter and belongs to the book it lives in and this is a different book. But the center of it. The thing it had been trying to say for three weeks while I was being careful.

The chapter was about a man named Daniel who has been living his whole life in the belief that the universe is a mechanism — enormous, indifferent, turning on its own logic without reference to the small creatures inside it. He is not bitter about this. He is a scientist. He understands that indifference is not cruelty. That a mechanism does not have intentions.

Then something happens.

Not a miracle. Not a vision. Not anything that would qualify as evidence in the system he has built his life inside.

Something small.

Something that arrives at exactly the right moment in exactly the right form to be useful in exactly the way he needed something to be useful.

And Daniel sits with this small thing and does the thing he has spent his life doing — tries to explain it within the available framework. Coincidence. Pattern recognition. The human tendency to find meaning in the arrangement of random events.

The framework holds.

The explanation works.

And Daniel knows, in the specific way that scientists know things that their framework cannot accommodate, that the explanation is correct and insufficient simultaneously.

That the universe is a mechanism and also something else.

That indifference and attention are not mutually exclusive at the scale the universe operates on.

That the timeline of care is longer than the timeline of a human life and therefore looks, from inside a human life, exactly like indifference.

That the small thing that arrived at exactly the right moment was not a miracle.

It was the universe operating at its own timeline. Which is longer than Daniel's. Which is longer than any individual life. Which encompasses all of them.

Which has, in its own way, at its own pace, without urgency, without drama, with the specific patient attention of something that is not in a hurry because it is not going anywhere —

Been paying attention the whole time.

Daniel sits with this.

Not converted.

Not healed.

Not arrived.

Just — expanded.

The framework large enough now to hold both things simultaneously.

The mechanism and the attention.

The indifference and the care.

The timeline too long for comfort and exactly right for truth.

Daniel puts the small thing in his pocket.

Goes back to his life.

Which looks the same from the outside.

Which is completely different from the inside.

Because a man who believes the universe is a mechanism that does not know he exists lives differently than a man who believes the universe is a mechanism that has been paying attention at a timeline he cannot see.

Not better necessarily.

Not safer.

Differently.

With the specific quality of a man who has been less for a long time and has just been told — not in words, not in visions, in a small thing arriving at exactly the right moment — that the less was not the whole story.

That something has been watching.

Not intervening.

Not protecting.

Watching.

With the patience of something that does not experience time as a limited resource.

Waiting for the man to stop being less and start being the whole of himself.

Which is all it has ever been waiting for.

Which has always been enough.

I finished reading.

The study was quiet in the Wednesday morning way.

The lake doing what it did.

The October light coming through the window at the angle it came through at this hour.

Wren sat across from me with her toast finished and her hands folded in her lap and her dark patient eyes.

She had not moved during the reading.

Had not shifted in the chair.

Had sat with the complete stillness of a child who is fully present in something and has no need to signal her presence.

I closed the laptop.

Looked at her.

That's about tonight, she said.

Yes.

And about you, she said.

Yes.

And about the field, she said.

Yes.

She was quiet for a moment.

The specific quiet of a six year old sitting with something large and finding it fits inside her without requiring her to expand in any uncomfortable direction because she has always been large enough for large things.

Grandpa, she said.

Yes.

The universe in the chapter, she said. *The thing that's been paying attention at a timeline too long to see.*

Yes.

Is that what we are, she said. *For Thomas. For Ellen. For all of them. We're the small thing that arrives at exactly the right moment.*

I looked at my granddaughter.

Thought about Gerald dying in his chair.

About the notebook in the box for sixty two years.

About Wren appearing at my elbow asking about Missy.

About all of it assembling itself in the specific way that things assemble when the timeline is longer than you can see from inside it.

Yes, I said. *I think that's exactly what we are.*

She nodded.

Filed it.

The small serious nod.

Then we should go be that, she said. *Tonight.*

Yes, I said.

Grandpa.

Yes.

The chapter, she said. *Daniel in the chapter. He puts the small thing in his pocket and goes back to his life.*

Yes.

What was the small thing.

I looked at my granddaughter.

The dark eyes.

The patience.

The field present in her like still water in the Wednesday morning light.

You, I said.

She looked at me for a moment.

Not surprised.

Not embarrassed.

The specific quality of a child receiving a true thing and holding it the way she held all true things — completely, without the defensive filtering of someone who needs it to be smaller than it is.

Okay, she said.

Two words.

The simplest thing she had ever said.

The most complete.

Not *thank you.*

Not *I know.*

Not *that's a lot of pressure* or *I'm only six* or any of the available responses that would have been completely reasonable from a child who had just been told that she was the small thing the universe had been using to remind a seventy one year old man that the less was not the whole story.

Just —

Okay.

The word of someone who has received the assignment and accepted it and is ready to go be it.

The word of someone who has never been less and does not intend to start.

The word of the field in its purest form saying yes to what it already was.

Okay.

I sat at my desk in the Wednesday morning.

The chapter finished on the screen behind me.

My granddaughter across from me with her hands in her lap and her dark eyes and her six years of being exactly what she was.

The thing in the corner of the living room quiet.

The lake doing what it did.

The October light doing what it did.

Twenty people coming to my house tonight.

The field becoming complete.

For the first time.

All of it.

Together.

Okay, I said.

She unfolded herself from the chair.

Stood up.

I'm going to get dressed, she said. *And then I'm going to call Thomas and tell him to wear his good jacket tonight. Not the big one.*

He has a good jacket, I said.

He does, she said. *He just doesn't wear it because he doesn't want to stand out.*

And tonight, I said.

Tonight, she said, *standing out is the point.*

She went to get dressed.

I sat at the desk.

Looked at the window.

At the October morning.

At the ordinary Wednesday that was going to become something else by evening.

Picked up the notebook.

Opened it to the man's section.

Wrote one line.

She said okay. That's enough. That's everything. We're ready.

Closed the notebook.

Put it in my jacket pocket.

Where it had been for three weeks.

Where it would stay through tonight.

The boy's record and the man's record.

The sixty two years between them.

The corn field and the rabbit and the cost of less and the long careful life of a man who had been less for too long and had stopped.

And the small thing that had arrived at exactly the right moment.

And had said okay.

And meant it completely.

The whole of herself.

No reduction.

No concealment.

Okay.

Outside the October morning continued its business.

Inside a six year old girl was putting on her good clothes for a Wednesday that was going to need all of her.

And she was going to give it all of her.

Because she had never learned to give anything less.

Chapter 32

Chapter Thirty Two — The Field Complete

Rudy arrived first.

This did not surprise me. He pulled up at five forty five in the truck he had driven to Petoskey and back and got out with the specific restored quality of a man who has been away from something draining long enough to remember what full feels like. He had color back. The eight pounds were not back but the steadiness in his eyes was and that mattered more.

He shook my hand at the door.

You look better, I said.

Danny's casserole, he said. *Four days of it. A man can only be so grateful before gratitude curdles into something else.*

He came in. Looked at the circle of chairs I had assembled from every room in the house including two folding ones from the garage that I had forgotten I owned and which had opinions about their hinges.

Cozy, he said.

Twenty two people, I said.

In this room.

Yes.

He looked at the corner. *Still there.*

Quieter, I said.

Hm, he said. The specific hm of a hardware man who has been told a structural problem is improving and is reserving judgment until he sees it himself. He looked at it for a moment. Then he went to find Ellen and the food because Rudy's relationship with problems has always involved eating something first and thinking second and this has served him adequately across seventy years.

They arrived over the next hour with the specific staggered quality of people who have been told seven o'clock and have interpreted this differently according to their personalities. Agnes arrived at six fifteen because Agnes is constitutionally early. She sat at the piano without asking — she never asks, it's a piano, she plays — and ran through something quiet that I didn't recognize and then stopped and looked at the corner.

Smaller, she said.

Yes.

Good, she said. And kept playing.

Margaret arrived with Ruth and Patricia in Margaret's car. They came in together with the specific energy of women who have been talking in a car for twenty minutes and have not finished the conversation. Ruth looked at the corner and stopped mid-sentence.

That's it, she said.

Yes, Margaret said, with the patience of someone who has already had this moment and is allowing someone else to have theirs.

It's smaller than I expected.

We've been working on it, Margaret said.

It's still — there's something wrong with the air near it.

Yes, Margaret said. *There is. Have some of Ellen's food. It helps.*

This was not strictly true but it was the right thing to say and Ruth went to get food and by the time she came back with a plate she had recalibrated sufficiently to sit down without further commentary on the air quality.

Thomas arrived with Diane at six thirty wearing a jacket that fit him which Wren had apparently specified in advance because she met him at the door and said *good* in the tone of someone whose instructions have been followed correctly. Thomas looked at the room full of adults with the amber eyes and the specific expression of a seven year old boy who has been told he belongs somewhere and is not entirely convinced yet but is willing to be shown.

That many, he said to Wren quietly.

Yes, she said.

All like us.

All like us.

He considered this. *Huh,* he said. Which was the right response. He went and found a chair next to Margaret who looked at him the way retired nurses look at children — with the professional assessment that becomes something warmer once the assessment is complete — and said *you must be Thomas* and he said *yes ma'am* and she said *I hear you've been doing the rabbit for two years* and he said *yes ma'am* and she said *me too, different version, thirty years* and he looked at her with the amber eyes and said *did it work* and she said *well I'm here* and he thought about this and said *okay* and they sat together in the specific comfortable silence of two people who have established the only common ground they needed.

Vera arrived with her sister Joan. Joan walked in, felt the corner, looked at it, looked at Vera and said *that's genuinely unpleasant* and Vera said *yes* and Joan said *all right* and sat down. I liked Joan immediately.

Nora and Dale arrived at six fifty. Dale stood in the doorway and looked at the room for a moment with the expression of a man who has walked into a space and is reading its structural integrity. He looked at the corner. Looked at me. Nodded once.

Foundation's good, he said.

Which was not technically what he meant and was exactly what he meant simultaneously.

He found a chair at the edge of the room. Not in the circle. The position of a man who understands his role is perimeter not center and has placed himself accordingly without being asked.

Nora moved through the room checking on people with the specific efficiency of a woman who holds the ordinary world steady by making sure everyone has coffee and somewhere to sit and feels that arriving was the right decision. She did this without drawing attention to doing it which is the highest form of it.

By seven fifteen everyone was there.

Twenty three people in my living room.

I stood at the edge of it and looked at what had assembled and felt something I want to be honest about — which is that it did not feel sacred or ceremonial or like anything you would want to set music to. It felt like a living room full of people who had each separately been carrying something confusing and heavy and were experiencing the specific relief of finding out that other people had been carrying the same thing and were also confused and had also found it heavy.

It felt like the world's most unusual support group.

Which is essentially what it was.

I looked at the corner. Quieter than it had been. The field present in twenty three people simultaneously not because we had arranged it that way but because that's what twenty three people who have been doing this their whole lives do when they're in the same room. They do what they do. The way musicians in a room together will inevitably start playing without deciding to.

I'm going to say one thing, I said to the room. *And then Agnes is going to play something and then we're going to eat Ellen's food which I'm told is non-negotiable.*

Several people looked relieved that the one thing was one thing and not a speech.

You've been doing this your whole lives, I said. *In hospital rooms and hardware stores and music studios and classrooms and at the end of tables with the ones sitting alone. You did it without knowing what it was called and without knowing anyone else was doing it. You're not here because I found you. You're here because you were always here. I just — connected the dots.*

I sat down.

Rudy said *that's it.*

That's it, I said.

Hm, he said. Processing. *Could have been shorter.*

It was four sentences Rudy.

I'm a hardware man, he said. *Two is usually sufficient.*

Agnes, who had been sitting at the piano this entire time with the patience of someone who has been waiting for her cue for forty minutes, played the chord. Three notes. Full and resonant. Let it fill the room. Then lifted her hands and held the rest.

She did not announce this.

She did not say *and now I will play something meaningful.*

She just played it because there was a piano and she plays and the chord needed playing.

The rest held.

In the corner of the living room where the light didn't quite reach something shifted. Not dramatically. No sound, no movement, nothing the official process would accept as evidence. The way a shadow shifts when every light in the room comes on simultaneously — not driven out, not destroyed, simply without a gap to occupy. The cloth was complete. The thing that had been hunting the whole of us found the whole of us and the whole of us was not a target.

It was a ground.

Agnes lifted her hands from the keys. The silence after was different from the silence before. Fuller. More itself.

Wren stood in the center of the room and looked at the corner.

It's gone, she said.

Matter of fact. Not triumphant. Not relieved. Just true.

The corner was empty in the way a space is empty when it has been returned to itself. Just a corner where the light didn't quite reach. As corners are.

The room absorbed this.

Ruth said *oh.*

Margaret nodded once like a nurse confirming a diagnosis she had already suspected.

Thomas looked at his hands. Then at Wren. *That's it,* he said.

That's it, she said.

Rudy looked at the empty corner for a long moment.

Huh, he said.

Which remained exactly right.

Dale looked at the corner. Looked at me. The nod of a man who has checked a foundation and found it sound.

Ellen stood with her hand flat against her sternum and said *Mom* very quietly to no one in particular and everyone simultaneously and nobody said anything in response because nothing needed to be said in response.

Agnes played the chord again.

Nobody asked her to.

She just played it.

Then she looked at the food on the counter.

Is that Ellen's mother's potato salad recipe, she said.

Yes, Ellen said.

Good, Agnes said. *I've been thinking about it for an hour.*

She got up from the piano.

Got a plate.

And the room, which had just done something extraordinary, did what rooms full of people do after something extraordinary — it became ordinary again. People got food. People found each other and talked. Margaret and Thomas sat together and Margaret told him about a patient she'd had in 1987 who she now understood in a completely different way and Thomas listened with the amber eyes and the focused attention of a seven year old boy who is being treated as someone worth talking to seriously and has decided to be exactly that.

Rudy found Vera and they stood by the window and compared notes on what the cold spot had felt like in the hardware store versus at the town meeting with the specific practical efficiency of two people who have been through the same thing and are comparing field reports.

Nora and Dale stood together in the kitchen doorway. Dale had his arm around her. She had her head on his shoulder. The specific posture of two people who have been through something together and are standing in the particular afterwards of it.

Joan cornered me by the piano.

My sister said you've been dealing with this for sixty two years, she said.

Yes.

And it took you sixty two years to find everyone, she said.

Yes.

That's terrible logistics, she said.

Yes, I agreed. *It is.*

We should fix that, she said.

Yes, I said. *That's the next problem.*

She nodded with the practical expression of a woman who has identified a systems problem and intends to address it.

I liked Joan very much.

Wren appeared at my elbow.

Leaned against my arm.

Good, she said.

Yes, I said.

The food is good too, she said.

Yes.

I'm going to get some.

You should.

She went to get food with the unhurried purposefulness of a six year old who has done what she came to do and is now approaching the remainder of the evening with the same complete presence she brings to everything.

I stood at the edge of the room.

Looked at twenty three people eating Ellen's food and drinking coffee and talking with the specific quality of people who have been carrying something alone and have just put it down in the same place at the same time and are now standing in the particular lightness of shared weight.

Not a revival.

Not a ceremony.

Just people.

In a living room.

In Bellaire Michigan.

On a Wednesday night in October.

Finding each other.

The weavers.

The cloth whole.

Chapter 33

Chapter Thirty Two — The Field Complete

Rudy arrived first.

This did not surprise me. He pulled up at five forty five in the truck he had driven to Petoskey and back and got out with the specific restored quality of a man who has been away from something draining long enough to remember what full feels like. He had color back. The eight pounds were not back but the steadiness in his eyes was and that mattered more.

He shook my hand at the door.

You look better, I said.

Danny's casserole, he said. *Four days of it. A man can only be so grateful before gratitude curdles into something else.*

He came in. Looked at the circle of chairs I had assembled from every room in the house including two folding ones from the garage that I had forgotten I owned and which had opinions about their hinges.

Cozy, he said.

Twenty two people, I said.

In this room.

Yes.

He looked at the corner. *Still there.*

Quieter, I said.

Hm, he said. The specific hm of a hardware man who has been told a structural problem is improving and is reserving judgment until he sees it himself. He looked at it for a moment. Then he went to find Ellen and the food because Rudy's relationship with problems has always involved eating something first and thinking second and this has served him adequately across seventy years.

They arrived over the next hour with the specific staggered quality of people who have been told seven o'clock and have interpreted this differently according to their personalities. Agnes arrived at six fifteen because Agnes is constitutionally early. She sat at the piano without asking — she never asks, it's a piano, she plays — and ran through something quiet that I didn't recognize and then stopped and looked at the corner.

Smaller, she said.

Yes.

Good, she said. And kept playing.

Margaret arrived with Ruth and Patricia in Margaret's car. They came in together with the specific energy of women who have been talking in a car for twenty minutes and have not finished the conversation. Ruth looked at the corner and stopped mid-sentence.

That's it, she said.

Yes, Margaret said, with the patience of someone who has already had this moment and is allowing someone else to have theirs.

It's smaller than I expected.

We've been working on it, Margaret said.

It's still — there's something wrong with the air near it.

Yes, Margaret said. *There is. Have some of Ellen's food. It helps.*

This was not strictly true but it was the right thing to say and Ruth went to get food and by the time she came back with a plate she had recalibrated sufficiently to sit down without further commentary on the air quality.

Thomas arrived with Diane at six thirty wearing a jacket that fit him which Wren had apparently specified in advance because she met him at the door and said *good* in the tone of someone whose instructions have been followed correctly. Thomas looked at the room full of adults with the amber eyes and the specific expression of a seven year old boy who has been told he belongs somewhere and is not entirely convinced yet but is willing to be shown.

That many, he said to Wren quietly.

Yes, she said.

All like us.

All like us.

He considered this. *Huh,* he said. Which was the right response. He went and found a chair next to Margaret who looked at him the way retired nurses look at children — with the professional assessment that becomes something warmer once the assessment is complete — and said *you must be Thomas* and he said *yes ma'am* and she said *I hear you've been doing the rabbit for two years* and he said *yes ma'am* and she said *me too, different version, thirty years* and he looked at her with the amber eyes and said *did it work* and she said *well I'm here* and he thought about this and said *okay* and they sat together in the specific comfortable silence of two people who have established the only common ground they needed.

Vera arrived with her sister Joan. Joan walked in, felt the corner, looked at it, looked at Vera and said *that's genuinely unpleasant* and Vera said *yes* and Joan said *all right* and sat down. I liked Joan immediately.

Nora and Dale arrived at six fifty. Dale stood in the doorway and looked at the room for a moment with the expression of a man who has walked into a space and is reading its structural integrity. He looked at the corner. Looked at me. Nodded once.

Foundation's good, he said.

Which was not technically what he meant and was exactly what he meant simultaneously.

He found a chair at the edge of the room. Not in the circle. The position of a man who understands his role is perimeter not center and has placed himself accordingly without being asked.

Nora moved through the room checking on people with the specific efficiency of a woman who holds the ordinary world steady by making sure everyone has coffee and somewhere to sit and feels that arriving was the right decision. She did this without drawing attention to doing it which is the highest form of it.

By seven fifteen everyone was there.

Twenty three people in my living room.

I stood at the edge of it and looked at what had assembled and felt something I want to be honest about — which is that it did not feel sacred or ceremonial or like anything you would want to set music to. It felt like a living room full of people who had each separately been carrying something confusing and heavy and were experiencing the specific relief of finding out that other people had been carrying the same thing and were also confused and had also found it heavy.

It felt like the world's most unusual support group.

Which is essentially what it was.

I looked at the corner. Quieter than it had been. The field present in twenty three people simultaneously not because we had arranged it that way but because that's what twenty three people who have been doing this their whole lives do when they're in the same room. They do what they do. The way musicians in a room together will inevitably start playing without deciding to.

I'm going to say one thing, I said to the room. *And then Agnes is going to play something and then we're going to eat Ellen's food which I'm told is non-negotiable.*

Several people looked relieved that the one thing was one thing and not a speech.

You've been doing this your whole lives, I said. *In hospital rooms and hardware stores and music studios and classrooms and at the end of tables with the ones sitting alone. You did it without knowing what it was called and without knowing anyone else was doing it. You're not here because I found you. You're here because you were always here. I just — connected the dots.*

I sat down.

Rudy said *that's it.*

That's it, I said.

Hm, he said. Processing. *Could have been shorter.*

It was four sentences Rudy.

I'm a hardware man, he said. *Two is usually sufficient.*

Agnes, who had been sitting at the piano this entire time with the patience of someone who has been waiting for her cue for forty minutes, played the chord. Three notes. Full and resonant. Let it fill the room. Then lifted her hands and held the rest.

She did not announce this.

She did not say *and now I will play something meaningful.*

She just played it because there was a piano and she plays and the chord needed playing.

The rest held.

In the corner of the living room where the light didn't quite reach something shifted. Not dramatically. No sound, no movement, nothing the official process would accept as evidence. The way a shadow shifts when every light in the room comes on simultaneously — not driven out, not destroyed, simply without a gap to occupy. The cloth was complete. The thing that had been hunting the whole of us found the whole of us and the whole of us was not a target.

It was a ground.

Agnes lifted her hands from the keys. The silence after was different from the silence before. Fuller. More itself.

Wren stood in the center of the room and looked at the corner.

It's gone, she said.

Matter of fact. Not triumphant. Not relieved. Just true.

The corner was empty in the way a space is empty when it has been returned to itself. Just a corner where the light didn't quite reach. As corners are.

The room absorbed this.

Ruth said *oh.*

Margaret nodded once like a nurse confirming a diagnosis she had already suspected.

Thomas looked at his hands. Then at Wren. *That's it,* he said.

That's it, she said.

Rudy looked at the empty corner for a long moment.

Huh, he said.

Which remained exactly right.

Dale looked at the corner. Looked at me. The nod of a man who has checked a foundation and found it sound.

Ellen stood with her hand flat against her sternum and said *Mom* very quietly to no one in particular and everyone simultaneously and nobody said anything in response because nothing needed to be said in response.

Agnes played the chord again.

Nobody asked her to.

She just played it.

Then she looked at the food on the counter.

Is that Ellen's mother's potato salad recipe, she said.

Yes, Ellen said.

Good, Agnes said. *I've been thinking about it for an hour.*

She got up from the piano.

Got a plate.

And the room, which had just done something extraordinary, did what rooms full of people do after something extraordinary — it became ordinary again. People got food. People found each other and talked. Margaret and Thomas sat together and Margaret told him about a patient she'd had in 1987 who she now understood in a completely different way and Thomas listened with the amber eyes and the focused attention of a seven year old boy who is being treated as someone worth talking to seriously and has decided to be exactly that.

Rudy found Vera and they stood by the window and compared notes on what the cold spot had felt like in the hardware store versus at the town meeting with the specific practical efficiency of two people who have been through the same thing and are comparing field reports.

Nora and Dale stood together in the kitchen doorway. Dale had his arm around her. She had her head on his shoulder. The specific posture of two people who have been through something together and are standing in the particular afterwards of it.

Joan cornered me by the piano.

My sister said you've been dealing with this for sixty two years, she said.

Yes.

And it took you sixty two years to find everyone, she said.

Yes.

That's terrible logistics, she said.

Yes, I agreed. *It is.*

We should fix that, she said.

Yes, I said. *That's the next problem.*

She nodded with the practical expression of a woman who has identified a systems problem and intends to address it.

I liked Joan very much.

Wren appeared at my elbow.

Leaned against my arm.

Good, she said.

Yes, I said.

The food is good too, she said.

Yes.

I'm going to get some.

You should.

She went to get food with the unhurried purposefulness of a six year old who has done what she came to do and is now approaching the remainder of the evening with the same complete presence she brings to everything.

I stood at the edge of the room.

Looked at twenty three people eating Ellen's food and drinking coffee and talking with the specific quality of people who have been carrying something alone and have just put it down in the same place at the same time and are now standing in the particular lightness of shared weight.

Not a revival.

Not a ceremony.

Just people.

In a living room.

In Bellaire Michigan.

On a Wednesday night in October.

Finding each other.

The weavers.

The cloth whole.

Chapter 34

THE QUIET ONES

Chapter Thirty Four — What Comes Next

Thursday morning.

Five forty five.

The specific grey light of a northern Michigan October morning that has not yet decided what it intends to be and is holding its options open above the lake while the world beneath it waits.

I was at the desk.

Coffee.

Notebook open to the man's section.

The last pages of it.

I had been sitting here since five with the pen in my hand and nothing written because what needed writing was larger than the available sentences and I was waiting for the sentences to arrive at the size of the thing rather than reducing the thing to the size of available sentences.

This is the fundamental problem of writing.

It is also the fundamental problem of living but writing makes it visible.

I sat with the coffee and the grey light and the notebook and waited.

The house was quiet in the specific way it is quiet after something has happened in it. Not the quiet of a house that has never held anything — the quiet of a house that has held something large and is settling around the space the large thing has vacated. The way a room feels after a long party has ended and the guests have gone and the furniture is back in its usual configuration but the air remembers.

The corner of the living room was just a corner.

I had checked it at five when I came to the desk.

Just a corner.

The cold without temperature — gone.

The pressing absence — gone.

The specific wrongness of air that has been occupied by something it was not supposed to hold — gone.

Just plaster and paint and the ordinary darkness of a corner where the light doesn't quite reach.

As corners are.

I had stood in front of it for a moment.

Not to confirm.

Wren had confirmed it last night and Wren's confirmation was sufficient.

I had stood there because after three weeks of looking at the corner with the specific attention of a man who knows what is in it I wanted to look at it with the specific attention of a man who knows what isn't.

Just a corner.

I went back to the desk.

Here is what I wrote when the sentences finally arrived at the right size.

Thursday. Early.

The thing is gone. The corner is a corner. The field held and the cloth was whole and Agnes played the chord and the rest was right and there was no room for the wrong note and the thing that had been hunting the whole of us found the whole of us and the whole of us was not a target.

This is true.

Here is what is also true.

The sewage still rises.

The conditions that fed the thing have not changed because we spent a Wednesday night in a living room in Bellaire Michigan being completely ourselves simultaneously. The cruelty is still ambient. The contempt is still comfortable dinner conversation in certain houses. The gaps still form in people who have not found the field and the gaps are what the thing fed on and the gaps are still there.

Gerald is still gone.

Carol Demming is still gone.

Roy Higgins who I barely knew is still gone.

Three people who became fully themselves and had no field around them when the opening came.

And there are more.

Not in Bellaire necessarily. But somewhere. The something that occupied my corner was one instance of a thing that exists wherever the conditions allow it. Wherever the gaps are deep enough and the cruelty is ambient enough and the people who see clearly are isolated enough and alone enough and being less enough that the absence can find purchase.

Which is — as Wren observed with the flat certainty of a six year old stating the obvious — very common.

Twenty three people in a living room in Bellaire Michigan.

That is not enough.

Joan said it last night. Terrible logistics. We should fix that.

She said it as a practical observation because Joan is a practical woman and she was right on both counts. The logistics have been terrible. One person at a time. One kitchen at a time. Three weeks to find twenty three people in a town of two thousand.

At that rate the gaps will always be faster.

The thing — or the next thing, the one already forming somewhere else in the lowest ground of the ambient cruelty — will always be faster.

Unless the field learns to spread the way the thing spreads.

The thing spreads by finding the gaps.

The field spreads by finding the people.

The ones who are doing it accidentally in hospital rooms and music studios and dark parking lots and hardware stores. The ones who have been the rabbit for too long and are paying the cost of less without knowing there is another option. The ones who are opening up — becoming more themselves — without the field in place to make the opening survivable.

Twenty three people who know.

Each of them knows others who don't.

Each of those others knows others.

The logistics can be fixed.

Not by me alone.

That was always the problem.

One man in a corn field learning it alone.

One man in a basement with a flashlight.

One man at a desk sending people to Petoskey and Traverse City one at a time.

The field does not grow by staying still.

It grows by spreading.

And it has twenty three people now who know what it is and know how to teach it and know how to find the ones who need it.

Twenty three people who are no longer alone.

Who know they were never alone.

Who have the name for what they have always been.

That is where it starts.

Not where it ends.

I put the pen down.

Read what I had written.

It was right.

Not careful.

Right.

The distinction being everything.

I looked at the notebook.

At the boy's section and the man's section and the sixty two years between them.

The boy's record had ended in November 1963 with *I am not going to write in here anymore. I am going to put this somewhere and not look at it. Right now I am nine and I do not understand it and I want to go play.*

The man's record had begun three weeks ago with *I know you're there* and had filled the remaining pages with the specific accumulation of three weeks of understanding arriving faster than expected and costing more than anticipated and producing something he had not known he was building until it was built.

The notebook was nearly full.

The last page had room for perhaps one more entry.

I thought about what that entry should be.

Thought about the boy in the corn field.

About the man at the desk.

About the sixty two years between them and what those years had produced and what they had cost and whether the cost had been the right cost for the thing produced.

I thought about what Wren had said.

Three weeks of everything is more than thirty years of less.

I thought about the field.

About twenty three people finding each other.

About the cloth whole for the first time.

About Joan's terrible logistics and what fixing them looked like.

About Thomas in his good jacket.

About Ellen carrying her mother's thread forward.

About Margaret who had been doing it in hospital rooms for thirty years without knowing it had a name.

About Vera practicing four times a day in Traverse City.

About Rudy returning borrowed tools.

About Agnes and the card and the forty one years of held silence.

About Nora driving four minutes in the dark.

About Dale checking the foundation and finding it sound.

About Briggs and the other line and Danny's cherry pie.

About all of it.

The small thing that had arrived at exactly the right moment.

Which was Wren.

Who had appeared at my elbow one October morning asking about Missy.

And had said okay.

And had meant it completely.

I picked up the pen.

Turned to the last page of the notebook.

Wrote the final entry in the man's section.

The notebook is full. The boy filled the first part with what he knew at nine and I have filled the rest with what the man knows at seventy one and between the two of them the sixty two years have been adequately documented.

But the documentation was never the point.

The point was always the field.

And the field does not live in a notebook.

It lives in twenty three people who know what they are and are no longer alone in knowing it.

It lives in the ones they will find tomorrow and next week and next month.

It lives in Thomas in his good jacket and Ellen carrying her mother's thread and Margaret who has been doing it for thirty years.

It lives in Joan who identified the logistics problem and intends to fix it.

It lives in Wren.

Who has never been less.

Who said okay and meant it completely.

Who is six years old and is the most complete thing I have ever been in the same room with.

The notebook is full.

The field is not.

The field is just beginning.

I closed the notebook.

Put the pen down.

Sat at the desk in the grey Thursday morning light with the coffee and the closed notebook and the corner that was just a corner and the lake doing what it did and the specific quality of a morning that has somewhere to be and knows the way.

The door to the study opened.

Small feet.

You're up early, Wren said.

So are you.

I felt you thinking, she said. *From the couch.*

I was writing, I said.

Same thing with you, she said.

She came to the desk.

Looked at the closed notebook.

Done, she said. Not a question.

The notebook is full, I said.

She looked at it for a moment.

What comes next, she said.

That, I said. *Is what I've been sitting here figuring out.*

She pulled the chair close and sat in it with her hands in her lap and her dark eyes and her hair still in its sleeping configuration and the blanket she had carried from the couch still around her shoulders because it was Thursday morning and she was six and some things are true simultaneously.

Tell me, she said.

So I told her.

About Joan's logistics observation. About the twenty three and the ones beyond the twenty three. About the field spreading the way the thing spread but in the opposite direction — finding the people instead of the gaps, filling instead of feeding, completing instead of draining.

About the ones who were opening up right now somewhere in the world without the field in place.

About the ones who had been less for too long and were paying the cost without knowing there was another option.

About the work.

She listened the way she listened to everything — completely, without the defensive filtering of someone who needs it to fit a predetermined shape, with the specific open quality of a child who has not yet learned that some things are too large to receive.

When I finished she was quiet for a moment.

It's not over, she said.

No, I said. *It's not over.*

It's different, she said.

Yes.

Before we were finding the field, she said. *Now we are the field finding others.*

Yes, I said. *That's exactly right.*

She sat with this.

The sitting of a six year old who has understood something large and is checking it for weight and finding it fits.

Grandpa, she said.

Yes.

The next notebook, she said. *You need one.*

I looked at the closed notebook on the desk.

The boy's section and the man's section and sixty two years and the last page written.

Full.

Yes, I said. *I do.*

I know where Mom keeps them, she said. *The spiral bound ones from the kitchen drawer.*

The practical ones, I said.

Yes, she said. *Is that okay.*

I thought about the speckled black and white notebook. The nineteen cent notebook from 1962 that had cost approximately nothing and had been carried in my jacket for three weeks and had held sixty two years of what a boy knew and what the man learned and the distance between them.

I thought about a spiral bound notebook from Nora's kitchen drawer.

Practical.

Unpretentious.

The kind that doesn't know it's important until after the fact.

Yes, I said. *That's exactly okay.*

She stood up.

Dropped the blanket on the chair.

Went to get the notebook.

I sat at the desk and watched the grey Thursday morning light coming off the lake and thought about what came next with the specific quality of a man who has stopped being less and knows what he is now and knows what the work is and is not afraid of the work.

Not because the work is small.

Because he is not alone in it.

Wren came back.

Handed me the notebook.

Spiral bound. Blue cover. The kind that costs approximately nothing and sits in kitchen drawers with batteries and good scissors and the ordinary equipment of a life.

There, she said.

I opened it to the first page.

Clean.

Empty.

Waiting.

The way first pages wait.

I picked up the pen.

Wrote the date.

Looked at the clean page.

At the pen in my hand.

At Wren sitting in the chair across from me with her hands in her lap and her dark eyes and her six years of being exactly what she was.

The field in its purest form.

Waiting.

The way first pages wait.

Okay, I said.

The same word she had used.

The same completeness inside it.

I began

Chapter 35

THE QUIET ONES

Chapter Thirty Five — The Field In Motion

Thomas had not been asked to do anything.

This is the part I want to be clear about because it matters to the story and because it says something about Thomas specifically that deserves to be said specifically.

Nobody had given Thomas an assignment. Nobody had told him to find anyone. Nobody had sat him down and explained that the field grows by spreading and that spreading requires people willing to do the finding. He was seven years old and had been in my basement exactly once for two hours on a Saturday morning and had attended one Wednesday evening gathering in a living room full of adults where he had eaten Ellen's food and talked to Margaret about hospital rooms and worn his good jacket because Wren told him to.

That was the full extent of his formal involvement.

And yet.

Thursday afternoon. Three fifteen. I pulled up in front of the school and Wren got in the car with her backpack and her homework and the specific expression she wears when she has information she has been waiting to deliver since approximately lunch.

Thomas found someone, she said before her door was fully closed.

Tell me, I said.

His name is Eddie, she said. *He's eight. Third grade. He sits at the back of Mrs. Kowalski's class and doesn't talk and the other kids think he's weird and he has been doing the rabbit for three years which means he started at five which is —*

Earlier than Thomas, I said.

Earlier than anyone, she said. *Even me.*

I pulled away from the curb.

How did Thomas find him, I said.

The same way I found Thomas, she said. *He sat with him at lunch. At the end of the table by the window. For three days. Without asking anything or explaining anything. Just sat there and didn't go away.*

I drove.

Thought about this.

About a seven year old boy who had arrived on my porch three weeks ago in a too-large jacket with the rabbit in his amber eyes and the fraction of himself that had knocked being most of himself by the time he left.

Who had gone back to school the following Monday with his spine slightly more vertical and his blue jacket that fit correctly and the beginning of the field in him.

And had apparently spent the intervening weeks doing exactly what Wren had done for him.

Sitting at the end of the table by the window.

Not going away.

On day three, Wren said, *Eddie asked Thomas why he kept sitting there.*

What did Thomas say, I said.

He said because you're like me, she said. *And I know someone who can help.*

I stopped at the light on Main.

Looked at it.

He said that, I said.

Yes, she said. *Eddie asked what kind of help and Thomas said the kind where you don't have to be less anymore.*

The light changed.

I did not go through it immediately.

The car behind me waited with the specific patience of a car in Bellaire Michigan where people understand that sometimes a man needs an extra second at a green light and this is not a crisis.

Grandpa, Wren said.

Yes, I said.

Green, she said.

I know, I said.

I drove.

There's a second one, Wren said. *A girl named Lily. She's in second grade. She found Thomas herself. She walked up to him at recess and said I heard you talking to Eddie and I think you're talking about me too.*

How old, I said.

Seven, Wren said. *She's been feeling something at the tree line behind the school for a month. The same tree line as Thomas. She thinks they're feeling the same thing.*

Are they, I said.

Wren was quiet for a moment. The frequency check.

Yes, she said. *It's smaller than the one in your corner was. But it's there. Near the big oak.*

The same one Thomas felt, I said.

Yes.

I drove through Bellaire in the Thursday afternoon thinking about the tree line behind the elementary school. About the big oak on the left side. About a nine year old boy in 1963 standing at the edge of a corn field feeling something at a different tree line in a different October and learning the rabbit alone because there was no one to show him anything else.

About three children at an elementary school in Bellaire Michigan finding each other the way children find each other when they are paying attention — without the adult apparatus of organization and outreach and logistics, simply by sitting at the end of the table by the window and not going away.

They want to come to the basement on Saturday, Wren said.

Yes, I said. *Of course they do.*

Is that okay, she said.

Wren, I said. *When has it not been okay.*

She considered this.

Never, she said.

No, I said. *Never.*

The field in motion looked nothing like I had imagined it would look.

I had been thinking about Joan's logistics observation since Wednesday night. About systems and methods and the practical problem of finding people before the thing found them. I had been thinking about it with the specific analytical attention of a man who has written fourteen novels and understands that structure serves the story and the story needs to be told efficiently or it doesn't get told at all.

I had been thinking about it like a writer.

The field was not moving like a writer.

It was moving like a field.

Which is to say — in all directions simultaneously, at its own pace, through the specific organic channels that fields use rather than the organized channels that writers imagine.

Ellen had found four more from her mother's book club connections. Not by going to them with a presentation or an explanation. By being Ellen — by talking to people the way her mother had talked to people, honestly and directly and without the managed distance of someone who is protecting themselves from the conversation. People had felt the quality of her attention and had said things they hadn't planned to say and Ellen had listened with the gap between what was said and what was meant clearly audible to her and had followed the thread.

Four more people who were opening up without the field in place.

Four more conversations in four more kitchens.

Four more people who now knew the name for what they had always been.

Margaret had called three former patients. Not the ones who had been ill — the ones who had been drained. The ones whose charts had said one thing and whose condition had said another. The ones she had filed in the unexplained folder thirty years ago and had been carrying since.

She had called them with the specific directness of a retired nurse who has decided that thirty years is long enough to carry something alone.

All three had answered.

All three had said some version of the same thing.

I knew someone would call eventually.

Agnes had identified three piano students whose parents she had been watching for years. Not the students — the parents. The ones who dropped their children off and sat in the waiting area with the specific quality of people who were listening to more than the piano. Who went still in a particular way when Agnes played. Who lingered after lessons longer than the logistics required.

She had invited them in.

Shown them the card.

Listen to what is actually there.

And then shown them what was actually there.

Three more.

Vera was running what she called a quiet correspondence from Traverse City — not emails, actual letters, the kind that arrive in envelopes and require a person to sit down and read them. She had found through her sister's network six people in the Traverse City area who were feeling something they couldn't name and were attributing it to anxiety or seasonal depression or the general ambient wrongness of the current age.

She wrote them letters.

Clear. Specific. Without the managed distance of someone protecting herself from the conversation.

The letters were working.

Rudy had done something that had not been discussed or planned or organized in any way that I was aware of. He had put a small card on the counter of the hardware store beside the register. The card said nothing about the field or the rabbit or the frequency or anything that would have made sense to someone who didn't know. It said simply:

Some things are real that don't have official names. If you've been feeling something you can't explain, talk to Rudy.

He had told me about this on Friday when I came in for the deck screws I still didn't need.

Is that wise, I said.

Three people asked me about it this morning, he said. *Two of them were relieved someone had put it in writing.*

And the third, I said.

Bought a box of nails and left, he said. *Which is fine. Not everyone is ready.*

The card doesn't say enough to explain anything, I said.

It says enough to start a conversation, he said. *The conversation explains everything. That's always been how it works.*

He was right.

It had always been how it worked.

One conversation.

One kitchen.

One person at a time.

The field does not spread by announcement.

It spreads by presence.

By the specific quality of people who are completely themselves in a room and make it possible for others to be completely themselves in response.

The way a tuning fork held near another tuning fork causes the second one to resonate.

Not by instruction.

By proximity.

By the simple fact of being fully what you are near someone who has forgotten they are allowed to be fully what they are.

Rudy's card was a tuning fork.

Ellen's conversations were tuning forks.

Margaret's letters to former patients were tuning forks.

Agnes and the card on the wall were tuning forks.

Thomas sitting at the end of the table by the window for three days not going away was the purest tuning fork of all.

Seven years old.

No instruction.

No assignment.

Just the simple understanding that the field spreads by finding the people and you find the people by being present and you be present by showing up and not going away.

He had learned this from Wren.

Who had learned it from the fact of being what she was.

Who had never learned to be anything else.

The field in motion.

Nora called on Friday morning.

Cooper, she said.

Yes, I said.

He came to me last night, she said. *About the thing he saw outside his window.*

Yes.

He described it, she said. *Accurately. In the specific way he describes things when he's been sitting with them for a while and has decided they are real enough to say out loud.*

What did you tell him, I said.

I told him it was real, she said. *And I told him what it was. The simplified version. The eleven year old version.* She paused. *He asked if Wren knew.*

What did you say.

I said Wren has known since before she could explain it, she said. *He was quiet for a while. Then he said — and this is exact — he said does she need help.*

I sat at the desk with the new notebook open.

What did you say, I said.

I said yes, Nora said. *She always needs help. She just doesn't always say so.*

What did he say.

He said okay, she said. *And went to bed.*

I sat with this.

The specific sitting of a man receiving information about his grandson who has been the ordinary one, the soccer and video games one, the eleven year old who had been given the one job of being able to make a phone call at the right moment and had accepted it with the gravity of someone told the truth for the first time.

Nora, I said.

I know, she said. *He's not like Wren.*

No, I said.

But he's not not like her either, she said. *He's something in between. He sees enough to know something is there. He doesn't see it the way she does. But he sees it.*

The ordinary world and the other one, I said. *Both.*

Like Dale, she said.

I thought about Dale.

Who checked foundations.

Who held the ordinary world steady.

Who had gone to the basement and looked at the corner and asked what do you need.

Who had driven six people to seven kitchens on a Sunday morning without requiring the thing to fit his previous understanding of what things could be.

Yes, I said. *Like Dale.*

That's not nothing, she said.

No, I said. *That's everything. The field needs the Dales and the Coopers as much as it needs the Wrens and the Thomases. It needs the people who hold the ordinary world steady while the others do what the others do.*

I'll tell him that, she said.

Tell him from me, I said.

He'll be embarrassed, she said.

Yes, I said. *Tell him anyway.*

She hung up.

I picked up the pen.

Wrote in the new notebook.

Friday. The field is moving faster than I can track it and this is correct. The field should not be trackable by one person. It should be larger than any one person's ability to account for it. It should be doing things I don't know about. It should be finding people I haven't met yet. It should be spreading in directions I haven't anticipated through channels I haven't identified.

This is not a loss of control.

This is what a field looks like when it is actually a field and not a project.

A project has a manager.

A field has ground.

I am the ground.

Twenty three people are the ground.

Eddie and Lily who haven't been to the basement yet are the ground.

Cooper who sees enough to know something is there and said okay I'll help is the ground.

Rudy's card on the counter of the hardware store is the ground.

Ellen's conversations and Margaret's letters and Agnes's parents and Vera's correspondence are the ground.

The ground is not managed.

The ground is simply itself.

Completely.

Without reduction.

And things grow in it.

That is what ground does.

I put the pen down.

Looked out the window at the October street.

At Gerald's house which was listed for sale now with a sign that had gone up Tuesday and which I drove past every day without stopping and thought about every day without resolution and would think about for a long time probably and that was the right and appropriate response to a good man who returned borrowed tools without being asked and was gone.

At the Millers' mailbox.

At the ordinary Thursday street.

At Bellaire going about its business in the specific way of small northern Michigan towns in late October — pulling inward, preparing, the particular industry of a place that knows winter is not a metaphor and gets ready accordingly.

The town looked the same.

It was not the same.

Twenty three people knew something in it that they hadn't known a month ago.

And they were telling others.

And the others were telling others.

And somewhere in the school three blocks away a seven year old boy in a blue jacket that fit correctly was sitting at the end of the table by the window at lunch not going away from an eight year old boy named Eddie who had been doing the rabbit since he was five.

The field in motion.

Not organized.

Not managed.

Not announced.

Simply spreading the way fields spread.

By being ground.

By being so thoroughly itself that things grew in it without being told to.

The way they always had.

The way they always would.

Saturday morning.

Eddie and Lily arrived at nine o'clock with Thomas.

Thomas had appointed himself the person who brought them which nobody had asked him to do and which was exactly right. He arrived at the front door with one child on each side and the specific expression of a boy who has done something he is proud of and is managing the pride with the restraint of someone who understands that the pride is not the point.

Eddie was eight. Small. Dark haired. The rabbit in his eyes so established that it had become structural — not something he was doing but something he had become, the way a habit becomes a posture becomes a shape. Three years of being less. Since he was five. Since something had happened that nobody had explained to him and he had explained to himself with the only available tool which was the rabbit.

He stood on my porch and looked at me with the specific assessment of a child who has learned to read adults quickly and accurately because quick accurate reading of adults has been a survival requirement.

He found whatever he was looking for.

You're Harlan, he said.

Yes, I said.

Thomas said you understand things, he said.

Some things, I said. *Come in.*

Lily was seven. Red haired. Freckled in the specific October freckled way of children whose summer freckles are fading but haven't gone yet. She had the specific quality of a child who has decided to be here and is fully committed to the decision. Not tentative. Not the fraction of Thomas on the first morning. The whole of herself. Present. Already.

She walked in past me and looked at the living room and looked at the corner and looked at Wren who had appeared from the kitchen and said:

You're the one who sees it completely.

Yes, Wren said.

Me too, Lily said.

Yes, Wren said. *I know.*

How, Lily said.

I could feel it from the school, Wren said. *When you were looking at the tree line.*

Lily stood in my living room and processed this.

Huh, she said.

Which was exactly right.

Which was always exactly right.

I looked at Thomas standing in my entryway with Eddie and the specific quiet pride of a seven year old boy who has done something that mattered and knows it and is not going to make a production of it.

Good jacket, I said.

He looked down at it.

I always wear it now, he said.

Yes, I said. *I can see that.*

We went to the basement.

The five of us.

An old man and four children descending the stairs into the specific quiet of a basement on a Saturday morning in October.

The flashlight still on the shelf.

The overhead bulb still burned out.

I had still not replaced it.

I was starting to think I would not replace it.

Some things earn their permanence.

We sat on the floor with our backs against the wall and the flashlight circle between us and the October light coming through the small window above the washing machine.

I looked at the four children.

Thomas in his good jacket.

Eddie with the rabbit structural in his eyes.

Lily who was already the field without knowing it had a name.

Wren who was always the field who had always been the field who had never been anything else.

All right, I said.

Four children looked at me.

I'm going to tell you something first, I said. *Before anything else.*

Okay, said Thomas.

Okay, said Eddie. Quieter. The okay of a child who has been less for three years and is not yet certain that okay is a thing he is allowed to say with full commitment.

Okay, said Lily.

Wren said nothing because she already knew what I was going to say and did not need to perform anticipation.

You are not strange, I said. *You are not broken. You are not too much or too little or wrong in any of the ways that rooms have probably suggested you are wrong.* I paused. *You are built for a frequency that most people don't know exists. That is not a malfunction. That is a specific kind of equipment that the world needs and has always needed and has never been good at recognizing or thanking.*

Eddie looked at his hands.

The specific looking-at-hands of a child receiving something he has needed for a long time and is not yet certain he is allowed to keep.

You've been alone with it, I said. *All of you. That's over now.*

I looked at each of them.

Thomas.

Eddie.

Lily.

Wren.

That's over now, I said again.

Because some things need to be said twice.

Because some things need to be heard twice before the body believes what the ears have received.

Eddie looked up.

The rabbit in the amber eyes.

And beside the rabbit — present, small, new, the way new things are present when they first arrive — something else.

The beginning of the field.

Same as Thomas had had it on the first morning.

The fraction that had decided to be here.

Okay, Eddie said.

This time with the full commitment of a child who has decided that okay is something he is allowed to say.

Which was everything.

Which was always everything.

I opened the new notebook.

The practical blue spiral bound one from Nora's kitchen drawer.

Right, I said. *Let's start.*

Outside the October morning continued its business.

Inside a basement in Bellaire Michigan four children sat with their backs against the wall in the flashlight circle on a Saturday morning.

The field finding itself.

One child at a time.

The weavers.

Learning the loom.

Chapter 36

THE QUIET ONES

Chapter Thirty Six — Marquette

The email arrived on a Tuesday morning at seven twelve.

I know the time because I had just opened the laptop to look at chapter thirteen of the new novel — not the one I had been writing when Gerald died, a different one, the one that had started arriving in the new notebook three weeks ago and had moved to the screen when the notebook pages ran out — and the email notification appeared in the corner of the screen with the specific intrusion of something that has decided your attention belongs to it regardless of what your attention was already doing.

I almost ignored it.

I ignore most emails on Tuesday mornings because Tuesday mornings are for writing and writing requires the specific quality of attention that email is specifically designed to fragment and I have been protecting Tuesday mornings from email for twenty years with the specific stubbornness of a man who has learned that the work does not negotiate and has decided to honor that.

But the subject line.

Rudy's card — I need to talk to someone.

I opened it.

Her name was Helen.

She lived in Marquette. Upper Peninsula. Three hundred miles from Bellaire on the other side of the bridge — a distance that in northern Michigan terms is not just geographic but cultural, the specific separateness of a place that has been shaped by its isolation into something distinct from the lower peninsula in ways that are hard to articulate and immediately felt by anyone who has spent time in both.

She had found Rudy's card description on a local community forum where someone had posted about it with the specific bemused quality of a person sharing something unusual they had encountered — not believing it exactly, not dismissing it exactly, posting it in the way people post things that don't fit their framework but are too specific to ignore.

Helen had read it at two in the morning.

She did not explain what she had been doing on a community forum at two in the morning but I understood without explanation because two in the morning is when people look for things they cannot look for in daylight — the questions too strange for daytime, the searches too specific for a world that is watching.

She had been feeling something for six weeks.

Not the cold spot. Not the corner. Something different in character from what had been in my living room — more diffuse, she said, more ambient, less located in a specific place and more present in the general quality of her days. A drain. A fatigue that sleep did not fix. The specific exhaustion of a battery that charges to eighty percent and stops.

She had been to her doctor.

Normal.

She had had her thyroid checked because her mother had thyroid problems and that had seemed like the responsible thing to rule out.

Normal.

She had tried going to bed earlier and drinking less coffee and taking the vitamins the internet recommended and all of it had produced exactly the improvement that placebos produce when the problem is not physical which is a brief and unconvincing improvement followed by a return to the original condition.

And then.

Her children.

She had two. A boy named Marcus who was nine and a girl named Sara who was six.

Marcus had told her three weeks ago that there was something wrong with the light in the corner of his bedroom. Not the light fixture — the quality of the light itself. The way it behaved. He was nine and scientific minded and had checked the bulb and the socket and the angle of the window and had concluded with the frustrated precision of a child whose investigative tools have failed him that the problem was not with any of the things he could measure.

Sara had said nothing about it.

Sara had simply started sleeping with all the lights on.

When Helen asked her why Sara had said because of the thing that doesn't have a inside.

Helen had sat with this for a day.

Then she had found Rudy's card.

Then she had found the community forum post.

Then she had written this email at two in the morning with the specific directness of a woman who has run out of the manageable explanations and has arrived at the place where the unmanageable one is the only one left standing.

I don't know what's happening, she wrote. *I know something is. My daughter described it exactly and she's six years old and she has never heard that language before so she found it herself. If you know what this is please tell me. I have been afraid for six weeks and I am tired of being afraid of something I don't have a name for.*

I read the email twice.

Looked at it for a moment.

Looked at the corner of the study that was just a corner.

Looked at the new notebook beside the laptop.

Thought about Rudy's card on the counter of the hardware store.

Some things are real that don't have official names. If you've been feeling something you can't explain, talk to Rudy.

Which had been posted on a community forum by someone who found it unusual.

Which had been read at two in the morning by a woman in Marquette three hundred miles away.

Whose six year old daughter had used the exact language that a nine year old boy had used in a notebook in 1963.

The thing that doesn't have a inside.

I picked up the pen.

Opened the new notebook.

Thought about Joan's terrible logistics.

About the field spreading faster than I could track.

About four children in a basement on Saturday morning.

About Ellen's conversations and Margaret's letters and Agnes's parents and Vera's correspondence and Rudy's card and Thomas sitting at the end of the table by the window for three days not going away.

About the field finding people in hospital rooms and music studios and dark parking lots and hardware stores and community forums at two in the morning.

About a woman in Marquette who was afraid of something she didn't have a name for.

Whose daughter had found the name herself.

At six years old.

The same age Wren had been when she found it.

I thought about this.

About what it meant.

About what it had always meant.

That the ones who see clearly find the language for what they see whether or not anyone gives it to them.

Because the language is not taught.

It is remembered.

The same way the field is remembered.

The same way Margaret had been doing it in hospital rooms for thirty years without knowing it had a name.

The same way Agnes had been teaching it in music studios for forty one years calling it something else.

The same way Vera had been doing it accidentally in dark parking lots.

The same way Helen's daughter Sara had found it at six years old sleeping with all the lights on and told her mother there was a thing that didn't have an inside.

I looked and looked, the boy had written in 1963. *There is nothing in there.*

Sixty two years later a six year old girl in Marquette had found the same words.

Without the notebook.

Without the basement.

Without anyone sitting with her at the end of the table.

Just the seeing.

And the language the seeing produces when you are built for the frequency and have not yet learned to explain it away.

I sat with this for a long time.

Then I wrote in the new notebook.

One line.

The line that had been arriving since I opened the email and had finally found the right words the way lines find the right words — not by being constructed but by being recognized.

The field was never something we were building. It was always something that was already there, waiting for us to stop being less long enough to remember it.

I looked at the line.

It was right.

Not careful.

Right.

I picked up my phone.

Called Rudy.

He answered on the second ring with the voice of a man who is at his counter and has been expecting this call in the specific way that people expect calls they don't know are coming.

There's a woman in Marquette, I said. *She found your card.*

Silence for a moment.

Marquette, he said.

Yes.

That's a long way, he said.

Yes, I said.

How did she find it, he said.

Community forum, I said. *Someone posted it.*

Hm, he said. The specific hm of a hardware man learning that a card he put on his counter has traveled three hundred miles through a community forum at two in the morning and found someone who needed it.

Her daughter is six, I said. *She found the language herself. The same language.*

Rudy was quiet.

The thing that doesn't have a inside, I said.

A longer silence.

Yes, he said. *All right.*

I'm going to call her, I said. *I wanted you to know.*

Why, he said.

Because it started with your card, I said. *You should know where it went.*

He was quiet for a moment.

The quiet of a hardware man standing at his counter in the specific weight of understanding that a thing he did without planning has traveled further than he knew.

Is she going to be okay, he said.

Yes, I said. *She is.*

Good, he said. *Call me after.*

He hung up.

I looked at the email.

At Helen's words.

I have been afraid for six weeks and I am tired of being afraid of something I don't have a name for.

I thought about what I would say to her.

Not the full version yet. Not the corn field and the sixty two years and the basement and the Wednesday night and all of it. Not yet. The sequence. The right amount at the right time.

But the beginning of it.

The thing she needed most before anything else.

The thing that was more important than the name or the mechanism or the field or the rabbit or any of the rest of it.

The thing I had said to Thomas on his first morning.

The thing that was always the first thing.

I picked up the phone.

Called the number in the email.

It rang twice.

She answered with the voice of a woman who has been awake since two in the morning and has been watching her phone since seven and is trying not to show how much she has been watching it.

Helen, I said.

Yes, she said.

My name is Harlan, I said. *I'm in Bellaire. I got your email.*

Yes, she said. Very carefully. The careful of someone who has decided to make this call and is now in the first seconds of having made it and is finding the ground.

I want to tell you three things, I said. *Before anything else.*

All right, she said.

The first thing, I said, *is that what your daughter told you is accurate. She is not imagining it and neither are you.*

Silence.

The specific silence of a woman receiving confirmation of the thing she has been most afraid was true and finding that the confirmation produces relief rather than more fear because fear of the unknown is always larger than fear of the known and she has been living in the unknown for six weeks and the known however large is smaller than that.

The second thing, I said, *is that it has a name. Several names depending on who you ask. The one we use is the field. And the field is the answer to it. Not a defense exactly. Something more complete than that.*

All right, she said again. Steadier this time. The ground firming up.

The third thing, I said.

I paused.

Looked at the new notebook.

At the one line I had written.

At the corner of the study that was just a corner.

At the October morning coming through the window.

At the lake doing what it did.

At the sixty two years between the corn field and this desk and what those years had produced and what they had cost and what they had made possible.

At the field in motion.

Moving faster than I could track.

Finding people in hospital rooms and music studios and dark parking lots and hardware stores and community forums at two in the morning and basements on Saturday mornings and ends of tables by windows.

All of them.

Finding each other.

The cloth.

Growing.

Thread by thread.

Kitchen by kitchen.

Conversation by conversation.

One person at a time.

In the only direction that mattered.

From the inside out.

The third thing, I said, *is that you are not alone. You have never been alone. None of us were. We just didn't know about each other yet.*

Helen was quiet on the line.

The quiet of a woman receiving the thing she has needed most for six weeks and possibly much longer than six weeks and possibly her whole life without knowing she needed it until this moment on a Tuesday morning in Marquette when a man in Bellaire said three things before anything else.

Thank you, she said.

Very quietly.

The specific gratitude of someone who has been carrying something alone and has been told the carrying is over.

Not because the thing is gone.

Because they have found the others who know the weight.

Tell me about Sara, I said.

And she did.

And I listened.

And the field moved.

Three hundred miles to the north.

Finding what it had always been finding.

Itself.

Chapter 37

THE QUIET ONES

Chapter Thirty Seven — The Bridge

We left at six in the morning.

Wren was in the passenger seat with her backpack and a thermos of hot chocolate that Nora had made the night before and pressed into her hands at the door with the specific look of a mother sending her daughter into something large and trusting the people around her to bring her back.

Call me, Nora said.

Yes, I said.

Both of you, she said.

Yes, Wren said.

And stop for breakfast, Nora said. *Not granola bars from a gas station. Actual breakfast.*

We'll stop in Gaylord, I said.

Good, she said. And kissed Wren's head and looked at me over it with the look that needed no words and we drove away in the six o'clock dark with the thermos and the backpack and five hours ahead of us.

Northern Michigan in late October from a car window is a specific kind of beautiful that does not photograph well and does not translate into description well and exists most fully in the experience of it — the birch stands gone bare and white against the dark of the remaining pines, the sky the specific grey of a sky that has weather in mind and is taking its time about it, the occasional lake visible through the tree line with the flat pewter quality of October water that has given up on warmth and is simply being water now without any further pretense.

Wren watched it.

Not the watching of a child on a car trip looking for distraction. The other kind. The complete present attention she brings to things that deserve it. The field receiving the landscape the way still water receives what passes over it.

I drove.

We stopped in Gaylord at seven thirty at a diner that had been a diner since before I was born and intended to keep being one without reference to current trends in breakfast. Eggs and toast and actual coffee and the specific quality of a diner that has been making the same breakfast for sixty years and has developed opinions about how it should be done.

Wren ordered pancakes.

They arrived the size of the plate.

She looked at them.

Grandpa.

Yes.

These are very large.

Yes.

I'm going to try anyway.

That's the right attitude.

She tried. Made reasonable progress. We drove on.

The bridge at nine fifteen.

The Mackinac Bridge is five miles long and crosses the strait between Lake Michigan and Lake Huron and connects the lower peninsula to the upper and is one of those things that photographs well and still manages to be better in person. The specific quality of being suspended over open water with the two lakes visible on either side and the wind always present and the sense of crossing from one thing into another that the bridge produces regardless of how many times you have crossed it.

Wren looked at it coming.

Then looked at the water on both sides as we crossed.

Then looked at the upper peninsula arriving ahead of us.

Different, she said.

Yes, I said.

The frequency is different up here.

Yes, I said. *It always has been.*

Older, she said. *Something older in it.*

I did not ask her to explain this because it did not require explanation. The UP has always felt older. The rock older, the trees older, the specific quality of the silence between human settlements older. As if the land up here has a longer memory than the land to the south and does not feel the need to pretend otherwise.

We drove through St. Ignace and north on 75 and then west on 28 through the specific Upper Peninsula landscape of long straight roads through second growth forest with the occasional small town arriving and passing with the self-contained quality of places that have decided they are sufficient unto themselves and see no reason to perform otherwise.

Wren was quiet for a long time.

The specific quiet of a child sitting with something.

I drove.

The road ran straight through the trees.

Grandpa, she said.

Yes.

Can I ask you something.

Always, I said.

She was quiet for a moment. Finding the words. Which Wren rarely needs time to do — she usually finds the words before the words know they are needed — so the time meant the something was specific.

Does it bother you, she said. *That you were alone with it for so long.*

I drove through the UP forest on the straight road in the late October morning.

Yes, I said. *Sometimes.*

What kind of bother, she said.

I thought about this.

About the honest answer versus the comfortable one.

About the fact that Wren heard the gap between them.

The kind where you wonder what was different about you, I said. *That you were alone with it when other people apparently weren't. Whether there was something you could have done to find them sooner. Whether the alone was necessary or just what happened.*

What do you think, she said.

I think it was both, I said. *I think some of the alone was necessary — it made me who I am in ways that the finding everyone wouldn't have. And I think some of it was just what happened. Circumstance. Bad logistics as Joan would say.*

Does that make you sad, she said.

Occasionally, I said. *Mostly it makes me glad it's over.*

She sat with this.

I'm going to tell you something, she said. *And I need you to hear it as true and not as something I'm saying to make you feel better.*

All right, I said.

The alone made you the right person, she said. *To find everyone else. Someone who hadn't been alone with it couldn't have recognized the alone in others. Couldn't have sat in Rudy's hardware store and seen what was happening. Couldn't have felt Gerald's living room. Couldn't have known what Thomas was from a description.* She paused. *The sixty two years weren't wasted. They were preparation.*

I drove.

The road ran straight.

The birch trees white on either side.

You sound like chapter twelve, I said.

Chapter twelve is right, she said. *That's why you finished it.*

I looked at the road.

At the specific straight northern road running through the specific northern trees in the specific northern light of late October.

Yes, I said. *That's why I finished it.*

She drank from the thermos.

Hot chocolate that was probably not as hot as it had been at six in the morning but that she drank anyway because some things you do for the ritual of them.

Can I ask you something now, I said.

Yes, she said.

What does it cost you, I said. *Seeing it the way you do. All of it. Not just the thing. Everything. The gap between what people say and what they mean. The underneath part. What does it cost.*

She was quiet.

Not the searching-for-words quiet. A different quiet. The quiet of a child sitting with a question that has been asked of her before — internally, by herself, in the specific private way that children ask themselves the questions adults forget to ask them — and is now finding the right version of the answer to say out loud.

It's loud, she said finally. *At school especially. Everyone saying things and meaning other things and the difference between them is — it's like a physical thing. Like static. Like everyone has their radio on a different station and I can hear all of them at once.*

Is it always like that, I said.

Less than it was, she said. *I've learned to turn it down a little. Not off. I can't turn it off. But I can choose how much I let in.* She paused. *Agnes helped with that. The rests. The held silence. If I hold the silence properly the static quiets.*

Does it hurt, I said. *The static.*

Hurt isn't the right word, she said. *It's tiring. Like carrying something heavy that you can't put down. You get used to the weight but you're always aware of it.*

I'm sorry, I said.

Don't be, she said. *It's also — it's also how I knew about Thomas. How I knew about Eddie. How I knew Vera could do the rabbit accidentally and Agnes had been doing the field for forty one years. How I knew what Ellen needed in the kitchen that afternoon.* She paused. *The static is how I find people. I'd rather have it than not.*

I drove.

What do you want, I said. *For your life. When you're older.*

She looked at the road ahead.

The long straight road through the northern trees.

I want to do what we're doing, she said. *Find the ones who are alone with it. Show them they're not.* She paused. *I know that sounds simple.*

It doesn't sound simple, I said. *It sounds like the hardest work there is.*

Yes, she said. *But it's the right work.* She looked at me. *Isn't it.*

I looked at my granddaughter.

Six years old.

In the passenger seat of my car crossing the Upper Peninsula on a Tuesday morning in October to meet a woman named Helen whose six year old daughter had found the language herself.

Going toward the work.

Without being asked.

Without hesitation.

Without reduction.

The whole of herself.

Yes, I said. *It's the right work.*

She turned back to the window.

Watched the trees.

Grandpa.

Yes.

Sara, she said. *Helen's daughter. I can feel her from here.*

What does she feel like, I said.

Like me, she said. *But newer. Less worn in.* She paused. *She's been alone with it longer than I was before I found you.*

Yes, I said. *She has.*

She'll be okay, Wren said. *Once she knows.*

Yes, I said. *She will.*

She needs someone to sit with her, Wren said. *Not to explain. Just to sit.*

Yes.

I'll do that, she said. *While you talk to Helen.*

Yes, I said. *I know you will.*

She turned back to the window.

The trees.

The road.

The late October light doing what it did in the Upper Peninsula — older, lower, more horizontal than the light to the south, the specific light of a place that has a longer memory and does not pretend the sun is higher than it is.

We drove in the comfortable silence of two people who have said what needed saying and are now simply present in the same car on the same road going toward the same thing.

The field in motion.

Three hundred miles from where it had started.

Carrying itself north.

Across the bridge.

Into the older country.

Finding what it had always been finding.

People alone with something they didn't have a name for.

And bringing them the name.

And the field.

And the one thing that was always the first thing and always the most important thing and always the thing that mattered more than the name or the mechanism or any of the rest of it.

You are not alone.

You have never been alone.

None of us were.

We just didn't know about each other yet.

I drove.

Wren watched the trees.

The road ran straight through the northern forest toward Marquette and Helen and Sara who had found the language herself at six years old and had been sleeping with all the lights on for a month.

We were an hour away.

Grandpa, Wren said.

Yes.

Thank you, she said.

For what, I said.

For turning left instead of right, she said. *That day you came to pick me up and I told you about Thomas. You turned left.*

I thought about the intersection on Main Street.

The green light I had sat through for an extra second.

The left turn toward Birch Street instead of the right turn toward home.

Yes, I said.

Everything started there, she said.

Everything started before that, I said. *Everything started with you asking about Missy.*

Everything started before that, she said. *Everything started with Gerald.*

Everything started before that, I said. *Everything started in a corn field in 1963.*

She was quiet for a moment.

Everything started, she said. *And is still starting.*

Yes, I said. *That's exactly right.*

She settled back into the seat.
Looked at the road ahead.
The long straight northern road.
Running through the trees.
Toward whatever came next.
Still starting, she said.
Quietly.
To herself.
Or to the road.
Or to the field.
Which were all the same thing.
In the end.

Chapter 38

THE QUIET ONES

Chapter Thirty Eight — Sara

Helen's house was on a street of similar houses in a neighborhood that had the specific quality of Marquette neighborhoods — built for weather, built for permanence, the houses of people who have made their peace with winter and have constructed accordingly. Deep porches. Storm windows. The specific practical beauty of a place that knows function and form are not enemies but have learned to work together out of necessity.

Helen was at the door before we reached the porch steps.

She had the look of a woman who had been awake since we called from Gaylord to say we were on our way and had spent the intervening hours in the specific productive anxiety of someone who needs to do something with her hands while her mind manages something too large for hands. The house smelled of baking. Not performance baking — necessity baking. The kind you do because the alternative is sitting still with the thing you've been sitting still with for six weeks and you have reached the limit of sitting still with it.

She was forty two. Dark haired. The specific quality of a woman who has been strong for a long time and is currently in the particular exhaustion that comes after a long time of being strong without anyone noticing the cost.

She looked at me.

She looked at Wren.

She looked at Wren for the half second longer that everyone looked at Wren. The recalibration. The unnamed recognition.

Come in, she said. *Please.*

The living room had two children in it.

Marcus, nine, dark haired like his mother, with the scientific minded precision she had described in her email — sitting at the coffee table with a notebook and a pencil doing something methodical that I recognized from a distance as an attempt to document what he had been experiencing in the specific way that scientific minded children document things that don't fit their framework. Making it measurable. Making it something that could be reported.

He looked up when we came in.

Assessed us with the quick accuracy of a boy who has been reading rooms carefully since something in his bedroom started behaving differently.

Found whatever he needed to find.

Went back to his notebook.

Sara was on the couch.

Six years old. Red haired where her mother was dark. Freckled in the specific way of children whose coloring produces freckles as a default. Small in the way that some six year olds are small — not the reduced smallness of Thomas when he first came, not the compressed smallness of a child who has been learning to be less — just small in the physical sense, slight, the smallness of someone who has not yet grown into the space they will eventually occupy.

She was sitting with her knees pulled to her chest and her arms around them and her eyes on the corner of the living room that I looked at when I came in and noted immediately.

Cold.

Not as concentrated as my corner had been at its worst.

Not as old.

But present.

The specific wrongness of air that is doing something it was not supposed to do.

Sara was watching it with the focused attention of a child who has been watching it for a month and has developed the specific vigilance of someone who has learned that looking away is not advisable.

She did not look at us when we came in.

She kept watching the corner.

Wren looked at Sara.

Looked at the corner Sara was watching.

Looked at Sara again.

She crossed the room without being directed or introduced or told what to do and sat on the couch beside Sara.

Not next to her exactly. Beside her. The specific placement of someone who understands that proximity has a right distance and has found it without being told.

Sara did not look at Wren.

She kept watching the corner.

For approximately thirty seconds the two six year olds sat side by side on the couch in Helen's living room in Marquette without speaking.

Then Sara said, without looking away from the corner:

You can see it too.

Yes, Wren said.

Does it go away, Sara said.

The one in our house went away, Wren said. *Three weeks ago.*

How, Sara said.

There were a lot of us, Wren said. *All being completely ourselves at the same time. In the same room. There was no room for it.*

Sara considered this. Still watching the corner.

How many, she said.

Twenty three, Wren said.

That's a lot, Sara said.

It took a while to find everyone, Wren said.

Where do you find them, Sara said.

They find themselves, Wren said. *Mostly. You just have to — be somewhere they can find you.*

Sara turned and looked at Wren for the first time.

The specific assessment of a child who has been reading people carefully for six weeks and has developed a sophisticated instrument for it.

She looked at Wren for a long moment.

You found me, she said.

Yes, Wren said.

How.

I could feel you, Wren said. *From far away. You were watching it very hard. I could feel how hard you were watching.*

I can't stop watching it, Sara said. *If I stop watching it it moves.*

I know, Wren said. *I'll watch it with you. Then you can look away sometimes.*

Sara looked at her for another moment.

Then she unfolded herself from the knees-to-chest position.

Sat normally.

Beside Wren.

Both of them facing the corner.

Both of them watching.

The specific quality of two children who have established in forty five seconds of conversation the working arrangement of people who have found each other on the same frequency and do not require further negotiation.

I stood at the entrance to the living room and watched this happen and thought about a nine year old boy in a corn field learning the rabbit alone because there was no one and a six year old girl in Marquette who had been watching a corner alone for a month and was now watching it with someone and the specific quality of the room when she had unfolded herself from the knees-to-chest position.

Something had shifted.

Not the corner.

Sara.

The specific shift of a child who has been carrying something alone and has been given the company of someone who knows the weight.

Helen had come to stand beside me.

She had seen it too.

She hasn't sat like that, Helen said quietly. *In a month. She's been — folded up.*

Yes, I said.

Who is your granddaughter, Helen said.

Wren, I said. *She's six.*

She just — Helen paused. *She just sat down and Sara unfolded.*

Yes, I said.

How.

She finds people, I said. *On the frequency. She finds them and she sits with them and she doesn't go away. That's all she does. It turns out it's enough.*

Helen looked at the two girls on the couch.

At the corner they were both watching.

At the specific quality of the room which had been different when we arrived and was different again now.

Not fixed.

But different.

The specific difference of a room that has had something added to it that belongs there.

Coffee, Helen said. *And then you're going to tell me everything.*

Yes, I said. *That's exactly what I'm going to do.*

We sat at Helen's kitchen table for two hours.

Marcus joined us after twenty minutes with his notebook and his pencil and the scientific minded precision of a nine year old who has decided that understanding something is better than being afraid of it and has come to gather data accordingly. He asked three questions. They were good questions. The questions of someone who is not going to accept comfortable explanations but will accept honest ones.

I gave him honest ones.

He wrote them down.

Filed them in whatever internal system a nine year old scientist uses for extraordinary information that does not fit the available framework but has been provided with sufficient credibility to merit documentation.

Helen listened the way she had written her email — directly, without the defensive filtering of someone who needs it to fit a predetermined shape, with the specific focused attention of a woman who has been afraid of something for six weeks and has arrived at the place where understanding it is the only available antidote to the fear.

I told her everything.

The sequence had ended for me somewhere around the third week and I no longer maintained it with new people. The full version was more useful than the edited version and took less time because it did not require the careful management of information arriving in the right order.

She received it the way Margaret had received it.

The way Ellen had received it.

The way Vera had.

With the specific quality of a woman recognizing something she has always known and has never been given permission to know.

The field, she said when I finished.

Yes.

I've been doing it, she said. *For years. I didn't know that's what it was.*

Where, I said.

Work, she said. *I'm a social worker. Seventeen years.* She looked at her coffee. *The clients who are the most — depleted. The ones who have been giving themselves to something that can't receive. I sit with them in a particular way and something in the room changes.* She paused. *My supervisor used to say I had a gift for the hard cases. I never knew what she meant.*

You were filling the rest, I said.

Yes, she said. *I just didn't know that's what it was called.*

Margaret's words.

Always the same words.

I've been doing it for years. I just didn't know it had a name.

The field had always been there.

In every person who had been doing it alone without knowing.

And here was another one.

A social worker in Marquette.

Seventeen years of sitting with the depleted ones.

Filling the rest.

The cloth adding another thread.

Your children, I said.

Sara sees it the way I understand Wren sees it, she said. *Completely.*

Yes.

Marcus —

Feels it, I said. *Without the complete picture. Like the outline without the detail. Enough to know it's there.*

Like his father, she said. *His father has always — he feels things in rooms. He won't say it that way. He says the vibe is off. But he's been saying the vibe in Sara's room is off for a month and he moved out of their bedroom two weeks ago because he couldn't sleep in there.*

Where is he, I said.

Work, she said. *He drives long haul. He's in Wisconsin.*

He needs to know, I said.

Yes, she said. *He'll be home Thursday.* She paused. *He's going to say the vibe is off and I'm going to say yes and here's what that means.*

Good, I said.

Will he believe it, I said.

He believes in what he feels, she said. *He just doesn't usually have language for it. Give him the language and he'll believe it.*

Rudy's card, I said. *That's what it did for him too.*

She almost smiled.

Rudy sounds like someone I'd like, she said.

Everyone likes Rudy, I said. *He returns borrowed tools without being asked. It puts him in a very small category.*

She did smile at that.

The first full smile since we had arrived.

The specific smile of a woman who has been managing something alone for six weeks and has just been given both the explanation and the company and has found that the combination produces something in the chest that presents itself initially as relief and expands into something warmer.

In the living room the two girls had moved.

Not apart.

Closer.

When I looked in at noon they were side by side on the floor with their backs against the couch facing the corner. The specific vigilant position of two people who have divided the watching between them and are doing it together.

Sara was talking.

I had not heard Sara's voice until this moment. She had been silent since the initial exchange with Wren — the forty five seconds that had produced the working arrangement — and had watched the corner with the focused vigilance of a child who has learned that watching is the primary available tool.

She was talking now.

Not loudly. The specific quiet conversation of two children who have established a private frequency and are using it.

I could not hear what she was saying from the kitchen doorway.

I went back to the kitchen.

At two o'clock Helen made sandwiches.

Marcus ate with the focused efficiency of a boy who has gathered sufficient data for now and is refueling for the next session.

Helen and I talked about the logistics. About Vera's letters and Rudy's card and Ellen's conversations. About the standing Thursday gathering. About Joan's terrible logistics observation and what fixing it looked like at a practical level.

Helen had ideas.

Good ones.

The specific practical ideas of a social worker who has been connecting people to resources for seventeen years and understands that connection is a skill and systems help and the best systems are the ones that look least like systems.

I wrote them in the new notebook.

At three o'clock Wren appeared in the kitchen doorway.

She had the specific expression she wears when she has something to tell me and has been waiting for the right moment.

Okay, she said.

Yes, I said.

Sara told me something, she said.

Tell me.

She came to the table and sat down and folded her hands in the specific way she folds her hands when she is about to say something she has been thinking about carefully.

She said, Wren began, *that the thing in the corner is afraid of us.*

I looked at my granddaughter.

Not of the field exactly, Wren continued. *She said it's afraid of what we remember. She said it can't stand the remembering. Not because it hurts the thing. Because the remembering is the thing it can never do. It has no inside so it has no memory. It can only exist in the present moment of the gap. The instant the gap closes — the instant we remember what we are — it has nothing to stand on.*

The kitchen was quiet.

Helen looked at her daughter through the doorway.

At Sara who was six years old and had been alone with something for a month and had found the language herself and had spent three hours with Wren and had arrived at something that neither of us had articulated in three weeks of notebooks and basements and Wednesday nights.

We don't defeat it by filling the gap, Wren said. *We defeat it by remembering. The field is memory. The remembering of what we are. The thing can't survive in a room full of people who remember.*

I sat at Helen's kitchen table.

Thought about what Sara had said.

Through Wren.

Across three hours of sitting side by side on the floor watching the corner together.

Thought about the notebook.

About the boy's section and the man's section and the sixty two years between them.

About what the notebook was.

A record.

Of what the boy knew.

Of what the man learned.

Of the corn field and the rabbit and the cost of less and the long careful life of a man who had been less for too long.

The notebook was memory.

Specifically.

The act of writing it down — the boy writing *it does not have a inside* and the man writing *I know you're there* — was the act of remembering.

Refusing to let the forgetting complete itself.

Refusing to let the gap widen past the point of recovery.

The notebook was not a record of the thing.

It was a record of the self.

The self refusing to be less.

The self remembering what it was.

Which was the field.

Which was exactly the field.

Memory of what you are.

Held deliberately.

Against the pressure of a world that finds it convenient for you to forget.

She said, Wren continued, *that the children who find the language themselves find it because they haven't forgotten yet. The adults had to find it again. The children never lost it. That's why the children see it most clearly. Not because they have better equipment. Because they haven't spent years being told to forget.*

Helen put both hands flat on the table.

The gesture I had seen in Rudy's hardware store.

The gesture of a woman steadying herself on a known surface while the ground rearranges.

Seventeen years, she said.

Yes, I said.

Seventeen years of sitting with the depleted ones, she said. *And I think I've been helping them remember. Not teaching them anything. Just — being so completely myself in the room that it reminded them they were allowed to be completely themselves.*

Yes, I said.

The field is memory, she said.

Yes.

And the thing feeds on forgetting.

Yes.

And the forgetting is what the world produces, she said. *The ambient cruelty. The contempt. The constant pressure to be less than you are. That's not incidental. That's the mechanism. The world produces forgetting and the forgetting produces the gap and the thing moves into the gap.*

Yes, I said. *That's exactly it.*

So the field is not just protection, she said.

No, I said.

It's resistance, she said.

Yes.

To the forgetting.

Yes.

Remembering who you are, she said, *is an act of resistance.*

She said it quietly.

To herself.

Or to the seventeen years.

Or to the clients she had sat with who had been giving themselves to things that couldn't receive and had been slowly forgetting who they were in the process.

I picked up the pen.

Opened the new notebook.

Wrote what Sara had said.

The whole of it.

And underlined the last line.

Remembering who you are is an act of resistance.

Not because Sara had said it.

Because it was true.

And had been true before Sara was born.

And would be true long after all of us were gone.

The field as memory.

Memory as resistance.

Resistance as the only weapon that had ever worked against a thing that fed on forgetting.

I looked at what I had written.

At the underlined line.

At the new notebook that was filling the way the old one had filled — with the specific accumulation of understanding arriving faster than expected and costing more than anticipated and producing something he had not known he was building until it was built.

Wren, I said.

Yes.

Tell Sara thank you.

She knows, Wren said.

Tell her anyway.

She said you would say that, Wren said. *She said to tell you that you're welcome and that she wants to come to the basement on Saturday.*

I looked at my granddaughter.

She said that.

Three minutes ago, Wren said. *While you were writing.*

I looked through the kitchen doorway at Sara on the floor in front of the corner.

Six years old.

In Marquette.

Three hundred miles from the basement.

Who had been alone with something for a month and had found the language herself and had spent three hours with Wren and had understood something about the field that had taken me three weeks of notebooks and basements and Wednesday nights to approach and had arrived at it in an afternoon sitting on the floor watching a corner.

Because she hadn't forgotten yet.

Because the children who find the language themselves find it because they haven't spent years being told to forget.

Tell her, I said, *that the basement will be there.*

She knows, Wren said.

Yes, I said. *She would.*

Helen was looking at her daughter through the doorway.

At the six year old who had been folded up for a month and had unfolded and was now sitting on the floor with her back against the couch watching a corner and talking to another six year old who had driven five hours to sit beside her.

She's going to be okay, Helen said.

Yes, I said.

She was always going to be okay, Helen said. *She just needed someone to sit beside her.*

Yes, I said. *That's always what it is.*

Helen looked at Wren.

Your granddaughter, she said.

Yes.

She's —

I know, I said.

She drove five hours, Helen said. *To sit beside a six year old she'd never met.*

Yes.

Without being asked.

No, I said. *She was asked. By the frequency. She felt Sara watching the corner from Bellaire and she came.*

Helen sat with this.

That's not nothing, she said.

No, I said.

The same words as Wren.

The same truth inside them.

That's everything, I said.

We left at four thirty.

Sara walked us to the door.

She looked at Wren.

Same frequency, she said.

Yes, Wren said.

I'll be able to feel you from here, Sara said.

Yes, Wren said. *And I'll be able to feel you.*

If it gets worse, Sara said.

Tell your mom, Wren said. *She knows now. And she'll call us.*

Okay, Sara said.

The same word.

The same completeness inside it.

She looked at me.

You're the one who was alone for sixty two years, she said.

Yes, I said.

That must have been very long, she said.

Yes, I said. *It was.*

You're not alone now, she said.

No, I said. *I'm not.*

She nodded.

The small serious nod of a child who has delivered a message and confirmed its receipt.

Went back inside.

We walked to the car.

Got in.

I started the engine.

Sat for a moment.

Wren sat beside me.

The Marquette street in the late October afternoon light. The specific quality of UP light at four thirty in October — already going, already making its preparations for a dark that arrives earlier up here than anywhere else.

Grandpa, Wren said.

Yes.

Sara said one more thing, she said. *When I was leaving.*

Tell me.

She said the thing isn't going to stop, Wren said. *Not this instance of it. Not all of them. She said as long as the world produces forgetting the thing will be there to move into the gaps.*

Yes, I said. *I know.*

She said the field doesn't end it, Wren said. *The field just means it can't win.*

I sat with this.

The specific sitting of a man receiving a true thing that is neither comfortable nor uncomfortable but simply accurate.

Yes, I said. *That's right.*

She said that's enough, Wren said.

Is it, I said.

Wren looked at the road ahead.

The road that would take us back to the bridge.

Back across the water.

Back to Bellaire and the corner that was just a corner and the Thursday gatherings and the new notebook filling and Thomas in his good jacket and Eddie and Lily and the field in motion.

Yes, she said. *It's enough.*

I pulled away from the curb.

Drove through Marquette toward the highway.

Toward the bridge.

Toward home.

The field carrying itself in two directions simultaneously — south in a car with an old man and a six year old and a new notebook with an underlined line in it, and north in a house on a Marquette street where a social worker named Helen was sitting with her daughter who had unfolded and her son who was writing in his notebook and the specific quality of a family that now knew the name for what they had always been.

The field in motion.

Still starting.

Always starting.

Because the world always produced forgetting.

And the field was memory.

And memory was resistance.

And resistance was enough.

It had always been enough.

It just needed people who remembered.

Chapter 39

Chapter Thirty Nine — The Bridge At Dusk

Wren fell asleep outside of Newberry.

One moment she was watching the trees with the dark patient eyes and the next she was asleep with the complete commitment of a child whose body has conducted a substantial day and is presenting the invoice without negotiation. Her head against the window. Her hands in her lap. The field present in her even in sleep the way it was always present — not performed, not maintained, simply what she was when she was not being anything else.

Which was always.

I drove.

The UP highway running straight through the darkening forest in the late October afternoon that was becoming evening faster than it would have south of the bridge. Up here October evenings arrive with the specific decisiveness of a place that does not negotiate its seasons. The light goes and it goes completely and the dark that follows is the dark of a country that has been dark for a long time and is comfortable with that.

The radio off.

The heater on low.

The specific quiet of a car carrying sleeping cargo through the northern dark.

I thought about Sara.

About what she had said through Wren.

The field is memory. The remembering of what we are. The thing can't survive in a room full of people who remember.

I thought about this the way I think about things that arrive fully formed — not constructing them, not analyzing them, just turning them over slowly in the available light to see what they show from different angles.

The field is memory.

I had been thinking about the field as a practice. Something you did. The rabbit and the held silence and the ground so thoroughly itself there was nowhere to land. Something that required cultivation and maintenance and teaching and the specific intentional effort of people who had found each other and were working at it together.

Sara had said something different.

Sara had said the field was not something you did.

It was something you remembered.

The distinction being — everything.

Because you cannot lose a practice if you are not practicing.

But you can lose a memory.

Memory requires maintenance of a different kind — not effort exactly, more like attention. The specific attention of a person who has decided that what they are is worth remembering. Who has decided that the pressure to forget — the ambient cruelty, the contempt, the constant message that less is safer and visibility is dangerous and the gap between what you are and what you present is the price of admission to the world — is a pressure they are not going to honor.

Memory as resistance.

Not heroic resistance.

Not the loud kind.

The quiet kind.

The kind that says — I know what I am and I am going to keep knowing it regardless of what the room prefers.

Which was what Gerald had done at the end.

Which was what Carol Demming had done.

Which was what Vera had done in the parking lot going still in a way that was not hiding but remembering.

Which was what Agnes had been doing for forty one years in a music studio calling it something else.

Which was what Margaret had been doing in hospital rooms.

Which was what Rudy had done at the town meeting saying true things when the room wanted comfortable ones.

Which was what all of them had been doing all along without knowing that's what it was.

Not building something.

Remembering something.

The field had always been there because the memory had always been there.

Buried sometimes.

Suppressed sometimes.

Covered over by decades of being less.

But there.

The way the notebook had been there.

In the box under the stairs.

For sixty two years.

Waiting.

Not gone.

Waiting to be remembered.

The bridge appeared at dusk.

I had been watching for it since the Mackinaw City exit and it appeared the way it always appeared — suddenly, after miles of trees, the specific shock of open water and open sky after the enclosed tunnel of the northern forest, and then the bridge itself.

Five miles long.

The towers going up into the last of the October light.

The two lakes visible on either side — Michigan to the west still holding some light, Huron to the east already dark, the specific quality of water at dusk that is neither one thing nor the other, the in-between time, the threshold.

I had crossed this bridge hundreds of times.

It was different every time.

Not the bridge.

The person crossing it.

I drove onto it.

The specific sound of the bridge under the tires — the grating sound of the open steel grid sections, the particular vibration that the bridge produces that is unlike any other road and that your body learns to recognize as the bridge specifically and nothing else.

Wren did not wake.

The sound of the bridge had always put children to sleep or kept them awake and Wren was apparently in the first category.

I drove.

The towers passing overhead.

The water on both sides.

The last light going out of the western sky in the specific way that October light goes out — not gradually, not with the long summer negotiations between day and dark, but directly, with the honest finality of a season that has decided.

The new notebook was on the dash.

I had put it there when Wren fell asleep. Not to read — I was driving. Just to have it there. In the periphery. The way you keep something nearby that you are not done with yet.

The underlined line visible from where I sat.

Remembering who you are is an act of resistance.

I drove across the bridge in the last light of the October day.

Wren asleep beside me.

The notebook on the dash.

The water on both sides.

And somewhere in the middle of it — not at a specific point, not at the exact center of the five miles, just somewhere in the middle where you are equally far from both shores and the bridge is the only ground available — something arrived.

Not a thought.

A knowing.

The specific knowing that does not construct itself from available evidence but arrives complete, the way certain things arrive, in the specific register below thought where the true things live before the mind has finished building the sentence.

I knew what the book was.

Not the novel on the screen at home. Not chapter thirteen or any of the chapters after it.

The notebook.

The boy's record and the man's record and the sixty two years between them and the three weeks of understanding and the field and the rabbit and the cost of less and all of it.

The notebook was the book.

Not for me.

For them.

For Helen in Marquette and the woman in Traverse City who had found it through the community forum and the ones who would find it through other forums and other cards on other counters and other Thursday nights and other basements.

For the ones who were alone with it right now somewhere and didn't know there were others and didn't have the name and were paying the cost of less without knowing there was another option.

For Thomas and Eddie and Lily and Sara.

For the children who hadn't forgotten yet and the adults who needed to remember.

The notebook was not a record.

It was a message.

The boy had written it for the man.

The man needed to write it for everyone else.

Not the notebook exactly. The notebook was mine and would stay mine. But what the notebook contained — the corn field and the rabbit and the cost and the field and the memory and the resistance and the weavers finding each other — that needed to be said in a form that could travel.

That could find people in community forums at two in the morning.

That could arrive in hospital rooms and music studios and hardware stores and the hands of social workers in Marquette and the hands of retired nurses and the hands of seven year old boys in too-large jackets and the hands of children who were sleeping with all the lights on.

The knowing arrived complete on the Mackinac Bridge at dusk on a Tuesday in late October.

I did not do anything dramatic with it.

This is important.

I did not pull over. Did not wake Wren. Did not reach for the notebook on the dash. Did not make a decision or form a plan or organize my thoughts into the shape of an intention.

I drove.

The bridge under the tires.

The towers behind me now.

The lower peninsula ahead.

The dark coming down on both sides.

Wren breathing in the passenger seat with the specific steady breathing of a child deeply asleep.

The knowing settled into me the way true things settle — not dramatically, not with the fanfare of revelation, but with the specific quiet permanence of a thing that has found its place and intends to stay there.

It was enough.

It was exactly enough.

To know.

The doing would follow.

It always did.

I came off the bridge onto the lower peninsula.

The trees closing in again on both sides.

The specific enclosed quality of the road after the open water.

The heater on low.

The radio off.

The notebook on the dash.

Wren asleep.

Home three hours ahead.

I drove.

Through the northern Michigan dark.

Thinking about nothing in particular.

Which is what you do when you have received something complete and have recognized it as complete and have decided to let it be complete without immediately doing anything to it.

The specific discipline of a man who has learned that not everything requires immediate action.

That some things require simply being received.

And held.

And carried home.

The way you carry something you are not ready to put down and are not ready to display.

Close to the body.

Warm.

Present.

Not displayed.

Not performed.

Just known.

We stopped in Gaylord again.

Same diner.

Wren woke when I turned off the engine in the parking lot with the specific instant wakefulness of a child who was deeply asleep and is now completely present without the intermediate stages that adults require.

She looked at me.

Gaylord, she said.

Yes, I said. *Dinner.*

How long was I asleep.

Since Newberry, I said.

Did I miss the bridge.

Yes.

She looked at the diner.

Was it good, she said.

Yes, I said. *It was very good.*

Tell me, she said.

So I told her.

Not about the knowing. Not yet. The knowing was still settling and was not ready to be told.

About the bridge at dusk. The towers in the last light. The two lakes. The specific quality of being suspended between one thing and another in the in-between time.

She listened with her eyes.

The dark patient eyes.

Taking in the description of a thing she had slept through and was now receiving secondhand and finding it sufficient.

Next time I'll stay awake for the bridge, she said.

Yes, I said.

Promise, she said.

Promise, I said.

We went into the diner.

The same waitress. The same booths. The same specific quality of a place that has been making the same dinner for sixty years and has developed opinions about how it should be done.

We ordered.

Ate.

The specific quality of a meal after a long day that is simply fuel and warmth and the ordinary comfort of food that does what it is supposed to do without asking anything more of you.

Wren ate everything on her plate.

The day had been substantial.

She was six.

She had sat beside a girl in Marquette who had been folded up for a month and the girl had unfolded.

She had earned her dinner.

We got home at nine thirty.

Nora was at my house.

Of course she was.

She was in the kitchen with tea and the expression of a woman who has been managing the specific anxiety of sending her daughter three hundred miles away with her father and has been managing it since six in the morning and is now in the particular relief of having them back.

She looked at Wren.

Wren went to her.

Nora held her with the specific quality of a mother holding a child who has been away and is back and the holding is both welcome and assessment simultaneously.

How was she, Nora said to me over Wren's head.

Perfect, I said. *As always.*

Sara, Wren said into Nora's shoulder. *She was watching the corner alone for a month. She unfolded.*

Nora looked at me.

She unfolded, I said. *Yes.*

Good, Nora said. *Good.*

She held Wren for another moment.

Then released her.

Practical again.

Bed, she said to Wren.

Yes, Wren said.

She looked at me.

Grandpa.

Yes.

The bridge, she said. *You said it was very good.*

Yes, I said.

Something happened on the bridge, she said. Not a question.

I looked at my granddaughter.

The dark eyes.

Hearing what was said and what was underneath it and the gap between them which in this case was no gap at all because I had not been hiding anything, had simply been waiting.

Yes, I said. *Something happened on the bridge.*

Tell me tomorrow, she said.

Yes, I said.

Okay, she said.

She went to bed.

Nora looked at me.

Something happened on the bridge, she said.

Yes, I said.

Good something or complicated something.

Complete something, I said.

She looked at me for a moment.

The look of a daughter who knows her father and knows the difference between the versions of him and is reading the current version with the specific attention of someone who has been reading him for forty three years.

All right, she said.

Go home Nora, I said. *I'm fine. We're home.*

Call me tomorrow, she said.

Yes.

She left.

I stood in the kitchen for a moment in the nine thirty quiet of the house.

The lake doing what it did.

The corner just a corner.

The new notebook on the counter where I had left it when I came in.

I picked it up.

Went to the desk.

Sat down.

Opened the notebook to the page with the underlined line.

Remembering who you are is an act of resistance.

Read it.

Then turned to the next blank page.

Picked up the pen.

And wrote the first line of what the notebook was going to become.

Not the record.

The message.

The thing that could travel.

That could find people in community forums at two in the morning.

That could arrive in the hands of the ones who were alone with it.

One line.

The first line.

There is a thing. It does not have an inside. I know this because I have been watching it since I was nine years old in a corn field in October and I am seventy one now and I am still here and I am going to tell you everything.

I put the pen down.

Looked at what I had written.

It was right.

Not careful.

Right.

Outside the October night was what October nights in northern Michigan are.

Inside a man who had been less for a long time was at his desk not being less.

The whole of himself.

Present.

Broadcasting at exactly the right volume.

Which was all of it.

Every frequency.

The field in its fullest form.

Remembering.

Resisting.

Still here.

Still standing.

Beginning.

Again.

As it always began.

As it always would.

Chapter 40

THE QUIET ONES

Chapter Forty — Morning

Wednesday.

Six fifteen.

The specific grey light of a northern Michigan morning in late October that is almost November and knows it — the light of a season that has made its decision and is living inside it without apology.

I was at the desk.

Coffee.

The manuscript open on the screen.

Not chapter thirteen of the novel I had been writing when Gerald died. That novel would wait. That novel was patient in the way novels are patient when the writer has something more urgent to say and the novel understands this and steps aside.

The new manuscript.

The one that had begun on the bridge.

One line on the screen.

There is a thing. It does not have an inside. I know this because I have been watching it since I was nine years old in a corn field in October and I am seventy one now and I am still here and I am going to tell you everything.

I had been sitting with this line since six o'clock.

Not because it needed changing.

Because it needed witnessing.

The specific sitting with a first line that you do when you understand that the first line is the door and once you go through it the thing is real in a way it was not real before you wrote it and you want to be certain before you go through it.

I was certain.

I had been certain since the bridge.

I picked up the pen.

Reached for the notebook.

The door to the study opened.

Small feet.

The blanket.

The dark hair.

You're up early, Wren said.

So are you, I said.

I felt you deciding something, she said. *From the couch.*

I already decided, I said. *Last night.*

I know, she said. *But you were sitting with it.*

Yes.

She came to the desk.

Stood beside me.

Read the line on the screen.

The dark patient eyes moving across it once.

Then again.

Then she was quiet for a moment in the specific quiet of a child receiving something and finding it fits.

That's the beginning, she said.

Yes.

Of the one that travels, she said.

Yes.

She looked at it for another moment.

It's right, she said.

Yes, I said. *I think it is.*

She pulled the chair close.

Sat in it with the blanket around her shoulders and her hands in her lap.

Ready.

The specific readiness of someone who has been here before in a different version of this morning and knows what comes next.

Tell me what it says, she said. *The rest of it. What you're going to say.*

I looked at the screen.

At the one line.

At the cursor blinking after it.

Patient.

The way first lines wait for what comes after.

It says what you already know, I said. *What Sara knows. What Thomas knows. What Margaret has known for thirty years and Agnes has known for forty one and Vera has been knowing in dark parking lots and Helen has been knowing in the chairs beside the depleted ones.*

What we all know, she said.

Yes.

But haven't all said at the same time in the same place in language that can travel, she said.

Yes, I said. *That's what it says.*

She looked at the screen.

At the one line.

You're going to write about the corn field, she said.

Yes.

And the rabbit.

Yes.

And Gerald.

Yes.

And me, she said.

Yes, I said. *If that's all right.*

She considered this with the seriousness she brings to questions that deserve it.

Yes, she said. *It's all right. As long as you say it true.*

I'm going to say it as true as I know how, I said.

That's enough, she said. *That's always enough.*

I looked at my granddaughter.

The dark eyes.

The blanket.

The six years of being exactly what she was.

The field in its purest form.

Sitting beside me at six fifteen on a Wednesday morning in late October in a study in Bellaire Michigan while the lake did what it did and the light came in at the angle it came in at and the coffee went cold the way coffee does when you are doing something more important than drinking it.

Wren, I said.

Yes.

Thank you, I said.

She looked at me.

The assessment.

Then the warmth beneath it.

For what, she said.

For asking about Missy, I said.

She was quiet for a moment.

Then she almost smiled.

The specific almost smile that is more complete than most full ones.

You're welcome, she said.

She settled into the chair.

Looked at the screen.

At the one line waiting for what came after.

Write it, she said.

So I did.

Here is what I wrote.

Not all of it. The rest belongs to the manuscript and the manuscript belongs to whoever needs it and whoever needs it will find it the way Helen found Rudy's card and the way Margaret found the name for what she had been doing in hospital rooms and the way Thomas found Eddie and Lily found Thomas and Sara found the language herself at six years old sleeping with all the lights on.

But the last part.

The part that is not the beginning of the manuscript but the end of this story which is not really an ending but a door.

I wrote it to the reader.

Which is what Sara had told Wren on the floor of Helen's living room.

Which is what the boy had written in 1963 without knowing he was writing it to anyone but himself.

Which is what the man had been moving toward for sixty two years without knowing there was a direction.

I wrote it plainly.

Without the managed distance of a careful writer.

Without the ceremony of a man who wants to be remembered for the quality of his sentences.

Just the truth of it.

In the plainest available language.

Offered without reduction.

You are not strange.

You are not broken.

You are not too much or too little or wrong in any of the ways that rooms have suggested you are wrong.

You are built for a frequency that most people don't know exists. That is not a malfunction. That is a specific kind of equipment the world needs and has always needed and has never been good at recognizing or thanking.

The thing is real. The cold spot in the corner. The wrong quality of the air in certain rooms. The drain that sleep doesn't fix. The specific exhaustion of a battery that charges to eighty percent and stops. The feeling at the tree line that is not a deer. All of it real. You are not imagining it.

But here is what is also real.

You have been doing the field your whole life.

In hospital rooms and music studios and dark parking lots and hardware stores and classrooms and book clubs and at the end of tables with the ones sitting alone. You have been filling the rests and staying present when leaving would have been easier and not going away just because the person beside you has gone away.

You have been doing it without knowing it had a name.

Without knowing anyone else was doing it.

That is over now.

There are others.

There have always been others.

We just didn't know about each other yet.

A six year old girl in Marquette who had been alone with it for a month told me this: the field is memory. The remembering of what you are. The thing cannot survive in a room full of people who remember. It feeds on the forgetting. On the gaps between what you are and what the world has pressured you to perform. On the accumulated residue of being less.

Remembering who you are is an act of resistance.

Not the loud kind.

The quiet kind.

The kind that says — I know what I am and I am going to keep knowing it regardless of what the room prefers.

This is what the field is.

This is what you are.

This is what you have always been.

You don't have to build it.

You just have to remember it.

And you don't have to remember it alone.

That is the whole message.

That is everything the corn field and the rabbit and the sixty two years and the notebooks and the Wednesday nights and the bridge at dusk have been moving toward.

You are not alone.

You have never been alone.

None of us were.

We just didn't know about each other yet.

We do now.

The field is here.

It has always been here.

It is you.

Remember.

I put the pen down.

Read what I had written.

Wren read it beside me.

The study was quiet.

The lake outside doing what it did.

The October light coming through the window at the angle it came through at this hour.

The coffee cold.

The corner of the study just a corner.

The morning ordinary in all the ways that mornings are ordinary.

Wren finished reading.

Was quiet for a moment.

Then she said the thing she said.

The thing that was the last line of this story and the first line of everything that came after.

She said it simply.

Without ceremony.

Without the weight of a child who knows she is saying something significant.

Just a six year old in a blanket at six fifteen in the morning saying the true thing the way she always said the true things.

That's it, she said.

Yes, I said.

That's what it's always been.

Yes.

Someone just needed to write it down.

I looked at my granddaughter.

The dark eyes.

The field in them.

Still water.

The whole of herself.

No reduction.

No concealment.

Present.

Completely.

The way she had always been present.

The way she would always be present.

The small thing that had arrived at exactly the right moment.

And said okay.

And meant it completely.

Yes, I said. *Someone just needed to write it down.*

Outside the northern Michigan morning continued its business.

The lake moved.

The light came in at the angle it came in at.

The October that was almost November held its cold honest position without apology.

And in a study in Bellaire Michigan an old man and a six year old girl sat at a desk in the early morning with a manuscript that said the thing that needed saying and a cup of coffee that had gone cold and the specific quality of a room in which something has been finished that has been trying to finish for a long time.

Not the story.

The story was not finished.

The story was not the kind that finishes.

The manuscript.

The first draft of it.

The door through which whoever needed it could walk.

Finished.

One line at the beginning.

There is a thing. It does not have an inside. I know this because I have been watching it since I was nine years old in a corn field in October and I am seventy one now and I am still here and I am going to tell you everything.

And at the end.

The last line.

Which was not a conclusion.

Which was a continuation.

Which was the only kind of last line worth writing.

Remember.

THE END

Don't miss out!

Visit the website below and you can sign up to receive emails whenever Brad L Raby publishes a new book. There's no charge and no obligation.

https://books2read.com/r/B-A-ATPGF-IKTDJ

BOOKS 2 READ

Connecting independent readers to independent writers.

Did you love *The Quiet Ones*? Then you should read *The Thin Places*[1] by Brad L Raby!

[2]

THE THIN PLACES is the first volume of a geological horror saga exploring humanity's response to continental-scale temporal correction. When fractures along glacial boundaries allow the Pleistocene to return, DNR officer Dave Pritchard and sixty-two others refuse federal evacuation from Antrim County, Michigan. Over seven years, they pioneer adaptation methods—partnering with displaced Paleo-Indian populations, defending against extinct megafauna, and building hybrid communities that exist in multiple eras simultaneously. As correction spreads beyond the Great Lakes, their survival model becomes humanity's template for adapting to a world where the past is literally overwriting the present. Book One

1. https://books2read.com/u/meYG6g

2. https://books2read.com/u/meYG6g

establishes the phenomenon, the rules, and the cost of survival in the first correction zone—ground zero for a transformation that will eventually reshape the planet.

www.ingramcontent.com/pod-product-compliance
Lightning Source LLC
LaVergne TN
LVHW090545110826
845146LV00001B/19

9798995411512